Pilgrims of Fire

Pilgrims of Fire

An Adepta Sororitas novel

Justin D Hill

BLACK LIBRARY

A BLACK LIBRARY PUBLICATION

First published in 2023.
This edition published in Great Britain in 2023 by
Black Library, Games Workshop Ltd., Willow Road,
Nottingham, NG7 2WS, UK.

Represented by: Games Workshop Limited – Irish branch,
Unit 3, Lower Liffey Street, Dublin 1,
D01 K199, Ireland.

10 9 8 7 6 5 4 3 2 1

Produced by Games Workshop in Nottingham.
Cover illustration by Darren Tan.

A CIP record for this book is available from the British Library.

ISBN 13: 978-1-80407-353-7

See Black Library on the internet at

blacklibrary.com

Find out more about Games Workshop
and the worlds of Warhammer at

games-workshop.com

Printed and bound in the UK.

---

*For Percy – as you set out on your own adventures.
Remember, a towel is the most massively useful thing you can carry.
And always bring a book.*

For more than a hundred centuries the Emperor
has sat immobile on the Golden Throne of Earth.
He is the Master of Mankind. By the might of His
inexhaustible armies a million worlds stand
against the dark.

Yet, He is a rotting carcass, the Carrion Lord of the
Imperium held in life by marvels from the Dark
Age of Technology and the thousand souls sacrificed
each day so that His may continue to burn.

To be a man in such times is to be one amongst
untold billions. It is to live in the cruellest and
most bloody regime imaginable. It is to suffer an
eternity of carnage and slaughter. It is to have cries
of anguish and sorrow drowned by the thirsting
laughter of dark gods.

This is a dark and terrible era where you will find
little comfort or hope. Forget the power of technology
and science. Forget the promise of progress and
advancement. Forget any notion of common
humanity or compassion.

There is no peace amongst the stars, for in the grim
darkness of the far future, there is only war.

The Neverborn pressed against the thin skin of reality, testing the limits of their imprisonment. Aeons had passed since they had been free. Stars had burnt themselves out, mountains had been ground down to grains of sand – and each moment had been a torment. But there was a weakening.

The anticipation was torture.

The Neverborn pulsed like blind maggots within a rotting carcass. Reality bulged and stretched, and for a moment the membranes were so thin that a few gobbets of warp energy forced their way through – gibbering creatures divorced from reality, created with illogical numbers of heads and arms and legs, exultant and ravenous. They tasted humanity and howled with lust and hunger. When the Faultline ripped asunder, they would spill onto the worlds below and devour them.

Those who were sensitive to such things felt a chill of fear, a cold breath upon their name, a sense of unease, like a shadow passing over the soul. But there was one that should never have been disturbed, and it felt the presence of its kin, and started to stir from its long slumber.

As quickly as it had torn, the rent closed behind them. The gravity of the empyrean dragged at them, like drips being drawn upwards, back into themselves.

But one remained. It hung in the air, a luminous green clot, and caught the eye of a hungry child, picking his way through the midden heaps.

The barefoot child caught at the clot of hanging energy and missed. But it led him on, and when he caught it he opened his hand in triumph, and found nothing but three small dots.

He heard his mother's voice, and he hurried towards her, palm throbbing.

He licked his thumb and rubbed at the marks, but they did not wipe away. They were part of him now. And they would kill him.

Part One

Then

Holy Cion

'Proclaim this to humanity!
Rouse the warriors,
Gather your armies,
The days of war have come!'

– Dictum of Mirabai

i

War was already raging on the Obscurus Front the year the pilgrim fleet set off from Ophelia VII. They were to retrace the route of Saint Katherine's first War of Faith, their ramshackle ships chained together in a Gordian knot of piety and hope.

The fate of one would be the fate of all, the pilgrim-chiefs declared, the believers suffering together the travails and privations of their holy expedition.

They were plagued by all the dangers of the galaxy. Millions were lost to sickness and starvation. Attacks by xenos, renegades and pirates took countless others, while those of brittle faith fell by the wayside to lives of penance and prayer.

Empty warp ships were cut free and abandoned to the void. But after a decade, a billion souls yet remained, joined firmly by a tightening bond of belief. Their last ordeal was the desperate crossing, through the Fey Straits to Holy Cion.

This journey had twice repelled Saint Katherine. They all understood the danger, and gave themselves over to days of prayers and sacrifice and self-flagellation. There was an air of mourning as the fleet moved towards the Mandeville point.

The augurs were not good, and the warp was in a state of ecstatic tumult. When, at last, the pilgrim fleet broke into real-space, the tethered craft hung together, too weary and broken and stunned to do anything but offer prayers of gratitude to the God-Emperor, after years of travails, for their safe arrival.

The paean of thanks was heard by the astropaths on the shrine world of Holy Cion. Their tower was set in the upper reaches of the Abbey of Eternal Watch, which sat atop the vast stone out-crop known as the Bolt. A great cylinder of black granite which loomed over the surrounding Pilgrim Plains, the Bolt looked as though it had been fired into the planet's crust from some titanic orbital cannon.

Upon its peak, the Sisters of Our Martyred Lady maintained their guard. A cherub brought the news to the high chamber of Canoness Ysolt, where the venerable warrior was at prayer.

The messenger entered the chamber on fluttering white wings, anti-grav generators humming, the iron skull-face speaking in deep, resonant tones.

'Canoness. Tidings have come. The pilgrim fleet has arrived.'

Cion's output of prayer and faith and devotion was as inte-gral to the Imperium of Mankind as the production of any forge world. But the canoness' mind was concerned with disturbing portents. Shadows seen at night, mad laughter coming from empty rooms, reports of ghosts of sobbing women. And now the population of Cion were approaching a state of starvation. A pilgrim fleet was the last thing they needed, a doubting voice said. But, she reminded herself, faith was like a blade. It was there to be used. The Emperor would provide.

Ysolt steepled her fingers. Her voice was strained. She said a brief prayer of thanks and addressed her cherub. 'Sound the Bell of Ancestral Transgressions,' she said. 'I will take the augurs. The Feast of Landing must take place. We must welcome the faithful upon our holy soil.'

There were five hundred Battle Sisters within the Abbey of Eternal Watch. They exerted a gravity upon the population of Cion like celestial bodies. In better times the festival had been a moment of due solemnity. But the better times were now a distant memory for the serving women who worked in the bowels of the abbey.

The years of gathering privations had ground the working young girls down to a state of hunger and exhaustion, and none were hungrier that evening than Branwen, a maid-of-all-work, scrubbing the abbey stairs. She had scoured all the way from the lower gallery to the Sisters' refectory, and now her knees were sore, her shoulders ached and her stomach was as empty as an ogryn's brain.

'Hurry, girl!' one of the serving women said, as she carried a bundle of dirty sheets down towards the laundry. 'They're serving repast downstairs.'

Branwen nodded, but she saw with horror that the woman had left dirty footprints across the wet floor, and she said a prayer of contrition as she wiped them clean again. The trail led her right across the vaulted space. She paused at the refectory door and looked up. The gothic arch soared into darkness, statues of Sisters towering over her. The heavy oak doors were closed.

'You, girl!' a voice said.

Branwen jumped.

'Come away from there! What are you doing? Are you listening in?'

'No, ma'am!' Branwen said, but she looked as guilty as the hanged.

Tula, the Mistress of Chores, caught her by the ear and slapped her across the scalp. 'Shame on you! Soiling the sanctity of this place with your presence. You're just a bastard foundling. Away from that door!'

Tula tutted to herself as she dragged Branwen away. 'What do they say about cleanliness?'

'It brings us closer to the God-Emperor,' Branwen said.

'Indeed,' Tula said. 'And it seems this corridor is a long way from Him, who sits in majesty upon His Golden Throne.'

Branwen had tears in her eyes as she sponged her way along the flagstone corridor, dunking her brush into the bucket of caustic soap and slapping it down onto the dirty steps.

It was true, of course. She was a foundling. Everyone knew the story. An unwanted babe, spat out of the city and left at the abbey gates with just a swaddling blanket wrapped about her and a few hours of life within her hungry frame.

She would have died but for the charity of maid-of-all-work Kolpitts, who had taken her in and raised her as her own. And Branwen had tried so many times to be worthy of the life of servitude and prayer. But it was so very hard… Especially when she was *so* hungry.

'Careful!' a voice said.

Branwen had not heard the Sister approach. And now she had splashed the Sister's armoured boot with filthy water. She did not dare look up. 'Forgive me, holy Sister!'

The Sister knelt beside her and put her hand out. Branwen flinched as the Sister's hand touched her chin and lifted her face. Through her tears the maid-of-all-work found herself looking directly into the Sister's eyes. Her suit of armour was black as night, with a curling tracery of interwoven stems, acid-etched into the ceramite. Her face was fine as marble, her gaze resolute.

Branwen was mortified. It was not just any Sister, but Lizbet of the Sacred Sword, the most sublime of the Battle Sisters in the abbey. Stories filtered down to the scullery maids of her skill with bolt and blade. Of terrible foes cut down in their pride. Heretics purged. Vengeance made real.

'Forgive me!' Branwen whispered and tried to pull away, but Lizbet held the maid's hands. They were scabbed and raw. Lizbet pressed them between her own and spoke a prayer of spiritual fortitude. At the end she said, 'For your enemies are brought down and broken, and we are risen and victorious.'

Branwen stared like one smitten. Sister Lizbet rose with the gentle whine of servos, her black power armour gleaming with reflected candlelight.

The refectory door opened and Sister Lizbet passed inside. For a brief moment the sound of prayer spilt out. Branwen could not understand a word, but the sound transfixed her. So pure, so transcendent was the song of angels that a wave of raw emotion swelled within her, filled her heart with fierce joy. She could still feel the touch of Lizbet's hands and as she looked at her own, she saw that the raw scabs were gone.

Tears of joy rose through her as she finished her scrubbing and hurried down to the abbey cellars, bucket in one hand, rag in the other. The edificium was a place of wide walkways, heavy with prayer, but the stairs wound down to the servant quarters. They were dark and narrow, the undressed stone marked with simple icons of faith.

Branwen rushed into the slop hall, tipped the dirty water away, hung her bucket onto its hook, dried her hands upon her skirts and hurried through the wide chambers to the scullery.

It was the only warm room, where the maids sat before the fire in the moments when they could draw breath. There was a long trestle table, with plain wooden benches along either side, and a cast iron candelabra hanging from the stone ceiling, the candle flames guttering in the draughty chamber.

Branwen saw the table was empty, the stacked wooden plates picked clean. The day's single meal had been eaten.

Branwen would not cry, she told herself, not when others were out there on the Obscurus Front, dying in their millions. The God-Emperor suffered for all time upon the Golden Throne, and what was her hunger compared to that?

She lifted her face to the candle flames to stop the tears from falling, and one of the cooks breezed in with a damp cloth and wiped the trestle boards clean.

'What's wrong, girl?' the cook called out. 'Don't you have work to do?'

'Yes,' Branwen said, 'but I have not eaten since yesterday, and I came down and–'

'Then don't be late next time!' the cook snapped.

'But–' Branwen started.

'Throne above! The pilgrim fleet has arrived, girl. We don't have time for your fussing.'

The dead boy's name was Antonius Balthabic. His mother was listed as a member of the houseless poor.

The local searcher of the dead, Gospar van de Myr, recorded pestilence as the cause of death. His mother and her three other children were taken to the local infirmary as Antonius' body was wrapped in a plain shroud, loaded onto the back of a handcart and taken to the pauper's grave.

Van de Myr went to the local chapel for the evening prayers. He was on his way home when he started to feel ill. His wife welcomed him, and they sat together to break the day's fast with an afternoon meal of posset and bread.

'You look unwell,' she said.

He forced a smile. 'A little chill, nothing more.'

Sister Dogmata Morgaulat stood in the refectory's high pulpit of Terran stone, shin-bone pointer in one hand. She read in her stern monotone as a handful of Sisters sat at the benches beneath her, picking at their meal, heads bent in prayer.

The mood was sombre as they meditated upon the day's lesson, the twenty-fourth verse from the *Strictures of Divine Felicity*. Morgaulat pronounced each line with due solemnity. The end of the strictures listed the sacrifices Saint Katherine's Sisters had made and the grief she had suffered at the loss of her standard bearer, Aoid of the Golden Gauntlet. Tears rose in her throat as she recited those. She barely even noticed the skull-faced cherub that hovered above her head. As she reached the bottom of the page, the cherub floated down. It turned the leaf with a creak of ancient leather. Morgaulat waited for the vellum to settle and her pointer found her spot, and then she went on.

Beneath her, Sisters began to rise from the benches. One by one they stood, made the sign of the fleur-de-lys and made their way out. When Sister Morgaulat brought the lesson to an end she said the prayer of Strength in the Face of Heresy, left the cloth marker upon the next day's reading and descended down the narrow stone steps, the prayers glowing within her like hot coals. She was already thinking of the heretics she had to burn. It was considered ill-luck to have unburnt heretics in the cells for the Feast of Landing.

Only Sister Lizbet remained sitting at the bench. Her white hair was stark against the gloss of her black armour. She made the sign of the fleur-de-lys and a quiet benediction of thanks.

'The Feast of Landing has been announced,' Morgaulat said to Lizbet. 'The canoness awaits.'

Sister Lizbet put her palms onto the table and pushed herself up, her meal unfinished.

'We will pray for you,' Morgaulat said.

Lizbet smiled briefly. 'Saint bless you,' she said.

* * *

The laundry air was hot and steamy. Maid-of-all-work Dysha dredged the load of laundry from the cauldron, slopped it into Branwen's basket, let the water drain through into the open gutter and then hauled the straps over her shoulders.

There was still so much to do, and Branwen said a prayer as she lifted the heavy basket and stumped towards the hanging room. She lifted each wet sheet and strung it over the long wooden slats and then hauled the pulley ropes, dragging the wet clothes up towards the ceiling.

She was carrying the next basket of wet sheets when her legs gave way. She shook herself and tried to push herself up, but the basket was so heavy.

Dysha came to help her lift the weight.

'I'm fine,' Branwen said, but then her legs gave way again. 'I'm sorry.'

Dysha pulled a crumb of carb from her pocket. 'Here!'

It hurt to swallow. Dysha gave her a sip of water.

Branwen pushed herself up, steadying herself under the weight of the basket.

Dysha looked at her. 'Wait for me at the time of the second watch!'

Branwen did not understand.

Dysha put a finger to her lips for silence. 'The second watch!'

The way to the Octagonal Tower ran along the Walk of Martyrs. A sense of dread grew within Sister Lizbet as she made her way along the sacred passage lit by candle flames of rendered tallow from those who had died on pilgrimage. Their scant light sketched out the ancient ornaments. There were carvings and murals, scrolls of pilgrims' skin tattooed with ornate calligraphy, and niches with ancient relics and the bones of ancient warriors – skulls piled one upon another – some so venerable that they had flaked into brown dust.

A few niches held the remains of whole squads. The empty sockets of their eyes stared out.

Their struggle was over, their martyrdom complete.

On either side were chambers set aside for prayer and reflection and training. They were all empty. The only Sisters she saw were the twins, Brace and Morcada, in the Scriptorum bent over their work, their faces obscured with bifocal goggle-loups, their quills poised over the vellum.

The Octagonal Tower was the tallest of the abbey's many spires. The scent of incense fell slowly down the stairwell as Lizbet arrived at the bottom. She climbed up through gloomy galleries of statues, paintings, murals and gold-worked reliquaries.

The broad stone stairs were flanked with golden prayer wheels that sent entreaties to the God-Emperor with each revolution. She put her hand to each and spun them as she climbed.

At the very top of the Octagonal Tower lay the canoness' chamber. Lizbet could feel the hum of the void-shield generators, and over it came the song of the robed prayer-servitors.

The canoness' cherub, Lanselos, was waiting at the top of the stairs, steel-skull visage blank, as its wings flapped slowly over its golden curls. 'Sister Lizbet!' its voice called out. 'The canoness awaits!'

Lizbet felt her mouth go dry, the air turn chill as the cherub pushed the door open and gestured her inside.

The canoness' chamber took up a whole floor of the Octagonal Tower. The chamber was lit with banks of candles set before a wide bookcase that filled two sides of the room – scrolls and parchments stacked in boxed shelves, while the lower shelves were packed with leather-bound tomes and grimoires. But otherwise the room was as plain and bare as any other Sister's cell – a stone cot, blankets of sackcloth and the canoness' own suit of sacred armour.

The canoness was kneeling at a carved wooden prie-dieu, open book and triptych images of Our Martyred Lady laid out before her.

'Please join me,' the canoness said.

They knelt together. The book was the canoness' personal book of hours. The bookmark had been cut from the skin of a penitent, the devotional tattoos still embossed across its length, the end weighted down with a miniature skull of carved bone. On the left page were lines of prayer, while the facing side had an illuminated page which depicted the moment Saint Katherine landed upon Holy Cion.

Back then, the planet had been a den of heresy, the Pilgrim Plains filled with the massed armies of the Oracles of Strife. The saint had landed alone against them. She had cut down their prophet and then routed the armies.

Lizbet took in the tenebrism scene. The Bolt loomed high in the background, but in the foreground stood Saint Katherine, dressed in golden armour, her sword drawn to smite her foes, illuminated by a single beam of sunlight.

Lizbet found herself gazing into the illumination. Such peerlessness. Such beauty. She felt emotion rise within her and made the sign of the fleur-de-lys as she joined the canoness in the Prayer of Servitude.

Serve with faith, serve with devotion and accept the moment of sacrifice.

As the two Sisters finished their prayers, the page turned by itself, onto the next hour's prayer, which showed Saint Katherine locked in mortal combat with a daemon.

The saint rocked back upon her heels, as she swung two-handed at the foe. Lizbet knew that stance. It was that of a fighter struggling for their life. A desperate strike to throw an enemy back for a moment.

Lizbet took in the daemon and felt the visceral instincts of the fighter within her.

It was a serpent of darkness with spreading wings, claws of steel, a great maw of barbed fangs. Lizbet made the sign of the fleur-de-lys once more. She did not know how she would fight that beast, but she knew that she would die trying.

The canoness walked across to a wooden bench at the bottom of the bookshelves. Next to it was a small side table, formed in the shape of the fleur-de-lys, upon which was a silver tray of light morsels and a silver ewer.

She poured them both a cup of water. It was the same water they drank in the refectory, drawn from the holiest springs on Cion, but somehow, being here in the canoness' presence, the water tasted sweeter and more wholesome.

She said, 'I have taken the augurs. The Ritual of Landing will take place seven days from now. I would like you to take the part of the saint.'

It felt like an expected blow; painful, no matter how much Lizbet was braced against it. Her composure slipped for a moment. 'Canoness, I am sure that there is a better candidate than I. I speak from honesty, not humility.'

'Are there faults that you need to confess?'

Lizbet blanched. 'Many,' she said. 'Pride. Fear. When I look inside myself, I see many more sins.'

Ysolt put her hand on the Sister's arm. 'Pray upon it. Seek the saint's guidance.'

Before the gates of the abbey, a row of iron stakes were set upon the edge of the Bolt. Beneath Sister Morgaulat, the Pilgrim Plains stretched out to the horizon. The temples, chapels and triumphal arch were diminished by distance.

One by one the heretics were brought out and lashed to the

stakes with blessed chains. It was human to be tempted, she knew, for she was human as well and she knew the pain of her charges. But heresy was an infection that had to be cauterised. There could be no mercy.

She offered each a last chance to recant. Those that did were granted the swift death of a bolt to the brain. Those that refused were anointed with holy promethium, before the spark of purity was put to their clothes.

'And they shall be purged with blade, bolt and flame,' Saint Katherine had said, and Morgaulat made the sign of the fleur-de-lys. Their souls were damned. The God-Emperor would show no mercy.

The shouts died away as night came on. One by one the incinerating fires dwindled to smoking embers, here and there a melted gobbet of fat burnt with a smoky flame.

The Bell of Ancestral Transgressions tolled as the sun set. Lizbet's lips moved as she ran through the High Gothic prayers, each word tumbling out as if she were in a race against time.

She wore a plain robe of undyed cotton, onto which had been carefully scribed Gothic minuscule devotional texts. She prayed with a rare fervour, eyes pressed closed, hands lifted, lips tumbling over her catechism with all the intensity of a long-suppressed confession.

This was a simple beehive chapel set in the abbey walls, with a small statue of plaster and pigment.

There were finer representations in the chapels and halls higher up in the edificium. Statues of polished jasper, dressed in cloaks of gold, with faces carved by masters of their art and inset with precious stones: wounds of sardonyx, garnet cabochon blood drops and eyes of blue topaz, sparkling like sunlight in a pool. But Lizbet liked the bare simplicity of this place.

The saint stood in her suit of power armour, one boot upon

the head of a heretic, her cloak flapping about one leg. Her helmet was off, and her unblemished face was stern and fearless.

She had always felt close to Saint Katherine. The saint's holiest images were tattooed upon her body: a red sword upon her left breast and a teardrop of blood on the skin of her left cheek. An image of Saint Katherine ran down her left shoulder and arm, a radiant halo about the saint's hooded head, a sword in one hand and a staff in the other, from which a banner curled bearing the skull and surmounted cross that were the symbol of her Order.

'Blessed are those that die for the Emperor. Blessed are the wound-takers and the wound-givers. Blessed are those who smite His enemies. And blessed is the mind too small for doubt.'

Under the bare cotton shift, Lizbet could feel a sudden chill in the air. She thought that someone had spoken to her, looked about and cursed the interruption. She took a deep breath and found the groove of her prayer and started again, from the beginning.

The chill came again. Lizbet knew that the words were in her imagination, a temptation designed to distract her prayer, and she focused even harder.

But when they came a third time, they were like a superior addressing a novitiate. It was as loud and clear as the chime of the bell. And her eyes blinked open.

Lizbet, my child, why do you doubt?

Lizbet stared at the statue of Saint Katherine the Triumphant.

Why do you doubt? The words came again, and Lizbet imagined she could see tears in the statue's eyes.

Lizbet struggled to answer. The words were plain. 'I am not worthy.'

The saint's face seemed to soften before her. *But if not you,* the statue seemed to say to her, the voice full of emotion, *then who?*

* * *

The daemon threw itself against the Faultline and reality stretched and bulged like a pregnant belly.

For a moment it seemed that the skeins of sanity might fray or snap. But they held, and at last the daemon Gloranthrax fell back, exhausted. But there was an answering call of pain and desperation from its brethren in the warp.

It did not have long to wait.

iii

Searcher of the dead Gospar van de Myr's fever came on suddenly. He died that first night, his body taken to his family tomb behind the chapel of Saint Jerome.

His wife was taken to the local infirmary as night fell over Holy Cion.

At the time of the second watch, maid-of-all-work Dysha came to Branwen's cot and shook her awake.

'Come!' she whispered.

Dysha took Branwen's hand and led her along the dark stairs that went down to the cellars. The ancient chambers had once been piled high with stores of food and drink, but they had been picked clean long before and now echoed to the sound of starving vermin. Branwen's guts were so empty they felt as though they had been twisted into rope.

The air was cool as they descended into the cellar. The only sound was the screech of a dying rat. Dysha led her past the yawning side chambers. At the third, there was a heavy cloth and a glimmer of light within.

'Here,' she said, and pulled Branwen through. Inside, a group of girls sat in a ring, their pinched and weary faces lit by a single candle flame.

'I have brought another,' Dysha said.

Branwen stepped forwards into the light.

'The foundling,' one of them hissed.

'What have you brought?' another called out.

'Nothing,' Branwen said. 'I did not know. I need not stay...'

Dysha caught her hand and pulled her down into the ring. Branwen could feel the mood in the room. 'Saint Katherine, hear me. I will bring food. I swear this by your sword and your blood.'

The girls had been waiting for this moment all day. Dysha passed a metal bowl from hand to hand. Each of them tipped in whatever they had foraged: beetles, worms, maggots picked out from the rotting grain sacks. She tipped them all into a pot of hot water, slipped on the lid to trap the steam and left them to cook.

'Who will lead us in prayer?'

They looked around for the most devout among them.

The candle flame reflected from each of their eyes, and Branwen returned their gaze. The light reminded her of the God-Emperor, who had suffered for eternity upon the Golden Throne and who was like a beacon to them all. None of them were worthy of the God-Emperor's grace; not a single one. *He* had sacrificed everything for humanity and yet they were gathered to feast on stolen food.

Branwen took a deep breath and made the sign of the fleur-de-lys. She tried to sound confident as she stuttered, speaking with deep feeling. 'There is one God, and He is the Emperor, and He

sits upon the Golden Throne, and He suffers for us all. We...'
She struggled to get her thoughts back on track, but hunger was
slow torture and she had been hungry for as long as she could
remember.

'We, your *miserable* servants, are unworthy of your care, and
we ask for your forgiveness for what we are about to do...'

At the end of the prayer the maids-of-all-work made the sign
of the fleur-de-lys, and Dysha lifted the lid. The maids leant for-
wards with anticipation as she ladled out the thin gruel. When
Branwen got to her own bowl, the maggots were almost gone.
'Have some of mine,' Dysha said, but Branwen shook her head.
The broth alone would be enough for her.

The girls were scraping the last of their maggots from the bottom
of the bowls when the curtains were thrown back. 'What are you
doing? Shirking from work?'

The maids leapt to their feet as the Mistress of Chores pushed
inside. She snatched the bowl from Dysha and dropped it in
disgust. 'Maggots! You are eating maggots?'

Dysha opened her mouth, but no sound came out. Only
Branwen spoke. 'No one else wanted them.'

Tula slapped her full across the face. 'You again! Throne above.
You know that these are the hours of fast?'

Branwen bowed her head. 'Sorry, ma'am. This is all my fault.
If you punish anyone, punish me. It was my idea. I was the one
who ate them.'

The Mistress of Chores looked around and they all nodded
to confirm what Branwen had said. 'Get out of here! Out of the
abbey. Before I think of something worse!'

Grief and recrimination boiled within Branwen as she grabbed
her meagre belongings and stuffed them into a hessian bag.

She had come, unwanted, to the abbey and now she was being thrown out again.

The abbey was asleep about her, but as she took the night-stairs to the herbarium, a shape was waiting for her.

'You can't go,' Dysha said.

'I have to.'

'She'll calm down.'

But Branwen was decided. 'She does not want me.'

Dysha could see that there was nothing she could say. 'Listen,' she said, 'my father works in the market at Jeromegate. Ask for him there. His name is Absalom. He will help you.'

Branwen nodded. She hated to leave like this, but she had transgressed and this was her punishment. There was not enough time for her to express all she wanted to say.

She briefly took Dysha's hand. 'Look after my mother.'

Dysha's throat was too tight to say any more.

Branwen hurried out into the herbarium. There were servitors at work with long poles, harvesting sheets of the stringy wet growth into their metal trolleys. She could smell the bubbling vats of algae as she rushed through to reach the back gate.

She knocked on the guardhouse door and a peephole window slid open.

'What is it, girl?' the gatekeeper snapped.

'I'm going down to the city.'

'At this hour?'

'Mistress Tula sent me.'

There was a rattle as the gatekeeper threw on a jacket and stumped out. A ring of heavy keys from his belt unlocked the tall wooden gates, and he pulled them wide enough for her to slip through. 'Be careful,' he told her.

She nodded as she looked out. A narrow stair had been

chiselled into the living rock, but the steps were cracked and chipped and broken in places. The sheer sides of the Bolt plunged a mile down to the city. Down there, the city of her birth waited under a pall of brown smog.

The gates banged closed behind her.

The city lay beneath her, an unfriendly and haunted place, as unknown and ominous as a stranger.

The sickness started in the habs surrounding the Bolt.

The infection spread faster than the parishes could deal with it. Sufferers bled freely from nose and mouth, and within a few hours the local infirmary was struggling to cope.

Bells began to toll.

The local enforcers were keen to contain the sickness and stop it reaching the Pilgrim Plains, where the wayfarers were crammed in cities of tents.

The hours of prayers were extended in an effort to halt the plague, but the infection continued to proliferate across the city until it had spread from the Boltquarter out through the neighbouring Leathermarket, Prayergate and Chantryside.

Throughout the night, lights burned in the infirmary wards and corpse-carts moved through the streets, taking the dead to their final rest.

After hours of treacherous descent, the sounds of the city began to loom up from the brown smog. Branwen could hear the rumble of iron-shod wheels grating over cobbles, worship-horns – the low hum of busy streets, of humanity.

The area about the bottom of the Bolt had been used as a midden. There was a deserted stretch of city filth, scattered with smashed glass, piles of rubble and rusted tins.

As she hurried across the wasteland, the Bell of Ancestral

Transgressions chimed high above her. On the eighth stroke she heard what sounded like a cat screeching.

It was a long, slow, haunting wail.

Branwen shivered.

It wasn't a cat, she thought. It was a human cry that turned into a scream of pain.

The screech came again, so close it felt as though it were coming from all about her. The dreadful caterwaul rang out, louder and closer. It felt as if she were being hunted.

Branwen went rigid as something touched her leg.

She jumped up, stifling a scream as fingers clawed up from the ground at her feet.

She stamped them back into the earth, but saw they were just worms, wriggling in the dirt beneath her. The soil was alive. Spiders, slugs and beetles were crawling away from the Bolt.

The caterwaul came again. Or was it laughter?

'Who is that?' she called.

The sound was closing about her now. A malevolent hiss.

'Who are you?' Branwen called, but there was no answer. 'I am Branwen, maid-of-all-work,' her voice came, trembling with fear. 'I am from the abbey.'

Snow began to fall. Branwen put her hands together and, thinking of Saint Katherine, she declared a prayer of courage in the face of darkness.

The flakes settled onto Branwen's head.

The danger was like a cloud passing overhead. Branwen felt a warm glow within her, and as the ice melted, the sound of the wailing faded away into the night.

Steeling herself, Branwen crept into the darkened city. Habs loomed up from the gloom, the narrow streets overhung with balconies and lit with spluttering gas lamps. Behind her, the Bolt rose like a snow-capped peak, the luminescent white marble of the abbey hanging like a moon over the city. She took a deep breath and pulled up her robe as she picked her way along.

The streets of the Boltquarter were awash with thin black mud. Piles of filth were stacked against the mouldering flakboard. Pinched and wary faces peered out from doorways as a corpse-cart rolled by, the cartier ringing his bell as he came.

The people had a haunted, wary look. From some of the houses came the sounds of weeping and pain, spilling through the closed shutters. Branwen hurried on, counting the turnings until she reached the top of Jeromegate.

At the end of the street was a chapel and a cobbled square. Branwen stopped before it. The sky opened up and a sudden movement made her jump.

It was an old lady, picking through a rubbish heap.

'Please, ma'am. Is this the Jeromegate market?' Branwen called.

The woman grabbed her bag of scraps and cowered as if Branwen were about to strike or steal from her.

'Is this the Jeromegate market?' Branwen repeated, coming closer.

The lady was small and hunched with a patched knitted shawl tied about her neck. She shrank back as Branwen approached, then turned and hurried away.

Branwen paused and looked about. It would be hours until dawn and she was in a state of shock. She wanted to crawl away, like a wounded animal, and await the release of death. She found a place behind the chantry chapel where the graves butted up against the hab walls.

It was dark and secluded. Old tombstones had been cleared away, the aquila monuments and statuary stacked against the chapel wall. She picked over freshly dug graves to a corner near the altar of the chapel, found a stone marked with the fleur-de-lys and nestled down next to it.

She was so close she could make out the carved letters:

Allyana Evanga, who gave her daughter to the Order of Our Martyred Lady, and was forever blessed.

Branwen felt comforted by this inscription. She pulled her knees up to her chest and wrapped her arms about herself in an attempt to keep warm, but sleep did not come easily. Her stomach ached with emptiness.

She could hear the scratch and shuffle of vermin, the creak of old timbers, the chime of brass bells inside the chantry chapel.

She should have said no, she thought. She should have had faith in the Emperor to provide. She should have worked harder. She should not have listened to Dysha.

Her guilt slowly wound in upon itself, and all the time her mind kept going back to the moment that Sister Lizbet had knelt down before her and pressed Branwen's hands within her own. The pale face, set against the black power armour, the intense green eyes, the sense of mercy – the touch of the Battle Sister's hands.

As she huddled in the darkness, the sounds of sickness grew about her.

She could hear coughing nearby.

The sound grew louder as the darkness began to pale, and Branwen rose and picked her way through the graves.

It was the hunched old woman. She was wrapped in her dirty shawl, sitting slumped upon the earth, her head bowed. The cough rattled the old lady's whole body. It was a rasping, hollow sound.

'Stay away!' she hissed, but Branwen came closer and put her arm about the old woman. The cough did not relent. It sounded like it was going to tear her apart.

Branwen thought of the times when she was a child and her mother had held her. And she did now what her mother had done, and put her hand upon the old lady's head.

The hair was stiff with dirt and Branwen could feel lice crawling over the woman's scalp, but she closed her eyes and spoke a prayer such as the Sisters recited, and bit by bit the old lady's cough relented.

iv

Sister Dogmata Morgaulat prepared, arming herself with bolter
and blade as the gunship waited for her outside the abbey's front
gates. The remains of the heretics were like charcoal drawings
of men, held to the stakes with blackened chains. She made the
sign of the fleur-de-lys as she stepped up into the craft.

Her gunship spiralled down the black granite column of the
Bolt and landed in the wasteland, with a roar of retro-thrusters
blasting up a dirty cloud of dust and debris.

The assault ramp slammed down and Sister Morgaulat stepped
out. She could smell fear and panic. She had served long enough
to know that crisis was the spark from which heresy ignited. She
would go into the city, find its source and uproot it.

The narrow street was crowded with people, but they fell back
before the figure of Battle Sister Morgaulat. The crowd fell silent
as she strode into Jeromegate Square.

Ahead of her she saw a young girl, dressed in the robes of the abbey. The girl looked tired, her cheeks pinched, her hair cut short and tied back with a folded cloth. Her hand was placed on the head of one of the multitudes, and she spoke solemnly in a language forbidden to all but the holiest upon Cion.

Morgaulat strode across the cobbles. Silence fell onto them all.

'How dare you wear the robes of the abbey?' she demanded.

The girl looked up in horror and started to speak as Morgaulat's power-armoured fist reached out and took hold of her.

Branwen knelt in chains as the gunship lifted up. She had never been in such a craft, and felt uneasy as it started to wind up the side of the Bolt. She thought she was being taken back to her place in the scullery, and dreaded seeing the Mistress of Chores again. Instead, the gunship touched down on the broad approach leading to the abbey gates.

As she exited the craft, Branwen noticed the path was lined with a row of iron stakes upon which blackened bodies hung.

'Heretics,' Sister Morgaulat said as she marched Branwen through a wicket and into the abbey.

A set of broad stairs stood before them, and the Sister led her forwards into the edificium, where the Sisters dwelt. Branwen had only ever come here to clean, but soon she was taken to one of the towers. She had never been so high up in the abbey before. It was so different to the sculleries below, which were hectic and filled with all sorts of noises; the edificium was almost silent by comparison.

'This way,' the Sister said, leading her through various richly decorated corridors. Branwen kept her head down, watching her feet as they swept over the worn stone.

Eventually, they stopped outside a door.

'Here.'

The Sister motioned her forward. Branwen bowed to her, then hurried inside.

There was a small chapel set into the wall of the abbey. The room was heavy with ancient faith – scarlet candle-lumens flickered in the draught, and golden icons lay under a thick rime of time and dust.

'Wait here,' the Sister said, and then shut the door behind her, turning the key in the lock.

Apart from a half-sized statue of Saint Katherine, Branwen was alone. There was a single window. It was little more than a narrow embrasure, thousands of feet up. She strained to hear the city. She wanted to be down there. There were sick people waiting for her help.

She could hear the bells tolling, and she knelt before the statue, praying fervently.

'Dear Saint Katherine, thank you for the grace to heal the sick. Thank you to Sister Lizbet, who gave me that grace by laying her hands upon my own. Please send the Sisters down to the city, where they could do so much more than I.'

The abbey was hushed as Ysolt made her way past the librarium and scriptorium and finally reached her own high chambers. The serving woman had been summoned and was kneeling outside her chamber door.

She was one of the maids-of-all-work, dressed in plain homespun.

'You are Kolpitts?' Ysolt asked.

'Yes, ma'am.'

'How long have you worked here?'

'I was born here,' Kolpitts said. 'And my mother before her and her mother before that. I don't think we know who was the first of our line to be entered into holy service here, but we have all done our best, lady canoness.'

'And who is your daughter?'

Kolpitts swallowed. 'Well, she's not mine really. She was a foundling, left before the abbey gates. She was just a babe. I was cleaning the steps when I found her. I heard her, and I walked over and there she was. A starving thing, swaddled in cloth. And I picked her up and brought her in. How could we leave her? I named her Branwen, forgive me, after the canoness. The one before Linelt, who was martyred like Our Lady. I didn't mean to disrespect her. Not at all. I meant it as a compliment. Not meaning anything by that, great lady.'

Ysolt paused. 'Canoness Branwen. A fine warrior. You chose well. She should bear that name with pride. I wanted to ask you about her. She was sent away. Why?'

'She crossed the Mistress of Chores. A secret feast. Just things they found in the cellar. Nothing that the Sisters would eat.'

'Indeed,' Ysolt said. 'And her education?'

Kolpitts paused. 'I taught her as well as I could. The same as all the girls. They learnt their prayers and thread work, and cleaning, of course.'

'Did she learn to write?'

'Well, we all learn our letters. Not that we have much use for them. But I don't think she ever read. There's no time, to be honest.'

Ysolt's eyes were intent. 'Was she ever taught by one of the Sisters?'

'No.'

'You are sure?'

'Yes. What would she learn? Forgive me. She's a good girl.'

'You know that it would be heresy to impersonate a holy Sister of Our Martyred Lady?'

Kolpitts nodded solemnly.

The serving girl seemed honest, Canoness Ysolt thought to herself, after Kolpitts had left.

According to Morgaulat, Branwen had spoken the finest High Gothic she had ever heard. As she finished lighting the candles, she stopped. It was a miracle.

She closed her eyes and felt a sense of calm. She looked at the flames before her. With a single taper Ysolt lit each candle, wick by wick. This was how faith worked. A lone flame could ignite the faith of a million.

But that was also how heresy worked. One small spark could tip a whole planet into madness. And heresy often came in beguiling forms.

Branwen had been kneeling for hours when the door creaked open. She tried to rise but her legs were so stiff that she stumbled as she rose.

The candles cast little light in the room, enough to show power armour and the tabard of Our Sacred Lady, but not the face of the newcomer.

'You are Branwen, daughter of Kolpitts, the foundling left outside the abbey gates?' the Sister asked.

'Y-yes,' Branwen said.

'You may stand. Tell me what happened.'

'I'm sorry, mistress. I was working on the stairs and I was late to the supper and–'

'Tell me about the city. What happened there?'

Branwen looked down at her feet. 'I was sent away. I slept next to the Chapel of Saint Jerome. And there was an old lady. She was sick, and I knew I could help her.'

'You healed her.'

Branwen paused. 'Yes, I did. You see, Sister Lizbet had healed my hands earlier that day, and I think a little of her essence remained within them.'

'And what did you say to her?'

'I just spoke as I felt.'

The Sister took in a deep breath. 'I am Sister Morgaulat, Mistress of Redemption. You understand that you are accused of heresy.'

Part Two

Now

Shrine World of Ayaan

'Fear not the terror of night,
Nor the pestilence or plague,
He is your shield, your blade and your light,
In Him you will find refuge.'

– Song of Dominica

í

The Fang Takers Revolt had been defeated, its leaders slain, its holy places purged and burnt with holy fire, its shattered remnants driven deep into the Ashgarths. To celebrate this reconquest of yet another world, the lord militant had brought the commanders of the Astra Militarum together at the Unification Palace. But Sister Dialogus Dovere, of the non-militant Order of the Illuminated Page, approached the garden party with a sense of dread.

She arrived early and was let through by an honour guard of Vostroyan Firstborn. She stood alone as waiting staff made the final preparations.

The formal walled garden was a dusty expanse of gravel paths, low parterres and wilting rose beds. Aquila banners hung from the metal lumen-posts, and there were long trestle tables set by the gate with lines of cut crystal glasses half filled with amasec. It was all very pleasing to the eye, but it was the socialising that she disliked. She was happier alone in the libraries of her Order, but her canoness had assigned her to attend and so she must.

She stood to the side as the gardens filled with Militarum top brass. They came through the garden gate, took a glass and moved past her, unsure how to address a member of the Adepta Sororitas.

She was aware that her stiff wimple and augmetic data-goggles did nothing to break the ice.

They slid past her, in buoyant mood, jovial groupings of silk velvet shakos, embroidered double-breasted greatcoats, cavalry boots and starched collars, sporting their fresh bars and badges and service medals.

They did not want to talk theology. They wanted to exult in victory. The front line was moving onwards, and the minds of all the assembled Militarum were looking forward to the next engagement. The next planet. The next sector to be brought back to Imperial rule by the Indomitus Crusade.

Dovere took up a position next to a ring of commissioned officers and stood, trying to think of something to say as they recounted the events of the recent weeks. They had turned the flanks of the Fang Takers again and again in a series of devastating tank battles, and kill teams had located their commander, a mutant named Pastor Scylus, deep in the Ashgarth Mountains, wiping out his entire entourage.

At last she spotted an officer standing alone, glass in one hand.

'I am Sister Dovere of the Order of the Illuminated Page,' she said to him. 'You must be Captain Ayling of the Valkenberg Kossaks?'

He was a commanding man, in tribal plaid and with steel-grey eyebrows and thick tufts of hair jutting out from either nostril. 'Yes,' he said, a little stiffly. 'I am. Who told you?'

She pointed to the sleeve of his black velvet overcoat which was neatly folded at the elbow and pinned up. 'Fact one – you are missing an arm. I assume it was lost in battle. Fact two – when the serving women brought the platter of crudites to you, you fumbled for a moment and clamped your glass to your side with the stump of your arm to free up your hand. Deduction – you lost your arm recently. Twelve members of your regiment have suffered limb-altering injuries, but only three recently, at the Battle of Itoji Ridge. But of those, only one was an officer of your rank.'

He laughed. 'Very impressive,' he said, then paused. The silence stretched on for an uncomfortably long time. 'Will you be joining us on the next push?'

'If the Emperor wishes it. Although there remains much work here.'

'Work?'

'Yes. Cataloguing the work of the sadhvus.'

'Sadhvus?'

She nodded. 'Yes. The local mystics.'

He frowned. 'Are they important?'

She turned her data-goggles full on him. 'They are. They have been here since the founding of the settlement. I believe there are matters of belief that date back to the very earliest days of faith.'

He nodded, not sure what to say. 'So… you don't fight?'

Over her power armour was a tabard inscribed with sacred texts, held in by a belt of knotted rope. 'I am of the Adepta Sororitas. Of course I am trained in war, but I am a Sister *Dialogus*. I fight against the darkness through the correct ordering of information. My realm is that of knowledge and faith. Knowledge especially. In its dissemination, and its limitation.'

She fixed him with her goggle augmetics and he seemed at a loss. At last she said, 'So, the campaign for Ayaan is winding up?'

'That appears to be the general consensus. We push on and leave the mopping up to the penal legions.'

'The Savlar Chem Dogs,' she said.

He shrugged. It appeared that he had little regard for the penal regiments. He noticed his crystal tumbler was empty and went to look for one of the servers. As he did so her vox-bead let out a whine. She grimaced in discomfort and put a finger to her ear, but the noise remained.

'So, these sadhvus,' he said, returning after having retrieved a fresh glass of amasec. 'Have you collected much information?'

'I have, but there is so much to work on. On top of that I am examining orphaned transcripts.'

'Orphaned what?'

'That is the name given to the data catalogue of unassigned astropathic messages.'

'Why are they unassigned?'

Her goggled eyes were blank. 'Many reasons. Missing hail credentials. Garbled imagery. Time signals that are out of date. Or, simply, they are so incomplete that their message proved indecipherable. Since the Great Catastrophe their number has increased disproportionately. I believe that some might come from beyond the Rift.'

'Is that so? And that is where we are all heading?'

She nodded.

'Do you think we will ever get there?' he asked.

'Of course. The Regent has said so.'

'I pray you are right.'

A century earlier, the fortress world of Cadia had fallen, and with its loss the Imperium of Man had been torn in two. A curtain of madness had been drawn across the galaxy. Shrine worlds, forge worlds, bastions of Imperial power had all been lost. And with them had gone all the temples, the ancient battlefields, the monuments, and all the art and beauty that had accompanied them.

The officer stood, considering this. Battle Group Phaedra was part of the Indomitus Crusade, whose mission was to reclaim the lost part of the Imperium.

'What do you think lies beyond?' Ayling said. 'A miasma of Chaos, or lone worlds battling bravely onwards?'

'I do not know. That is what we will find out.'

The sense of discomfort was growing stronger. Dovere tapped her vox-bead again and frowned.

'Excuse me,' she said.

The afternoon heat was waning, and in Holy City sadhvus and mendicants took their places on the broad stone stairs. They wore loose gowns of undyed homespun, and they prepared themselves to expound on the nature of faith, the forms of the God-Emperor, and the lives of the ancient saints. Acolytes also came, finding their own spaces in the crowd in which to sit, and watching over all of them was Sister Superior Helewise.

This was her first command. She stood in her black power armour before the heavy doors of the Great Minster, her power sword, Reckoning, sheathed over her back, white hair framing her face like a bascinet. A scar marred one cheek, the tattoo of a fleur-de-lys was inked onto the other. Her power armour's systems kept her body cool, but as she stood, head exposed to the intense heat, beads of sweat glittered on her forehead.

Sister Ephraina stalked across the square. To the folk of Holy City, it was hard to differentiate her from Helewise. She had the same white hair, boltgun and black armour adorned with fluttering purity seals. But she was older than Helewise, and her face showed it. She had lost an eye, and now a red augmetic lens glowed in its place.

'Something is wrong,' she said.

'You can feel it too?'

Ephraina nodded. They looked about, but all seemed normal, for a warzone...

Helewise and her Battle Sisters had been fighting alongside the Imperial forces for the last six months. They had appeared in the front line, where attacks were faltering, or where troopers were starting to lose faith. They'd led by example, inspiring the wavering troops with prayers and hymns. It had been ruthless and dangerous warfare. They had lost seven Sisters in the campaign against the Fang Takers, and their martyrdoms were still fresh. Helewise remembered them all. But she remembered the deaths of Lalott and Nifach most clearly. Their martyrdoms had been sublime. They fuelled the faith within the remaining Sisters like hot coals.

Helewise voxed Josmane. There was no answer.

These buildings interfered with vox-systems, but Josmane could not be that far off, even if she was at the other end of the Great Minster complex – a three-acre sprawl of chapels, cloisters, scholams, meditation gardens and pilgrim-halls, where the mendicants were housed in long vaulted chambers and fed the holy langar.

She touched the bolt pistol mag-locked to her thigh, tapped her vox-bead onto the short-range codes. 'Aiguell. Something is wrong.'

Aiguell was in the Rhino, stationed behind the Great Minster, manning the vox and pintle-mounted storm bolter. *'Confirm,'* Aiguell replied. *'Only short-range vox is working.'*

'How long's it been down?'

'Five minutes. Something is blocking it. Militarum bands down as well. Only personal bands still functioning.'

'I can't raise Josmane.'

There was a pause. *'I have her,'* Aiguell said.

'And all is well?'

'Confirmed.'

'Who is at the tomb?'

'Dominora.'

'Good,' Helewise said. 'Send Lucitta there as well.'

'Confirmed.'

Ephraina and Helewise looked out.

The Sisters of Our Martyred Lady were stretched thin within Battle Group Phaedra. Her commandery was deployed where they were most needed, bringing faith and drive to the forces of the Imperium. The next nearest Battle Sisters on Ayaan were hundreds of miles distant. Their void-cathedrum, the *Daughter of the Emperor*, was two systems away, spearheading the crusade on another battlefront. On the scale of the Indomitus Crusade, Ayaan was just a sideshow. If anything happened at Holy City, then they would have to deal with it alone.

This was her first command. She could not break the trust placed in her.

'Our orders are to defend the saint,' Helewise said, half to herself.

Ephraina nodded. The saint was Saint Elaire the Anchorite, who had lived her entire life within the Minster complex.

Helewise had already scoped the city out. The fabric dated from the later Imperial colonial era, but it had been constructed on a much older street plan – a confused tangle of alleys and lanes, overshadowed by the five-storey habs and ornate covered balconies. Enemies could be anywhere, and she only had nine other Sisters with her, spread about the minster complex.

Helewise lifted her helmet onto her head and Ephraina did the same. Both Sisters felt the cool wash over them. Helewise's targeting matrix appeared within her ocular display.

Ruslana had been leading prayers in one of the side chapels. Josmane came round from the other end of the minster. Both of them took their place on the steps, Ruslana with bolter, Josmane's underslung pilot flame hissing on her flamer. Each of them was ready, and alert to danger.

The tension was palpable.

'Morgandrie. See anything?' Helewise voxed.

She pictured Sister Morgandrie in the bell tower, heavy bolter resting on raised knee, saying a brief prayer as she slammed a fresh magazine into her weapon.

'Nothing,' the other Sister said.

Helewise drew her bolt pistol from her thigh. She scanned the narrow street for anything: a glint of metal, a gun barrel hidden in a shaded window. The startled flight of a bird. The black eyeball of a gun muzzle.

Their isolation did not daunt them. It was a test of their faith and their ability. And they were Sisters of Battle: the finest human warriors the Imperium could field. And more than that, they were the loyal servants of the God-Emperor. He was with them. Each of them could feel His presence. She was ready for whatever He had in store for her. Battle, dismemberment, martyrdom. She welcomed them all.

One of the waitresses held a platter of food out to Sister Dovere.

'No,' Dovere said. The waitress nodded and moved on. Through the armoured glass panes of the Unification Palace, Dovere could see figures making their way to the doors. Lord General Sandvig stood out in his ornamental breastplate. She stepped over the box hedging, her power-armoured boots crushing the carefully manicured hybrids as the garden doors of the Unification Palace swung open.

Lord General Sandvig looked magnificent in his black iron

breastplate, embossed with an aquila in silver, and a smart uniform of pressed Navy worsted. He was a traditionalist who had risen through the ranks and survived a hundred wounds. He looked like he'd been zipped together with scars, and from his gait it was clear that at least one of his legs was augmetic. But he had brought them victory, and lifted his hand in response to their cheers. Victory had the power to forge many into one.

A waitress stepped forwards and handed the lord general a glass of amasec. The cut glass glinted in the sunlight and Dovere's data-goggles suddenly zoomed in on the symbol etched into it. It was a deeply heretical glyph.

Dovere shouted a warning as streaks of warp energy crackled in the air.

The lord general staggered back as the wild voltaic energy engulfed him. Lightning lashed out at the officers about him, transfixing them by the eyeballs. In an instant a chain of warp lightning threaded through the crowd, the force lifting each of its members off their feet.

There was a brief moment of unnerving silence before the bodies exploded with the force of ordnance. Fragments of cloth, muscle, skin and bone tore through the tightly packed crowd. Dovere's ocular feed captured it all in terrible detail before she was thrown sideways, engulfed in flames and screams.

An octopus of smoke, dust and flames swirled up into the air as Sister Dovere recovered and forced herself to stand. Her power armour had protected her, but the sight that greeted her through her goggles was appalling.

It was like the shambles of a mad butcher. Bodies – and bits of bodies – hung from the roses, the box hedging, and were splattered up the walls. Servants were already dragging the lord general inside and had got him to the shattered doors by the time she reached him. His body had left a broad smear of blood on the flagstones.

She knelt at his side, put her hands upon him and spoke a prayer of fortitude in the face of death. His eye opened for a moment, and what remained of his hands seemed to reach for her. He tried to speak, but all that came up was a gout of blood.

She laid her hands upon his head, pressed her eyes closed and prayed harder. But she was no Hospitaller, and too much damage had been done.

Lord General Sandvig died before her. His last battle was done. But her struggle still remained.

The Fang Takers were not finished if they had the power to strike here, at the very heart of the battle group. She cursed herself for her failing. She had been trained to understand data, and yet she had clearly missed something vital.

ii

The 17th Savlar Chem Dogs were twenty miles out into the desert, trudging along the metalled bahn in a long dusty column as the afternoon heat cooled. The Chem Dogs were a penal legion, listed by Munitorum scribes as light infantry, but the truth was they equipped themselves and only stole what they could carry.

The Chem Dogs had a few helpers to carry their heavy gear – a pair of Munitorum half-tracks, five Scout Sentinels, and seven bad-tempered mukaali that grumbled and farted every inch of the way.

They were divided into large packs, grouped about their leaders. It was the turn of Major Chalice's lot to lead the way. They tramped along, ammo belts draped across their bodies, weapons slung over their shoulders, rebreathers filtering out the worst of the dust.

The regimental motto of the 17th Savlar Chem Dogs translated into Low Gothic as 'Never Stop'. Lord Commissar Aebram had told them it more times than Trooper Shin could remember.

It was a shit day to march, but they kept on, heads down, shoulders bent under the weight of their kit, sweating under the intense sun as heat waves shimmered about them, rippling the landscape.

'You all right?' Shin called to Wythers.

'You all right?' Echo said.

No one took any notice of him. Especially not Wythers. The big man stumped along beside him, sucking on his rebreather.

Wythers had been their colonel once, but nitra-chem addiction had tipped him into decline. He was as big and hunched as a cudbear. His swollen gut hung from his frame, and a rough mane of dirty-blond hair fell in matted dreadlocks about his face.

Wythers grunted in reply as he slipped another nitra-chem canister into his rebreather. It was a non-committal sound, and he sucked on his pipe, letting a thin stream of blue smoke escape from the corners of his mouth. 'This is a lot better than Savlar.'

Shin laughed. That was true enough. Anywhere was better than picking through the slag heaps, scavenging for chemical deposits.

Shin offered Wythers a strip of dried meat.

Wythers shook his head. The skin of his face sagged from narcotic use, and his eyes looked sad and weary, but thankfully sane.

Shin tore a strip and stuck it in his mouth, savouring the salty flesh. He chewed as they stumped along, humming an old mining song. The tramp of boots kept ringing out as the melody caught on. The song rippled down the column, then fell away again, as the sun began to sink towards the horizon, stretching their shadows across the road.

'How long's it been?' a voice rasped.

Shin turned. Dimok looked pale as he limped along.

Shin scratched the stubble on his scrawny neck. 'Six months.'

'No, you bastard. Today!'

Shin paused. He couldn't tell. 'Ten hours?'

'How much longer?'

'I don't know.'

They were on a mopping-up operation, which meant they'd be here hunting the Fang Takers down into every desert hellhole. They could keep marching for hours. Weeks. Months!

'Frekk,' Dimok winced. He'd taken a round in the backside two days ago and the wound wouldn't close. The rear of his trousers was stained dark with blood. But he could just about keep up by using his rifle as an improvised crutch. 'All right,' he said. 'Once we get there I'll rest up for a bit.'

Shin nodded, though he wasn't sure where 'there' was. 'You'd better not be asking me to help you out,' he said.

'I wasn't,' Dimok spat.

'Good. If you want help, you should see Sawbones.'

Sawbones was the regimental medic, a hissing, malevolent bundle of rags.

'Frekk you,' Dimok shot back.

'Frekk you,' Echo said.

Shin shouldered his backpack. Coming towards them, along the bahn, was an armoured column. The sun glinted off the ceramite facets of the tanks. Pennants flew from their antennae. They filled the road.

'Who the frekk are they?' Shin cursed as he took a bare swig from his bottle.

Echo repeated the question.

Wythers barely lifted his head. He was beyond caring, but Dimok spoke through his pain, 'Don't know. They've got barrel covers on.'

'Covers on,' Echo said.

Wythers sucked on his chem-pipe. He'd cut this rubber mouthpiece from some frekker in the medicae. The rim was gone and the rubber was starting to crease and split, making a rattling sound in his throat.

'I don't think those bastards are going to move,' Dimok hissed when the tanks were barely a hundred yards off. They were coming four-wide, filling the bahn. The Dogs waited for the order, which came almost too late as one of the Mercies saw the danger. A gun fired, and a whistle blew. 'Move aside!'

Wythers was too high on nitra-chems. Shin had to knock him sideways as the tanks swept towards them. The two men tumbled into the drainage ditches, ate dust as the tanks swept past, whipping skirts of sand about them.

'Frekking bastards!' Shin hissed as he pulled his rebreather from his mouth, and wiped off the grit. But the fall had knocked Wythers' nitra-chem canister free and the liquid drained out into the dust.

His fury was sudden.

He lashed out. The nearest person was Dimok. Shin could hear the wheeze of breath being knocked out of him as Wythers went for the wounded man's face.

'Hey!' Shin shouted over the roar of the tanks. 'Calm down! Here. It's all right. It wasn't us. It was those bastards!'

Wythers had Dimok by the throat, and the other man was already turning purple.

A whistle blew. It was Major Chalice, pushing his way through the crowd. 'Here!' he shouted, holding up a canister of chems. 'Let him go. No killing anyone today.'

Dimok dropped to the floor and gasped for breath. Wythers pushed the curtain of lank hair from his face and grabbed the nitra-chem canister, screwing it into place.

'That's it,' Chalice said. 'Keep sucking on that. Now, move along, Dogs. And you, Dimok!'

Shin helped Dimok up. 'Thanks,' the other man said as he

struggled to his feet and heaved up his pack, one shoulder strap at a time. He glared at Wythers. 'Frekking bastard.'

Echo repeated the words as the Mercies drove the Dogs on. Shin slapped Dimok on the shoulder. 'Come on! Keep up.'

'Keep up,' Echo said.

It took half an hour for the Vostroyan column to pass by. Only the commanders were visible, though their faces were obscured behind thick goggles and headscarves. Shin glared at them as they passed south. He could read their minds. Battle duties were done, and they were already thinking about the flesh pots of Main Camp.

He yearned for the decadence of a main-line trooper. Food, supplies, reconstitution camps. They should try life as a penal legionnaire, he thought. Nothing to look forward to but your own death.

When, at last, the convoy had disappeared into the haze, the Chem Dogs moved back onto the road. The tar was tacky, the surface torn up by the tank tracks. The black surface radiated the day's heat as the marching Chem Dogs fell into step.

The tramp of boots helped everyone keep their pace. Helped the endless miles pass as the afternoon started to tilt towards evening.

Dimok's wound still hadn't closed, and he was visibly struggling.

'You should have seen Sawbones,' Shin said.

Dimok grimaced as he tried to laugh. He caught sight of the hated medic. The old murderer had wrapped himself in a Vostroyan greatcoat, its hems torn, the left side singed and one of the sleeves stripped away. He shuffled along like a bundle of rags with legs. 'I'd rather die than see that mad bastard,' Dimok hissed.

A few moments later, Dimok tripped and fell. Shin tried to help him, but the man had lost too much blood. He started crawling forwards, along the bahn.

'Pick him up!' Major Chalice ordered.

Shin dragged Dimok up but the injured man's legs gave way, and he rolled off the road into the drainage ditch.

Shin grabbed Dimok's lasrifle, compared it to his own, then threw it back down.

'Let him be,' Wythers said. 'He's dead meat.'

'Dead meat,' said Echo, and Shin cursed.

It was true. A waste of good meat.

From the back of the column came the Mercies, black flak-coats flapping about their booted legs, bolt pistols cocked and loaded. Mercy Cody stopped over Dimok's body.

'I command you to rise!' he shouted.

Dimok's face was a determined snarl as he crawled, arm over arm.

'Stand!' the order came, but Dimok could not stand. Cody drew his bolt pistol, pointed it down and fired. The movement was practised, casual, perfunctory. Indifferent.

Dimok's body jumped as the round went through him, and he lay still.

Cody pulled the penal tag from Dimok's neck and stuffed it into a chest pocket. The column of Dogs left Dimok's corpse, his head lying in a growing pool of his own blood. His suffering was over. His sentence was complete.

iii

As the sun set, a stain darkened the eastern skies. Morgandrie's ocular reading screened out the glare of the setting sun and within seconds she had assessed the danger. 'Helewise! There is a brigade-strength armoured column. Twenty miles off. Approaching at speed.'

'Militarum?'

Morgandrie paused. She couldn't tell.

'Aiguell,' Helewise ordered. 'Get me the Militarum commander!'

There was a pause as Aiguell tried to raise the long-range vox. '*I'm trying…*' she said as she reeled through the wavelengths. '*Nothing yet…*'

But Morgandrie was already moving. 'Helewise!' she shouted. 'Explosion at the Unification Palace.'

Helewise felt her heartbeat slow. She had little patience for subterfuge, and exulted in the simplicity of combat: swordplay was her supplication, battle her worship, purging heretics the most sublime form of prayer. She braced herself. Reckoning sang to her. It yearned for heretic blood.

She was ready for battle, but the people in the square before her were not. The meat-stick sellers, sadhvus, sellers of shaved ice – they were all blithely ignorant as she waited for confirmation.

Morgandrie swung her heavy bolter up over the parapet and saw the flare of a missile soaring towards them. Her helmet's augmetics assessed its trajectory. 'Get the people out of the square!' she shouted. 'Missile incoming!'

Helewise had a few seconds. There was no time to get them to safety. She would have to lead them all in prayer. She began to chant the Fede Imperialis and the Sisters next to her joined in.

The whole square seemed transfixed. Mendicants, worshippers, traders, pilgrims – all of their eyes were fixed upon the four Sisters. 'A spiritu dominatus, Domine, libra nos – from the lightning and the tempest, our Emperor, deliver us!'

Their voices were drowned out as the Deathstrike missile passed overhead. It impacted a quarter of a mile to the east with roiling thunder and black smoke.

The shockwave of the explosion shattered every pane of glass. Sheets fell like buckets of water, lacerating those beneath. Gouts of dust and smoke and rubble flowed along the narrow streets and rolled out into the square, shrouding man, woman and vehicle in white dust.

A sudden silence dragged on for what seemed like minutes, although it could only have been seconds. Hands covered mouths. Eyes were wide open. No one moved or spoke. No one even seemed to be breathing. No one dared to exhale.

And then the screams began.

The Sisters were already moving. Ruslana herded the people out of the open square. Ephraina raised her bolter to her shoulder as Josmane stood beside her, flamer ready. Helewise was cold and calm. 'Aiguell, use the short-range vox. I am Sister Superior Helewise of Our Martyred Lady. I am assuming command of the city. Relay that to all units within range.'

Alarm klaxons wailed as another rocket slammed into the city, and then a third.

'There are two companies of Ayaan Carabineers,' Aiguell reported after a pause.

'Summon their commander at once.'

Helewise was frantically issuing orders as auto-fire sprayed the minster's facade. She recognised the Fang Takers at once. They had been hiding amongst the populace, and revealed themselves as they threw off their robes. They were all brute muscle, heretical tattoos gouged into flesh, faces hidden under executioner's hoods.

Helewise drew her bolt pistol and fired. Her skill was exemplary. Each shot was a demonstration of her skill and faith and training; a prayer to the God-Emperor, punishment upon the impure. Three shots knocked three insurgents backwards, then Morgandrie's heavy bolter opened up, its rounds hammering down from the minster tower. Their mass-reactive cores threw up a murderous cloud of shrapnel, and the remaining heretics were ripped apart, the settling smoke and dust revealing only dismembered gobbets of blood and flesh.

Helewise yearned to rush into battle, but she could not. Though she was the highest-ranking Sister here, she had her orders. 'South!' she shouted. 'Sister Ruslana will protect you!'

Ruslana waved the people south, out of the square, towards the only hope of safety. The people followed her directions. She could do no more. Her orders were to protect the relics of Saint Elaire the Anchorite.

Major Sire of the Ayaan Carabineers appeared a few minutes later, still buttoning up his jacket. The sight of the dead Fang Takers sobered him at once. He pushed his way through the fleeing crowd, his troops behind him dressed in longcoats and feathered shakos, their nervous hands fumbling with ornate laslocks. They were not a line unit but a local defence force, suited more to ceremonial duties. But they were all Helewise had and she would use them, just as she would use a knife when her chainsword malfunctioned.

'North-west?' he said as he continued to button up his jacket. 'The Ashgarths? That's impossible. An army cannot cross the Ashgarths.'

Another Deathstrike missile thundered overhead and landed in the northern habs. The warhead punched through the stonework, and blasted blocks of mortared sandstone out into the street. The boom rolled over them all.

'What strength of heavy weaponry do you have?'

'Two autocannons,' he said as his troops ran into the square, teams of four pushing the antique guns on their ornate carriages. She held her counsel. These troops needed missile launchers and meltaguns to resist an armoured spearhead.

'Ephraina, Aliciel and Josmane will go with you,' she said. 'Have faith! The God-Emperor has called you all to this moment.'

Ephraina stopped to make her battle vow. 'I will hold the enemy back. My body will be a shield to the weak. A scourge upon the heretic.'

Helewise nodded. She wished she could take Ephraina's place. 'Take my sword!' she said.

Ephraina looked at Reckoning.

It was a sacred blade, a relic of her Order.

She put her hand to the hilt, but shook her head. 'I cannot,' she said. 'It is yours, and you are the only one worthy to carry it.'

Helewise pursed her lips. She yearned to throw herself at the enemy in search of martyrdom. But she had to stay and command.

'The Emperor protects,' she promised.

Helewise paused as she focused. She had to still the bellicose spirit within her. She was the youngest Sister Superior within her commandery, but she was Sister Superior nonetheless, and so she had to take upon her the weight of leadership.

This stationing at Holy City had been intended to be a ceremonial duty. A chance to rest and restock themselves before they were sent to the next front line between faith and doubt. But now this was a moment of crisis, and one where she could not plunge into the thick of battle. Where she had to stand back and command others.

She considered her options. Her priority was the body of the saint. Elaire the Anchorite was as much a part of Holy City as the flagstones that Helewise stood upon. And more than that, she was a symbol of all they had fought for; not just on Ayaan but across the whole system. It was inconceivable that the saint's body should fall into the hands of the heretics. But it was also inconceivable that she should leave. She had been born within the city, had spent her whole life within the minster environs – the last forty years as an anchorite, bricked up within its walls with only a hatch through which she was passed her daily sustenance. The loss of her tomb to the enemy would be sacrilege.

Helewise's first order was to transfer the saint's remains to the Rhino.

'*Remove the saint?*' Aiguell demanded over the vox.

'Confirmed. Our priority is the saint. Then the relics. Then the people.'

* * *

Trooper Shin shielded his eyes, and called out the warning. 'Tanks!'

The column of troops grumbled as they reached for their rebreathers. Something was wrong. The tanks weren't on the road. They were coming across the Ashgarths, kicking up a cloud of dust in their wake.

As they stood watching, they saw the flash of missiles launching. Lord Commissar 'the Marshal' Aebram lifted his monocular.

His face was expressionless as he focused in on the symbols daubed upon the tanks. Fang Takers, in attack formation.

'I thought we had defeated them,' Colonel Salem said.

'If they had been defeated, we would not have been left behind to mop them up.'

'Should we be concerned?' Salem said.

Aebram put the monocular down. His tone was scathing. 'It seems to me that they have saved us the effort of flushing them out of their hole.' He looked about. The setting sunlight highlighted a few bumps and hollows amidst the featureless wastes.

'We will hold here,' he ordered. 'Three lines. One in reserve with the Sentinels. We will need them if any of these bastards break through.'

Colonel Salem called his company commanders to him. They stood as he gave commands. 'A column of Fang Takers,' he said.

'I thought they were beaten?' Major Chalice said.

Salem smiled coldly. 'Clearly they didn't get the vox-script. That, or they're going out with a final flourish. Either way, they're heading in our direction.'

'And what are we supposed to do?' Chalice said.

'The Marshal's orders are to hold and then counter-attack.'

Chalice laughed.

'You think that's funny?'

'For us to counter-attack an entire armoured column? I think it's ridiculous.'

'Congratulations, Major Chalice. Your company will lead the front line of defence.'

Captain Dokona laughed and Chalice's cheeks darkened. 'And how the frekk are we to hold tanks back?'

'Faith,' Salem said, and Chalice cursed. Salem wasn't happy either. 'Think you can do better?'

'Yes,' Chalice said. 'I think I can.'

Mercy Quinn heard the disturbance. 'Anything wrong?' he said.

Salem nodded. 'Yes, sir. It seems that Major Chalice does not have faith in our ability to hold. It seems he doubts his Dogs' combat effectiveness. I recommend a double complement of Mercies to accompany the major's unit. We would not want his lack of confidence to weaken the resolve of the troopers.'

Salem smiled as Chalice stalked off, a pair of Mercies standing behind him.

That's the last time he'd have to deal with that cocky bastard, Salem told himself, as he went to give orders to the rest of the regiment.

IV

The mukaali tugged against their electro-leashes as the crates of heavy kit were unloaded. There were a few stubbers and heavy bolters, the weapons and ammo scavenged from the hands of the dead.

The munitions and stimms were shared around. Salem's Dogs got best pickings. Chalice's lay in sullen silence. They laid out whatever they had: demo charges, grenade launchers, krak grenades – but there was never enough to go around.

The column of dust grew steadily closer.

Shin stuck a piece of dried meat into his mouth to stop himself grinding his teeth. He was lying in the drainage ditch. Wythers was next to him, sucking furiously on his chem-pipe.

The tanks were nosing forwards, looking for the road. There were a pair of Leman Russes and then Chimeras, with Fang Takers sitting on the hulls.

Wythers switched to his rebreather.

'Don't take the stimms too early,' Shin told him, but Wythers was beyond caring. He was muttering to himself. He seemed to be listing all his crimes.

Shin thought about how he had been sentenced to Savlar. He didn't like to think about that past. He gritted his teeth and focused on the moment. Around him the Chem Dogs were slipping their stimms into their rebreathers. Shin slipped his in as well. It stopped the pain, if nothing else. And it would stop him reminiscing.

He wanted to take a drag of his rebreather. 'Wait...' he whispered to himself. 'Wait.' As the tanks pushed forwards, dust swirled up from their tracks.

All along the line, the chems were kicking in. One by one the Dogs charged. The first were mown down by heavy bolter fire. Shin held back, but sucked in an acrid lungful of chems and felt his rage rising. He needed to kill.

Wythers went first and Shin followed right behind. Multi-laser bolts blinded him as he ran. He saw one of the Dogs go down before him, the las-bolt setting the trooper's robes aflame. Shin knelt to grab the demo charge the man had been carrying. The tank was twenty feet before him, dust skirts billowing up around it as its turret spun sideways, its nose-mounted heavy bolter barking.

Shin pulled the fuse, and stumbled forwards, mag-locking the charge to the tank's side.

It slammed home with a satisfying *clunk* and held, and Shin threw himself to the floor.

The tank ground on for a few seconds before the shaped charge went off.

He thought it was a dud at first.

The tank rolled onwards and Shin pushed himself up, just as a tongue of fire licked out of the commander's turret. A second later, the tank's ammo exploded, sending the turret spinning fifty feet into the air. A man tried to climb out before the inferno claimed him, and Shin had to shield his face as an incandescent white flame roared up through the turret hatch like a firework. The sudden blaze lit the desert. Shin could see Dogs all around him stooping and firing as the hooded Fang Takers charged towards them, just as eager to get into combat.

One of them ran towards Shin, gunning his chainsword as he shouted heresies. The stimms kicked in, and Shin met the Fang Taker with equal fury, swinging his lasrifle round and connecting with the heretic's head.

There was a spray of teeth and blood as the man went down, head slamming sideways into the dirt. Three more Fang Takers appeared before him, and Shin charged at them.

The largest had a necklace of human teeth about his neck. Shin put his bayonet into the heretic's chest, ducked and twisted as the blade snagged, dropped his rifle as a las-bolt hissed past his head, dragged his war-knife free.

A club slammed into his back and he was thrown to the floor, rolling as he desperately avoided the next blow. And then there was a roar as Wythers barrelled into the Fang Taker above him. He charged, pistol in one hand, trenching tool in the other. The crude weapon slammed into one man's chin, shattering the bone as the blunt metal kept driving upwards.

The Marshal watched his first line surge forwards into the Fang Takers' armour with grim satisfaction. The heretics stalled, their warbands dismounting from the half-tracks behind and rushing into hand-to-hand combat.

He gave the order for the second line to engage.

Colonel Salem led the charge. He was a ferocious fighter, and the Marshal watched him go as he signalled to Captain Dokona to ready the reserves. Dokona blew the signal to advance on his whistle, as one of the Dogs brought the mukaali to Aebram.

The saddle was mounted upon the shoulders of the beast. Its sinuous neck was writhing in fear at the sudden firefight. But Aebram was a man of fierce will. He grabbed the leather reins, wrapped them round one wrist, and hauled himself up.

The whole reserve advanced as a tank shell whistled past and exploded a long way behind the line. 'Forwards, Dogs!' the Marshal shouted, kicking the beast along. The Sentinels joined in the charge, their piston legs creaking as they kept up with the four-legged, low-bellied mukaali.

Aebram's beast crested the bahn causeway in a lumbering trot, and for a moment he could see the whole battle laid out below him. It stretched out for half a mile on either side, a square of desert burning bright and filling up with the dead.

He knew his Dogs would not flee. They engaged the foe with chem-enhanced fury.

A las-bolt slammed into Aebram's armoured chest. He felt the impact as the mukaali drove onwards, looked for the shooter, and fired back a quick salvo.

The beast stomped down into the fray, crushing a dying man under its hooves.

His mukaali shied away from a burning tank, and Aebram heeled the creature forwards, bolt pistol raised, and crashed through the enemy as the Fang Takers turned their fire towards him. The mukaali's thick hide shrugged off the shots, which only served to enrage the great beast. Aebram used its bulk to smash the heretics aside, then lobbed a grenade into the open turret hatch of an immobilised Chimera.

He kept going until he had gone through the combat, then wheeled around and took it all in. The Dogs fought with a fury unsurpassed by even the crazed Fang Takers, and in the middle stood the hunched shape of Wythers, fighting with his trenching tool, like a man possessed.

He felt proud of his Dogs. They were the scum of the earth, but, by Throne, they knew how to fight!

Aebram heeled his mount forwards, leading the charge once again.

As the desert battle raged on, the main column of Fang Takers pushed south. Within a few hours Holy City was in sight.

Its mud-brick walls were thick, but they were never designed to withstand an assault of this magnitude.

Major Sire's carabineers were untested troops, suddenly thrust into mortal combat. Ephraina led them in the Prayer of Self-Sacrifice. It was one that she had recited many times, but for the young troopers the words were fresh and full of moment.

By the end some had tears of faith streaking their faces while their chests swelled up with pride and self-belief. Major Sire was too emotional to speak. He watched his carabineers hurrying towards their positions, their voluminous flak-coats flapping about their embroidered felt boots, inherited laslocks thrown over their shoulders.

Ephraina put her hand on Sire's shoulder. 'The Emperor protects,' she whispered, and radiant belief surged through him.

His voice croaked. 'Thank you.'

In the outskirts of Holy City the carabineers knelt, laslocks braced, waiting for a target, feeling the thunder of the assault through the hard ground. Many would have thrown down their weapons and fled, but the three Sisters moved among them, giving them all confidence. As the Fang Takers came into range, Sister Ephraina revealed herself, standing on the top of the city gate, resplendent in black armour, calling death and doom upon their enemies.

The autocannons spat out a furious salvo and return fire came, las-bolts flaring about Ephraina, but she was utterly fearless, her voice cutting through the carabineers' off-tune efforts. She held them all together, and filled their hearts with faith as the rain of suppressing fire slammed into the buildings about them, blasting holes through the dry earth, and slamming into the buildings behind.

The staccato thud of heavy weaponry set the dry earth jumping. One of the attacking Chimeras caught fire and slewed sideways. The gunners riddled the thinner side armour, and the tank caught fire as the ramp slammed down and a handful of troops stumbled out. They were cut down by salvos of las-fire.

Ephraina fired her bolter one-handed, the rocket-propelled rounds streaking towards their target. The lead tank was a Leman Russ Demolisher with a full set of heavy flamer sponsons. Her rounds bounced uselessly off it as it fired off a cloud of white smoke for protection.

There was a moment as the smoke cleared, and the turret swung to pick the right spot.

The carabineers kept their heads down.

The massive projectile impacted with the wall, igniting its fuse, and detonated a second later, tearing a great hole in the mud-brick facade. The blast threw anyone standing to the ground. The carabineers were blind. The air was acrid with fyceline smoke. Dust billowed out and through the gloom all they could hear was the rattle of tank tracks rolling towards them.

The song had faltered at the first gunshots. Major Sire was shouting panicked orders. Gouts of fire roared towards them from hull-mounted flamers. The carabineers fell back, unable to respond. Major Sire screamed orders, but they went unheeded.

Aliciel seized her moment. She braced herself, aimed and fired. Her multi-melta drove a slug of molten metal into the tightly packed interior, igniting the shells inside and setting off a sudden fireball that blasted the Leman Russ turret a hundred feet into the air. A raging firestorm poured from the open turret, and the Demolisher went up in flames. Then a second tank, and then a third. The flaming wrecks turned night into day.

Within minutes the ground before the breach in the city wall was clogged with burning wreckage.

Aliciel and Ephraina pulled back, Aliciel's twin multi-melta barrels still steaming as the superheated metal cooled.

As the Fang Takers' attack on Holy City stalled, their commanders pushed around the flanks, seeking weak spots.

Even with the Sisters' aid, the carabineers could only offer a rudimentary defence. The Fang Takers' armoured column smashed through on either side, and the carabineers fell back from the city walls. The fight was spread across the whole northern city as the Guardsmen fought a desperate battle, hab to hab, to hold the enemy back.

Sister Ephraina remained with the main body, directing and inspiring the untrained warriors. The longer they held, the more relics could be carried out of the Great Minster. She could almost weigh their lives against the sacred objects being salvaged.

Sister Aliciel sortied out, her multi-melta vaporising enemy vehicles. But the weight of numbers told. The Fang Takers' column finally broke through, and Aliciel let them pack into the main street.

When the whole street was full of grinding armour, she took out the lead tank. The multi-melta shot flared from the second-floor balcony, and there were a few seconds before the tank went up in flames. Wild fire raked the building she had been in, but she was already moving to a new vantage point in one of the covered balconies.

She kicked the carved wooden screens out, lined up the rear-most tank in her sights, and fired.

The Chimera disappeared under a cloud of black smoke. The whole column was trapped within the narrow defile and Sister Josmane stepped out, her black armour reflecting the flames. She sang hymns as she fired her flamer from the hip, filling the streets with gouts of burning promethium.

The Sisters took a terrible toll on the armoured columns. But as the night wore on, the Fang Takers outflanked the dwindling carabineers. The battle was close-up and ferocious, Leman Russes firing point-blank into habs. Carabineers were blasted apart, or crushed by collapsing buildings that slewed out into the streets, blocking further progress.

A piece of shrapnel hit Ephraina in the arm, piercing armour and sinew. She ducked back out of the way and loaded the final magazine into her bolter. It was a struggle, and it was her last. The understanding came to Ephraina.

She fell back to the Chapel of Saint Thor.

'We are spent,' she voxed Helewise. Blood gouted from her injury. 'I am sending Aliciel and Josmane back.'

'You have served well,' the Sister Superior told her. 'Fall back.'

'I will keep them at bay here,' Ephraina said.

'Ephraina. Do not martyr yourself needlessly! Our Sisters are on their way.'

Ephraina gritted her teeth against the pain. 'How long?'

'They will not be here until the morning.'

'Not soon enough,' Ephraina hissed.

Helewise heard the pain in her Sister's voice. Reckoning weighed her hand. It willed her to charge out. She knew she could save Ephraina. She yearned to sally forth, to lead a counter-attack, to rescue her, but if she did so, others would die. She did not try to argue. She was restrained by her rank.

And, she told herself, sometimes a Sister knew when she was called to martyrdom. 'You are sure?'

'The Emperor protects,' Ephraina said.

Ephraina prepared herself. She had always known that her life would end in martyrdom. Her only concern was to be worthy of it when it came. Ephraina reassured her Sisters. 'Do not weep for me. I can hear His choirs already!'

Ephraina made her last stand in the Chapel of Saint Thor. It was an island in the middle of the two roads that led to the Great Minster, the heavy stone blocks defence against all but the heaviest ordnance.

She stood, alone on the steps of the chapel, bolter spitting with fury and singing hymns of joy. When her ammunition ran out, she flung away the weapon, drew her chainblade and cut down any heretic who drew near.

The Fang Takers charged again and again, but she fought them off until she was weak with blood loss.

Finally, her voice raised in righteous defiance, she charged at the traitorous mob.

The Sisters all felt Ephraina's death. The martyrdom flowed through each of them. They had gutted the minster of paintings, scrolls, the bones of ancient teachers, warriors and holy men. Loaded them up on half-tracks, and sent them towards safety.

But now it was time to go.

Morgandrie took Helewise aside. 'Sister. It is a grave matter to take the saint from this sacred place. It would be better if we stood here. Made our sacrifice.'

'Fear not, our sacrifice will come,' said Helewise.

'Let me stay.'

'No.'

Morgandrie started to argue, but Helewise took her hand. 'We need you. I promise you this. We keep the saint within the city. If it means we are martyred, then let it be His command. Our Sisters are on their way. Let us hold out until dawn.'

* * *

As the last half-track loaded with relics pulled out, Morgandrie sensed a new presence. She spun round, finger on the trigger of her heavy bolter, night-optics showing warm bodies hiding in the shadows.

'Halt!' she commanded.

A voice came back, 'Hail, Sister!'

'Show yourself!'

Three figures crept forwards as a mortar shell landed fifty feet distant.

Morgandrie grabbed the leader and pulled him inside.

'Who are you?'

'Thaddeus, son of Dalmor. And these are Gormina and Calor.'

'And why are you here?'

Thaddeus lifted his shirt. There was a laspistol stuck into his belt. 'I have come to fight!'

The girl, Gormina, stepped forwards. She had an autocarbine cradled in her arms, a kitchen knife thrust into her belt. She nodded. 'This is our world. The Emperor calls on us to protect it!'

As the night wore on, more and more citizens came to defend the saint. By the time the Rhino pulled out of the minster, there were hundreds of faithful. They were young and old, men and women, their faces lit by strobing tracers and the light of flames.

They were untrained, poorly armed and filthy, but they were filled with faith.

The Sisters looked about. They had no doubt of the danger.

'This is because of Ephraina,' Morgandrie voxed. 'Her martyrdom has inspired them.'

'She inspires us all,' Helewise said.

'*Praise be to the God-Emperor!*' Aiguell voxed back. '*It is good to see His hand at work.*'

The Sisters formed an honour guard as the Rhino drove away from the enemy.

Though the militia fought hard, they were no match for the Fang Takers. But they died with the name of the God-Emperor upon their lips.

Slowly but steadily the Sisters and their militia were driven back, right to the factorum quarters, on the very perimeter of the city. They barricaded themselves inside the lower hangar of what had once been a printing house.

There were only a handful of militia left. Thaddeus and Gormina were two of them. He still had his laspistol, and she her auto-carbine, but their faces were streaked with dust and soot, and there was a hastily bound cut across her forehead.

Helewise turned to them. 'You have fought well. The God-Emperor knows. Guard this door. We must hold out until dawn. Let none approach.'

'We shall!' they called out, their eyes burning with bright ferocity. She put her hands on their heads. She had seen many like these two in her time. They would probably be dead by morning. But they would fight to the last, and they would worship the God-Emperor with their deaths.

The Fang Takers were here to kill and to die.

They charged without thought of their own lives, and the Sisters and their militia gunned them down until their guns were too hot to touch.

Aiguell tried to get through to someone in command, but the Astra Militarum headquarters were in chaos. It was only when she got through to Sister Dovere that she was able to grasp what was happening out there on the planet.

Dovere managed to get hold of a Navy officer and demanded an air strike, conveying the Sisters' location. They awaited support, as Josmane guarded the main approach. She squeezed out the last drops of fuel from her flamer canister, then hurled the weapon aside and drew her bolt pistol. The heavy rounds tore through the Fang Takers as their charge led them up to the door where she stood.

The enemy brought everything to bear upon them. Sister Dominora died defending the lower wing – a hard round punching through her helmet's eyepiece and killing her instantly.

They heard the roar of incoming fighters, and braced themselves for the explosions.

They looked like Thunderbolts, coming low and hard over the city. The building rattled as the wing of fighter-bombers tore overhead, the bombs blasting the habs and manufactoria about them.

The strike halted the attack for a few minutes, but then the Fang Takers came again, from the south, mobs dashing forwards through the loading bays.

A mortar shell shattered Lucitta's hip. She braced herself against the wall, kept on firing even as she bled to death. Gormina's autocarbine ran out of ammunition, and she was forced to swing it two-handed in a desperate defence. One of the Fang Taker's chiefs, a large, red-faced man wielding a heavy-bladed cleaver, singled her out. A human head hung from his broad belt, and iron bands clamped his huge arms. He caught the butt of her rifle in one hand and tore it from her grasp as he closed in for the kill.

She had her back to the wall. He came in for her, his hood cut away about the mouth to reveal barbed iron teeth. 'The God-Emperor protects!' she shouted in defiance, as he lifted his cleaver. It flashed with a dull red light, and struck home with a dull, wet sound. It landed twice more as he hacked her apart.

Thaddeus did not see his sister's death, but he felt it as he was dragged back through the factorum's halls, until he and the remaining Sisters held the last generator chamber at the rear of the printworks. Before them was the long, cluttered print room, and it was through the machinery that the Fang Takers crept.

'Stay back!' Helewise shouted as she stood in the doorway, legs braced, bolt pistol in one hand and power sword in the other. She felt the God-Emperor's will surge through her. He was with her, she knew. She never doubted it. 'I am Sister Superior Helewise, of the Order of Our Martyred Lady! I shall serve you with the wrath of the God-Emperor!'

Her shouts were met with laughter. She could feel the Fang Takers creeping near but refused to give ground.

She willed them to charge her, desperate to gun them down, felt Morgandrie's imposing presence next to her, heavy bolter panning for targets. Across the vox, Helewise whispered, 'We stand here. We can retreat no more. Our lives are now in the Emperor's hands.'

Morgandrie felt the thrill of approaching death. 'We stand,' she repeated. 'And we lay our necks open for His judgement.'

And then with a shout, the Fang Takers charged. Reckoning sang as traceries of voltaic power crackled along its well-forged edge, and Helewise let out a paean of prayer and joy as she met the charge.

For hours in the Ashgarths there was a ferocious night battle lit only by tracer rounds, the white light of illumination flares and the flames of burning tanks. The Dogs met the ferocity of the Fang Takers and matched it. At last, as the dawn approached, the last of the heretics were routed.

By the time the sun rose, the sky was streaked with columns of black smoke, rising from mile upon mile of burnt-out and blackened wreckage. The Chem Dogs were hunting down the last survivors, who had trickled out into the desert.

A piece of shrapnel had cut a gash along Major Chalice's thigh, but to Salem's annoyance he was still alive. 'Where's Quinn?'

'With the Emperor,' Chalice said.

Salem found the body, under the black flak-coat. He turned it over. 'Shot in the back.'

Chalice nodded.

Salem turned away. 'You! What is your name?'

The man he addressed had been picking his way through the dead, looking for gear. 'Shin, sir.'

'Shin, did you see Mercy Quinn die?'

The trooper came forward. 'Yes, sir.'

'Who shot him?'

'The Fang Takers, sir.'

Salem turned away. Wythers was sitting, head slumped between his knees, hair hanging over his face.

'Wythers!' Salem shouted. 'Hey!'

Wythers toppled sideways, his stained teeth clamped about his rebreather as he wheezed.

Salem cursed.

He looked around and shook his head. 'Get your lot together. There are more of them. We march for Holy City.'

A pile of dead lay before Helewise's feet. Beside her, Morgandrie was unbowed.

The reinforcements were drawing close to the city. They could hear the rumble of their tracks, and the song of their hymns. The Fang Takers could hear it too; they were drawing off to face the new threat.

The voice that came over the vox had the unmistakably crisp Ophelian accent. *This is Sister Superior Lanete. We are coming to relieve you.*

Helewise pulled off her helmet and spat a curse. Sister Lanete had only recently been assigned to their abbey and she and Helewise had rekindled an old enmity. But she could not think of that now. There were only six of them left. Ruslana was too injured to fight, and as Sisters of Our Martyred Lady, they had to rely on each other.

But Ruslana disliked Lanete as much as Helewise. She lay in the back of the Rhino, a hole in her power armour's torso, leaking blood. 'We must be the ones to retake the city.'

Each of Helewise's remaining Sisters removed their helmets as well. Their white hair was wet with sweat and pressed to their skulls. None of them wanted Lanete to take the glory.

Helewise looked to Ruslana.

'Put me in the turret,' Ruslana said. 'I can man the storm bolter.'

Helewise turned to the others. 'Are we agreed?'

They nodded, one by one.

'What about the boy?' Morgandrie asked.

Helewise turned to Thaddeus. He trembled before her. It must have been like looking up at the angel of death, her armour splattered with blood and dust, a gore-crusted sword crackling in her hand.

'I will fight!' he said.

Helewise nodded. Thaddeus had lost his sister in the night, but if it was the God-Emperor's will then she could not resist.

Helewise placed the point of Reckoning onto the floor, both gauntleted hands folded upon it.

'Let us pray,' she said, and one by one the Sisters knelt, their weapons of war still in their hands. The sun broke the horizon as they intoned the words. 'He is the salvation of mankind. We obey His words and tremble before His majesty. For He is the salvation, the hope and the future of us all. Those who stand against Him shall suffer the purity of our righteous flame.'

Her Sisters stood, slammed rounds into their bolters, and fixed their helmets into place. Helewise took a moment for her suit of armour's visual feeds to kick in. She scrolled up, blinked away all non-necessary material as she checked on her squad's status. She put her hand to the factorum door, felt the tears well up and blinked them away. She felt His presence rise within her. It was like a tide of anger.

In the last moment she said a silent prayer inside the silence of her mind. A personal prayer between her and the God-Emperor.

The long printworks' gallery was cluttered with Fang Takers dead. They would not go that way.

'We cannot let Lanete get there first! We will be the ones to see this through!' she hissed.

The other Sisters all nodded. They understood. And they felt Helewise's passion burn within her with all the intensity of a white-hot flame.

She stood back as Aliciel's multi-melta blasted a hole in the factorum wall. She tore a passage through, and shouted Ephraina's name as she led the charge.

It was fifty feet of open ground to where the Fang Takers were dug-in in the lower storeys of a broken hab-block. They were hiding in the shadows of the ruined buildings, firing wildly at the charging Sisters.

Helewise did not need to look back. They all followed her, roaring their hatred, as their Rhino powered behind them, storm bolter barking out.

Dressed in power armour and armed with blade and bolter, the Sisters of the Order of Our Martyred Lady were one of the most ferocious weapons in the Imperium's arsenal. Helewise felt rounds slam into her battleplate as her bolt pistol bucked in her outstretched fist.

Her ocular feed identified each heretical soul. Each round

smashed through a heretic, the rocket-propelled rounds punching through wall, flesh, flakboard, bone and armour with ease. She was the Emperor's blade, and she rejoiced in the killing.

Throughout the morning, the Chem Dogs marched south.

They chewed through any stragglers in a series of encounters. For twenty miles there was nothing but twisted metal, burnt-out tanks, corpses lying where they had fallen, and the thick pall of smoke and fumes. And before them the habs of Holy City had been ground down. Now they were like the teeth of a bare-knuckle fighter: broken and jagged stumps.

Their next battle, Shin thought, as he rested in a hastily dug trench, one boot up against the rough-hewn wall. He'd run out of dried meat. But he'd plundered a grenade launcher from a dead Dog, and had swapped a silver-hilted battle knife for a bandolier of grenades and that was almost as good as a full belly.

'How are you doing?' he called to Wythers. The big man pushed the hair back from his face.

The nitra-chems gave him an unhealthy pallor. His skin hung in slack hammocks under his eyes. It had a translucent quality to it, like tallow wax. His bloodshot eyes were the only colour. 'It's running out,' he said. His voice was a raspy whisper, and a thin trickle of blue smoke climbed from his mouth.

'You should see Sawbones.'

Wythers laughed.

'Carry his pack,' Shin said. 'You'll be fine.'

Wythers thought about it for a moment.

'You'll be fine,' Shin said. 'You were our colonel.'

'I was,' Wythers said, as if reminding himself, chewing the mouthpiece of his rebreather absent-mindedly. At last he looked at Shin. 'Was I good?'

Shin smiled. 'Yeah. You were. The best.'

Wythers nodded, but said nothing.

What Wythers gave to the medic Shin didn't want to know, but the big man came back with a fresh canister of nitra-chems. His hands were shaking as he unscrewed the spent one, bit off the cap, and screwed the new one in.

All this time he had the pipe in his mouth, and he closed his eyes as the blue smoke filled the pipe.

'Wake me,' he croaked as he took another drag and his eyes rolled up into his skull.

Shin didn't like to see that. He pulled Wythers' hair down over his face and left him to dream his chem-dreams. It was true. He had been the best. He'd fought like a bear to keep them all alive. They all owed him. And they knew it.

Three hours later Major Chalice appeared, limping through the wreckage, using a rifle as a crutch. 'Still on your feet?' Shin said.

'Afraid so.'

Shin laughed. 'What happened?'

'Shrapnel,' Chalice said.

'You all right?'

'Still alive,' Chalice said. He lowered himself gingerly to the floor. His trews were dark and wet with fresh blood. He winced as he cut the wet cloth away. The metal was still embedded in his leg.

He grimaced as he tried to pull it out, and stopped, took a deep breath and tried again.

On the third go, he pulled it out, and held it up with finger-tips stained red. 'There!' he said. 'The bastard.'

He tossed the shrapnel away. 'Get me some cloth,' he said.

Shin found the nearest body. It was a fellow Dog.

'No!' Chalice said. 'Find me a cleaner one than that.'

Shin looked around. 'Well, it's Gunter or a Fang Taker.'

'Fang Taker,' Chalice said.

Shin cut a long strip of cloth. He held it up. It was clean enough.

Chalice's teeth were clenched against the pain. He was breathing through his nose as he took the cloth and wrapped it just above his knee. He worked slowly, tightening the knot each time, and finally tying it closed.

He was sweating by the time he had finished. 'There,' he said. 'That should keep me going.'

It took him a few moments to get back to his feet. He swayed. The lasgun crutch steadied him.

There was barely time for a rest. The order came to move out.

Chalice slapped Wythers on the shoulder and the big man pushed himself up. He shook his head, smacked his lips.

'We're moving out,' Chalice said as he made his way along the line. 'Ten minutes. Final assault.'

Sister Superior Lanete stood in the cupola of her Immolator, *Fire of Wrath*. She had a lean face, shaped like a blade, with a high nose and deep-set eyes. She led the relief column of Adepta Sororitas armour – five Rhinos, with full battle squads, and three Penitent Engines – as they smashed through the barricades that blocked the southern gate.

Neural amplifiers and iniquity augmenters drove those piloting the latter to a state of heightened guilt and penance. Their berserk minds were unleashed into the ruins to hunt out any heretics. There was scant time for a brief blessing before the Penitents set about their task. The relief force had raced all night to get here, and now they took in the scene of destruction and were filled with righteous anger.

Fang Takers had hastily set up a kill-zone just inside the perimeter wall, but Lanete called in a strike from a pair of Exorcists she had stationed outside the city. The conflagration rockets slammed down into the area, a salvo of two dozen warheads that filled it with smoke and flame and shrapnel.

Dust and smoke still roiled about the open space as *Fire of Wrath* smashed through the roadblock, turret-mounted heavy flamers spraying a wide arc across the square.

A few Fang Takers remained to return fire, but squads of Sisters burst through behind the lead tank, singling the enemy out and cutting them down with precision salvos of bolter and flamer fire.

'Death to heretics!' Lanete called out, and as she did the Penitent Engines crowded through the gap. They thundered past the Sisters, buzz saws spinning in their blind fury, heavy flamers hissing, desperate as hunting dogs to sniff out and destroy the enemy.

The Fang Takers had come to Holy City to die.

They had been broken in battle, abandoned by their commanders, but in the depths of their torment, the Chaos gods had been generous to them. The cultists had delivered Holy City to them, and they had repaid that gift with an orgy of destruction and murder. Holy men had been strung up and tortured. The population had been slaughtered, their heads piled up in gory heaps. And the Fang Takers had gloried in the bloodbath.

As the Sisters counter-attacked, they were unrepentant. Most of the cultists died with shouts of heresy upon their lips. They were flushed out, room by room, building by building, quarter by quarter, with flamer, bolter and melta.

Lanete's column drove through them, *Fire of Wrath* grinding through the tight streets, flamers hosing the enemy down with righteous fire.

But ahead of Lanete's onslaught went Helewise, with the saint in her Rhino. She could hear Lanete's commands through the vox, and was determined to be the first to reach the minster complex. They looked upon the ruin with horror. The pilgrim hostelries and lodge-houses were burnt out, the ornate wooden balconies punctured and burnt, the Imperial colonial facades defaced with heretical images and the scars of battle.

It was nearly midday when Helewise's squad approached Minster Square. She could hear Lanete's tanks crashing through the ruins on the other side of the square. The bark of bolters reverberating through the ruined cityscape as gouts of flame and black fumes rose into the air. The ignition of distant promethium tanks and the crack of las-fire as they flushed out isolated pockets of heretics.

Fire stabbed out of a ruined hab. Helewise ran across the road, and pushed through into the central courtyard.

There was a fountain shaped in the form of a stone sadhvu. The head of the sadhvu had been broken off. Three dead bodies floated in the red water.

Stubber fire hammered about her. It was coming from the first-floor window.

She took out the shooter with a single bolt, swung around to take out another two in the balcony above her.

The last one fell forwards, slamming onto the flagstone floor. He left a wet smear as he tried to throw the demolition charge with his dying gasp. Helewise slammed through a carved wooden screen, leading the counter-attack street by street.

Another flight of Thunderbolts came in low over the city. Helewise could see the pilots' faces as the autocannons roared and underslung missile pods fired, their payloads slamming into the buildings only thirty feet from her.

The broken spires of the Great Minster drew closer.

The few remaining Fang Takers had made improvised strongpoints, bunkering down behind rubble and scraps of broken furniture. Morgandrie's heavy bolter drove them out of their positions. The self-propelled shells tore a line of chunks out of the building opposite, tracking to an open window and filling the area with hard rounds.

Helewise paused for a moment to take in the approach to Minster Square. Ruined habs had been blown open. Their guts spilt over the cobbles, curtains flapping where windows had once stood; broken chairs, beds and a table were mixed in amid the rubble, daubed in heretical scrawl. Amongst the bricks and timbers she could see a hand, a boot, an arm, a face – white with dust.

As she neared Minster Square, she heard a metallic clank. She pushed herself up and as she reached the last crossroads, she turned and found her-self standing face to face with a Penitent Engine, pistons hissing as it stumped forwards, clawed steel feet skidding on the rubble.

The construct turned towards her. The two-legged walker carried a penitent on its torso. He had been crucified onto a rebar cross, the limbs lashed with sacred chains, tormenter-cap covering his face from the nose up. It swung round, auto-feeder spitting out spent cartridges as its drum magazines reloaded, underslung buzz saws spitting gobbets of flesh and blood.

One of its metallic arms had been shorn off, the stump twitching as it sought a target.

'Heretics!' She pointed and the construct spun slowly as its targeting matrixes passed over her, and she turned towards the foe.

Helewise's visual feed located a number of heretics in the minster ruin.

'I see them,' Morgandrie voxed, and she hosed the ruins with heavy bolts.

Helewise's first shot killed the sniper in the upper window. The second killed a man who was struggling to clear a jam in his stubber. She stepped out into the square as one of them fired a missile. The explosion ripped through the fragile bones of the building behind her. The facade fell in one flat piece, and then shattered across the street as one of the heretics stood to fire a salvo of autocannon rounds.

It was a wild salvo, but three shots hit home, ricocheting off her power armour. Helewise fired again. Her shot hit him full in the chest. The rocket-propelled bolt exploded within his chest cavity, and tore him apart.

The burnt-out remains of an armoured troop carrier stood at the entrance to the square, a blackened body lying half out of the open ramp. The human flesh had been calcified by the heat of flames, its extremities – nose, ears, fingers – all burnt away, leaving the remains looking like a half-finished sculpture. She strode past, looked on without compassion. The rear ramp had slammed down, but the troops inside had died, their blackened bodies sprawled across the benches, deathly rictuses grinning out under burnt helmets.

Helewise pushed on until she could see the minster steps, a hundred yards across the square.

She waved Aiguell forwards. The Rhino's metal tracks ground over the rubble.

Ruslana was getting weak. Helewise could hear her prayers in her vox.

'We are nearly there,' Helewise voxed to Ruslana.

'*Praise to the Emperor,*' Ruslana whispered back.

Helewise paused. The square was deserted, but there were Fang Takers barricaded at the top of the steps. There were barrels, flakboard pews, lumps of masonry. Helewise picked out at least five of the heretics. One of them had an autocannon. It fired a staccato salvo, tearing chunks off the masonry behind them.

'Lanete is getting close,' Morgandrie warned.

'Into the Rhino,' Helewise ordered. They clambered in and the doors slammed closed. The saint's coffin lay on the cabin floor. Helewise put her hand to it, as Aiguell called out a warning then set off at full speed across the square.

The storm bolter casings rattled off the Rhino's roof as auto-cannon rounds rang against the tank like a bell. It careered across the open square, mounting the broad steps and slamming into the makeshift barrier. 'Ramps down!' Aiguell shouted, and a second later the Sisters piled out.

Morgandrie went out of the left side, her heavy bolter spraying rounds across the palisade. Josmane and Aliciel followed her, Josmane rushing to engage the enemy in hand-to-hand slaughter.

Helewise ducked out to the right. There were two Fang Takers before her. One was lying wounded against the wall, the other was manning the autocannon. He tried desperately to swing it round, and died to a headshot from Helewise's pistol.

The wounded man died a moment later.

It was all over within a matter of seconds. Sister Helewise put up her hand for her Sisters to stop firing.

The thunder of the heavy bolter fell away into silence.

'Here!' Helewise called out. She kicked a dropped flamer to Josmane.

The Sister said a prayer of purification and picked it up. As she checked it over, the rest of the squad refreshed magazines and holstered their weapons. Helewise looked about. Minster Square lay behind them, broken, burnt and filled with the bodies of slaughtered locals, black and stiff. Every statue in the portico had been defiled with crudely chiselled images, while the head of a wolf and a three-taloned claw had been crudely added to the statue of the Emperor.

Helewise braced herself as she stepped forwards.

The Great Minster had been emptied and now it stood, hollow and disfigured as a gutted corpse.

Helewise strode into the Great Minster of Saint Elaire, her boots stepping into the lake of blood. Bodies lay where they had been decapitated. Men and women, young and old. Piles of heads rose up on either side. The dead mouths were open, their skin grey, features fixed in expressions of pain and anger and doubt.

She moved past them and felt the weight of the destruction. It settled on Helewise's shoulders as she stopped at the top and looked back. The Fang Takers had wired the pediments with fyceline. The massive portals now hung from their hinges and slumped against a lump of shattered statuary. The ribbed vaults had collapsed, the broken remains silhouetted against the sky, and blunt stubs of columns pointed up to the jagged tear in the ceiling above them. Daylight shone through the collapsed domes. The floor was littered with smashed bosses, fragments of colonnette and the traceries of gun embrasures.

Helewise held her breath as she stepped deeper into the once hallowed building. The sacred place was now strewn with glassaic, rubble, spent shells and the severed heads of the city's sadhvus. Even the bas-relief on the iron doors had been defaced. The heads of saints had been sawn off, their eyes drilled out, and the holy imagery had been splashed with blood and scrawled with heretic symbols.

At the top of the stairs was a wounded heretic. He had blasphemous symbols inked into his skin. His face was pale, his beard was stained with bloody spittle, his face half hidden behind the daemon-faced bascinet. He felt her shadow fall across him, and his eyes opened as she drew her bolt pistol.

'Sister!' he whispered and put up his hand.

Despite the tattoos and the ritual scarring, it appeared as if his hand was trying to make the sign of the aquila. 'Forgive me, Sister,' he whispered. But it was the sound of his voice, not the words that held her finger. He shared the same accent of her home world.

'You are from Liepra?' she demanded.

'I am.'

She felt a strange mix of emotions rise up as the scraps of memory returned to her. She knew her home world had fallen to the Archenemy. She had often thought of the people she had grown up with. Of the children she had once played with. And now she saw how they had ended up: they had become the foot soldiers of the heretics.

'May the Emperor's light shine upon you,' he said, in the Liepran cant.

Helewise suddenly had an image of her mother, gathering her in when she was just a child. There was a set response. 'And may His light…' It had been so long and her lips were too slow.

'…shine in all our hearts,' the man said, bloody spittle foaming at the corners of his mouth. He winced against the pain and choked. 'What chance has brought us both here?'

She knelt next to him. 'It is not chance,' she told him. 'This is the working of the God-Emperor. I am here to bear witness.'

Bloody foam caught on the corner of his lips. 'You will hear my confession?'

She nodded.

'They took the planet. They took us all. They made us reject the Imperial creed. And the Imperium did not come. The Emperor abandoned us.'

'It was a test and you failed. There is no force that can make you repent. It is a choice.'

He coughed blood. 'I was just a child.'

'That is no excuse,' she told him. 'I have fought with people little older than children this night. They died for their beliefs. But you did not. You betrayed your faith. Your people. Your Imperium. For those who break their oaths there is no forgiveness. The only contrition is death.'

He nodded and fumbled with the straps on his elaborate bascinet. 'Forgive me,' he said. He lifted the half-visored black helm free. The effort exhausted him, and the helm tumbled to the side.

His head was shaved, apart from a greying mohawk. His smooth skin gleamed with serpent swirls of heretical runes and skull images inked across his scalp and down beneath his carapace gorget. Helewise sheathed Reckoning. She would not soil the blade with the blood of this heretic.

She put the barrel of her bolt pistol to the side of his head. Her eyes were hard.

'There is no forgiveness for the heretic,' she said, and fired.

Helewise led her Sisters as they carried the saint's lead coffin back to its tomb.

It lay in the heart of the minster complex in a private chapel. They processed through the dark aisles and stopped when they came to the holy of holies. An artillery shell had blown a hole through the floor. The undercroft beneath was exposed. People had sought sanctuary here, but not one had been spared the arcane rituals. Their bodies hung from the galleries, nooses of flaywire cutting into their necks and blood dripping from their toes.

And the tomb of the saint had been daubed in their blood.

'Return her,' Helewise said, and they lifted the coffin up the stairs and slowly placed her into the marble sarcophagus.

Helewise led them in prayers. She knelt, resting both hands upon her power sword, and closed her eyes. As she concluded, she stood and turned to Josmane.

'Purify this place.'

Josmane disengaged the spent promethium tank and slammed a new one into place.

Her voice called out, in High Gothic, the Prayer for the Ignorant and the Innocent. 'In the name of the Emperor!'

Her words echoed back from the empty chamber, as if the hanging dead had been given voice. She squeezed the trigger, and a torrent of holy promethium roared out.

VI

Trooper Shin picked his way through the rubble of Holy City. He had not slept for nearly a day and a half. His feet ached, and he was starting to feel the weight of the grenades hanging from his webbing.

The city had a haunted feel. He and Echo led Wythers through the ruins. They had got separated from the rest of their platoon, who'd gone off to plunder.

'Keep up!' Shin called back to Wythers. They had to keep ahead of the Mercies. At one point they came to an intact hab, where Captain Dokona sat on a stack of wooden crates marked 'Starch'. His top pockets were bulging with what looked like lho-sticks. He saw Shin. 'The Marshal wants you lot up at the south gate.'

'Where the frekk is the south gate?' Shin said.

'How should I know?'

'How should I know?' Echo said.

* * *

It took Shin and Echo an hour to find the remains of the south gate. Wythers stumbled behind them, sucking on his rebreather. The streets were cluttered with the burnt-out remains of tanks, the tracks shed and the turrets lying where they had landed.

'South gate?' Shin asked another one of Dokona's lot, picking through the remains for anything of value. He had a bandage over one eye that was stained with blood.

'Yeah,' he said, and made a vague gesture Shin took to be pointing towards it.

Shin shouldered his pack and pushed forwards. He regretted picking up the grenade launcher now. After this long it weighed a ton.

They stumped through a ceremonial entrance that had once been adorned with statues of Imperial saints. Now they lay smashed, the arch had collapsed, and there were bodies lying everywhere amidst the ruins.

There was only one hab still standing in this whole quarter. It was a small, flat-roofed shack with a haalwood door hung on heavy iron hinges. The Dogs of Chalice's lot were sheltering inside.

Their packs were stacked against the wall. There was a wide entrance room. Someone had cleared away a space and set up a pot over a small fire. Shin led them through into another chamber. One wall had been taken up with the family shrine. The Fang Takers had seen to that; now it was daubed with an eight-pointed star.

Shin stopped and looked about. 'Filthy bastards,' he said. It seemed that the sadhvus of Holy City had eaten in communal kitchens. But at least there was a vat of drinking water in the back courtyard, the metal tap at the bottom of the terracotta tank strapped up with cloth to stop an old leak.

Wythers threw his pack down. His hands were shaking. He needed his chems.

'Wythers. Try that,' Shin ordered.

Echo repeated his words, his mouth moving soundlessly as he looked on in thirsty anticipation. Wythers watched as Shin filled his canteen and handed it to him.

His hands shook harder as he lifted it to his mouth and started to drink.

'How's it taste?'

'G-g-good.'

'Sure?'

Wythers didn't answer. He nodded, and took another gulp.

Echo tried to take the mug from Wythers, and Shin shoved him back. 'Hey! That's mine.'

Shin took a gulp, then slung the mug on his belt. 'You lot stay here. If the major comes, tell him I'm going to scout about.'

No one said anything. Shin had unsavoury appetites, and no one wanted to know what he was up to.

Salem's command squad had found a block of slab, and they were boiling it in an upturned helmet as evening began to fall. Colonel Salem stood in the doorless opening of a five-storey hab and looked out. The dead city stared back. The only thing that moved was a stray canid, picking its way along the road.

'It's the silence that gets me,' he said.

No one answered. They were more intent on the food before them.

'They killed every one of them,' Salem said. He could hear the rumble of Chimera engines as they ground through rubble-filled streets, shouts of tank drivers, and the occasional thunder of a collapsing building.

The lights of the column appeared at the end of the street. They moved slowly around the piles of rubble and burnt-out armour. The lead tank took a few minutes to reach him. It bore the red-and-gold livery of the Niwara Janissaries.

They looked down at the Dogs with contempt. Salem returned the look. Bastards.

The last of the Chem Dogs were limping into the city as darkness enveloped them.

They were worn out and haggard. Some of them had pushed their goggles back from their faces. Their rebreathers hung about their necks. Bandages were wrapped about legs and arms and bound unhelmeted heads. Behind them came the regiment's last Sentinel, their remaining mukaali and, of course, the unmistakable silhouettes of Mercies in their flak-coats, peaked caps and knee-high boots.

Salem could see a Chem Dog crawling towards the city perimeter. He was not going to make it, Salem was sure, and he stood to watch as one of the Mercies stopped over him. The man put a hand up. It was hard to tell what the gesture meant. It could have been a plea for clemency or an attempt to ward off the shot.

He saw the muzzle flash first, then the sharp retort, and then the man's arm fell, and the Mercies continued on.

The sound of the gunshot hurried the walking wounded. They filed past Salem with barely a nod, their faces hollow, their eyes angry, scavenged weapons slung from their shoulders or cradled across their bodies.

At last, there was one survivor left. He limped into town just before the Mercies caught up with him.

'Of all the bastards!' Salem called out. 'So, you made it?'

Major Chalice limped towards him. 'I did,' he said. His foot was swollen as large as his head, and the flesh was putrid. His face was pale and drawn with pain as he limped along with a length of rebar as a crutch.

'Fit for combat?'

Chalice slapped his laspistol to prove that he had not thrown away his weapons. 'Try me.'

Salem laughed and pulled a pack of lho-sticks out of his pocket. 'Here!' he said and tossed one to Chalice.

Chalice caught the stick and swayed for a moment, before straightening. He stuck the lho in his mouth. 'Where's Sawbones?'

'There,' Salem said, pointing to a hab three doors down.

Major Chalice paused at the open doorway. It was dark inside. 'Sawbones?' he called.

There was a grunt from the shadows.

Chalice shoved the door open.

A slanting light fell through the open doorway from a passing Chimera, the blue-white glare of the searchlight briefly illuminating the room. There were dead bodies lying against the wall. Civilians, not Dogs. It looked like they had been lined up to be shot. The walls were scarred with smears of blood and gunshots. In the heat, they smelt as if they'd been dead for days.

Another Chimera passed along the road, its machine-spirit grumbling.

Major Chalice stood to let his eyes grow accustomed to the gloom. From the darkness he could hear the wheeze of the stimms-pump.

'Where are you, you bastard?' he called out. There was the sound of snorting from the corner of the room and a dishevelled shape rose and peered out through thick goggles. If Sawbones had a name, narcotics and stimms had long since driven it from memory. The medic was sucking on a black corrugated tube that reached over his back. In his hand was a twin-barrelled shotgun.

'No guns!' Sawbones hissed.

Chalice made a show of taking his pistol from its holster. The sidearm clattered down into the doorway. Sawbones waved the shotgun to signal him in.

Sawbones beckoned him forwards as he took a long drag on his chem-tube, held the breath in and patted his lap. 'Show me your leg.'

Major Chalice hopped into the room, pulled a chair out and lowered himself down. He swung his foot up. It landed in Sawbones' lap and he started to cut the bandages away.

The strips of dirty cloth were stained with ash and promethium, pus, and blood. Sawbones pulled them away and a putrid stink filled the room.

Sawbones made a sucking sound as he inspected the wound.

'It's bad,' he said, and fumbled in one of the greatcoat pockets for a band-mounted headlamp. He muttered to himself, and a cloud of fumes gathered about his face as he felt for the lumen-stud. He tapped the lumen until it came on with a flickering white light.

'It will hurt,' he said.

'I'm a big boy.'

Sawbones chuckled as he pulled a knotted leather rag from a pocket. 'Here.'

Chalice slapped the rag away.

'It's genuine,' Sawbones insisted and held it up. *Biting Rag, Munitorum Issue*, the label read. Sawbones had an offended air as he picked the rag up and stuffed it back into one of his pockets.

When the light came there was a loose connection. He tapped the battery pack behind his head, and the lumen shone steadily.

Chalice saw his injured foot properly for the first time. It was so swollen that the skin looked as though it would burst.

Sawbones sucked his teeth. 'You should have found me earlier.'

'I know,' Chalice said.

Sawbones adjusted the lumen, focusing it into a narrow cone

of light. He pressed the tip of a scalpel into the taut red flesh and a river of pale pus oozed out.

Sawbones pulled out his buzz saw from within his jacket. The circular blade was scabbed and rusted. He shook it for a moment, and then with an audible click he started the rusty wheel-blade spinning.

Chalice reached inside his greatcoat, and from his inner pocket he pulled something he had carried since they had ransacked the upper hives of Minerva Prime. An ornate little pistol of ivory and blue steel. Small, easily concealed, but a gun nonetheless, with six barrels fashioned in a circle about the central spine.

'Put the buzz saw down,' Chalice said. 'You clean it up, give me counterseptics and I walk out of here, or I will cut your liver out and use it for stir-fry. Understand?'

'It'll have to come off.'

'No chance.' There was a click as Chalice put the gun against Sawbones' forehead and pulled the firing pin back. 'Put it down.'

Sawbones' eyes narrowed and the buzz saw's whine died away.

'Now,' Chalice said. 'Clean that wound nice and slow. Any tricks, we're both going to hell.'

'The Emperor protects,' Sawbones hissed, and Chalice laughed.

'Oh, He doesn't care about us.'

vii

The sun had long set over Holy City by the time Colonel Salem had finished his dinner of boiled slab and ordered his Dogs to empty their pockets.

There were buttons, a copy of *The Imperial Infantryman's Handbook* bound in buckskin, a neatly ironed white pocket handkerchief, even pictures of other soldiers' spouses, parents, children.

Anything that might conjure up a normal life.

'Throne!' he said as he went through the pile. 'You're a pitiful bunch. You'll steal anything!'

Salem picked one of the pictures up. The name was embossed in what had once been gold lettering: *Mamzel Hilma*. The picture showed a woman sitting on a high tubular stool. She wore a long dress of black lace and net gloves that reached up to her elbows. One of her hands had hold of her skirts and had pulled them up to show her ankles. They were shackled together with penal bar and clamp. Her face was young and pale, but it was her eyes that drew him in. There was a haunted, guarded look in them.

'Who found her?'

One of his Dogs, Tick, put up his hand. 'On a Fang Taker.'

He reached out for the picture and Salem backhanded him. 'Keep your filthy hands off her.'

Tick came at him again, and this time Salem punched him on the side of the head and knocked him sprawling. 'You grubby little shit,' he said. Mamzel Hilma was young and defenceless in a cruel, cruel world. And none knew better than Colonel Salem how vicious this world could be. He wiped the photo on his fatigues and then slipped Mamzel Hilma inside his flak armour. 'She's mine now.'

'Frekker!' Tick hissed.

'The Marshal's coming!' one of his orderlies called out.

Colonel Salem took one last, long drag of his lho-stick before throwing it out into the rubble of the street.

Everyone was standing to attention as the Marshal entered. He was short, especially for a commissar, and that only made him more dangerous. The numerous duelling scars on his face showed how many times others had mistaken a short man for an easy opponent.

He wore his black leather overcoat loose over his shoulders. If he could smell the smoke then he made no comment, but took the aquila salute from them all, and then let them stand smart. 'Colonel. It has been a long fight. And we are victorious!'

'Praise the God-Emperor!' they all shouted.

He nodded. 'I am going to rest. By the time I wake up I expect a full audit of how many Dogs we lost.'

Sawbones put down the scalpel and wiped it on his overcoat.

'There!' he said and took another drag of his rebreather.

Sweat ran down Chalice's face. He could barely speak. 'Finished?'

'Finished,' Sawbones said. The corpsman sat back on his haunches and took a long suck of his pipe. 'I've cut out the infection and stitched it back together.'

Chalice nodded. He looked at the wound. It hurt like frekk.

'You'll live,' Sawbones said, as he always said. Sometimes he was right, and sometimes his medical judgement was impaired.

'Does it need counterseptics?'

Sawbones nodded. 'Yes.'

'Got any?'

'No.'

Chalice reached down for the crutch he had fashioned for himself. It took some jiggling to get it under his arm. 'Thanks,' he said, and pulled a ration pack from one of his pockets and tossed it onto the floor.

'I see you kept your foot,' Colonel Salem called out as Major Chalice limped out into the street.

'Looks like I did.' Chalice said.

'Sawbones gone soft?'

'Clearly.'

The two men eyeballed each other. 'The Marshal wants a full report of casualties by morning.'

'I'll get it to you.'

'Your lot are up at the south gate.'

'And which way is that?'

Salem smiled. 'It's not here.'

'Colonel,' Chalice said. 'Do you know what a frekker you are?'

'Yes,' Salem said. 'I know perfectly well.'

Chalice limped through the dark ruins. The only illumination came from smouldering fires. The only ones who acknowledged him were other Dogs. No one offered to help, and nor did he expect it. He found his way, eventually.

It was nearly midnight when he finally saw one of his Dogs. It was Shin, crouching over something.

'That you, major?'

'Yeah. Where's the south gate?'

Shin pointed. Chalice didn't want to know what the other man was eating. He stumped along, feeling the throb in his leg. He saw the dome of a chapel and limped towards it.

He pushed through the broken door and saw a woman standing before the altar. It was a Sister of Battle, black power armour covered with dust. She spun around. Her face was stern, the cheeks coated with dust and ash, the white hair hanging about her head in a sweat-stained bob. She was a warrior through and through, but he also thought her the most beautiful thing he had ever seen.

'Who are you?' she said.

'I-I am Major Chalice,' he stammered.

'Chalice?' the woman said, stepping towards him. 'A curious name to give a child.'

Chalice's cheeks coloured. He wanted to explain he had got the name from a grisly gang initiation ritual but stopped himself. 'My mother was religious.'

'I am Sister Helewise, of the Order of Our Martyred Lady.'

'Oh,' he said. His throat was so tight the words had to be squeezed out. 'I'm a Chem Dog.'

Her eyes narrowed in recognition. 'Savlar Penitens. Penal world, in the Armageddon System? So, you are–'

He didn't want her to say the words. 'I thought I would come and say a prayer.' He looked at the state the heretics had left the city in, but didn't know where to start.

'Then speak. He will still hear you.'

Chalice paused. He didn't know what to do, but he knelt down on the bare stone. The truth was, he didn't know any proper prayers. He pressed his eyes closed and tried to find the words.

'You do not pray?'

'I do,' he said, though if he was honest with himself he only prayed in craters, or when he was scared shitless.

'Shall I lead you?'

'Yes. Please.'

He heard the soft whine of armour as she knelt beside him.

Helewise spoke in words he did not understand, but he felt their meaning. They went on and on, and he felt his fear lift from him. He felt as though a shaft of golden light had surrounded him, bathing him with its warmth. Then she finished and the light faded, and he felt bereft.

'You're right,' he said at last. 'I felt the God-Emperor flow through me.'

But when he turned back to her, she was gone. Where she had been kneeling beside him there was now only a strip of parchment with a red wax seal at the end.

His fingers shook as he reached towards it. He cupped the parchment in his palms. It was so clean and pure it felt as though it came from a different existence. Carefully dusting it off, he slid it into his inner pocket. It was the most beautiful thing he had ever possessed.

Helewise waited for Sister Lanete at the Chapel of Saint Thor.

Lanete arrived in her Immolator, waiting for her honour guard to dismount before she did so. Dominion Naoka was there, bolter resting casually upon her shoulder. She nodded to Sister Helewise. They had fought together, and that had forged a strong bond between them.

But not so with Lanete. Her parents had been officers in a Cadian regiment. They had both been killed on a planet named Malouri, and as an orphan she had been entrusted to the care of the schola progenium – the very same establishment in which Helewise had been raised. She had been vindictive and judgemental ever since their first meeting. Now she was a veteran Sister, who looked down upon the newly appointed Sister Superior with a hard and unforgiving gaze.

She strode in through the ruined entrance and took in the scene before her.

'Sister Helewise.'

'Sister *Superior* Helewise,' Helewise said.

Lanete ignored the correction. 'You will have much to explain.'

'Indeed?'

'This is your fault.'

'It is not!' Helewise snapped, and regretted it already. She was weary, and she should not have let her old rival annoy her so.

'Were your orders not to protect the city?'

'No,' Helewise said. 'I was here to protect the saint.'

'And did you?'

'Yes,' Helewise said. 'She has been returned to her tomb...'

'You removed her?'

'I had no choice. It was that or leave her to the heretics.'

Lanete paused. It was as if she were thinking of another insult. But then she saw what Helewise was looking at. It was the remains of a Sister of Battle lying in the middle of the chapel floor.

Charred, dismembered, beheaded, but the suit of power armour was unmistakable.

'That is Sister Ephraina,' Helewise said.

Lanete was quiet for a moment. She had served with Ephraina for many years.

Her tone changed. 'Did she die well?'

Helewise nodded. 'She died with the Emperor's light upon her. She knew it was her time.'

Lanete and Helewise knelt in prayer. When they were done, Ephraina's remains were gathered up. The bones and armour were lifted with care and placed in an old ammo crate, though a more suitable reliquary would have to be found when the time came. The manner of her death was such that these objects had power. They could be used to help focus faith and devotion, or be strapped to the front of a tank as it roared to battle.

Lanete waited for Helewise to say her last farewells to Ephraina's remains. When she came out into the daylight, the older Sister said, 'I am now taking command of Holy City.'

Helewise did not argue. They were both Sisters Superior, but Lanete was Helewise's elder by some years. It was part of the reason the older Sister disliked Helewise so. She regarded Helewise as a spoilt upstart, promoted far above her station. Helewise forced a smile.

'Take good care of it.'

Major Chalice eventually found the south gate, and pushed into the hab his lot were using.

Wythers looked up through his curtains of dirty hair. 'You made it,' he said.

'Clearly,' Chalice said. 'I think the God-Emperor loves me after all.'

Wythers started to laugh so hard he made himself choke.

Chalice sat down but he couldn't get the Sister of Battle out of his head. 'Got a spare canister?' he said.

Wythers took his own out, and shook it. It was half full. He tossed it across to the major and Chalice caught it one-handed. He'd sworn himself off, but the urge was growing more and more insistent.

He found a secluded spot and reached inside his pocket and found the wax seal. He held it for a moment as he said a prayer to the God-Emperor – simple words, spoken from one warrior to another – and then he left it there, pressed close to his skin.

He felt that the God-Emperor heard, and with that consolation he slipped the cartridge into his narcotic pump. It took a moment for the chems to flow into the rebreather system. They tasted sweet as perfume. He put the rebreather into his mouth, took a long, deep breath, and his pain eased as the stimms kicked in.

viii

There were too many bodies for the usual practice of burial upon Ayaan, and as the heat brought out the stench of rotting flesh Sister Superior Lanete gave the order for excarnation to be carried out with all haste.

Bodies were butchered and boiled, and within days a noxious fug hung over the city: a mix of ash, dust and the steamy wet stink of boiling flesh. Workers were picking through a drained vat as Sister Dovere passed by. The cooked flesh was taken to the agri-plants and the separated bones were stacked to dry in the hot sun.

A penitent held an icon of the God-Emperor in his arms, and he moved along the line of heaps, pressing his head to the floor, lips moving in a ritual of absolution.

Sister Dialogus Dovere did not have time to stop and record this prayer. She made her way to the library hall, and climbed the steps. The long gallery had been burnt and plundered, but the Fang Takers were too ignorant to know what treasures lay within. They had just set incendiary charges along the carved shelving.

'Sister Luis,' she said.

Her fellow Sister was standing halfway along the gallery, her pole-mounted book standing out amidst the piles of torn papyrus and half-burnt tomes. Luis was a transcriber and illuminator. The large tome above her was the *Fide Imperialis*, the page opened to the Lessons on Human Frailties.

Luis turned to her. Her face was strained. It was the same look they all had as they came to understand the damage that had been done to what was an ancient repository. 'The Fang–' she started, but Sister Dovere cut her off.

'We should not honour them with a name. They are beneath contempt. They are *vandals*.' It was an old word she had found in ancient annals that described those who exulted in wanton destruction. Lovers of ignorance. Enemies of learning and art. Destroyers. And here they had wreaked their mindless destruction on five thousand years of holy artefacts accumulated over generations.

'Indeed,' Luis said.

At that moment, a pair of Battle Sisters appeared at the other end of the gallery. They made their way along the long room.

'Sisters,' Helewise said. 'I trust your work goes well?'

The two non-militant Sisters bowed. 'It is painstaking,' Luis said, gesturing to the piles of half-burnt manuscripts she was working her way through. 'I think this will take me years to complete.'

Helewise nodded. 'We all serve in our own way. And you, Sister Dovere?'

'I am coming with the fleet,' Dovere said. 'I have catalogued the items that you saved. You did fine work.'

Helewise half smiled. 'You should tell Sister Superior Lanete that.'

'I will,' Dovere said. 'Meanwhile my scribes are already at work on a list of the lost manuscripts of the Great Minster of Saint Elaire. It will have its own chantry chapel, and will be an object of veneration for centuries to come.'

'And your work with the sadhvus?'

'I have taken the last survivors into the care of her Order. Their words were already being recorded by servitor scribes. Again, Sister Luis will remain to supervise this work.'

They looked at Sister Luis. She nodded. 'And where next?'

Helewise looked about. Their work on Ayaan was done. 'The next war front,' she said.

'I have heard rumours that the lord general has summoned all the fleets to him. That Battle Group Phaedra is to make the crossing at last.'

Helewise's eyes twinkled. 'I have heard that too.'

Luis clearly wanted to return to her work, and Helewise had come here looking for Dovere. She made her farewell to Luis and took Dovere aside. 'I have to thank you.'

Dovere's data-goggles had been fixed, and they gave her a blank appearance as she stood before the Sister Superior. 'What for?'

'I met Captain Ayling of the Valkenberg Kossaks this morning. He spoke very highly of you.'

Dovere blushed.

'I heard you were instrumental in organising the defence in the aftermath of the attack. You are the one who coordinated with the Navy.'

'There was much confusion, and many of the staff officers had been killed. I had the ability to process data. And I did so.'

'You saved our lives.'

'We serve in our own way,' Dovere said, and Helewise laughed. The sound made Luis turn. Laughter had not been heard here for what felt like an age, but it was a sign that wounds were starting to heal.

'We do indeed. But I owe you.'

Dovere's cheeks blushed again. 'No.'

Helewise looked up. Before, this library had been a living place, with teachers and their acolytes clustered around. It would be returned, she knew, but it would never be as fine as before. So much had been lost.

'How did they do it?' she said suddenly. 'The attack. At the palace.'

Dovere had made a full report to her Order and no doubt any who needed to know the details had been informed. Such heretical sorcery was a matter for the Inquisition.

Her face was inscrutable as she said, 'I am sure the culprits will be found.'

Helewise nodded, but as she stood there, the face of the Fang Takers war chief came back to her, along with the memories of her home world of Liepra. The culprits might be found and killed, but there would be more.

The seed of heresy lay in each heart. All it needed was a chance to grow.

'What are you thinking?' Morgandrie asked Helewise that night, as they stepped out of the drill pit.

Helewise hung her helmet upon its stand, ran her fingers through her damp hair to loosen it, and placed her training sword on the weapon rack.

'Nothing.'

Morgandrie sat next to her. She didn't ask any further questions, but just let her mind drift off as well – to Ephraina's death in the Chapel of Saint Thor.

The heretics had hacked her apart and burned the remains in

the middle of the chapel. The indignity added to her martyrdom. Morgandrie closed her eyes. The God-Emperor had only given her one death, and she hoped that her martyrdom would be like Ephraina's. Or Lalott and Nifach. They had shared that moment, and it bonded them for all time, in the prayers and annals of their Order.

'It's Sister Lanete,' Helewise said. 'I have history with her.'

Morgandrie stopped. Lanete had joined them a year before, and she knew that there was friction between the two women.

'The first time I met her, I was nine.'

'And she was in the Order already?'

Helewise nodded. 'Yes. She was assigned to the abbey on my home world of Liepra. My uncle was seigneur there. I grew up in his court. He doted on me. But...'

She took in a deep breath. She could no longer recall her mother's face, but when she thought back to those days she could still remember many things: the smell of rosewater; the stiff brocade and lace skirts; the feeling of being pressed into her mother's bosom and the touch of her hands that were hot and fine as carved ivory.

'The barons revolted against him. I think my mother must have known. She locked me in her private chapel and we hid in the darkness. She prayed and I knelt there beside her, terrified. The palace guard were slaughtering everyone they could find. They came for us.

'My mother took my hand and pulled me through the vestibule. I remember the chests of vestments, the hanging robes and the flickering lumens. She dragged me to the abbey of the Sisters. One of them brought me inside, but she would not let my mother in. I heard the rebels gun her down, right there, at the gates of the abbey.

'That Sister was Lanete, just a novice back then. And as I stood there by the gates, crying, do you know what the first thing she said to me was? "Silence! Your mother is dead and you are a princess no longer!"'

Morgandrie was not surprised. 'You are lucky you remember your mother at all.'

'You don't?'

Morgandrie shook her head. Most of the schola progenium did not. The Imperium's many wars supplied a constant harvest of orphans, and the Adepta Sororitas could afford to be picky, selecting only the most malleable and serviceable.

Helewise paused. Maybe Lanete was right. Maybe she was a spoilt aristocratic brat after all. She would pray on the matter, she told herself. And she would do what she did best, which was to kill the enemies of the God-Emperor.

They were preparing to leave Ayaan when Sister Helewise came to visit Sister Dialogus Dovere in her quarters.

The non-militant Sister was sitting over her papers. She looked up suddenly, the light catching on the panes of her goggles as a figure stepped inside.

'Sister Helewise!'

Helewise had a natural grace. There was a feline menace in the way she walked, like some feral-world jungle cat. She stopped and looked about at the piles of tomes, papers and scraps of vellum. 'Not working on the sadhvus?'

Dovere's mouth opened for a moment. 'No. Well, my servitors have transcribed the oral records. And they have been logged in the cogitator data banks, as well as being sent to Ophelia. The rest of the work will be done by Sister Luis.'

Dovere blushed. She felt awkward and clumsy about Sister Helewise. She was everything that Dovere would have liked to be. Strong. Beautiful. Accomplished.

'Something happened at the Great Minster,' Helewise said. 'I met a man from Liepra, and he stirred up memories for me – ones that I've kept buried for years. Do you know the circumstances of my youth?'

Dovere nodded. She had researched Sister Helewise in a spare few hours.

'It always seemed strange that a delegation of Sisters had come to see my mother... at the time the outbreak took place,' Helewise continued, then caught something in the Dialogus' manner. 'Why was Sister Lanete upon Liepra?'

'I don't know.'

Helewise looked into Dovere's data-goggles and saw her own face reflected back at her. But for Sister Dovere it felt as though the other Sister were staring into her soul.

'No?' she said.

Dovere pursed her lips to stop herself from speaking. She shook her head.

'Tell me,' Helewise said.

Dovere thought that she might scream. No matter what, she could not tell Helewise what she knew.

Lanete established the local hierarchy, set in order the raising of a new regiment of carabineers, and turned over the protection of the planet to a regiment of the Bifrost Huscarls, who would put the fear of the God-Emperor into the local recruits.

But there was no time to linger. Battle Group Phaedra was already behind schedule. They should have crossed over with the rest of Fleet Quintus. Great deeds awaited them. The governance of Ayaan was the duty of those who were being left behind.

The hundred or so Sisters of Our Martyred Lady and the lesser Orders assigned to them were to be loaded up on the battleship

Vigorous. Only Sister Luis was to remain. She came out to watch the other Sisters leave.

She had never had much to do with the Battle Sisters, but Sister Dovere came out, and stood before her, data-goggles giving her an impersonal look.

'May the Emperor protect you all!' Luis said.

Dovere nodded. She never knew what to say in moments like this.

'You have a lot of work ahead of you,' she said.

And with that she turned, and followed the other Sisters onto the lighter.

Their tanks went first. They still bore the scars of battle, still carried the dust of Holy City in their tracks and across their armoured panels. One by one the great weapons of war were loaded, and lashed down, and then the Sisters carried their relics back with them. Among the loads, Luis saw the crate that carried Sister Ephraina's relics.

She stood alone, as the last Sister, Helewise, mounted the ramp, paused at the top and turned to look one more time upon Ayaan and the ruins of Holy City. Luis hoped that she would turn to her as well, but Helewise did not. She made the sign of the fleur-de-lys, and stepped inside. The ramp closed behind her, and shut with the sound of mag-locks engaging.

Two days later, the last of the troops were lifted off Ayaan.

The 17th Savlar Chem Dogs were granted the honour of joining Battle Group Phaedra as a reward for their role in quelling the Fang Takers.

'Is that an honour?' Shin asked.

'It's better than being dead,' Chalice told him.

Shin nodded. He paused as he sat on his pack. 'How's the foot?'

Chalice held it up. 'It's good,' he said.

'Where did you get the counterseptics from?'

'I didn't. I prayed.'

Shin looked at Major Chalice and burst out laughing, but he realised his mistake as Chalice kicked him.

'Frekk,' he wheezed. 'You're serious?'

Chalice nodded. 'The Emperor protects.'

Part Three

Now

Thought for the day:
   Faith in your commander is your strongest armour, your sharpest blade, your wellspring of courage.

í

The Indomitus Crusade was made up of ten great fleets, named according to their number, and each of those was divided into lesser battle groups.

Battle Group Phaedra was one such, assigned to Fleet Quintus, the 'Cursed Fifth'.

It gathered at the edge of the Great Rift, drawing its splinter fleets to it.

The fleet was commanded from the bridge of the battleship *Pax Imperialis*.

The old dame had been built in the great shipyards of Cypra Mundi a thousand years before. She had served under a dozen commanders, including Admirals d'Armitage and Aarke. Their portraits hung on the wall, severe faces looking down on those that followed after. Lord General Gnaerac felt their judgement. He stood with broad shoulders bent, his head bowed, as his assistant, Bennigsen, announced the Munitorum ambassador.

'What is his name?' Gnaerac sighed.

'Lord Raglann, sire.'

Gnaerac nodded. 'Show the bastard in.'

Lord Raglann's robes were embroidered with the sigils of his order. He was a man who could break planets with his demands, but he was contrite as he bowed low.

Gnaerac's forced smile was almost a grimace. 'Ambassador,' he said. 'I hope you have good news for me.'

Raglann remained bent. 'No, sire. Alas, I have none.'

Gnaerac's gaze was stony. 'It is lost?'

'Yes, lord general.'

Gnaerac's voice was a bare whisper. 'The entire fleet?'

The ambassador coughed to clear his throat. He felt the news as deeply as the lord general.

'Yes, lord general. The whole fleet.'

The words fell across the room like lead.

No one spoke. No one even dared to draw breath. The sombre portraits stared down from the walls as if in judgement.

He cursed. Supply Fleet Gamma had set out a year ago, on what should have been a short hop from the neighbouring system. He had been *promised* it. It *should* have been here waiting for them. It *had* to be here. How could they make the jump without their supply fleet?

These thoughts beat in his brain like the blows of a hammer. 'Ambassador. What are you going to do?'

Lord Raglann turned pale. Battle chewed hungrily through armour, supplies and munitions. 'Supply Fleet Gamma was carrying the output of a hundred forge worlds… It would take years to build up another supply fleet.'

'Years.'

'Yes.'

'Do we have years?'

'No.'

'Think of the men and women over there!' Gnaerac shouted.

Raglann said nothing. Gnaerac paced up and down. He was too angry to speak. He was the leader of Battle Group Phaedra, but he felt powerless. His force would rot waiting for another supply fleet to be raised, and he could not cross over without the materiel it carried.

'Throne!' he said at last. 'If we can't make warp jumps within sight of the Astronomican, then what hope is there that we can cross the Warpscar?'

The ambassador looked desperate. He had no answers.

Gnaerac went on, 'What do you suggest we do, ambassador?'

Raglann remained silent.

'Is there nothing you can say?' Gnaerac demanded.

Raglann shook his head, but the silence stretched on uncomfortably. The ambassador felt the eyes of all the Astra Militarum officers upon him. He was a man without answers, and so he turned to faith. 'The Emperor protects,' he said.

Gnaerac turned on him. 'Does He now? He didn't protect Supply Fleet Gamma, did He?'

'Lord general, I assure you, the augurs were good. The crew underwent all the necessary rituals.'

Gnaerac waved him away.

He stopped at the sideboard, and poured himself a cup of recaff.

Bennigsen and his attendants exchanged glances. None of them wanted to be the lightning rod for his fury.

The air was electric.

Gnaerac drained his cup and swilled the recaff as if it were mouthwash. He remembered them all: the missing regiments, fleets, forge worlds, shrine worlds, places of pilgrimage, planets... friends, too. All sundered from the light of the Emperor.

He looked through the void window, put his fingers to his forehead and massaged the pain.

'Dismissed!' he said suddenly.

The command staff filed out in silence. As soon as they were off the command deck, Gnaerac heard them begin to speak. He didn't know what they were saying, but he heard the tone. Only Bennigsen remained. She was his most loyal servant.

She stepped forwards. 'I have set the savants to work out our options,' she said. 'I will urge them on, sir.'

'Whip the bastards,' Gnaerac said, half in jest. She did not laugh. It was too dire for that. Or not quite dire enough, yet.

There was a long silence. He turned the empty recaff mug in his hand. 'They blame me!' he said. 'Those scum.'

Bennigsen had always imagined putting her body before Gnaerac's own, taking blade or bolt in her flesh. But this was so much more difficult. This was a proxy war where Bennigsen's valour, experience and veteran fighting skills were as naught against an enemy unseen.

At last Gnaerac sighed. 'We cannot wait any longer. Summon a great council.'

Gnaerac spent the rest of the ship-day with Admiral Karlien going through possibilities.

The Navy man was stiff as a rod of iron. He spoke plainly. 'The crossing can be made, but without supplies, how long can your regiments fight? A forced crossing without adequate logistical support would be folly. Why bring millions of mouths to feed?'

Gnaerac nodded. The truth was that many Navy commanders considered the *Pax Imperialis* too ancient and valuable to risk in such a venture. He stood at the armoured viewport, looked out and caught sight of a recent arrival.

'I see the Adepta Sororitas have arrived.'

Karlien nodded. 'Yes. It is the *Daughter of the Emperor*. Seconded from the Order of Our Martyred Lady.'

Gnaerac paused, gazing out towards the great craft. It was a void-cathedrum with vaulting fabric domes and pinnacles that caught the light of the sun like a faceted jewel. Atop the craft was a statue of Saint Katherine, sword raised in defiance. An object of sublime beauty.

But he was not fooled. He had seen the craft close up. It was a dreadful weapon of terror and war. Macro cannons, sonic disruptors and an organ-mounted array of attack-suppressing weaponry were all touched by the light that spilled out from the glassaic windows, illuminating the void like a tiny star. Just the sight of it brought hope to his heart.

'Maybe they will change our luck,' he said.

ii

The heart of the *Daughter of the Emperor* was the Great Prayer Hall, with serried ranks of wooden thrones that rose up the sides like the rows of an amphitheatre. At the centre of the chamber was an ancient brass prayer wheel, turning endlessly on vast cogs, sending prayers across the ether to the Golden Throne. Its bas-relief surface showed images of the God-Emperor, His palace on Holy Terra, and the life of Saint Katherine, and etched in fine script were the names of all those martyred in service to the Master of Mankind. Over it, cherubs circled slowly with heavy censers trailing sacred smoke.

It was turning now, as Palatine Albreda led her Sisters in their nocturnal prayers. The summons had come from the *Pax Imperialis*, and they had prayed together to seek a solution.

But as the prayers came to an end, one voice spoke in dissent. 'Palatine Albreda. I have heard that the light of the Astronomican is not visible across the Rift. How then can we cross?'

The words were greeted with silence. All they could hear was the low creak of the massive prayer wheel and the hiss of disapproval from Sister Superior Lanete.

Palatine Albreda turned to make out who had spoken. Sister Superior Helewise stood to show herself. 'Apologies, Palatine. I should not have spoken, but the question has been nagging at me and I do not know the answer.'

The Palatine's face was stern, but not unkind. 'Speak, child. What is it you fear?'

Helewise stammered. 'Palatine. If I had my way, we would send a lesser force across. Let them light a beacon that we might follow. We are the finest warriors within the whole battle group.'

The silence that greeted her words was stony.

Palatine Albreda's jump pack hummed as she lifted from the floor and hovered above the prayer wheel. Her voice was amplified by the curvature of the chamber. She did not need to speak in more than a whisper and all could hear.

'You think we should wait until it is safe?'

'I do not want safety,' Helewise said. 'All I want is to meet our enemies in battle, and to crush them. But if we are lost in the warp, how can we aid the Imperium?'

The great prayer wheel turned slowly beneath the Palatine. 'Sister Helewise. We have no power to decide the manner of our own deaths. Our lives are His gift. Some great warriors die in their beds, while civilians often die in battle. Who knows when our time will end or what manner of death it will be? We would all choose to die in battle against some evil of the warp. Or, like Saint Katherine, in crushing the heretics underfoot.'

'Exactly!' Helewise said, and she knew that there were many who felt the same way.

Palatine Albreda paused. 'Imagine if we were to sacrifice ourselves in the crossing.'

'That would be a waste of our prowess.'

'But if that is the will of the God-Emperor?'

'We are His holy blade. Why would He throw us away like that?'

Albreda smiled. 'But think. How might our deaths serve the God-Emperor? Perhaps our souls would burn in the warp. It is possible that our souls would be a light that Navigators might steer by. Would that not be a great service?'

Helewise hesitated. 'It would,' she said. But she prayed that it would not be so.

After the prayers, the Sisters filed out.

Sister Superior Lanete was waiting for Helewise. Her face was like stone. 'How dare you question the Palatine?'

'The Emperor put the thought into my mind, and I spoke it aloud.'

Lanete snorted at the idea.

'None of us are perfect,' Helewise said.

Lanete laughed coldly. 'Indeed we are not.'

The next day, both Helewise and Lanete were on board the Palatine's personal lighter as it crossed the void to the *Pax Imperialis*.

The great battleship was so large that it filled the viewport of the shuttle despite still being far away, and the Palatine studied it closely. 'A fine craft.'

Her personal guard stood about her, looking strangely alike in their black armour, and with their white hair hanging about battle-scarred faces.

'Forged in Cypra Mundi,' Albreda said, as the lighter slowed on its approach to the void dock, retro-thrusters whining as it slid into one of the central hangar bays. As the atmospheres stabilised, the Palatine readied herself. She had spent the night in prayer, looking for guidance, and had found none.

She led the Sisters in a brief final prayer before marching

down the ramp and onto the deck of the *Pax Imperialis*. A row of Fury interceptors were being armed across the hangar. The vast, sleek craft dwarfed them all.

A Naval party was waiting for them. A squad of ratings were led by an officer, her velvet jacket and trousers pressed to razor-edge creases, her left arm an augmetic claw.

She bowed her head. 'Welcome, Lady Palatine. I am Captain Rela. Please, let me accompany you to the council chamber.'

The officer led the Sisters across the hazard warning stripes, then along a metal-panelled service corridor, wide enough for missile and torpedo carts. Caged lumens lined the walls. There was a faint flicker in time with the ancient ship's slow heartbeat.

'*Pax Imperialis*,' Albreda said. 'An illustrious history.'

'Indeed,' Rela said, speaking with evident pride. 'She has fought for nearly a thousand years.'

'I know,' Albreda said. 'First confirmed kill was the *Hollow Sigil*, in the Siren Straits. Three hundred years in the Gothic Sector and a string of assignments that have taken it as far as the asteroid mines of the Crinan System and the gas clouds of Creke. And in the last century, she has fought in over thirty major engagements, including the Battle of Faith's Anchorage.'

The Naval officer smiled. 'Very good, Palatine, though that was before my time. In our last engagement we destroyed the *Bloody Cauldron* and the *Bilious Spawn*.'

'The Battle of the Brethren Hollow.'

'Yes,' Rela said. 'One more flight run and we would have destroyed the *Foebane* as well.' There was a pause. 'We'll get her, next time.' Rela stopped. 'I'm impressed. I don't think I could list them all...'

Albreda smiled as she started forwards. 'My father was an admiral. Port Maw.'

'Oh,' Rela replied. Her tone said it all. Port Maw was one of those worlds lost in the Imperium Nihilus.

Albreda nodded. 'My father was of the von Ravensbergs.'

'That is a name of great potency within the Imperial Navy.'

'Indeed. And no doubt I would have followed my forebears into the Navy. But my father was lost. Indeed, all contact was lost when the galaxy was sundered. My mother never recovered. She took her own life when I was five. So the crossing of the Cicatrix Maledictum is very important to me. In a way, my whole life has been bound up with it.'

There was a long pause, then Albreda went on. 'But if these things had not happened, I could not serve the God-Emperor as I do. It is the trials in life that make us who we are.'

'Indeed.' Rela half laughed. 'Though I don't think I could ever have been like you.'

'Do not be fooled by the armour,' the Palatine said. 'We are not like the Adeptus Astartes. They are gene-altered to give them extraordinary strength, size and power. We go into battle without their gene-enhancement. But our humanity gives us our greatest asset – faith. We shape and channel it, and hone it until it is a blade.'

Rela said nothing for a long time as they arrived at the mag-lift. As they rose up through the guts of the old warhorse, Helewise could see that the officer was thinking on the Palatine's words. Albreda had a powerful charisma. Helewise had seen it work upon others many times. In the quiet moments like this, she radiated faith and belief. But in battle she was like an angel, always soaring before them, leading them – if she wanted – into the very pits of heresy.

They were halfway through their ascent when Rela said, 'So many of us are starting to lose ours. Since we set out from Holy Terra, we seem to have suffered travail after travail.'

Albreda nodded. 'It is difficult at times, to look around at the Imperium of Man and to see all the flaws – the crimes, the indignities, the stupidity, the cruelty – and to still have faith. But even in the face of misfortune, you must believe. Despite all the misfortunes, the Imperium endures.'

Lord General Gnaerac and Bennigsen stood in his personal chambers and watched through the view-portal as the command deck filled. It was a fine collection of men and women, from worlds that stretched from one end of the Imperium of Man to the other. Velvet jackets, smart shakos, duelling scars, hardened and scarred faces – bodies that had been ruined by war and yet still fought on, missing limbs and eyes replaced with bespoke augmetics.

Gnaerac wished he had good news for them. He had spent the night working with the savants, and yet they had kept coming up with the wrong answer, and he had sent them back again to refigure the details.

His face was drawn and grey. 'Listen to them! They're like vultures, lining up along the branch, waiting for the old grox to die.'

'Are you comparing yourself to a grox, sir?'

The lord general laughed. 'Yes, damn it!' He punched his fist into his hand. He slapped his aide's shoulder and the woman was knocked sideways. 'Now, I faced worse than this lot while I was a rank-and-file Guardsman. Throne! I've faced worse than this in a damn bordello!'

He ran a hand down the braid buttons that lined his long-coat, stood at the doors and took a deep breath as he put his hand to the knob. He felt the tension as the portal swung open, and he stepped inside.

But the sense of foreboding only grew stronger. Only Commissar-General Oskarr Qartermayne, of the Terrax Guard, approached him. The 74th Terrax Guard were one of the finest regiments in his fleet, and their leader led the Fifth Void Army – one of the few detachments that had succeeded in their objectives.

'Commissar-general!' Gnaerac said. 'Congratulations on the reconquest of Hathea.'

Qartermayne bowed his head. 'I was overproud,' he said, reflecting and gesturing towards his arm. He had lost part of it in the final battle and the augmetic limb hung in a sling. The steel fingers twitched. 'Nerve-splicing is still bedding in.'

'Sometimes a commander has to lead from the front,' Gnaerac said.

Qartermayne nodded. 'Very true.'

Gnaerac felt those own words prod him forwards as he made his way to the dais.

Silence fell throughout the room as he turned towards them. It had been a long time since they had all been gathered in one place.

'Commanders,' Gnaerac started. 'We have secured all the primary and secondary targets. I have assured high command that we are ready to make the great push across the Cicatrix Maledictum.' The words fell like lead. 'I have asked much of all of you. But now it is time to take the next step. We must cross into the Imperium Nihilus.'

For a while, his words were greeted by silence, then a voice shouted from the back.

'Where is the supply fleet?'

Gnaerac paused. He drew in a deep breath. 'Our supply fleet has been lost.'

Gnaerac could feel the mood of the room start to unravel before him. There were questions, and statements masquerading as questions. The audience started to hum like an angry psych-neuein and one officer called out, 'Lord general, is a crossing even possible?'

Gnaerac approached the confrontation like a battle. He tried to pummel her with a long list of figures and particulars, but another voice shouted, 'It's suicide!'

There was a low murmur of assent. Ever since the loss of the *Embrace of Fire*, things had gone wrong. Now many were convinced that they were cursed.

'You are brave warriors all,' a voice called out. 'But your lack of faith does you no credit.'

It was Palatine Albreda, of the Order of Our Martyred Lady.

She had been standing at the back, but now she strode through the officers to take her place at the front of the command dais. The officers stepped aside to let her pass.

They took her in, in wonder. Embroidered tabard hanging loosely over her power armour, her rough-shorn white hair hanging about a battle-scarred face.

All talk was stilled. She took her place before the dais.

'Your fears are valid. What hope can we have indeed, that the first of us who attempt the crossing will be successful? None of us wish to end our days lost in the warp. I have many years, I pray, before me. But our lives and our deaths belong to the God-Emperor to use as He wishes. Only He can decide how and when we will die.' She paused as she took them all in.

'Fifteen years ago, you paraded on the Muster Plains of Holy Terra and you swore to Fleet Master Prasorius that you would join him in this great venture. And you would let misfortune impede your vows?'

The words were greeted with silence, but Helewise could tell that the Palatine had changed the mood of the room.

'Battle Group Phaedra has fought its way to this point. And now the next step is the transition to the Imperium Nihilus. On the other side of the warp curtain humanity prays for our intervention. For a hundred years they have looked to the skies in blind hope for the lights of our warships, glittering in orbit. And for a hundred years their hopes and prayers have lain fallow. At last, after years of fighting, we have reached this moment. This great opportunity where we are ready to send the vanguard across. Our task is to bring faith and hope to those who dwell in darkness. This is not a time for dissent. It is a time for leadership. Which of you will step forward?'

Gnaerac found himself kneeling on the dais. 'I will lead,' he said.

At that moment one of the officers moved towards her and knelt down, his head bowed under a black peaked cap.

One by one, the generals started to kneel. She looked at them with obvious pride.

She joined them, dropping to one knee, her hands resting upon her sword hilt. A thrill surged through the room. The air began to turn cold. A rime of frost sparkled from the lumens as the room darkened about them, Albreda's inner light the only source of illumination.

'The Sisters of Our Martyred Lady shall lead the way,' Albreda called out. 'Together we will sear a white-hot path of prayer through the warp. And the loyal and the faithful will look up and see in the sky a great light. And we will bring death to our enemies, vengeance to the faithless, and light to those who have held true to their vows.'

There was a roar of approval. It was decided. Gnaerac and the Sisters would lead, and the others would follow.

Albreda motioned them all to stand. The officer in the peaked cap stepped back into the crowd, but the Palatine called him out. 'Sir. You were the first to step forward. What is your name?'

'I am Commissar Aebram. I lead the Seventeenth Savlar Chem Dogs.'

'Welcome, Commissar Aebram. Will you join us?'

'I would be honoured, lady.'

'Lord General Gnaerac, please have the Savlar Chem Dogs brought aboard my ship. Together we will carry the torch of faith into the darkness of the Imperium Nihilus.'

iii

The *Daughter of the Emperor* was three miles in length, its super-structure lined with lancet windows, buttresses, fleur-de-lys pinnacles and finials, and blind arcades filled with statuary and divine scripts.

It was a wonder of the Mars shipyards, fashioned centuries past by Fabricator General Raskian. His finest fabricators spent three centuries on its decoration under the tutelage of Ecclesiarchy artisans. Yard by yard, its flanks were acid-etched with sacred texts, and glassaic windows were set along its length, displaying the trials that Saint Katherine had undergone in a wonderful mosaic of colour. Finally, the inset reliquaries were filled with sacred objects, and the great prayer wheel in the prayer hall was set in motion.

It was the terror of heretics, combined with the fiercest weaponry the Imperium of Man could provide. The heartbeat of the great vessel quickened as Palatine Albreda returned from the *Pax Imperialis*.

This void-craft had been her home for longer now than she

could remember. Piety hung heavy throughout the corridors. It was in the mouldering tapestries hung at the ship's launch depicting worlds and fortresses that no longer existed, and the niche-shrines piled with objects of faith and devotion, covered with centuries of dust and incense-motes. It lay in the sacred candles, and in the song of the great craft, piped out through a thousand ornate brass vox-grilles.

The corridor was lined with golden prayer wheels, the spindle bases lubricated with the tallow of martyrs, fibre-bundles carrying the resultant grace up to accumulators within the dorsal lance batteries. The Palatine put her hand to each as she swept back to the Great Prayer Hall. Helewise and the other Sisters marched behind her, past galleries, cloisters, chantries, reliquaries, barracks, battle halls, side chapels for private contemplation, and gloomy tombs lit only by occasional wicks floating in the liquid fat of ancient martyrs.

The whole mission awaited them in the prayer hall. Even the shutters to the Repentia cells had been opened, casting cracks of light onto the Sisters within, and letting the sound of their incessant prayers tumble down among the others.

The Battle Sisters were arranged in tiered balconies according to rank – five hundred of them, enough to compel a planet to the Emperor's will.

Helewise and the other Sisters Superior took their places high up in their carven thrones. Sister Helewise's seat was set just beneath the Repentia cells. The line of the fleur-de-lys-shaped grilled windows marked each one out.

As she knelt, Helewise saw a face pressed against one of the metal grilles, and had a brief impression of chains and a leather hood.

Palatine Albreda lifted her arms and rose to hang in the middle of the chapel as the cherubs clustered about her.

'Sisters! Rejoice! The God-Emperor has chosen us to lead Battle Group Phaedra across the Cicatrix Maledictum! This will be a journey from which few, if any, of us return. But we will carry the flame of faith into the desert of the Imperium Nihilus. Scourge your souls of doubt. Make yourselves worthy of this great honour.'

The Sisters heard the words in silence. There were no questions. No argument. Each Sister accepted the future they had been given and looked within themselves for any faults or flaws.

From the Repentia cells came shouts of ecstatic joy. They welcomed the crossing. It seemed that their martyrdom was assured.

Helewise's first squad commander, Muroki, had taken the vows Repentia. She had been stripped of her armour and vestments, her white hair shaved to her scalp, her wrist, neck and ankles bound with chains, and then, finally, a hood lowered over her head and locked in place.

Helewise looked across the chamber and caught Morgandrie's eye. She knew exactly what the other Sister was thinking.

This journey meant death for them all.

Helewise closed her eyes and drew into herself.

They prayed for a long time, but after half an hour, the battle for Holy City returned to Helewise.

Visions had troubled her since Ayaan. And most frequent were those of the Great Minster, the leader of the Fang Takers, and the bodies hanging from nooses of razor wire.

She meditated on the lessons within. Two souls plucked from her home world, choosing such divergent roads. Her a Sister and him a heretic, brought back together at the hour of his death.

Her mind returned to her last days upon Liepra. The last moments with her mother.

She had not dared ask what was happening.

'Pray,' her mother had told her as she had dragged her through corridors littered with the dead to the gates of the Abbey of the Unstained Vow. She remembered the heavy metal gates, the palace guard dressed in bulky flak armour. She saw clearly her mother banging with both fists.

The wicket opened. Sister Lanete had been much younger then, and even more stern. 'We cannot let you in.'

Helewise pondered on that moment as she knelt in the prayer hall. Her mother had sacrificed herself for her daughter. And now, it seemed, it was her turn to pass on that sacrifice, for the Imperium Nihilus.

As the Battle Sisters stood and left the hall one by one, Albreda found the Sister Dialogus. 'Sister Dovere. How is your work on the orphaned transcripts progressing?'

Dovere's data-goggles reflected the lights of the flickering torch-lumens. 'It goes well,' she said, and tried to hold her enthusiasm back. 'In fact, I think I have found something of importance.'

'Oh?'

Dovere froze, mouth open. 'Sorry, ma'am. Progress, but no conclusions yet. I came here to check the names on the prayer wheel.'

Albreda gestured for her to continue and Dovere moved to the great brass wheel. Her goggles focused. She took in the information and then she turned and saw, with surprise, that Palatine Albreda was still there, watching Sister Helewise as she finished her prayers and made her way out.

'The Emperor has great things in store for that one,' Albreda said.

Dovere nodded awkwardly. It was true. Helewise, for all her flaws, was a paragon. Her faith and spirit burnt so much brighter than all the others.

* * *

Each of the Battle Sisters prepared themselves in their own way, and Sister Helewise felt the need to hold a blade in her hand. She made her way down to the drill pits to pronounce the catechism of the *Fide Imperialis*.

It was a low domed chamber, a sunken floor strewn with cinders.

She fought helmless so she could smell and hear and take in every detail.

She dropped down onto the cinder floor and thought of the dangers that they would face upon this expedition.

There would be daemons and Traitor Space Marines, she had no doubt. When the moment came she would match them blade for blade, and she would vanquish them.

From the gloom above her head, hydraulic arms lowered the first pit fighter towards the chamber floor. It was a hulking combat-servitor, armed with a powered blade. Its armoured shape was enhanced with slab-muscles, and stimm feeders tubed directly into the meat of its brain.

She destroyed the warrior-construct with ease. She wanted a tougher opponent. The strongest kind that they kept in the drill pits.

Helewise felt the weight of the blade in her hand, visualising her blows in her mind as she paced about the cinder pit. It took a long time for the cogitators to bring the requested grade forward.

The hydraulic armature creaked with the weight of the warrior. The steel groaned as it lowered the massive servitor to the floor.

She was deadly calm, and did not even grace the creature with a look, but knelt, hands cupped upon her sword's hilt, praying. The pit shook as the warrior was set down just ten feet from her. She smelt sweat, corruption, hatred; heard the snarl of anger as combat stimms were fed intravenously into its system, and then the roar of a weapon.

The ogryn berserker's head was hidden within a heavy sack sewn onto its face.

Chains wound about its wrists. In its massive fists, a two-handed buzz saw.

Reckoning rested point down as the ogryn-servitor came forwards with a roar, gunning the saw as its blade screamed through the air at the kneeling figure before it.

At the last moment Helewise leapt up. Reckoning flashed with voltaic sparks as she parried the first blow.

Another attack came down from above, then another, and a third.

She blocked each of them, slanting them aside, running through her daily catechism. 'From the lightning and the tempest!' she hissed, swinging around and parrying another blow. 'From plague, deceit and temptation!'

The ogryn stepped in close, its knee slamming into her chest. She was thrown backwards, rolling back to her feet as the beast came on again, snorting its fury.

She remained composed, even as the terrible blade screamed through the air.

'From the blasphemy of the fallen!' she shouted as she drove the ogryn back with a flurry of attacks, left and right. 'From the begetting of daemons!' she snarled, parrying a pair of wild chops to her head, and chose her moment for a decisive blow.

'From the curse of the mutant!' she hissed as she drove her blade into the creature's torso, burying it up to the hilt. The beast dropped the buzz saw and grabbed at her, but she ducked away, dragging her blade out with a gush of hot blood.

The beast kept coming, its steps faltering as its life ebbed away.

'From the curse of the mutant,' she sang again, 'our Emperor, deliver us!'

And with those last words her blade swung with a flash of steel, cutting through sacking, flesh and bone.

The ogryn stood for a moment, as its head slipped slowly from its shoulders and landed in the cinders with a heavy thud. Its massive fists twitched in death, and then the heavy body tipped forwards, its lifeblood coming out in an ebbing torrent.

Helewise knelt once more to finish her catechism as hydraulic claws picked up the dead body and hauled the dripping corpse into the gloom. 'A morte perpetua,' she prayed, her words ending in a whisper. 'Domine, libra nos.'

Helewise stood. She called out to the fighting pit's cogitator. 'Again!'

Dovere returned to her chambers. She had been working for years on these orphaned stacks of vellum, but she felt that she was just starting to break through.

She searched through the piles of text and found the one she wanted. It was written in the neat, impersonal script of an astropathic servitor. The ink was still dark, despite its age. At some point an unknown scribe had written *Arcius Sector?* in red ink. A seal that had been attached to the parchment's top-left corner showed an Imperial aquila, and the given name *Kryre*.

A second slip had been stapled to the side, imprinted with the name *Quage*. Upon it, in neatly written Gothic minuscule, *Arcius unlikely. Scelilus' Hope?*

Scelilus' Hope was a planet in the Morhet Sector, but there were no other comments. Both trails of research had run out.

Dovere had cloth-wrapped weights to hold the vellum down. She bent over it.

Astropathic communications usually began with a salutation. That was missing, and the rest of the text was largely absent, with missing sentences, words and word endings.

Astropaths – and choirs – had their own particular styles, still observable even when they had been processed through the scriptorium services of the receiving choirs.

It was something that a non-Sister would not recognise, but Dovere was sensitive to such things. To the choice of High Gothic, and a High Gothic that had a preponderance of religious terminology.

On the other side of the table lay sample correspondence that stretched back to the earliest days of Saint Katherine's War of Faith. They had been grouped chronologically. She blinked and sorted them in order of priority.

Data scrolled up Dovere's retinal display, cataloguing past communications from the world. She sat still as her goggles conducted a search, looking for salient features. Words. Images. Patterns of informational relay.

She was bent over for so long that she lost track of time. It took her hours to find the one that she was looking for.

At last she sat back and let out a long exhalation, allowing herself a quick, tight smile.

The Chem Dogs had journeyed from Ayaan in the bilge decks of the *Vigorous*. The only time the gates were unlocked was when the cooks delivered their daily meal. That day, the cook detail was met at the doors by Mercy Cody. 'Eighty hundredweight of slop,' the lead cook said.

'Eighty hundredweight?'

'That is correct.'

Cody nodded to one of the Dogs, who lifted the thin pressmetal lid. Steam escaped from under the lid. It had the strong, yeasty scent of nutrition paste. He ordered them all in.

'Us too?' the chief cook said.

'Yes. You too.'

One of them started to sweat. The beads trickled down his face as he held out a chit for the stamp. 'Is it safe?'

Cody smiled. 'It's never safe.'

'What happens if they try something?'

Mercy Cody had an assault shotgun inside his longcoat. He lifted it up, and pumped the magazine full of shot. 'Know how to stop a line of marching ants?'

The cook shook his head.

'Stamp on the first ten.'

Major Chalice's lot were on security detail. The Dogs were armed with cudgels of rebar. Fifty lengths had been issued, and fifty pieces would be returned – upon Chalice's life.

He still had a faint limp as he paced along his Dogs. He waited until the meal line was nearly done, and went over to check on Shin. 'Got it?'

Shin slid his hand from his pocket and held it out, over Chalice's open hand. The press-board packet was stamped with the Munitorum symbol. A canister of nitra-chems.

'Well done, lad!' Chalice nodded and lifted a mess plate that he had put aside especially and handed it across.

Shin looked down. In the middle of the grey slop was the distinctive round of a sawn bone with gelatinous tendons, gristle and a few scraps of meat. It was hard to tell what animal it had come from.

'What's that?' Wythers asked as Chalice walked past.

'Spares,' Chalice said.

'For me?'

Chalice nodded, and Wythers was so overcome he didn't know what to say. 'Thanks,' he managed at last.

'Just in case,' Chalice said. 'Maybe I'll need it.'

Chalice took in all the lengths of rebar as he escorted the

cooks out. Shin was gnawing on his bone. He tore at a lump of gristle, crunched it down and swallowed.

The cooks gave him a look and Chalice smiled darkly. 'No one sleeps with Shin about.'

At the end of the meal, the Marshal's black-booted feet padded into the room. One of the Chem Dogs was slow in getting out of his way and the Marshal's boot knocked him sprawling. The hangar went silent. They had known the Marshal long enough to know that he only brought bad news. They stood frozen by his presence.

'We are transferring to another craft,' the Marshal told them. 'One hour.' He turned his back on them and marched from the room.

After a few moments of silence, Chalice spoke. 'What the frekk does that mean?'

No one knew. But they did exactly as they were told, and an hour later the Mercies opened up the hangar doors and drove them out.

At the end of the line came Sawbones, pushing a rusted medicae trolley piled up with old, dirty plastek bags. All manner of stolen implements poked out. There were bloody bandages, sutures, saws and a bundle of scalpels.

He stopped before Chalice. 'You're still alive.'

Chalice nodded. 'Thanks to the Emperor.'

The Chem Dogs were herded into a lighter.

'Where are we heading?' Shin called out.

Major Chalice ignored him.

'Are we going to fight?' Shin asked Mercy Cody.

Cody lashed out with his neuro-whip. There was a crackle as the lash caught Shin on the arm. The Dog let out an involuntary yelp, and crashed to the floor, where he lay twitching.

The Dogs moved away from him. When Shin came to, his trousers were warm and wet.

The others refused to look at him. Weakness was not something they tolerated.

The Chem Dogs spent three hours sitting in cramped darkness as they crossed the void.

When they arrived, Shin's trousers were still damp. They heard the clang and rattle of loading gear, and then the hiss of stabilising atmospheres.

'Well, we're somewhere,' Chalice called out.

And then they smelled incense. It was faint at first, struggling through the miasma of sweat and fear and unwashed bodies.

But it lifted all their spirits as the lights came on and they were herded down the ramp.

They stepped out in wonder. The air smelt sweet. There were candlelit shrines set into the walls, and from a row of vox-grilles came the sound of prayer.

'What the frekk is this place?' Shin asked Chalice, but Chalice didn't know.

'Looks like a frekking chapel,' he said.

'You're aboard the *Daughter of the Emperor*!' Mercy Cody shouted.

'And what's that?'

'It's the craft of the Sisters of Our Martyred Lady.'

'What do they want with us?'

'Frekk knows,' Cody said. 'Now move along.'

iv

Helewise's muscles were burning as she was forced back onto her heel, her back pressed against the pit wall. She let out a shout of anger as she swung her sword two-handed.

There was a wet thud as another head was severed from its body.

'How many is that?' a voice said.

Helewise spun about. She had not heard the intruder approach. It was Morgandrie. One side of her scalp had been shaved, the other half bound into a rudimentary plait, clasped at the end with a spent round from a heavy bolter.

'Eight,' Helewise said.

'More?'

Helewise shook her head as claws descended to lift the dead body from the floor. Helewise waited until the ogryn's torso was rising before she wiped both sides of her blade clean.

She slammed the blade into its sheath and clambered up the ladder.

'I think I am done,' Helewise said. 'You?'

Morgandrie nodded. She had been practising with her blade as well.

The two of them walked back to the mag-lift. The heartbeat of the void-craft was slow and sure.

They stood in the lift as the doors swept closed and the mag-lock engaged.

Helewise had the sense that Morgandrie wanted to speak. She waited until they were out, in the corridor, walking to their cells.

'Are you troubled, Sister?'

'No,' Morgandrie said.

They walked on a little further.

'I think of Ayaan,' Helewise said.

Morgandrie said nothing.

They stopped at Morgandrie's door. Helewise turned to her Sister, but Morgandrie would not look her in the eye. They each made the sign of the fleur-de-lys, and then Morgandrie slipped inside and Helewise was left, staring at the closed door. She passed Naoka's and Ruslana's cells, and reached her own.

They were all the same, no matter the rank. A plain beehive chamber, with painted ceiling, choir vox-grille, incense censer hanging from the apex, armour stand and hard cot.

The ship had switched into its night cycle.

The light within her chamber dimmed and the note of the hymn through the choir-grille deepened, until it was a low bass rumble, singing praises to the God-Emperor.

She knelt to pray, but she knew, and the God-Emperor did as well, that Helewise's true prayer was not here, kneeling on the floor of her cell, but in combat. In the swing and parry of her blade. As she finished her prayers, her mind's eye relived each sweep and thrust of battle.

The satisfying thud of severing heretical heads from their bodies.

As she stood, she turned the page of her psalter and saw a strip of paper had been inserted there.

It read: *Order of the Veiled Mantle. Liepra.*

'Dovere,' she said aloud, and spoke a prayer of gratitude. 'So that was why Lanete was on Liepra...'

There were only a few hours' sleep before the Sisters woke for their night prayer. In her dream, Sister Morgandrie stood on the turret of the Great Minster and slammed a fresh round into the heavy bolter's firing chamber as heretics swarmed into the square. As she set her booted foot upon the parapet and aimed down, the square had gone. Now she was standing upon the top of a mountain, and beneath her rivers of Neverborn were clawing up towards her.

It was hard to distinguish one from another. In truth, she had no idea how she could kill them. They were like a thousand-headed hydra, and when she looked to her heavy bolter it had gone.

A terror gripped her. She would die like this, alone and unable to defend herself.

Then she found herself sitting up in her bed, sucking in breaths. There was a knock at the door. A gentle sound. Morgandrie rose quickly.

'Hello?' she called, trying to sound normal.

'It is I, Naoka,' a voice called back. 'I heard a noise and did not know if you were well.'

Morgandrie was at the door in an instant. Naoka had the cell next to hers, and was one of the oldest Dominions within her squad. She had suffered a geas long before Morgandrie's time and had shaved her head ever since.

It was a few days since the last shaving, and the pale stubble furred her scalp, but it did not hide the scripts that circled her skin, swirling up to the crown of her skull.

The text was the Lesson of Saint Thor. But now Naoka looked at the other Sister with concern.

'I heard shouting,' she said.

Morgandrie knew she could not hide. 'I was dreaming,' she said.

Naoka nodded. She knew what it was to face the horrors of the galaxy, and to bear their scars. 'I will remember you in my prayers…' she said.

Morgandrie put out a hand and touched the other woman's arm. 'Bless you.'

V

A sombre air permeated Battle Group Phaedra as the *Pax Imperialis* and *Daughter of the Emperor* made preparations for the transfer.

Gnaerac prescribed twenty-one days of prayer and fasting. Masses took up most of the day cycle as the ships were prepared for the upcoming transition. There were nearly half a million souls involved in that expedition. Almost all of them considered their mission to be a death sentence, and they prepared accordingly.

Platoons of scriveners arrived to assess the belongings of those with anything to bestow. Landers carried cargos of wills, written, sealed, signed and safely consigned to the care of the Munitorum. Over the sound of chanting and prayer came the rumble of industrial thunder as each craft was made fit for the crossing. Welding arcs flared, rivets were stamped closed, and supply craft queued for a berth as the loading bays and orlop decks were stacked with backup systems and generators. Lesser ranks penned last messages to loved ones left behind on distant planets, and finally the last dispatches and memorandums were parcelled up and loaded in the departing ships.

Among those who had been selected for the vanguard, the long hours were filled with forced prayers. There were vast rallies held in the hangars of the transports, with Imperial preachers lining up to read from the scriptures, sermonise, and offer consolation as well, for those who were coming to terms with their imminent mortality.

Even those who were not involved in the first wave were herded into great prayer meetings. The advance fleet spent three weeks in preparations and there was no one who did not feel the pressure. Across the fleet, Navy maintenance teams conducted round after round of essential checks. Blast doors were tested while the Navy ratings ran through containment drills for days upon end. There was no sacrifice too extreme – they all knew that if any part of the Geller field failed and there was warp contamination anywhere within the craft, then that section would be sealed off and those within would be left to their grisly fate.

Crews repeated the drills until it was second nature and they were inured to the consequences of their actions. If the worst happened, then whole regiments could be culled in order to allow the ships to survive. This was discussed at the highest level of command. And it was a sacrifice that they were willing to make. As Gnaerac stated, 'There are hundreds of thousands of worlds across the dark veil. Trillions of souls waiting for liberation. And we are their best hope.'

He issued orders across the fleet for the utmost preparations. Tech-priests spent hours in binharic communion with the ancient machine-spirits, Geller-field generators were blessed and tested.

Any mishap or bad omen was reported back to the high command. Savants worked through the data-streams – running probabilities of success through their best algorithms. But the truth was that they were excluded from the chief source of information, which was jealously guarded by the Navis Nobilite.

The Navigator house of Benetek had a reputation for handling difficult warp transits. Their potentates recommended a narrow strait between areas of great warp tumult. They were too illustrious to lead the crossing, but recommended a daughter house of Navigators who would manage the crossing itself.

They were treated with great honour as the fleet prepared.

It was three days before the scheduled crossing. Chief Navigator Hemponia Benetek descended from her high chambers to meet with Gnaerac. Before her came a procession of acolytes and a banner-bearer carrying the emblem of her house – a winged shield emblazoned with the lion's maw, embroidered with golden thread on black velvet.

Stitched into the banner were purity seals and tokens of safe crossing and peaceful and timely arrival. Ahead of the banner, censer bearers carried heavy brass thuribles, each fashioned in the shape of a skull marked with three eyes.

All of the House Benetek servants wore tall conical hats of black, embroidered with the third eye. Their robes were of the same material, hanging down to the ground, so that the only parts of their bodies that were visible were their hands. They chanted a hymn as they approached.

Gnaerac's skin prickled. He had always felt there was a strange intensity to Navigators. They had seen things that would drive others mad, and despite their training and warding they always seemed as though there was a tension beneath the glassy surface of their eyes.

They ran through the ceremonies, and then a stool was produced for Benetek. At last they sat down, and the servants stepped back and left her alone with Gnaerac and his attendants.

'You asked me here,' she said, 'to see how our work is progressing. We have consulted ancient texts and logs and warp charts. We have studied the warp, looking for eddies or currents that might aid our passage. But I have to tell you, we have found no evidence that the old routes remain.'

'What does that mean?'

'In short,' the Chief Navigator said, 'we see no way across.'

'Nothing?'

She shook her head. 'No.'

Gnaerac stood and paced up and down. 'We have to make the crossing. Other fleets have crossed over. There has to be a way.'

'There may be a way,' Benetek said. 'But if there is, it is not yet clear to us.'

'So, what do you recommend?'

'I cannot recommend any course of action.'

'Chief Navigator, are you telling me that there is no way across?'

'No. But I am telling you that there is little hope of success.'

'So there is no point in this crossing?'

She sighed. 'It means, simply, that we could be throwing ourselves to our deaths. Akin, in simple terms, to jumping off the roof of a hab-spire. Except, of course, the end would not be so straightforward.'

Gnaerac paused. 'I have no choice but to risk the crossing. The question is, are there members of your household that are prepared to cross over?'

The Chief Navigator's face was set. She gave nothing away. 'I will. But you do not know how much you ask.'

Gnaerac paused. 'No,' he said. 'You are right. But I ask it nonetheless.'

'It is a weighty matter. You might think that this is no more than asking a man to march into battle. There are many dangers. When I was twenty years old, I was assistant to my uncle and we were navigating a troop transport. It was a straightforward mission from a planet named Thracian Primus to Lethe Eleven. It wasn't until we started the process of re-entry that things went catastrophically wrong.

'We had been stalked through the warp by an entity of great power. It waited until the last moment, when my uncle was weary. For just a fraction of a second his concentration wavered...

'We waited six months for a salvage craft to find us. Black Templars brought us out. Their Chaplain led us through a charnel house of deformed and twisted bodies. I only had a glimpse as we were evacuated. The rescue crew did not dare to attempt to cleanse the craft. It had been possessed as well, and the superstructure was infected with a kind of living flesh.

'But worst of all were the crew who had not died. They had been absorbed into the walls and bulkheads. They were bound by veins as thick as rope, which trembled with the pulse of a vast heart, hidden somewhere within the ship. And it kept them all alive, yet they were not alive. Some of them were just faces, or mewling forms wrapped in tentacles and translucent veins.

'"Do not look!" the Space Marines told us. But I could not help myself. There were bits of body beneath our feet. They were clutching at us. And all about us I could *hear* the crew. They were still alive. Sobbing. Mewling. Slobbering. They were still *alive!* Oh, Throne! They all suffered terribly. One of them called my name. I knew the voice. It was the captain. "Hemponia Benetek! Save us!" I could not help myself. "Forwards!" the Astartes ordered. But I stopped and looked...'

There was a long pause. Hemponia shuddered with the memory. Her face had turned pale. She paused as she calmed herself. She smoothed her palms on her skirts to straighten out the cloth. Then she took a deep breath. When she spoke, it was in a whisper. 'I saw him.'

Trained as she was to face the horrors of the warp, Gnaerac could see the memory clearly still haunted her.

'I saw him,' she repeated. 'The Astartes thrust me forwards. "Hemponia!" the thing called again, and then there was the report of a bolter. His fist caught my shoulder and he steered me through the corridors as a mother would guide a child through a hive-market crowd. Then the... creatures all started to call my name. All of them. Their faces were everywhere. The veins pulsed – the pulse quickening as the heartbeat began to accelerate.

'The Astartes started to fight their way out. Gunfire was all around us. I could smell the rancid stink of blood. I kept my head down. I was terrified. I, who had looked into the warp. But I have always been protected by the Geller field. Here, the warp was alive and all about me, reaching out to me. It was a nightmare made real.'

She took in a deep breath and settled herself. 'As far as I know, the crew would still be suffering if it were not for the fact that our rescuers destroyed the craft with a series of broadsides, until at last its generators were overwhelmed and ignited like a starburst. But the debris was not lumps of steel, or superstructure. It blasted out gobbets of blood and flesh. I have never forgotten. Even though many years have passed since then. Many lives of mortal men.'

'Have you spoken to the canoness about this?'

'Of course. She is deaf to all but words of faith and piety.'

Gnaerac stood and paced up and down, his head bent in thought. At last, he said, 'Thank you, Lord Navigator. The Emperor protects.'

'I wonder, at times,' she said.

Palatine Albreda's deep reverie was broken by a knock upon the door. The face that greeted her was framed by a harsh bob, two goggled eyes staring out blankly. 'There is something that I wanted to bring to your attention,' Dovere said.

She handed a leaf of parchment to the canoness.

Albreda was left unenlightened. 'Dovere, I am sure that you have a story that you want to tell me...'

Dovere took three steps and then stopped suddenly, her goggle eyes staring straight at the older woman. 'Yes. I have compared the fragments to extant communications from before the Cataclysm. I believe that this communication comes from the world of Aoid's Sepulchre.'

Albreda sat forwards. 'Aoid's Sepulchre?'

'Precisely!' Dovere said. She could barely hold her excitement back. 'The world where Saint Katherine's first War of Faith began.'

Albreda paused to think about this.

'There is more,' Dovere said. 'It is possible that the message was sent after the Great Rift divided us from them.'

'Are you sure?'

'No,' Dovere said. 'But if you put these three transcripts together, they appear to be sent by the same astropath, *after* the sundering happened.'

'So there is life across the Great Rift.'

'There was...'

'I pray so,' Albreda said. 'Who knows, our Sister may even remain, yet unbroken. Emperor be praised!'

VI

On the night before transition there was a formal handover of power. The hierarchy of Battle Group Phaedra stood together to witness Lord General Gnaerac transfer the seal of authority to his designated deputy, Commissar-General Oskarr Qartermayne.

Qartermayne was now dressed in the red-corded black drill of his regiment, his chest an expanse of medals. Gnaerac presented him with the symbols of office, the cyphers and codes, and the authority to lead Battle Group Phaedra in his absence, as the servitor choir sang a hymn of benediction.

There were prayers, and another blessing, and then the two men met again, in private, for a final briefing. They had been through it all before, but it was hard for Gnaerac to let go.

The old man held his emotion back, as he gave Qartermayne a final handshake.

'Good luck,' Qartermayne said. 'We will see you in the Imperium Nihilus.'

'I hope so,' Gnaerac said. 'Who knows, you may make a better commander than me.'

'Impossible,' Qartermayne said, and Gnaerac smiled.

The mood was dark on the bridge of the *Pax Imperialis*.

As Admiral Karlien gave the order for the generators to be brought up to full power, Gnaerac stood at the void window and gazed into the darkness.

He had done his best, he told himself, and checked the chronometer.

One by one the last supply craft disengaged. Void gates were closed, sealed, triple-blessed and stamped with purity seals. It was impossible to look at the departing ships and not feel a deep sense of loss and loneliness. All the crews could do was entrust their prayers to the God-Emperor and the Imperial saints – there was a busy trade in religious tokens imprinted with the image of Saint Asceline of the Order of the Opening Eye, patron saint of Safe-Passage-through-the-Warp.

Long before ship-dawn, wheel-gears started to turn, winding in the grav-anchors and the mile upon mile of anchor chain.

Adjutant Bennigsen spent a last, sleepless night listening to the repetitive sound of the thudding links. She lay awake waiting for the lights to announce ship-dawn.

She tossed and turned in the narrow cot.

Prayers were chanted as the plasma generators were fired up. One, two... five engine cones began to glow blue and then white.

Grav-anchors were disengaged, and the *Pax Imperialis* started forwards with a creak of its superstructure. It slipped slowly out of its orbit, and then accelerated towards the designated

Mandeville point, pulling away from the rest of Battle Group Phaedra, with the *Daughter of the Emperor* sailing alongside.

As they approached the Mandeville point, the devotion of the Sisters of Our Martyred Lady grew more and more overt. Reliquaries were brought out from the sacred vaults to magnify their prayer. There were ancient blades and blessed guns, and the stasis-coffins of ancient canonesses, their mortal wounds on display.

But chief of all the relics here was a lock of hair, cut from the body of Saint Katherine. The hair was held in an open-sided box, carved from the marble of the Imperial Palace on Holy Terra. Its windows were framed with slag-glass taken from craters on the planet of Mnestteus, where the saint had given her life to the Holy Cult.

Its appearance was greeted with a reverent gasp from the assembled Sisters. And from the high cells where the Sisters Repentia were locked away came inhuman howls of zealotry.

Albreda led them all in the strict devotion. She was in the middle of a prayer when one of her attendants came to her and whispered in her ear.

'I will come,' Albreda said.

A man was standing outside. He was tall, and gaunt, almost to the point of being skeletal. His long gown was black and he exuded a strange aura, as pungent as heresy, but tempered. It was his face that gave him away. He had a third eye, set in the middle of his high forehead, its baleful light hidden behind an embroidered patch.

'Lord Navigator Siles,' she said.

'The warp is in a state of some...' He paused as he considered the right word to describe the warp to one who did not have the third eye. At last, he settled upon, 'convulsion. We are all… uncertain.'

'What can I do?'

'Hemponia asks if there is someone of great purity who could pray with her as we make the transition.'

Albreda paused. She thought of who she could send, but the truth was, the best person was herself. Her faith would sustain the Navigator through the trials ahead, but more than that she would bring relics too.

The grav-generators were running strong. It made the Sisters' footfalls echo as they marched through the deserted corridors. They were lit only by the guttering flames of the bracket lumens. The light flickered off the jewelled reliquary which held Saint Katherine's hair within its crystal case. The bier was carried on the shoulders of four Sisters.

Albreda led them as they approached the mag-lift. It took nearly a minute to carry the bier up to the peak of a lonely pinnacle, high on one of the great spurs of the Astral Cathedrum. The guards at the top were dressed in heavy carapace emblazoned with the emblems of House Benetek, and wore mirror-visored helms with psychic dampers on either temple. They stepped aside as the Sisters passed through.

Helewise was one of the four bier carriers. She had never been in a Navigatorium before. The chamber was a dome of clear glass, with a heavy metal throne set in the centre, laced with circuitry. It was strangely empty.

'Put it down here,' Albreda said.

The Sisters did so, and then they made their way to the door. Helewise paused. 'I would stay with you.'

The Palatine shook her head. 'In battle, I would be honoured to have you at my side. But not in this struggle.'

Helewise understood the danger and started to argue, but Albreda's smile cut her short.

'Have faith, my Sister.'

As the two craft approached the Mandeville point, Navigator Hemponia handed Albreda a cloth. Albreda knelt beside the throne, and knotted the cloth about her head.

Throughout the ships, void ports were closed and sealed, strict edicts of isolation issued. Armed ratings took their places in the corridors and hangar decks. It was death for any to break isolation without permission.

'Whatever happens. Whatever you hear. Do not open your eyes,' Hemponia reminded her as the armoured dome was withdrawn and she looked out into realspace.

The rest of the fleet held their breath as they observed the ships' departure.

All that those who were watching saw was a brief blue flash of Geller fields, and then the craft blinked out of existence. And as far as many were concerned, those who had taken part in the transition were as good as dead.

Hemponia moaned through gritted teeth as Albreda knelt in prayer at the Navigator's side. The canoness held the Navigator's left hand within her own.

Hemponia had never faced such hatred. The warp was bloated and swollen with emotion and reacted to their presence as if it had been stung. Clouds of emotion boiled up about them. They formed fanged maws, a host of faces, clawed hands, tentacled monsters that snapped and grasped and threatened to swallow them whole.

It was madness and she could see no way through. And as insanity reached out for her, Navigator Hemponia sat upon her throne, her mouth fixed in a rictus scream.

vii

Commissar-General Qartermayne chose the Victory-class battleship *Vigorous* as his flagship – a brutal old warhorse, with miles of heavy macro cannons lining its superstructure, and an underslung nova cannon running halfway along its length. He began to draw up plans for a translation.

It was only a few hours after Gnaerac's craft had entered the warp that an adjutant rushed inside.

'Yes?' Qartermayne said as he looked up from the hololithic display which hung in the air before him.

'Sir!' the adjutant said, saluting smartly. 'The admiral begs your attendance. The *Pax Imperialis* has returned.'

'Already?'

'Yes, sir.'

Qartermayne could tell that there was more to this story. 'It is wounded?'

The adjutant did not want to be the one to bring bad news, but he was blunt. 'Sir. I am afraid that it appears dead.'

Qartermayne hurried to the bridge. Admiral Jayn was buttoning up his jacket as his craft started to move from anchor. The gunnery commanders were rushing to their positions.

'Sir!' Jayn said, as Qartermayne appeared. 'The *Pax Imperialis*–'

'I can see,' Qartermayne said. 'Any signal?'

'None.'

'And no sign of life?'

'Nothing as yet, sir. The picket ships are sending a landing squad.'

The *Vigorous* bristled with weaponry, but its most fearsome armament was the nova cannon, which propelled a vast warhead at astronomical speed. It was already starting to charge.

The picket ships' pict-feeds were fed straight to the cogitators of the *Vigorous*.

'It does not look good,' Jayn said.

The *Pax Imperialis* was dark, and it was, without a doubt, dead. There were rents within the metal superstructure. But as they watched, they saw movement within one of the tears in the battleship's hull.

The pict-feed focused closer and showed what was moving within the ship. It was not human. It was like no xenos they had ever seen. It inhabited the old battleship as a hermit crab occupies another shell. And as they watched in horror, a fleshy appendage emerged and seemed to reach towards them.

'Holy Throne,' Qartermayne hissed, blanching as he shut the pict-feed down. 'Destroy it at once!'

The bridge of the *Vigorous* was set well back along the dorsal spine. The wide windows looked along the length of the grand cruiser towards the gunnery tower, its augur discs slowly spinning, alert for any danger. The chief gunner did not ask for confirmation, but set the nova cannon to fire.

A hum ran through the ship. Qartermayne held his breath as he waited for the optimal moment. Then he gave the order.

The whole craft shuddered with release.

Propelled at hypersonic speed, the warhead left a tracer-streak across the void.

It hit the *Pax Imperialis* amidships, and ripped the battleship in half. There was a blinding salvo of lance strikes as the ancient vessel broke up into burning scraps of wreckage. And still they fired in fury.

Qartermayne witnessed it all. It was only when the last fires dulled that he finally turned away and gave his final instruction. 'Orders for the entire fleet. A day of prayers for Lord General Gnaerac, the *Pax Imperialis* and all who made the attempted crossing. And give the order that we will make the crossing in a week's time.'

Qartermayne was silent as he made his way down to the planning room. He could feel the lesson sinking in to all those around him. They were terrified of him and he liked that, even as he started to consider the future.

He slid his thumb onto the gene-lock. The door slid sideways, and his servo-skull lifted off its stand as he swept inside.

The holomaps and charts were all in place, the cogitator fans were still whirring, and the scribe servitors stood poised, the quills waiting for his return.

Qartermayne closed the door behind him. His command team were standing waiting for him.

The commissar put both hands to the chart table: one human, one augmetic. He paused. There was no doubt about it. The Emperor had shown His will. Lord General Gnaerac had lacked faith. He had attempted to cross with a mere escort of Battle Sisters.

Qartermayne was a man of sterner mettle. He was not going to make the same mistake. He would take the whole battle group, and smash a way across.

Part Four

Now

Immaterium

'Sisters, every voyage into the nothing is a confrontation with horror, with the implacable things of the warp, and with our innermost fear, but remember this. Faith is your shield. Your blade. It is the strength in your right hand.'

– Epistles of Saint Katherine

í

According to the ship's own chronometer, it took the *Daughter of the Emperor* forty-three days to cross the straits. But time in the warp did not move normally. Sometimes it doubled back upon itself. Sometimes it simply broke – like a rope stretched too far. For those aboard the craft, only the ship's internal day-night schedule gave time any meaning. The team of Navigators worked one after another, constantly vigilant, labouring to steer them through to the other side of the tumult as the warp smashed into the craft, throwing it continually off course.

Behind them the Astronomican faded from a dull orange, to red, and then it was lost – like sunset – amidst the roiling tides of the warp, and they were plunged into the darkness of end-less night.

Without its light to steer them, the *Daughter of the Emperor* was buffeted like driftwood, tossed about upon the seas of the warp. It was a struggle to keep the craft within the narrows of the straits. Time and again they scraped past the clutches of monstrous warp entities. A number of times they thought they could see the far side of the Cicatrix Maledictum only to find themselves plunged into another tempest.

At last the eddies diminished. Hemponia struggled to re-enter reality, but the warp refused to let them go. A fanged black hole sucked them in, and sealed about them.

Alarms sounded as they spiralled down the gnashing guts of the warp spawn. Klaxons wailed. There was a succession of Geller field breaches. Whole sections of the craft were sealed off as the crew responded to every rupture.

Navigator Hemponia moaned as she struggled to tear a route back to reality. The sound was inhuman, emanating from the depths of her body. She could see the Imperium Nihilus, just there... but she could not reach it.

The *Daughter of the Emperor* flickered on the edge of reality, a ghostly apparition poised between two realities.

At last, Hemponia screamed in pain and triumph as the craft tore through and plunged with a jolt out of the warp.

The *Daughter of the Emperor*'s superstructure groaned. It was quite alone as it settled back into realspace, wounded and broken.

It took long moments for those aboard the *Daughter of the Emperor* to realise that at last the nightmare was over. A sense of desolation seized them all. The decks were awash with vomit and throughout the craft came the sound of weeping and madness, and the sporadic crack of gunfire.

The cathedrum was crippled and broken, its air-scrubbers silent, the motive force barely ticking over. The air grew stale as the recyclers were shut down, and the walls began to film with bone-white hoar frost as teams of tech-priests struggled to restore the engines.

Emergency lighting strobed across every deck as klaxons and alarms wailed. The *Daughter of the Emperor* had suffered catastrophic injuries: the equatorial castellations had been ripped away, there were structural faults that ran throughout the great craft and entire sections had lost power. Without the oxygen pumps, it was a race to get the emergency generators firing.

In the lower decks, a third of the crew had been lost to warp sickness, insanity or catastrophic hull breach. Helewise led her team in culling those who had lost their mental faculties. Her bolter kicked out as she hunted them down.

It was brutal but necessary work, a simple declaration of her creed.

When she had finished, the dead were gathered up, but there were too many to shroud them all. The corpses were loaded onto covered gantries and expelled by the hundred into the void, the bodies freezing within moments as they spiralled away.

As Albreda descended from the Navigatorium, she found an honour guard waiting for her.

'Palatine…' Lanete said in welcome, but her words caught in her throat as she saw Albreda's face. She looked as though she had aged a century. Her skin hung in wrinkled bags from her skull and she moved stiffly, like a woman twice her age.

The Sisters gathered in stunned silence as Lanete helped Albreda along the corridor. The Palatine had not gone far before she stopped and leant against the wall.

Lanete caught the eyes of her Sisters, all of them mortified by the transformation. At last, Lanete asked the question. 'Palatine. What trials did you face?'

Albreda wet her lips, eyes closed, sucking in breaths, and whispered, 'I would not burden you with that knowledge.'

* * *

On the tenth hour of the third day after the crossing, the *Daughter of the Emperor* was finally declared secure. The ship's generators were blessed, refreshed with holy unguents, and then reignited.

Quadrant by quadrant, life and motive energy returned. Helewise led her squad into the abandoned sectors, guns ready.

As the lumens flickered back to light, they illuminated scratched graffiti, puddles of blood, piles of the shrouded dead. The air-scrubbers rattled back to life, and from the vents the stale air was sucked away, and with it the taste of smoke and fyceline.

It took days for the stink of warp contamination to be cleansed as the augurs attempted to locate the *Pax Imperialis*. But there was no trace.

The chief communications officer approached Palatine Albreda. 'We cannot locate the flagship,' he said. 'The Navigators are not clear where we are. All we know is that we have successfully crossed the veil.'

The Sisters gathered in the Great Prayer Hall.

It was a sombre place. But what was most shocking was that they were alone. Profoundly alone. All of them felt it, but it hit the Sisters hardest of all. They were beyond the grace of the God-Emperor.

Each of the Sisters felt the loss in their own way. Some knelt in prayer, even though they were beyond the Emperor's hearing. Others wept.

The younger ones looked to Palatine Albreda, and she tried to show courage. But she barely had the strength to lead them in prayer.

The shutters to the Repentia cells were locked, but from high up, they could all hear the screams and moans of pain.

Helewise felt it as strongly as the others. She felt as though she had lost a limb. Her voice was a croak as she ran through her prayers. One by one the Sisters took each other's hands. They had passed beyond the eye of the God-Emperor. It was as if they had tumbled into hell.

Helewise remained kneeling as the other Sisters filed out. The scent of dead men's blood clung to her as she finished her prayers and pushed herself up.

She made her way down the stairs to the bottom of the hall. The muffled sounds of the Sisters Repentia echoed through the vaulted chamber.

'They feel it,' a voice said.

It was Sister Dialogus Dovere, her data-goggles blank as she stared at Helewise.

They all felt it. 'We have travelled beyond His gaze,' agreed Helewise.

Dovere nodded. Her gaze was empty, yet she tried to sound confident. 'But we are still alive...'

'Yes. And we can still fight,' Helewise said, smiling. 'Faith without deeds is worthless.'

Helewise went back to her chambers after that. Her armour was splattered with gore, her sword stained. There was no time for the proper purification rituals, so she took a cloth to wipe her power armour down with holy unguents. The black surface gleamed in the light of her lumen. When she was done, she drew Reckoning and wiped it clean until the ancient broadsword gleamed. She slipped a fresh powercell into the hilt, pressed the power stud, and watched the crackle of energy feel its way along its shaft.

Reckoning felt no fear, it yearned to cleanse heresy.

As she turned it in her hand, there was a scratch at the door.

Helewise hung Reckoning upon its stand, and turned as Morgandrie entered. She had removed her armour and now wore a simple cotton robe, belted at the waist. 'May I come in?'

Helewise nodded and Morgandrie shut the door behind her. Her eyes looked hollow and she had taken a las-bolt to the cheek in the fight to cleanse the craft. The wound had cauterised, but her raw lips were purple and inflamed and it gave her face a strained look. 'Forgive me, Sister Superior, I have not slept.'

'None of us have.' Helewise paused.

'Now I understand why they named it the Imperium Nihilus,' Morgandrie said. 'When I pray, I feel nothing. No consolation, no hope. It is as if my words fall into a bottomless well.' She fell silent. It hurt to even explain how she felt. She paused. The enormity of what they had done had hollowed her out. 'We're never going back again, are we? We shall die this side of the Rift.'

Helewise nodded.

'I wish I'd known,' Morgandrie said.

'What would you have done differently?'

'I would have branded His presence into my soul.'

She had been quiet for a few minutes before she whispered this.

Helewise nodded. You never knew when it was to be the last time. As a warrior she felt that more than others. They always slipped by without notice: the friend killed in battle, the home world that you would never see again, the feeling of the God-Emperor's grace.

'He may not hear us, but…' Morgandrie paused. 'Would you pray with me?'

Helewise nodded.

The two Sisters knelt together.

When they had finished praying, Morgandrie stood and made her way to the door.

'Helewise… there is something that I have not told you.'

Morgandrie had a hard, battle-scarred face, but her brown eyes brimmed briefly with tears. 'When I was a novitiate, there was a

Sister named Grace. She had the art of ceromancy. At prayers she would examine the wax that had dripped from the great candles. Sometimes they would fall to one side and mount up in great crags of melted wax. Other times the drops would fall equally. And, occasionally, the candle would burn down without any drips. That was when the most terrible things would happen.'

Helewise was confused. 'And what does this have to do with you?'

Morgandrie paused. 'I have always felt a close connection to Saint Katherine.'

Helewise nodded. They all felt close to Saint Katherine, but Morgandrie had taken that to extremes. In her quest for purity she had covered her body with tattoos of the saint and her victories. The inked images ran up her arms, across her back and legs. On her chest, above Morgandrie's heart, lay the saint's figure in the sacred moment of her death.

'I have started to see what some might call coincidences,' Morgandrie said, pulling aside the shoulder of her gown. The chaplet ecclesiasticus was strung three times about her neck, each of the adamantium beads representing an act of great penance. But she pulled the heavy weights aside and exposed the naked flesh beneath. 'Here,' she said. 'Look. This was the first wound I took.'

The dark skin was puckered with thick scar tissue in the round shape of a las-shot.

'I did not think anything of it,' Morgandrie said. 'But then I was struck here.' She pulled her robes up and revealed another wound, this one covering half her leg.

Helewise did not understand, but Morgandrie seemed to notice her confusion.

'That first shot hit me in the script of Saint Katherine's Prayer for the Heretic. Look, the shot has obscured the words *smite the unholy*. And the shrapnel – there are two prayers here. The Blessing of the Bolter and the Love of the Matriarch. These wounds came before our battle on Kanzaz Ridge, when Palatine Hadley gave her life to save us. I started to think that there were messages in the wounds.' She laughed at herself. 'That I might be granted visions of the future.'

'And have there been any wounds recently?'

'Yes,' Morgandrie said. 'On Ayaan. I did not notice it at first. It was not until the battle was over. I was disarming, and I found my leg was smeared with blood. I think it was a bolt-shell. A glancing shot. Or perhaps the bolt had exploded, and a fragment cut through the joint between my greave and knee-plate.'

'And is there a prayer there?'

Morgandrie nodded. Her dark skin gave nothing away, but she looked chastened. 'It is the Prayer for Safe Transit.'

'And you think that this is more than a coincidence?'

Morgandrie paused. Like all the products of the scholams, she had been raised to love and cherish, and to honour the God-Emperor and Saint Katherine above all others. To consider herself a servant. Part vessel, part fount. Both to fill herself with holy essence, and to find within herself the magnificence of sublime faith. To always be secondary to the saints that ruled her life, certainly not to have the pride of putting herself in the centre of the story. To consider herself the primary participant.

'Something else happened in the transit,' Morgandrie said. She unbelted her girdle and pulled her robes open.

There was a wound just below her collarbone, a neat round scar. 'On the morning we transitioned, this mark appeared upon my chest.'

Helewise stood. 'But you were not wounded?'

Morgandrie shook her head. 'No.'

'Stigmata?' Helewise whispered.

Morgandrie nodded. She appeared uncertain. She appeared fearful. She appeared hopeful as well. All that mixed in her face, in her expression and in her brown eyes.

'And have any more of these marks appeared?'

Morgandrie nodded again. Tears started to well in her eyes. She pulled her left sleeve up, revealing a scar that ran around her forearm, cutting through the tattooed script. If it had been a blow, it would have cut through her limb.

Helewise shook with the understanding. 'These marks...' she said. 'These are the wounds that Saint Katherine suffered...'

Morgandrie nodded. When Saint Katherine had fought the Witch-cult of Mnestteus she had been shot in the arm, and then her hand had been cut away. Finally, she had been stabbed through the heart...

Helewise made the sign of the fleur-de-lys. 'Are you frightened?'

Morgandrie shook her head. Her voice was a bare whisper. 'No,' she said. 'I am blessed.'

Commissar Aebram's face was impassive as he made his way down to the decks where the Dogs were quartered. His Mercies came with him, their bolt pistols loaded, as did a detachment of ratings, who had prepared as if ready to repel a boarding. They wore home-made armour comprised of metal plates stitched onto overcoats, and clenched improvised weapons in their gloved fists.

Mercy Cody looked to the Marshal for permission to open the bulkheads, and the commissar unfolded his arms and nodded slowly.

Aebram waited for the blast doors to open. He expected little of his Dogs, and he knew what they would find when the bulkheads finally opened. Mercy Cody pushed the unlock stud, and slowly the doors slid upwards.

The first thing they saw was a puddle of blood. And then the stink rolled out. It was the stink of death.

A figure appeared, hand raised against the sudden light.

'Hold your fire,' the Marshal ordered.

It was Colonel Salem. He straightened up and stopped ten feet before the Marshal.

The Marshal said simply, 'How many?'

'Thirteen.'

'What happened?'

'Wythers.'

The dead were dragged out. The Marshal stood over the grav-trolley, looking down on the corpses as they were loaded for feeding to the plasma generators. Mercy Cody was collecting their number tags as the Marshal took in the faces.

He felt thwarted. They should have died in battle, the name of the Emperor upon their bloody lips. 'I don't see Wythers,' he said at last.

Colonel Salem paused. 'No, sir. I subdued him.'

'Why didn't you kill him?' the Marshal asked.

'I owed him,' Colonel Salem said. Aebram remembered. Wythers had saved many of them, during his time. 'We all owed him.'

Aebram said nothing. But after a long pause, he said, 'Is he calm?'

Salem nodded. 'For the moment.'

Wythers was too valuable to execute, as long as his ferocity could be harnessed. 'If that changes let me know at once.'

The Marshal stalked ahead, arms behind his back, and looked about the hangar. His boot falls were deadened by the mass of bodies crouching in the darkness.

Even the Chem Dogs felt the dread of the Imperium Nihilus. They knew the ritual. They lined up in rows, kneeling down, their heads bowed as the Marshal paced along the line, his bolt pistol loaded and primed. He smelt the air; there was no hint of taint. No trace that alerted him.

When he got to the end, he retraced his steps. At last, he came to the end of the line, where Sawbones was mumbling to himself.

'Silence!' the Marshal shouted.

Sawbones shook himself but Echo called out, 'Silence!' and someone snickered.

The Marshal pulled his bolt pistol and fired. The bolt hit Echo in the chest. He was thrown back against the hangar wall and slumped down, neck bent at an unhealthy angle, the hole in his back leaking blood.

ii

The *Daughter of the Emperor* had started the journey with forty-five thousand, three hundred and ninety souls aboard. They had lost eleven thousand, three hundred and forty-seven in the transition. The dead were all honoured. Chief were Sisters Nimue and Eirad. They had fallen holding back the entities of the warp. Their bodies were washed and wrapped in holy shrouds, and interred in niches about the Great Prayer Hall.

Once they had been remembered, the chief officers were honoured by the Sisters personally. Their names were read out that evening as the Sisters gathered for their nightly prayer. Then they were added to the *Book of Martyrs*, and their names were inscribed onto the brass panels of a vast prayer wheel that slowly turned in the centre of the cathedrum, remembering the thousands that had been lost on crusade.

The others were simply listed by the scriptorium. Silver quills were dipped into inkpots, as casualty lists were pasted onto the brass prayer wheels.

The drone of remembrance mixed in with the piped sound of servitor choirs and cherubim.

Hours turned into days, and then a week, and they hung alone in the void, with the hostile darkness of space surrounding them. The Sisters joined together in prayer each day, but their words fell into emptiness.

His absence was like a death. They were all in mourning, and at night the Sisters lay awake, eyes open to the darkness, and wept in silent despair.

They returned to the Great Prayer Hall day after day.

The air of hopelessness hung over them. They had no idea where they were, stranded far out in the void between systems.

In the hours between prayers, Albreda summoned Sister Dialogus Dovere to her chamber. A little colour had returned to the Palatine's cheeks, but her skin still hung about her face, and the back of her hands were blotched with liver spots.

The Sister Dialogus bowed. 'Palatine. Thank you for all you have done.'

The Palatine winced. She nodded. 'Thanks to the grace of the God-Emperor, we have made it across. But the question remains – where are we?'

Dovere blushed. 'I wish I knew.'

'Are there any signs? Any astropathic communications? Anything?'

Dovere paused. 'Nothing. Well. Nothing that we can construe. The astropaths did attempt to make contact, but their initial efforts were overwhelmed. They spoke of a madness of voices, all shouting heretical thoughts. Sister Superior Lanete was on guard the last time. We lost two of them and the remaining members' minds are fragile. I am wary of exposing them to the tumult.'

Albreda nodded. They were all fragile. Even the Sisters, who had bolstered themselves with years of training, prayer and faith.

'Is there any word of the *Pax Imperialis*?'

'None.'

There was a long pause. Albreda closed her eyes. Her hands found the beads that were slung about her neck. She grasped them, remembering what she had done to earn these.

'Are there any other clues as to our location?' she said at last.

Dovere's expression was blank as she shook her head. Albreda sighed. This seemed to be the final punishment. To be utterly lost in the darkness of the Imperium Nihilus. At last the Sister Dialogus stepped forward. 'If I may suggest something...'

Albreda shook herself and nodded.

Dovere took another step towards her. 'There is a system a month's journey away. If we can verify the identity of that planet, comparing it to the old charts, assuming this area of the void has not changed, then there might be clues for us.'

Albreda said nothing. She closed her eyes again, and her lips seemed to be moving in silent prayer. Dovere did not know whether she had been dismissed or not. At last Albreda opened her eyes.

'You are correct. Give word to the captain. In the meantime let us all pray.'

The Sisters filled each day with drills and prayers, snatching sleep where they could.

Sister Morgandrie's dreams were dark and sinister. She suffered the blows that Saint Katherine had, and after each dream she awoke in a cold sweat, knelt by her cot and wept.

She found comfort in the rituals. All the Sisters did, even when they did not feel His grace. They gathered in the Great Prayer Hall, and lifted their voices up in devotion and song, praising the God-Emperor.

Palatine Albreda had never felt so lost. In the end, she resorted to her tome of prayers for answers. Each night she closed her eyes, opened the book to a random page, placed her finger upon the text, and only then did she open her eyes to read what it said.

The first time, she read: *Faith in the Emperor is its own reward.*

The next stated: *From the lightning and the tempest, our Emperor deliver us!*

Each night the lines spoke to her, and while she did not see the route ahead, she did find comfort in the scripture.

But as they approached the nearby system, their hope began to fade.

The sun was dying. It burnt with a dull red light, its roiling plasma slowly devouring the planets, like a ghastly old matron devouring her own children. The remaining planets were dead. A gas giant, three habitable rocks, and a moon marked with the unmistakable pattern of an Anphelion-pattern settlement. But it was clear that the base had been destroyed. Its burnt remains were cold and lifeless, the generators dead.

They continued on until they reached the system's innermost planet. The Sisters looked upon it through the foot-thick armaglass.

Its surface was bare, bleak, burnt.

Dovere was the one who reported these findings to Palatine Albreda, who sat in her chambers, a closed book upon her lap. 'What news, Sister Dialogus Dovere?' the Palatine asked her.

Dovere shook her head. 'We have tried all the old codes, but the augurs have revealed nothing.' There was a long silence. Dovere wished she could have brought good news. 'I am working through the possible systems, but as yet there is no clear match.'

Albreda nodded. She had her eyes closed. She opened the book before her, picked a page, and placed her finger upon it.

She opened her eyes, and read the line before her.

It was a line from the Song of Josmane.

The faithful shall be sacrificed on the altar of battle.

It was a startling line. She did not know what she should take from this. But one thing seemed clear, that they should expose themselves to death and danger.

She prayed on this for over an hour, and at the end she sent out the order for lighters to be prepared to go down to the planet.

'Who should lead the expedition?' Dovere asked.

Albreda paused, wishing that the God-Emperor would speak to her. At last she said, 'Sister Superior Helewise.'

Helewise received the orders with calm. She was to command three squads.

Ruslana was in charge of one. Naoka another. Helewise would lead the third herself.

She looked around at her Sisters as each of them prepared for battle, and spied Morgandrie anointing her armour with holy oils. Helewise's gaze fell to the Sister's arm.

I will keep her with me, she thought to herself, and then continued her own rituals. *If she dies I will witness her martyrdom.*

Once each of the battle squads were armed, Helewise brought them to one of the chapels and led them all in prayer.

Finally, they made their way into the gunship.

It was a sleek black craft, with a dorsal turret and wings slung with racks of missiles. Each squad was assigned a Rhino, and an Immolator was to provide fire support to the expedition. The tanks had already been driven into the craft, and tech-priests were tending to the holy vehicles, making last checks and blessings as they woke the machine-spirits.

The Sisters followed them up and took their places at the side of the craft. Helewise had Reckoning strapped over her back and her inferno pistol mag-locked to her right thigh. Each of them carried their weapons with fierce pride. They stood in their full battleplate, their helmets tucked under their arms as they went through the final equipment checks.

An alarm sounded as the ramp began to rise and the void-craft prepared to leave. A warning lumen started to flash and the Sisters' voices rose in a brief prayer. It was a paean of courage in the face of death, conviction in the depths of battle. But Helewise had composed new words at the end of the prayer.

'…and for those of us beyond the veil, remember us. We still serve, beyond hope, and we pray that our sacrifices will not be forgotten.'

Dovere had picked one of the equatorial regions for landing.

The thirty Sisters stood with their backs to the cabin hull, and Helewise led them in hymns of courage. She watched Morgandrie as they roused their warlike spirit.

When at last the approach klaxon rang, they brought their prayers to an end.

The last minutes were spent in silence as they each prepared themselves.

Morgandrie was quiet and detached. Helewise watched her as they mounted their transports.

As the gunship settled down upon the planet, Helewise closed her helmet with a slight twist. There was a clunk as the locking system engaged, and then a low hiss as her helmet filled with breathable air and the retinal display linked with her optical implants. Her gunsight appeared, and a scrolling series of power-armour readings, as well as those of her squad.

As they prepared to disembark, Helewise recited the Fede Imperialis over the vox. She tried to sound hopeful, but Ruslana voxed her over their personal link.

'This is going to be a waste of time,' she muttered.

'Have faith,' Helewise told her, though in truth even she found it hard at times.

'It is in short supply,' Ruslana said.

The atmosphere evacuated as the gunship's doors began to part. The Rhinos powered down the ramp and out across the landscape. Each had a series of objectives to assess. Markings that Dovere had identified as points of possible interest.

Helewise clambered through the Rhino until she was at one of the forward hatches. It opened with a hiss of venting atmosphere.

Ruslana's Rhino ploughed across the flat, dusty, featureless landscape. 'Nothing to see,' she voxed after half an hour. In fact, it seemed to her, the nothingness was striking.

Naoka's Rhino had a curling route towards a line of hills or mountains. She experienced the same blank landscape of dust, which rose behind them in climbing columns.

There was nothing to report. Nothing to see but dead, cold sand. After a few hours, Helewise climbed back into her tank. She removed her helmet. It was covered in fine dust that slewed off the smooth surfaces.

There were hymns playing through the vox-grille.

It was the Choir of Holy Terra singing Saint Katherine's Lamentations. The mood was sombre. Helewise had always hoped to make the pilgrimage to Holy Terra, but that chance was lost to her now. She felt the distance yawn open, and still, she told herself, she had faith.

It was harder now, she thought, like a flimsy sheet of foil crushed into a tight ball.

She caught Morgandrie's eye, and the other Sister looked away.

'Anything?' Aliciel said.

Helewise shook her head.

'How long until we get to the hills?'

Helewise checked her helm display's chronometer. 'An hour.'

Aliciel nodded.

They sat in silence. After a while, Aiguell voxed that they were approaching their destination.

They could feel it. The landscape was becoming rockier, and the Sisters were knocked back and forth, their armour tapping against the cold metal of the cabin interior.

'We're here,' Aiguell said. *'But I don't see anything.'*

The Rhino trundled forwards and then came to a halt.

The Sisters were finishing their prayer, their lips moving in unison.

'...that thou shouldst spare none,

That thou shouldst pardon none,

We beseech thee, destroy them.'

One by one they engaged their helmets, and then Aliciel slammed the ramp door power stud with her open palm.

It did not take them long to prove Ruslana wrong.

It was not a line of hills. There had been a city here once. Barely two stones still stood upon each other, and from the stamped remains were the twisted lengths of rusted rebar, upon which hung the mouldering corpses of impaled dead. A helmet here, a skull there, at the bottom a pile of blighted bones, a belt, the charred remnants of a uniform or scraps of flak armour.

'Annihilated,' Morgandrie said.

Helewise nodded. She knelt down and picked up a handful of slag. The soil of the planet was a mix of metal, beads of silicon and burnt rock.

'Nothing,' she said. No clue as to what it was, or where it had once been, or who had lived here. Or, indeed when. Not a single stone still stood. It had been blasted, scorched and ground into rubble.

* * *

The Sisters climbed back into the Rhino.

The mood had changed. They had seen destroyed cities before, but nothing like this. This had been obliterated.

It was five hours to the second point they were set to investigate. This was revealed to be the remains of another city; the stumps of hab-blocks and chapel spires rose up from a pale sea.

Helewise approached. At a closer look, the surrounding dust was given its pallor by the white fragments of human bones. She waded waist-deep and looked about.

'How many died here?' she whispered, almost to herself, but Aiguell answered.

'It's as if the whole population of the planet had been herded to this spot.'

Helewise nodded. The weight of death hung over this place.

She stood in silence as the rest of the squad walked along the shoreline. Even Aiguell limped along on her augmetic leg, bending down to pick items up, and limp on again.

'Has anyone found anything?' Helewise demanded after a long pause.

The negatives came in one by one.

'Morgandrie?'

'Nothing. Only death. I can feel it. It hangs like a miasma about the place. The stink of terror, violence, slaughter.'

The mood was sombre as they returned to their Rhino.

Helewise stood at the command hatch, and watched the planet sweep past.

Ruslana and Naoka's expeditions were as unfruitful. Ruslana's depression looked like it had once been a sea. Naoka's mountain range had also once been cities. Perhaps hives.

The Sisters reassembled at the gunship. Helewise's squad was the last to return. As she approached the grounded craft, she could see the storm sweeping in across the landscape. It was a wall of boiling dust, rolling towards them. It would be upon them within minutes.

'Let's get out of here,' Helewise ordered.

The gunship started to rattle as the Rhinos drove up. Aiguell's was last to mount the ramp and by now the gunship was shaking violently. The engines were already firing and the craft lifted up as the ramp sealed them in.

Sheets of dust blasted in before it closed with the sound of engaging mag-locks. They waited for the atmosphere to stabilise before removing their helmets.

The planet had been scrubbed clean, the population massacred. Even the atmosphere had been consumed.

Helewise looked about. The Sisters' black armour was stained with pale dust. She did not need to ask. She could read their faces.

They had found nothing that hinted to the identity of this place. They were still alone, and lost.

Albreda met them in her private quarters.

Though a little colour had returned to her cheeks, Helewise could only see the wrinkles and the stoop. But as she recounted what they had seen, she saw that Albreda's eyes were as sharp as ever.

'Nothing?' Albreda said at the end.

Helewise shook her head.

Albreda looked away. She took in a deep breath and nodded. 'We shall pray for guidance upon this matter,' she said.

The Sisters did so, all of them gathered together in the Great Prayer Hall.

Helewise prayed, but felt no answer. She left the hall. She needed to feel a blade in her hand again.

The lumens came on as she reached the drill pits, and the servitors' hydraulics began to warm up. She drew Reckoning and engaged the power stud. The blade crackled with traceries of voltaic energy.

She dropped down into the cinder pit and called out for her first foes. Three battle servitors were lowered into the chamber. She felt the menace as their targeting matrixes locked upon her, and they started to twitch as their stimms kicked in.

The first one came for her, and she sang the Fede Imperialis, 'A spiritu dominatus, Domine, libra nos!' as the blade swung. She imagined the servitors as those who had defiled the Emperor's domain as she tore them apart.

Palatine Albreda had never known such silence. She knelt and prayed and yet had little sense of the best course of action.

She broke her fast with a light meal of carb and slab, and then retired to her chambers for a day of private prayer. At the end she took *Consolations of the Warrior* from her shelves, and sat to consider the ancient words.

'Fortune has not yet turned her hatred against you. The storms of misfortune have not yet broken upon you. Have faith, while you yet have strength to hold a blade. Put your faith in the bolter, flamer and melta. Let that holy trinity be your guide.'

Albreda was deep in thought when Sister Dovere asked for permission to enter. She came in, leading a lectern-servitor that stumped forwards. On one side its metallic arm hung in reverse, and it was bent under the weight of the heavy leather-bound tome upon its back. Dovere's goggles were blank, but Albreda could feel the excitement within her.

'The search parties came back without news,' Albreda said.

'Correct,' Dovere said. 'None of the features I identified brought any useful information.'

'So, what next?'

Dovere signalled to the servitor, and the holo-pict in the middle of its forehead lit up. An image of the planet appeared before them, in its charred and ruined state. She set the holo-map to spin before her. 'I have run the planet's dimensions through the cogitator.'

Alongside the image of the planet appeared a scrolling column of names in pale white script – too small for Albreda to read. 'I eliminated those whose systems had the wrong sun, wrong number of planets. And then those that had orbiting satellites.'

Each time she ran through the search criteria, the scrolling list reappeared, each time getting shorter. 'At last, I have a list of twenty-nine possible worlds,' she said, and looked up. Albreda could not hide her weariness, but she nodded.

Dovere went on. 'I removed those that were clearly not this one. This planet was not a hive world, and appears to have been too populated to be an agri world. Which leaves these.'

Dovere clicked her fingers, and the holo-pict projected the image of five planets. She brought the first one forward. 'This is Kicury – a mining world. Large augemite deposits. Next Gonoe Prime. Forge world. Believed lost. Resettled five thousand years ago. Depler's Hope. Merchant world. Home to the Depler family – rogue traders who can trace their lineage back to the earliest days of the Imperium of Mankind. Elania, medicae world. And finally, this one.'

Dovere looked to the Palatine as the planet's holo-image spun before her. 'The fifth planet is Aoid's Sepulchre.'

A flush of colour returned to Albreda's cheeks as she sat forwards and put a hand to her chest. 'Aoid's Sepulchre?'

Dovere nodded. 'The world of Aoid's Sepulchre was where Saint Katherine launched her first War of Faith. It was the start of a pilgrimage route known as the Pilgrimage of Fire. The last world was Holy Cion, which marked the place where the first War of Faith ended in victory against the Witch-cult of Mnestteus.'

Albreda was silent as she made the sign of the fleur-de-lys. 'What are the chances?' she said at last.

'Minuscule,' Dovere said.

Albreda stood and paced back and forth.

'No!' she said after a long pause. 'We cannot think that we have been blessed. To do so would be a sin of the utmost pride!'

Dovere instructed the servitor to turn. The construct stumped round so that the book was facing them, and the augmetic arm turned the pages.

'This is the best pict I have found of the site where Aoid was buried.'

She expanded the image. It showed a vast ziggurat of white marble surrounded by statuary, each sculpture showing one of the ten thousand Sisters of Battle lost in the fight for the planet.

Pennants flew over the whole complex, and there were servo-skulls and cyber-cherubs circling about the soaring incense towers. Fires burnt at their summits, and the heavy, scented smoke tumbled down the tiered marble stairs.

'If this planet is indeed Aoid's Sepulchre, the data-screens say her tomb was located on the northern continental mass.'

'And have you searched that area?'

Dovere nodded. 'We have,' she said, 'but dust storms have been raging there since we arrived.'

'Then we must return,' Albreda said. 'I will lead the expedition.'

iii

Three gunships descended into the raging dust storm. Each one shook and rattled with the elements as the pilots spent hours combing back and forth over the seas of rubble and rust looking for the place that Dovere had identified.

The pilots were flying by instruments only, close enough to the ground for the augurs to scan the landscape. But the storms made the search impossible.

Palatine Albreda heard the vox-traffic with a sense of despair. She prayed, and for the first time she felt the answer come to her.

'Set the gunship down!' she ordered. She confirmed her instructions to the pilot.

The touchdown was bumpy.

Palatine Albreda led a party of Celestians out onto the surface. It was the same rubble that Helewise's team had found, a mix of bones and charred rockcrete.

Albreda led the Celestians away from the gunship, and through the storm they could see a shape, dark against the horizon.

They were bent into the storm, the servos of their suits of power armour whining with effort.

Albreda led them as the structure slowly came into view. It was a pyramid.

The realisation quickened the Palatine's heartbeat, but as she drew close to the base, she saw through the whipped dust that the structure was built of skulls.

She refused to give up hope.

The pile of skulls rose up before Albreda like a mountain. She set foot upon the base, and the skulls fractured and tumbled beneath her weight, the burnt ones crumbling under her boots.

'They were all slaughtered,' she voxed her team as she took in the magnitude of this devastation. 'Such suffering.' She knelt. Liquid seams of melted gold ran through the fissures, and she pulled a lump of carved stone from the ash.

It was a fragment of a gargoyle – the face of a Battle Sister, with the image of a burning heart carved into it.

'This is the spot,' she voxed. 'This is where Aoid was laid to rest.'

Sustained salvos of melta shots cleared the skulls. It took hours before they reached solid footings and found a step of intact stone – not a facing slab, but part of the construction layer. They eventually found a tunnel and the entrance was cleared of skulls and rubble.

Bèle wanted to go first, but Albreda would not let any go before her.

The tunnel mouth moaned as the wind blew over it. Albreda wiped the dust from her eye-lenses as she paced down the dark tunnel. It was wide enough for two Rhinos to drive abreast. The walls were carved with images of Sisters in battle. The heads had been chipped away, and profane symbols had been scrawled across them all.

The roar of the storm fell away as they processed into the ancient structure. The tunnel ended with a bent and misshapen door.

The name carved above the door confirmed their worst suspicions. *Aoid's Sepulchre*, it read.

'This is it,' Bèle said.

Albreda nodded. The tomb door had been blasted through with melta shots.

Bèle put her hand out to stop her.

'No,' Albreda said. 'We must go in. We must bear witness.'

Albreda stood in the middle of the domed chamber and looked about and felt the breath go out of her. She tried to draw in another, but her body rebelled against her and she had to put her hand out to steady herself.

In her mind's eye she could see it as it had been centuries before, with attendant cherubs trailing silken pennants, and a trail of noble pilgrims winding out of sight to the edges of the plains. The contrast between that and the scene before her was staggering.

Aoid's tomb was cracked and burnt and broken. The marble lid had been smashed open, the shattered fragments tipped out and scattered. Albreda forced herself up the stairs.

Inside the stone sarcophagus lay a lead coffin. The metal had been ripped open. The scorched and melted edges of the tear were unmistakably the work of a power fist. The tomb itself was empty. Aoid's body had been stolen.

The air aboard the *Daughter of the Emperor* was tense as word spread through the Sisters. They gathered at the Great Prayer Hall as the name of Aoid's Sepulchre was added to the prayer wheel.

The Sisters looked on with cold fury. Helewise felt a deep

chasm of grief open up within her, and from the Repentia cells came the sharp crack of self-chastisement.

The rituals. The festivals. The sacred sites. Hallowed shrines. Five thousand years of history and worship. All had been lost and profaned.

It was three days later that the whole company of Sisters stood on the planet and filed silently into the burial chamber. Even the Sisters Repentia were brought in, muzzled and hooded.

Nothing had been cleaned away. The profane scrawl remained. The defilement was plain.

Albreda's voice was trembling as she led them all in prayers of revenge.

As they sang hymns of righteous anger, the Sisters were led forward to touch the tomb. The Sisters Repentia went first. The torment they felt was visible. Some screamed, some howled; others thrashed, berserk, against their confinements, and as they were led away they lashed themselves with chains and knotted cords.

After them the other Sisters came forward, one by one, and placed their hands upon the empty tomb. Ruslana heard the screams of the dead and swore an oath to protect the innocent. Morgandrie felt as though she were Saint Katherine standing over Aoid's tomb. Helewise brought Reckoning, laid the naked blade upon the ancient stone and swore a vow of utter fearlessness, whatever the foes she faced, whatever the danger.

Next came Sister Dialogus Dovere, trembling as she knelt and stretched out a hand. She screamed as the sanctity of the place ran through her like lightning. Her voice was a shrill note of pain, such as Aoid suffered in her martyrdom, but there was a word within that scream: *wrath*.

Last to step forwards was Palatine Albreda. Anger gave her

voice a new strength. She roared out her vow, which all of them took for themselves. 'Witness the desecration of our most holy places! I shall not rest until I have taken vengeance upon the defilers of this tomb. Until I have purged their souls in flame, brought calamity upon their armies, and brought the Emperor's doom upon their commanders.'

The ancient stone shook as the Sisters' voices rose in a fearsome battle cry. 'Cleanse your foes with bolter and blade!'

In the days that followed, Palatine Albreda took tarot readings and auguries to decide the best time and place to begin the journey. At the end she was clear, and she announced her decision in the Great Prayer Hall. She hovered above the prayer wheel and looked about.

The faces she saw were fiercer and grimmer than she had ever seen them. Each eye burned with righteous anger. Each jaw was clenched in fury. Each mouth was fixed in an expression of focused passion.

They had been transformed by their experience upon Aoid's Sepulchre. They had stood in Saint Katherine's own footsteps, and the spark of the martyred saint had kindled a burning flame within them all.

She felt it within herself, and she saw the light in their faces, and she stood a little straighter as she called out, in her battlefield voice, 'Sisters! We have been plagued with doubt and uncertainty. But you have had faith. And our faith has been rewarded. We promised to act as a beacon for Battle Group Phaedra, and so we shall. It is not mere chance that we arrived here, at Aoid's Sepulchre. The way ahead of us is clear.

'We shall retrace the steps that the saint took. We must undertake the Pilgrimage of Fire.'

iv

Each of them prepared for the transition as the *Daughter of the Emperor* made its way to the Mandeville point.

Helewise spent hours with Reckoning. There was a freedom to combat. A thoughtlessness. A pure expression of the Emperor's mercy. She exulted in it, cutting, stabbing, thrusting, disembowelling.

One night Morgandrie joined her. Afterwards, as they took the mag-lift back up to the cells, Helewise said, 'Do you still dream?'

Morgandrie nodded.

'Are they still of our saint?'

Morgandrie hesitated. 'No. But they…' She paused, looking for the right words. 'When I wake. The feelings are intense.'

Helewise did not understand.

'Last night, in my dream I was climbing a mountain. The steps rose ever before me, and the journey was wearying, but I knew that at the summit of the mountain, He waited. As bright as sunrise.

'When I reached Him, His radiance was so fierce that my skin blistered and puckered and cooked lumps fell from my body. He was as hot as plasma. As fierce as a melta shot. My flesh was so weak. So pitiful. It fell from my bones as I stepped towards Him. I was just a skeleton, striding towards Him, and then my bones started to char and blacken and crumble with each stride. At last I was nothing but a skull, tumbling forwards onto the ground, and I felt my life drawn out of me, like a silk cloth, pulled from a pocket.

'I felt it rise up, almost weightless, hanging in the air above me. Then I woke. And I was myself, not Saint Katherine. And I was here. Just Morgandrie, the picture of mediocrity.'

'You are a Sister of Our Martyred Lady,' Helewise told her, and Morgandrie nodded.

'I am,' she said after a while. 'But I think of Ephraina. She knew and she welcomed it. I feel my death coming. And I welcome it.'

Helewise said nothing. She thought on the name of her Order. Martyred Lady. They would all end up martyrs, in time.

As far as those they had left behind in the Imperium of Man were concerned, they were already dead.

When they reached the Mandeville point, Palatine Albreda returned to the Navigator's chamber. There was a sense of the familiar. They had spent so long together in the last crossing.

'I pray this will be shorter, and easier,' Hemponia said as Albreda had the relics set down and took her place at the Navigator's side.

Once the necessary rituals were undertaken, Palatine Albreda asked, 'Are you ready?'

'I am.'

Albreda sang a hymn of sacrifice as Hemponia removed the

cloth that had been bound about her head, opened her third eye and looked onto the raging insanity of the warp.

Albreda could feel the sudden tension go through the Navigator. Hemponia let out an involuntary moan, like one possessed.

'I do not see a way!' she hissed, a note of panic rising in her voice. 'I cannot find a path.'

Albreda took her hand in both of hers and begged the God-Emperor for guidance.

The hours stretched on, and Hemponia was transfixed. 'We are lost,' she said, finally.

Albreda's voice was calm. 'Pick a road and we will journey it without complaint.'

'I cannot...' Hemponia hissed. Her third eye looked upon insanity. It was an experience that would send most into instant madness, and that time it strained even the seasoned Navigator. But again, Albreda's voice was like oil on troubled waters.

'He has guided us this far,' Albreda said. 'He has a purpose for us. Be stout of heart. The pilgrim's path is never easy.'

The Chem Dogs remained locked in their hangar, enduring each warp transit with fraying strength.

Wythers found the journeys harder than any of the others. He spent the warp crossings fastened to the wall with a length of chain. But even so restrained, no one wanted to be near him. Not after what they had seen him do during the crossing of the Cicatrix Maledictum. He sat, hunched, sucking on his rebreather, even though the canister was done.

'I need Sawbones!' he moaned, as they brought him food or water, gingerly sliding the tray towards him. 'Bring me Sawbones!'

He wailed and moaned, refusing to eat, and his pain was an added nightmare for all of Chalice's company.

On the third transit, from Praesteum's Forge to the Stalost, the Mercies arrived to deliver supplies to the Chem Dogs' hangar, and found that Wythers had caught the man that brought him his food, Dokona, and torn out his jugular.

'With his own teeth?' Mercy Cody demanded.

Chalice nodded.

'The bastard took some subduing.' He had the scratches and bite marks to back his words up. 'Dokona's lot did him over. I thought they were going to kill him.'

He paused. 'They would have done, if it weren't Wythers. I got Sawbones in the end. He slipped something into his nitra-chems. Knocked him out. But we can't keep him around for much longer. His service to the Emperor is done.'

Mercy Cody nodded. 'Keep him alive for the moment. I'll speak to the Marshal.'

Aebram cursed when he heard. He slammed his hand onto his desk, making Cody jump.

'Where's that bastard Salem? He's supposed to maintain command.'

Cody nodded. 'It's the chems. They've fried his brain.'

The Marshal stood up and turned his back on Cody. 'Wythers saved my life, you know.'

'So I've heard, sir.'

'More than once.'

Cody could well believe it. So many of them owed Wythers over the years.

Aebram sighed. 'There were men, in the distant past, who, it was said, turned into bears, and when they were in this state, their bodies were invulnerable to blade or shot. Wythers is like that. He does not seem to feel pain when the battle-anger takes him. He is unstoppable.' He sighed. 'But it seems his battle is done.'

'Do you want me to shoot him?'

'No,' Aebram said. There was a long pause. 'I should do it.' He turned and Cody saw that there was emotion glistening in the commissar's eye. 'I owe him that, at least.'

Cody nodded. 'Sawbones laced his chems. He is sleeping at the moment.'

Aebram understood. 'Get Sawbones to wake him. I'd like to say goodbye to him first. If only for myself.'

The Marshal waited within his cabin for Sawbones' stimms to kick in.

He sat at the small table where he broke fast each morning, the bolt pistol lying next to the ceramic cup he used for the ash of his lho-sticks.

The pistol was loaded. He was ready for whenever the big man came to. The minutes dragged on, and he took another lho-stick and smoked it right down to the last pinch.

Cody knocked gently. 'He's come to, sir,' he said.

Aebram took one final drag, then ground the last bit out into the cup. He stood up in the smoke-wreathed room and paced up and down, his lips pursed in thought. 'I'm on my way.'

They used the storeroom as a cell. The lock was broken. The sliding metal doors had been spiked closed. Shin had used his hammer to knock the wedge out.

Wythers was chained to the far wall. Aebram lifted his head up. The suppressors had not taken any risks. Half of them were Dokona's lot and they'd beaten the hell out of Wythers. His face was bruised and swollen, his lower lip was split, and one eye was closed, the purple skin bloated and swollen. Bloody drool hung from the corner of his mouth. The stubble on his chin was crusted with other men's blood. Gore stained his front in a sticky, scabbing mess.

'Marshal,' Wythers hissed. 'I know why you're here.'

'Your service is over,' Aebram told him.

Wythers cursed. 'It's not,' he said. 'It's not, I promise you. I can still fight. Just put me on the battlefield. I will fight for you, the Dogs and even that bastard on the Golden frekking Throne.'

Aebram knew that Wythers was right. He paused. 'I believe you,' he said. 'But you cannot remain with the Dogs.'

'Send me away, then,' Wythers said. 'I don't care. I will still fight.'

Aebram paused. 'There might be a way. But it will be hard.'

'I trust you,' Wythers said.

Aebram nodded, but said nothing.

'Is he dead?' Mercy Cody asked when Aebram came out of the storeroom.

'No,' Aebram said. He appeared distracted. 'I gave him more chems. Keep him locked up.'

'Where are you going?'

'To pray.'

The corridors were dark, the lights on low, the grav-plates humming, as Aebram made his way to one of the lesser chapels in the bowels of the cathedrum.

The pomp and frippery and costume of the Ecclesiarchy did nothing to bring him closer to the God-Emperor. He was a man of simple tastes and simple faith. When he prayed, he liked to do so alone, and this place set aside for novitiates and Naval thralls was usually empty.

The Marshal's gloved hand was firm as he ground the stiff levers open and looked inside. The chapel was barrel-vaulted, lit by the flicker of flaming sconces set about the chamber. There was no one here.

He was glad of that as he entered the chamber, his boots echoing on the tiles. His footsteps led him towards the banks of votive candles. They had all burnt out. It had been a long time since anyone had come here to pray.

The misshapen stumps of candles reminded him of his Dogs, which in turn reminded him why he was here. Wythers was burnt out, he was sure, but perhaps there was a way for him to yet serve.

There was a basket of fresh candles, each one wrapped about with golden strips. He picked one from the top.

It read: *There is only the Emperor, and He is our shield and protector.*

The sentiment was not what the Marshal wanted. He took out another.

In an age of insanity, look to the madman to show the way.

The Marshal paused, and tapped the candle in his hand as he thought on the implications of that quote. He slid the candle into his pocket. He would keep that one for another time.

The third read: *Let the barrel of your gun answer to heresy.*

He kept that one, too.

There was a brass kindler crafted in the shape of a dragon, its tail curled up beneath it. He pressed the ignition stud and there was a short cone of hissing blue flame. It took a moment for the wick to catch.

The candle smelt of tallow. He pressed it into the bed of sand and then went to pray.

There were three narrow lines of wooden pews. He ignored those and made his way to the wrought-iron altar rail. It was fashioned in the form of scrolled vines, each curling frond ending in a fleur-de-lys. There was a kneeling rail, padded with red velvet.

He stood at the front for a moment, and pursed his lips to one side, in a moment of indecision.

Before him, in the flickering light of a pair of altar candles, was the form of the God-Emperor, sitting in His Golden Throne. The face was hard and set. It was the kind of face that brooked no weakness. The kind of face that the Marshal wore himself.

It took the Marshal a long time to bend the knee. This was not a natural gesture for him. But at last, he made the sign of the aquila and bent his head, and he asked for strength for what he had to do.

He said his prayer silently. It was between him and the God-Emperor. It would be easier to shoot Wythers, of course, but he wanted to fight, and he deserved a good death. It was only through battle that a penal legionnaire could hope to earn the forgiveness of the Golden Throne.

The Marshal moved up through the decks of the cathedrum.

The Sisters' quarters were still and quiet and thoughtful. He passed a skull-faced cherub in the corridor, white feathered wings flapping as its anti-grav generators hummed. It threw handfuls of red petals into the air and they fell slowly to the ground, like bloody snow.

His hobnailed boots crushed the petals underfoot. He could smell the perfume, rising slowly about him, and it softened his mood a little.

'I am looking for Sister Superior Lanete,' he said to one of the Sisters.

She came out in a red-and-black robe, her pinched face looking stern. Regardless of rank, she had a holiness that he did not.

He coughed to clear his throat. 'Sister,' he said. 'May I have a word?'

He found himself fumbling for words, an unfamiliar sensation, but at last they started to flow. He held the power of life and death over his regiment. It was a request, and he was not used to asking others for permission for anything.

She heard him out. At the end she said, 'Is he worthy?'

'None of them are worthy.'

She nodded and considered. 'I will have to see him first.'

Major Chalice walked into the hangar and picked six others. 'Up!' he said. 'Come with me.'

The six Dogs stood before him. 'We're bringing Wythers out.' There was a silence.

'Only six?' Shin said after a moment.

Chalice held up the mag-cuffs. 'We've got these.'

They nodded, but none of them were keen to join in.

Chalice pulled the spike free and they braced themselves as the door swung inwards. The room was dark. Shin shone the lumen inside. It was a bar of white light swinging through the darkness.

'There he is!' he said. The light remained on the shape in the far corner. Wythers was slumped sideways. They moved in. Tentative steps took them across the empty space. Wythers did not move.

'Is he dead?' Shin whispered.

'Let's hope not,' Chalice said. 'Cover me.' He crept forward and slipped a fresh canister into the rebreather.

The big man jerked awake.

'What is this shit?' Wythers said.

Three men took each of Wythers' long arms as they dragged him out. The 17th Savlar Chem Dogs turned out in their own way to say goodbye to their old commander. They stood as he approached, called out to him, swore at him, said nothing. It felt to them like the passing of an era. The chems had worn his nerves away, made Wythers a shell of his former self.

At the end of the line, one of the Dogs caught Chalice's arm. 'What are they going to do with him?'

Chalice didn't know.

'Better to die in battle,' the trooper said, 'than to be put down like a rabid dog.'

Part Five

Then

Holy Cion

'Whosoever slayeth mine servants, vengeance shall be served upon them sevenfold.'

– Epistles of Cludhari

í

A company of Sisters removed Lizbet's power armour, piece by piece. They gave her a simple tabard of undyed cloth to wear, inked with High Gothic script, prayers and images.

Lizbet spent the day purifying herself, and when the hour came she stood in the doorway of her cell, looked back, and knew that when she returned, she would have been changed by her experience.

The abbey was so quiet she could hear the low hum of the generator as she made her way down to the front gate.

The canoness' lighter was waiting for her, engines running, hot air rippling the air about it. Beneath she could see the countless lights on the plains, twinkling through the smog.

The canoness stepped out of the lighter, and waited for her by the door.

Lizbet's boots rang out on the worn cobbles. Dark against the horizon were the burnt remains of heretics. The carrion birds startled at her appearance, and flapped up into the breeze with caws of alarm, circling before settling back down on the dead.

The cadavers gave the open space a gloomy, forlorn feel. It was made worse by the chime of bells from the city below.

'Ten years ago, I remember how joyous the time of the feast was,' Lizbet said. 'And now there is plague and all we hear is the toll of mourning.'

'It is a trial, but we must remain faithful,' Ysolt told her. 'Remember the struggles that the saint went through. Our troubles are but foothills to her mountains.'

The two women embraced, and then Lizbet climbed up, alone.

Ysolt stood as her lighter lifted up into the wind, turned, and set off across the plain.

Far off was the white dome of the Shrine of Landing, which marked the very spot where the saint had landed on Cion to conclude her first War of Faith.

Ysolt had once taken the role of the saint. She remembered the time clearly, and wished that it could have been as joyous for Sister Lizbet.

Lizbet knelt in the lighter and prayed as she flew.

Beneath her were the tents of the pilgrims that covered the plains. The multitudes had turned the land dark. Trails of smoke drifted up in a thousand threads as the fires twinkled in the gathering gloom.

She felt the craft descending, finished her prayers and looked out of the window.

The people were held a mile back by a perimeter of local troops. The ground about the shrine was empty, and the lighter landed a hundred yards from it.

Lizbet stepped down. She could feel the beating of great drums, the wail of holy pipes, the songs of exultant pilgrims.

Millions of faces strained to see her, so many that they blurred into the distance, each one lit with hope and faith and expectation. Over the tumult of worship, the roar of a million voices rolled towards her like a wave. It was the sound of joy and ecstasy and exultation.

The enormity of the saint's action struck her. While Lizbet faced the millions of worshippers, the saint had landed amid an army of heretics. While Lizbet faced adulation, the saint had faced blasphemy and hatred.

The boom of great drums continued as she lifted a hand in a salute and turned on her heel, acknowledging each part of the crowd, until she had turned a full circle.

The shrine was built of white stone, like a foil to the dark mass of the Bolt.

It had been conceived on a monumental scale, five thousand years before, and each generation had added to it until it was a sprawling edifice of gothic splendour rising a mile into the sky.

Lizbet mounted the marble staircase, head down, lost in reverie – unheeding of the cries and weeping of the horde of pilgrims who crammed the plains. Her eyes picked out arches and galleries soaring above her, each one studded with gargoyles and gun emplacements, prayer flags flapping in the night breeze, tapestries hanging stiff with their embroidered threads of precious metal. Only when she had reached the top did she stop and look back the way that she had come.

The towering blackness of the Bolt rose from the dust, rising up from the city with the pale spires of the abbey set atop. Nothing seemed amiss.

She thought of her Sisters, and the canoness, and the quiet of her cell, then said a silent prayer. She bowed her head and stepped inside.

The broad path led her into the inner chapel through galleries and side chapels, each one lit with candlelight, glittering off golden icons and faceted stones.

There were relic stores locked up with heavy chains and iron padlocks; ossuaries of those who had died on pilgrimage, stacked to the arched ceilings with mouldering remains; and chantry chapels, piled one upon the other, ten thousand choir-servitors singing hymns for the souls of the beneficiaries: bishops, warmasters, planetary governors and their ilk.

The deeper she went, the more the noise of the crowd fell away, until all she could hear was a sound like a distant wind, the clear note of her boots ringing on the marble flags, and the drumbeat like a distant vibration, or the thudding of a heart.

It took Lizbet an hour to reach the tiered amphitheatre that was at the centre of the chapel. The space plunged down before her, rank upon rank of misericords set in steep tiers. At the bottom was a small dais where her vigil would take place.

The emptiness struck her. She was alone, apart from robed servitors lighting candles, refilling lantern oil, and ministering to their mundane tasks.

Step by step she descended. When she reached the bottom, she stood and looked up and felt almost as if she had been buried in some primaeval tomb.

A thin shaft of light plunged down from a single fleur-de-lys-shaped window above her. She took in the stillness and felt her breathing slow. She stood for a long time before she closed her eyes and knelt.

Usually there was something to focus her faith upon. An icon, or reliquary, or song. But there was only silence.

She focused on the emptiness and felt the stillness seep into her soul, and calm her troubled mind.

* * *

The maid was kneeling before the two Sisters, facing away from the door, her wrists and ankles shackled with sacred chains.

She felt a number of Sisters enter the room behind her. She could not say how many. She could hear Sister Dogmata Morgaulat as she laid out her instruments of confession one by one. Her expertise was in the frailties of the human body; she could heal just as well as she could cause pain. She listed all of these instruments one by one. Last of all she lifted the Blessing, the captive boltgun she used to dispatch the condemned.

The mechanism clicked as she pulled the bolt back, and she laid it down on the table.

'Open your eyes, child,' said Sister Morgaulat.

Branwen obeyed. She made the sign of the fleur-de-lys, and looked up.

'Do you know why you are here?'

Sister Morgaulat had a thin, severe face, her white hair hanging in a short-cropped bob about her face. Her lips were pursed, her eyes hard.

Branwen felt no fear. 'You believe me to be corrupted.'

'And are you?'

'No.'

Morgaulat's eyes flickered briefly to the one who stood behind the maid. 'I have heard many say that of themselves. And they have turned out to be the foulest of heretics.'

Branwen said, 'Forgive me, Sister. What is my crime?'

'Do not question me,' Morgaulat snapped.

Branwen bowed her head as Sister Morgaulat picked an electro-scourge from the table.

Her voice was a low monotone. 'You healed the sick.'

'I laid my hands upon them.'

'You spoke a blessing?'

'I did.'

'Tell me about those prayers.'

Branwen paused. 'I felt the words come to me.'

'From where?'

Branwen paused longer this time. 'I do not know.'

'Did you have an image in your head?'

'No. Nothing like that. But I had a sense. It was like a shaft of golden light falling onto me. And the words came to me. And I spoke them, and told each of the sufferers to have faith.'

'And where did you learn to speak like this?'

'Like what?' Branwen said.

Morgaulat stepped forwards so that she could look down into Branwen's face. 'Are you mocking me?'

'Of course not.'

Morgaulat turned her head. 'Child. This conversation has been conducted entirely in High Gothic.'

Branwen's cheeks coloured.

'Where did you learn to speak like this?'

Branwen shook her head. She did not know. 'I cannot say,' she said.

'Cannot or will not?'

Branwen paused. 'All I can surmise is that it is the Emperor's will.'

Morgaulat said no more and stepped out of Branwen's line of sight. There were footsteps as the room emptied, and then the door closed behind her. The latch fell. The key turned in the lock and left her in silence.

Branwen was alone again.

Alone, apart from the light that burnt inside her like a sun.

Canoness Ysolt and Morgaulat paused at the end of the corridor.

'I believe her,' Morgaulat said in a bare whisper.

The canoness nodded. She agreed, which was more troubling. 'It is more miracle than heresy.'

Morgaulat nodded. It was easier to deal with heresy. You gave them the opportunity to repent, and then purged them. But a miracle?

Ysolt could not deal with this just as the festival was beginning. If this was a miracle, then it needed to be handled with utmost caution.

'Take her to one of the lesser chapels. I will pray upon this matter when the festival is done.'

Morgaulat took Branwen through the upper cloister to a chapel of prayer.

None of the maids were ever allowed so high up in the edificium. Branwen lifted her head in wonder as she stepped inside. She put her hand to her mouth as she looked about.

Tenebrism murals covered the ceiling, depicting Sisters in black power armour, the foes they faced, and the extreme light of the saint, whose golden paint exaggerated her beauty.

The maid-of-all-work walked barefoot across the tiles to the altar. A prayer rail ran before it and Branwen knelt and closed her eyes.

Branwen sang a hymn of praise. Morgaulat's skin goose pimpled. The beatific song was sublime, and she had never heard it before. This was a miracle at a time when they needed one more than ever.

Morgaulat found herself kneeling as well. Tears were brimming and she could not hold them back. She was here to witness the saint at work. And despite the darkness and the hunger, her faith was renewed.

The God-Emperor protected them yet. But if the saint was with this child, then should she not be taking the mantle of the saint upon her shoulders?

ii

Night fell over Holy Cion and the ecstatic prayers carried on through the darkness, alongside the constant thunder of holy drums.

Lizbet felt the night draw on about her as she meditated on her faith.

She was left in silent vigil until the last watch of the night when the Sisters returned, each carrying a part of the saint's suit of armour.

They descended to where she knelt. She was so intent on her prayers that they seemed almost like ghosts.

None of them spoke, and they moved silently, anointing the neuro-sockets in the flesh of her shoulders, upper arms, her thighs, her chest, her hips, calves and skull with holy oil. The touch of the cold oil sent a shiver through Sister Lizbet.

As the ancient suit of armour was fitted piece by piece onto her body, she felt the amphitheatre fill with worshippers. She could feel their joy, their faith, their expectation.

Next came the Wings of the Vermilion Path, the winged power pack that had been crafted on Holy Terra for the saint to allow her to soar above the earth.

As soon as the power pack was connected, Lizbet felt its holy power flow through the ornate suit of golden armour. It was the very same armour that Saint Katherine herself had worn.

The realisation ran through Lizbet like a shot of combat stimms.

She had never been so close to the divine. The last piece to be fitted was the saint's halo.

As it was lowered onto her shoulders, it hummed to life and glowed like molten gold.

A shaft of light plunged down into the chamber.

Dawn, at last, had come.

Branwen's lips were moving, as if she were speaking in her sleep.

Sister Morgaulat put her hand out and touched her shoulder. 'Child. It is dawn.'

Branwen's eyes opened. They heard a distant roar roll towards them. The procession was beginning. It was the sound of a billion voices. It was the sound of a hurricane in the mountains. The roar of a forest fire. It was the sound of faith and belief and righteous anger, and it stirred Branwen's soul to hear it.

'The saint!' she said.

'Yes.' Morgaulat nodded. 'Come.'

Lizbet knelt in the shrine and sang the Fede Imperialis. Last of all, Chalybix, the saint's own sword, was brought to her, the jewelled sheath almost hidden under the weight of prayer strips and embossed red wax seals. The gilt had been worn away on the exposed surfaces, but it was a work of beauty and wonder, such as might come from the armouries of the Palace on Holy Terra.

Lizbet wanted to reach out and touch it, but her hand trembled and would not move. At last she reached out for the wire-worked grip and lifted it from its bed. She mag-locked the holy artefact to her belt.

At that moment a titanic horn sounded from the central tower of the shrine. It was a deafening bellow, a defiant blast against disbelief and heresy. The ground shook, and then, from the side of the temple, a chorus of other horns announced the great unfurling as the long, dark night of liturgy ended, and hydraulic generators slowly hauled the mile-high iron doors open and daylight flooded down through the smog-brown sky.

Lizbet felt the humming as the gravity well activated beneath her, and then a shaft of golden light stabbed down into the darkness and illuminated her.

The amphitheatre was full, and Lizbet heard the gasps of awe and wonder as the Wings of the Vermilion Path spread behind her. She rose, a glowing golden figure, through the shaft of light, arms outstretched, Chalybix held in her gloved hand.

There were shouts and prayers and calls to witness the miracle as she was lifted up, through the song of circling cherubs, until she rose through the fleur-de-lys opening at the top of the dome and appeared like a golden star for all those who waited on the plains.

The pilgrims roared in religious ecstasy. They had suffered for ten years to reach this place and this moment, had suffered all manner of privations. The ground shook as the multitudes called out or threw themselves down and wept. Lizbet was the centre of all this adulation as she hung, transfixing all who saw her, bright as a golden star, a mile above the Pilgrim Plains.

This was how the saint had landed. Lizbet could picture the scene. From her height, the masses of pilgrims could be the heretic tribes that had stood against her, their totems and heretical emblems.

Lizbet felt the thrill of battle as she sang in a clear, confident, high voice; a paean of praise to the God-Emperor. Her voice rang out across the planet. And then the massed choirs answered her call in a rolling roar of voices, as the twins, Sisters Brace and Morcada, led a host of Seraphim into the air about her, and Chalybix flashed in the light of the rising sun.

'Death to the unclean,' she sang, and the choir answered her. 'Death to the heretic. Death to the xenos.'

The call was answered by the sound of worship-horns booming out across the planet. The sound was primaeval. Deep, haunting wails folded one on top of the other, like a herd of mastodons crossing the great plains of Hamooth.

As the noise blasted out, a hundred servitors began to winch open a vast banner from the southern wall of the Shrine of Landing. The tapestry was as tall and broad as a Titan.

It showed Saint Katherine, rampant: a golden figure upon a field of black. Her eyes were diamonds, her skin was silver, and upon her cheek was a blood-red teardrop that signified the compassion she felt for humankind. In her right hand she bore a sword, in her left a shield, emblazoned with the fleur-de-lys. And in each corner of the banner were the emblems of her Order. Droplets of blood, red roses and the golden skull of the God-Emperor.

Lizbet's winged power pack held her up in the air. The wings felt like an extension of her body, and with a thought she slowly descended. Beneath her, the procession waited. It snaked off across the plains, out of her sight. And she was to lead it. Sister Lizbet hung golden among the Seraphim. The devout roared as she approached, shouted petitions to her, begging for the grace of a look, or just to touch their hands.

She felt their roars deep within her body.

Lizbet felt the adoration rise towards her. She transfixed the plain as drums boomed out, horns blared, marching choirs began to strike up hymnals and cherubs trailed censers above their heads.

Morgaulat stood behind Branwen on the tower top.

The plains hung under a haze of smoke and dust. Lizbet was a golden speck against the dark background, her golden armour glinting in the sunlight. Branwen stood transfixed.

She remembered that moment she had splashed the saint's boot, and felt that the saint must have moved her. The chances of it all happening were so slight. The blessing she had given to the sick of Jeromegate was just her passing the blessing along.

But as she stood, she felt a cold hand upon her neck.

It was as if a shadow had passed over her.

The clouds above the Bolt were coiling in upon themselves. A shape was forming. It looked like a human face at first. The saint, perhaps? A woman's face with locks of swirling black hair. It was hard to tell.

'What's that?' she said.

She put her hand to Sister Morgaulat's shoulder, but the Sister did not move.

Nothing was moving. Only Branwen, and the swirling clouds above her head.

A voice called her name.

It was insistent. Branwen could not refuse. She found herself descending the broad stairs, under the chandeliers of ancient brown bones, towards the chapel. Her bare feet were soft on the steps. She was now walking on the same tiles that she had been scrubbing just a few days before.

Across space and time, she had been summoned to this moment, and the Bolt began to shake.

Her sovereign awaited.

* * *

Sister Lizbet led the procession along the mile-wide Road of Purification. It led in a straight line for ten miles across the plains and the outskirts of the city to the base of the Bolt, under which Saint Katherine had buried a creature of nightmare.

Golden reliquaries were carried on tracked chassis: the bones and armour of ancient warriors encased in sarcophagi of gold and precious stones, and draped with embroidered tapestries, pennants and flags, and banners hand-stitched with holy scripts.

Cherubs fluttered above them, proclaiming the same hymnals and the deeds of those interred beneath.

Canoness Ysolt led the Sisters of the Abbey of Eternal Watch. Her cloak was a holy pennant, the corners carried by floating cherubs.

About her was an honour guard of Sisters Repentia. Chains clanked with each step. Their heads were covered with white hoods, and listed, in black Gothic minuscule, upon their plain cotton tabards were the accounts of the transgressions that had brought them to this sorry state. Upon their shoulders sat their two-handed eviscerators, the chains lovingly cleaned and hung with seals of purity.

Next came the visiting delegations from the Convent Sanctorum and the three Orders of the Convent Prioris, all of whom stood or knelt in attitudes of prayer and devotion. Then a float with a fleur-de-lys censer, hanging like a bell from a great crosspiece, smoke pouring through ten thousand perforations. The abbess of Aoid's Sepulchre rode alongside in her floating pulpit, her fist punching the air, her voice ringing out in a searing sermon about the dangers of temptation and excess. At her side marched two columns of Penitent Engines, the interred bodies screaming with ecstatic pain as their pistons hissed with each lurching stride.

Behind her came the Order's greatest warriors, who led their commanderies with all their accoutrements of war. At the head came Imagifier Lyonesse with Saint Katherine's own banner. About her, Celestian Alird with the Commandery of the Risen Sacrament, marching to the Song of Divine Anger. Then company upon company of stern warriors in black power armour, with Paragon Warsuits marching alongside, and the tanks of their Order: Rhinos; battle chapels walking on articulated limbs; the Cathedral of Woe, its vast bulk rising like a miniature hive, with grav-repulsors crackling about its skirts and dwarfing the Exorcists and Immolators that advanced at its flanks.

The air shivered to the blast of annunciation engines and laud hailers as Sister Gahene led a company of Dominions through the promethium fumes, their fearsome flamers and meltas ready for battle. Iblis the Stern came at the head of the Retributors, who carried heavy flamers and bolters and multi-meltas across their chests.

The might and power of the Ecclesiarchy was laid bare for all to see, united in prayer and worship.

The planet rocked with the boom of voices lifted up in ecstatic reverie, and then the tramp of the procession as it started towards the Bolt. Mobile shrines mounted atop the tanks of her Order, walkers carrying embroidered silks, holy men and women, the Sisters of her Order, and then mile upon mile of robed penitents, a hundred abreast, bare feet, ragged grey robes, their skin raw with sackcloth and severe chastening.

And above the whole procession floated a river of banners and symbols and icons which bore all manner of devout iconography. But chief among them and repeated in many forms was the image of the Martyred Lady. And behind her, five hundred men carried the golden statue of Saint Katherine upon a bier, their tread in step as the weighty statue swayed with their movement.

The air vibrated as they marched along. Behind came

representatives of daughter churches and ecclesiarchal dignitaries – the priests and pastors led by Cardinal Anamel, the earth shaking beneath the iron claws of his walking throne, his bearded face thrust forwards.

The chancellor of Holy Cion and his whole household followed, with the Great Standard of the Emperor – a silver Imperial aquila – lifted square by a flock of golden cherubs. Figures waved, or wept, or stared out in stunned awe at being part of this glorious commemoration.

Neat squares of the Cion Rifles marched behind in full dress uniforms, the feathered plumes of their brass helmets quivering with each step. Behind them, a thousand standard bearers marched in neat echelons, the battle colours of the regiments flapping in their wake. Each had fought in the original War of Faith and were still honoured among the Adepta Sororitas, with their senior officers occasionally granted the right to have their ashes interred within the catacombs of Cion.

Elite units from the Aquarian Guard were led by a Macharius Vulcan named *Judgement of Seth*. Behind it came a hundred and fifty tanks of the line, barrels elevated in salute; five hundred Aquarian Chimeras, their commanders standing in their turrets, the pennants stiff with the wind of their own passing; and then the attendant detachment of tech-priests and savants, the robed figures hidden inside their black-painted tanks. The earth shook as they rumbled past, a brown smog of promethium fumes swirling in their midst. Behind marched the 37th Sanctuary Rifles, then the Cion Vanguards, and then the Osiron Revellers, each trooper marching in step, bayonets sparkling in the growing light of day.

Ossuaries followed, interred within super-heavy hulls, the mouldering remains of revered dead gathered from the planets that Saint Katherine had purified during her first War of Faith.

Each one was covered with ornate filigree and the names of the regiments who had fought alongside the saint five thousand years before.

Ten thousand barefoot Ecclesiarchy hierarchs strode behind, prayer beads in hand, mumbling personal devotions. Then, the long train of pilgrims, each fulfilling a lifetime's ambition to walk the steps that Saint Katherine had trodden. A tide of humanity washing across the Pilgrim Plains.

The pilgrimage trail followed a ten-mile route along the Road of Purification. It ran under a series of monolithic gates that overshadowed the processional. First was the Lisanors Gate, of black oolite, the smooth stone glittering with embedded quartz that looked like faces staring out from the past. It was Sister Jorea Lisanors who had protected the saint's back as she strode heedless through the enemy, and she had taken the blows aimed at Saint Katherine and been cut down in the process. Lisanors' Memorial was lit with banks of votive candles.

The racks rose, as tall as habs, the millions of lights glimmering in the darkness with hooded attendants moving round, removing any that had burnt out and adding the newly lit.

The inner surfaces of the monumental arch were covered with sprawling murals showing the Sister putting her own flesh between the enemy and the saint, and in niches on either side stood soaring statues of Sisters of Battle, their hands resting upon their chainswords, their heads bent in a gesture of remembrance.

The next was the Sanguine Gate. Heavy columns held up a monumental dome over the place where Saint Katherine spilt her blood upon the planet, and a small marble shrine was set into the midmost column, marking the site of her wounding.

Last was a vast torii gate, so massive that a morning cloud had caught upon one corner, wreathing the hanging bells with veils of mist.

As Lizbet reached it a great hush fell upon the crowd. A hissing silence that spread backwards through the massed bodies. It took five minutes to reach the rearmost, and then there was the low hum of a crowd, billions strong. But after the roar and tumult, the stillness was sudden. This was the place where Katherine had fought her battle against the arch-heretic Orneus, a psyker of awesome power who drew on the ancient spirits of the planet.

The sky over the Pilgrim Plains suddenly darkened. It was as if a celestial body had slipped before the sun. The chill was abrupt. A billion faces looked upwards. The note of consternation was like an earthquake rumbling over the land.

Only the sight of Lizbet stilled their panic. She hung golden in the air. She tapped her vox-bead. Her mouth was dry, her heart thundering.

Sister Morcada was soaring beside her. She caught the look in Lizbet's eyes.

She felt it too.

'What's happening?' Lizbet hissed across the vox.

Canoness Ysolt's face was white. She shook her head. 'I do not know.'

The sky grew yet darker. It was as if the dawn had been reversed. Wind whipped over the plains as the gloom deepened. A clap of thunder boomed over the plain and a bloody rain began to fall, the gobbets as large as fists, freezing as they fell. There were screams from the crowd as the hailstones broke bones and caved in skulls. The Sisters were already dashing ahead. Panic began to spread as the darkness fell, and there were howling voices high in the air above her head as, one by one, the Seraphim fell like burning torches from the sky.

'Heresy!' Ysolt shouted as voices called out in crazed chanting.

* * *

Lizbet felt impotent. She hung in the air, sword in hand, but there was no enemy she could fight. Rage filled her that this should happen when she was the saint. Along the column of Sisters, boltguns were raised, swords drawn, battle companies formed about their Sisters Superior. They were ready as the darkness thickened about them and the music of the marching bands took on a discordant, sickening note.

The dancing pilgrims lost restraint. Lewd cavorting broke out along the route of the procession, the singing of the pious turned to hellish howling. Or was it laughter? And then reality screamed as it was ripped apart from within.

The tear started half the galaxy away as the world of Cadia fell.

It was a cosmic crisis the like of which had not been seen for over ten thousand years. Around the epicentre, the vortex sucked the souls from every life upon the planet. In an instant all that remained were empty streets, haunted ruins, heaps of corpses.

The rent tore across the material realm, swallowing whole worlds and systems within it.

From the Eye of Terror to the fringes of knowable space, the rip tore sanity apart, extinguished reason. On every world in the scar's path, screams of terror turned to those of ecstasy and pain as entire planets were swallowed in intoxicating clouds or showers of blood.

Macabre scenes were multiplied wherever humanity dwelt. Where hands had been, there were now claws. Where fellowship had once existed, there was deepest depravity. In an instant, the Imperium fractured.

The air above Lizbet turned purple as witchfire freckled the sky. Within the etheric clouds were faces. There were hands as well, pushing against the limits of reality. Clawed, two-fingered, grasping hands. Tentacles with mawed suckers, biting and snapping for flesh.

They were dim, contorted shapes, like half-formed lumps of clay scattered around a potter's studio. Some took the form of maggots. Others were like human foetuses. Others were mere lampreys of emotion – blind, bloodsucking worms seeking release. They seemed to strain and bulge against a hidden barrier, stretched so thin it was translucent.

The skies of Cion sagged over them like the belly of a rotting carcass struggling to contain the putrefaction inside. A single claw punched through from within and tore the sky asunder.

Bolts of unreality crashed to the ground. Lumps of soil started to fly up into the vacuum that was opening above them, and typhoons of moaning winds began to whip across the plains.

There were voices within the storms. Howling, screaming voices.

Tornadoes swirled into ever-tightening circles as they roared over the plains.

The screams of terror rose over the tumult. The violent wind flashed with swirling razors. A soup of human debris whipped into the air. A rain of blood lashed into Lizbet's face. Her nostrils flared in pain and fury. The horror of this moment drove her to a state of catatonia as shapes started to materialise inside the whirlwinds.

The Sisters sang hymns of battle, but their song was drowned out as the fabric of reality tore. The sky was awash with an unholy deluge. Gobbets of corruption rained onto the world as the Neverborn poured through the rent.

Insanity reigned. Pilgrims fell upon each other with vehement fury. Preachers screamed hatred, and holy men were consumed by daemonic fire. A billion voices screamed in unison.

'Not me,' Lizbet hissed. 'Not on this day. I knew that I should not have been chosen!'

She wished that someone else had taken the role of the saint upon themself. But as she hung paralysed by doubt, another voice spoke to her. It was not her own. It was experienced, old and calm. 'Fight, my child. Have faith. Be strong. The Emperor protects!'

Lizbet was filled with fury. Her fingers closed about the handle of Chalybix as she shouted her battle cry, but it was a thin, shrill sound in the thickening air.

In response, the mouths of the pilgrims stretched open. From their lungs came a single shout multiplied across millions of voices.

A scream of wordless hate.

The answer from the Sisters was the bark of bolters. Blades flashed, chainswords raged as their metal teeth shredded flesh and bone.

The Road of Purification was a scene of slaughter even as the forces of the Imperium rallied to their leaders. At one end of the road the Cion Rifles, the Aquarian Guard and the Osiron Revellers massed under the hundreds of banners, the edges of which smoked and smouldered with witch flame.

The crew of *Judgement of Seth* were driven mad and fired upon the tanks that trailed behind it. Sisters and Guardsmen made their stand under the dome of the Sanguine Gate as the roaring daemons raged towards them, axes clutched in blood-red fists.

Sister Hospitaller Gwenet was ministering to the pilgrims on the plains when reality fractured. The pilgrims were driven mad with despair and terror. They dropped their icons, threw down precious bundles of bones, stampeded like terrified animals, trampling the weak and the small, and being trampled in turn as they sought shelter.

Their only hope was the Adepta Sororitas. There were hundreds of Sisters like Gwenet, each one a rock within the maelstrom of madness to which the pilgrims clung.

Gwenet called out prayers as a gale of blood whipped across her face. She quelled her panic. Her faith was like a weighty bulwark, honed and chiselled with years of study, prayer and learning – to guard her at just a moment like this, as terror's tentacles slithered up her spine.

'Stand firm!' she called. 'The God-Emperor protects!'

Her voice was strong and clear as she sang the Gloria Sellam Aureum. Their voices swelled up like a dome of golden light. Waves of unholy darkness boiled and tumbled about them all like waves in a storm, crashing upon each of them and sweeping a few castaways off the rocks of piety.

On one side, rotting Neverborn fell upon them, laughing as their corruption spread, while on the other daemons of blood hunted the pilgrims like wolves, picking at the edges of the flock. Chunks of blood and flesh were flung from feasting jaws and the crowd of pilgrims packed even tighter.

Gwenet's knuckles were white as she held the hands of those about her, who looked to her for strength and aid and sustenance. Their hands reached up for her as if she were an anchor onto which they could cling. They crawled and fought over each other, and those who could not hold on to a hand grasped a foot, or the hem of her robe.

Far across the plains, her eyes were upon the golden star of Lizbet.

She was a lighthouse, a white light shining out amidst the roiling warp storm. But the storm was engulfing them all. Gwenet's eyes glittered with tears as she saw Lizbet's light shine out. And then she turned away from the light, and confronted the darkness that surrounded her.

One by one, the islands of the faithful were overwhelmed by a gathering tide of insanity. Gwenet stood among the last of them, even as they were pulled from her grasp. She knew she was going to die, but she sang in the face of death, hymns and paeans of faith and resolution. She kept encouraging the faithful who clung to her with all the desperation of drowning men. Her song was sublime. She felt a sense of calm, even as the madness intensified into a swirl of blades.

She had given her life to the service of the Emperor. She had healed the sick, terminated the unclean, burnt the heretics.

At the end she felt the storm lashing at her robes. She staggered as it pulled at her, but her song did not falter. She sang the Finis Dierum, a hymn that celebrated the end of days, as the ground gave way beneath her.

Her song ended abruptly as the blades shredded her.

From horizon to horizon was filth and corruption. Ysolt wept tears of fury as daemons manifested all about her. They were a flood of depravity, gibbering, insane monsters with fanged maws and clawed, suckered limbs.

She fought for what might have been aeons or bare moments, and felt as though she were alone, battling across a landscape awash with a rotting soup of blood and entrails. Putrid maggots rose wriggling to the surface, popping like bubbles and transforming into clouds of hissing flies. She was witness to horrors no sane mind could absorb.

Ysolt fought her way through the insanity of the daemon-infested hellscape. But there were too many hideous daemons with lashing tails and bat wings, surrounded by a fog of corruption. She cut them down, but they were too numerous, too unfeeling.

The host of daemons fell on her like hyenas and she lashed about, bleeding from a dozen wounds. She called on the God-Emperor, but she could feel His power draining out of her. It was as if the sun had set, and His light was quickly failing.

There were now only a bare handful of Sisters where once there had been thousands. The twins, Brace and Morcada; Celestian Alird, who carried her holy banner; and Elaifor the Pure, whose blade dripped unholy ichor.

'Leave me,' she told the Sisters as she looked out upon the floor of daemons that was rising about them. 'I am tainted.'

They formed a ring about their canoness, refused to leave her behind as the surviving Sisters fought their way to her.

Ysolt ripped the broken plates of her armour away and saw boils and maggots eating at her flesh. It was an unholy corruption, rising up her legs. Hospitaller Avalla of the Ebon Sword put her hand to the depravity, and only the strength of their combined prayers held the poison at bay.

Ysolt let out a cry of grief and despair. She had been tested and she had failed, and in her pride she had been struck down and maimed.

iii

Sister Lizbet felt it before she saw it. It was a dread wave, a sickening nausea. She turned as the Bolt began to tilt. Fragments sheared off the granite rock and tumbled into the habs below, and from beneath she could see a dark form taking shape from the maelstrom of blood.

It was a behemoth of brass and flame and iron with legs like hab-blocks, its titanic form framed by a pair of black, bat-like wings. Eyes blazing like hot coals, its first breath for five thousand years sucked the souls of countless pilgrims out of their bodies. Lifting a double-headed axe to the heavens, it bellowed in bloody rapture, howling its name over and over at the sky through fanged jaws that roared fire.

Gloranthrax was free, and the daemon had woken to hunger – and before it lay the Pilgrim Plains, packed with prey.

First to die was a Penitent Engine. It was batted aside with the massive axe and sent flying through the air, crashing back down to the ground and shedding arms and metal casing. Another charged and was knocked aside in the same manner, skidding in a ruin of limbs.

Gloranthrax howled in bloody exultation as the golden figure of Lizbet flew towards it, Chalybix glowing like a shaft of sunlight.

It had waited five thousand years for this moment. The earth shook as it crashed towards her, calling her name with a dreadful voice that was half rage and half the call of a long-abandoned lover.

The axe burst into flames as it swung.

With divine strength Lizbet parried the first blow with Chalybix. She stopped the second swing, and the third.

Gloranthrax bellowed.

With each breath it grew yet stronger as the warp's influence waxed, and the flame of the daemonic axe came closer to her with every swing. Across the plain, the Militarum and pilgrims were consumed by insanity. Neverborn melded with their human hosts and set upon each other with wild blows. Brother fell upon brother, fathers slaughtered wives, and the flame of faith flickered and died.

The end of this world had come.

Part Six

Now

Imperium Nihilus

'Why have you cast us down, O Lord? the hopeful called,
Why are we plunged into turmoil?
Rely not upon hope, the God-Emperor answered.
Trust in blade and bolter, and righteous anger.'

– The Book of Thor

í

Sister Lanete summoned Aebram. He came at once.

'Your man…' she started.

'Wythers?'

'Yes. He is suitable for incarceration.'

'Good,' he said.

'You understand that any interred within my engines are sinners who are beyond clemency. We grant them the absolution of extinction.'

Aebram paused. 'He will die fighting?'

'I can assure you of that.'

'Good. Thank you. That is all he wanted.'

There was a pause.

'May I speak to him before he goes?'

They had left the big man slumped against the wall. His system had been dragged off its nitra-chem addiction, but it had left his nerves shredded. He sat on the press-metal floors, his knees drawn up before him and his mag-cuffed hands set against his temples, holding the mane of hair back from his face.

'Wythers,' the Marshal said.

Wythers looked up through a face distorted with swellings, his one good eye bloodshot, with clots sprawling in the corner. Wythers did not twitch or look away, but held the commissar's steel gaze.

'Marshal,' he said. Wythers and the Marshal had faced down all manner of enemies, but now, he felt, something had changed. 'Is this it?' he said.

The Marshal nodded.

'Are you going to shoot me?'

The Marshal shook his head. 'No. The Sisters have another way you might serve.'

A shudder went through Wythers. That was all he wanted. 'How?'

'There is a machine that will march into battle beside them. I have seen them. It will allow you to carry death to the enemy.'

Wythers used both his manacled hands to push his hair back. The chems had left him a shell of a man, his skin aged and grey. He'd lost a lot of weight, the Marshal saw. In fact, he looked like his clothes were hanging off him.

'Will it hurt?' he asked in a bare croak.

The Marshal paused. He had once seen a Penitent Engine close up. The interred body had hung, crucified in the crucible at the front of the walker, scraps of penal legionnaire uniform caught by the iron clamps and heavy padlocks that held it about the ankles, neck, waist and wrists.

The Marshal nodded. 'It reminds you of your sins.'

'All of them?'

'All of them.'

Wythers' hands were shaking. 'Any nitra-chems?'

'No.'

'Shit.' Wythers forced a smile. 'So this will be the end?'

'Yes,' the Marshal said.

Wythers wiped his eye with the heel of his palm as the Marshal put his hand out and pulled Wythers to his feet. Wythers was a good foot taller than him. He tried to salute, but the mag-cuffs made the gesture impossible.

'Good luck,' the Marshal said.

Wythers smiled, but his face was pale, and his hands were trembling. 'Thank you, sir.' He paused for a moment, thinking. 'Who leads the regiment now?'

'Salem.'

Wythers raised an eyebrow. 'I'm surprised. I thought it would be Chalice. Who are the others?'

'Umbata. Gred. Heba. And we need a replacement for Dokona.'

'Dokona's dead?'

Aebram nodded.

'Who killed him?'

'You,' Aebram said.

Wythers said nothing. The Marshal could see how he felt. But here, at the end, Wythers was more lucid than he had been for years. The Marshal forced a smile. 'I've missed you.'

'I've missed me too,' Wythers said.

The Marshal laughed. 'The Emperor protects.'

'And He judges,' Wythers said.

Four Sisters of the Order of Our Martyred Lady came to take Wythers away.

The Marshal stood alone to watch. Wythers had to bow to pass under the door lintel as he was taken to the mag-lift. Wythers turned so that his back was against the far wall and he was staring back down the corridor to the Marshal.

Aebram lifted a hand, not in the sign of the aquila, or even in a salute, but in a friendly gesture of parting, from one man to another.

The doors closed, the lift dropped down into the bowels of the cathedrum, and the Marshal turned away with a sigh.

News spread through the legionnaires that Wythers had been taken away. A sombre mood hung over them all. Chalice and his Dogs returned to the hangar. As they arrived, Colonel Salem was standing within the door to meet him.

'He's gone?' Salem said.

Major Chalice nodded. 'Yup. Gone.'

Colonel Salem sighed. 'I'll miss the old bastard.' He took a crumpled brown paper packet of lho-sticks from his breast pocket and offered one to Chalice.

Chalice shook his head. He wasn't stupid.

Colonel Salem took one for himself, put the packet back into his pocket, and then lit the stick, blue smoke wreathing about his head.

'I'm offended you don't trust me,' Salem said.

Chalice felt Salem's Dogs gathering behind him. One of them shoved Shin.

'Hey!' Shin shouted.

Chalice didn't need to count. He only had six Dogs. Salem had over twenty.

There was a scuffle as Chalice's men were shoved away. Chalice started to run, but Salem's lot caught him. It took four of them to hold him tight.

They dragged him to Salem and the colonel smiled as he smoked his lho-stick.

Salem's smile was chilling. 'Now, Mr. Miracle. What was it you said to me on Ayaan?'

Chalice tried to break free, but he ended up pinned to the ground with Salem kneeling by his side.

'"Yes. I think I can",' Salem said.

He took a long drag, until the embers glowed red. He exhaled smoke as he savoured those words. 'I don't like that, major. It's what they would call insubordination…'

Chalice spat his fury, but there was nothing he could do. Salem brought the glowing embers close to Chalice's face and his men held his head still as Salem forced one of his eyes open. There was a wet sizzle as Salem stabbed the hot embers into the pupil.

Wythers trembled as the lift descended. He didn't want anyone to think it was nerves.

'Stimms,' he said, but none of the Sisters were listening.

At last the descent ended. The grate door slid open and his one good eye blinked at the sudden light, as ungentle hands took him by each elbow and moved him forwards. Each footstep was a struggle, and he tripped on the ledge. They caught him with iron fingers.

All Wythers could think about was nitra-chems.

His mouth was dry. The tremors were coming on again. His mag-cuffs rattled about his wrists.

Wythers closed his eyes and inhaled deeply. There was so much in that one long breath. His stomach lurched. He started to unpick the scents. There was the metallic smell of power armour, the greasy tang of holy unguents. But there were other odours too. The lingering scent of sandalwood incense, a bookish smell, carbolic, counterseptic creams.

He felt as awkward and uncomfortable as an abhuman. But there was something else as well… He couldn't quite pinpoint it.

No one spoke to him. He was as good as dead. They walked

him along a press-metal corridor. To either side were dark, vaulting chambers, the alcoves lit by candlelight. He could see the shapes of metallic bodies standing twenty feet above him. And at the front of each hung a penitent.

They pushed him onwards at a rapid pace. They led him along the corridor, the vaulted ceiling lost in shadows. From ahead an arc light crackled, throwing out a stark blue-white glare. He could see a menial dressed in a heavy leather apron, a dark-slitted visored helmet covering her face. Wythers saw the thing that she was working on, and his mouth went dry.

It was a Penitent Engine, standing tall above him. The body chamber was empty.

A shroud lay at the side. The body within it had just been cut down, and fresh manacles were being welded into place.

'Still,' a voice said.

Hands pushed him down and he fell to his knees. He felt cold metal touch the nape of his neck and tensed.

A lock of hair fell onto his shoulders. And another. The cutters worked their way up his head, cutting strips of hair away. A finger under his chin lifted his head. They started again at his forehead and moved backwards towards his crown. They caught a couple of times on the matted hair, and his whole head was jerked back.

He felt blood start to run down his scalp. The skin was suddenly exposed. The hands lifted him up and he saw the machine again. It was scratched and pitted, but it was the weapons that caught his attention.

Each arm ended with an underslung buzz saw. Above those were a pair of flamer nozzles, the metal distorted and discoloured purple. He could smell the promethium.

He would now wield these.

The baser levels of his nature stirred. Now he would kill in the name of the God-Emperor. Hands gripped him on either side and manoeuvred him into position. His hands were locked into place, the metal clamp closed about his neck. The clunk of locks sealed him in and then the arc torch flared as the clamps on his ankles were welded shut.

He looked across to the opposite alcove, where another penitent hung in their rigging. The face was twisted in a rictus of pain.

The arc torch flared at his bare ankles and Wythers gritted his teeth as it crackled. Each time his flesh burnt and began to smoke. He snarled with pain as someone started to recite the Blessing of Internment. A censer was being waved around the chamber. The welder climbed up next to him. She had taken off her helmet, revealing a shaven head covered with fine white stubble. Through it he could see inked emblems of her Order and the white streaks of old scars.

A servitor gantry rolled towards them, bearing an old crone with a red candle. She pressed prayer strips about his cage, her arm a stump fashioned as a brass seal, a fleur-de-lys surrounded with High Gothic text.

She had one eye, the other augmented with a red-glowing orb. She had a busy, brusque manner. He wanted to speak to her, but knew that it would not be acceptable. She mumbled prayers as the last strip went upon his bare chest, affixed with searing hot wax.

A second woman clambered up the gantry. She had short, bleached hair, and held a stud-gun in one hand and holy strips in the other.

'I am Sister Superior Lanete,' she said. 'This was your name.'

Lanete put one of the strips to his bare chest, pressed it down and pulled the stud-gun's trigger. 'And these were the crimes for which you were condemned.'

He grunted as each metal staple pinned the crimes to his flesh. At last, she slung the tool onto her belt.

He tried to joke. 'That's all of them?'

The woman squinted at him. 'I doubt it.'

Sister Lanete reached up and brought the neural amplifier down onto his head. He flinched as the cap settled over his scalp. She screwed the cap tight. He heard the metallic clang of gears and levers, and something suddenly pressed against each of his eyes.

'That hurts,' he spat, but the pressure grew even worse. He swallowed and felt the raw wounds tug as the gantry was pulled back.

'Ready?' a voice called out. The speaker was not addressing him.

'In the Emperor's name,' the woman next to him said.

Wythers told himself he was ready, puffing out his cheeks as he waited for whatever came next.

Lanete pulled the last lever.

The neural implants pierced his eyeballs and plunged into the wet fat of his brain.

Wythers screamed as he fought and struggled against the pain, tearing the flesh about his wrists and ankles, but the clamps held him rigid. Blood ran in rivulets down his face.

The machine-spirit was not easily shocked. It savoured the anger as pain amplifiers followed the neural pathways, searching for the strongest emotions of guilt and self-recrimination. His crimes, his fears, his phobias – the things that made him feel deep shame.

Wythers writhed as the engine absorbed him into itself, wiring its rage-generators into this human battery. He was the prey.

The ravenous machine would devour it all, and there was plenty to feast upon.

* * *

Chalice left a bloody smear as he crawled across the metal plating, his broken lips hissing prayers.

Salem's lackeys had broken his fingers one by one, but he gritted his teeth against the pain. He used his knees to propel him towards his men. No one helped him. That was not the Dogs' way.

Shin and the rest of the men watched him crawl.

At last Chalice made it, and they clustered around him, dragging him to safety.

Blood was running from his nose. He spat out a fragment of tooth. 'Get Sawbones!'

ii

The discovery of Aoid's Sepulchre gave new purpose to Albreda's mission, but as the *Daughter of the Emperor* progressed along the pilgrimage route, hope began to fade once more.

It took them from Aoid's Sepulchre to the Surtelo System, where Katherine had removed the poison from the world of Xirior. But the toxic atmosphere and carnivorous jungles had returned, and the landing parties who went down to secure the holy spots were forced to abandon the world, bringing back their dead.

Next was Praesteum's Forge, where Saint Katherine had cleansed the Daughters of the Pallid Lord and set up temples and chapels to the God-Emperor in their stead. But the world had suffered Exterminatus, and the Sisters could only salvage the altar-stone from the Great Chapel, set amidst the ice of the southern pole.

The stone was brought back to the craft, and the pieces set up in the Great Prayer Hall. But in the mission they had lost five Sisters to a void breach, and only recovered the remains of three of the dead.

Soon afterwards, they become aware that unidentified craft were following them along the route. They kept well back, on the edge of the system, or faded in and out of the immaterium.

But there was no doubt. The light of their faith was drawing the forces of heresy to them, as a light in the depths will draw out unholy creatures of the darkness.

Nedes Citadel was a voidport that controlled the Straits of Infirius' Fall. It was an ancient structure, shaped like a cartwheel, with spokes running out from a central hub. It was clear that the citadel was held against them. They had barely transitioned when the augurs lit up, indicating that the citadel's great defence batteries were targeting them.

Their void shields crackled to life, and they returned fire. Palatine Albreda was presented with a choice: fight or flight.

'We can take it,' Dovere advised her. 'But the citadel was a challenge even for Saint Katherine's forces, and she had a fleet behind her. We are but one ship.'

The Sisters gathered for prayer. They were hungry for battle, and Albreda decided that they should fight.

The *Daughter of the Emperor*'s shield generators were brought to full power as she moved towards the citadel, cutting a way through minefields.

The void battle raged until the citadel's guns fell suddenly silent. *An invitation*, thought Albreda. She was inclined to accept.

Albreda ordered boarding parties to be prepared. Two hundred Sisters were sent aboard a battle chapel.

Sister Superior Helewise prepared herself for combat as she stood with her Sisters. A voice spoke out from a laud hailer, telling the Sisters to prepare to fight a transhuman foe.

She closed her eyes, and thanked the God-Emperor for this opportunity.

'Astartes,' Morgandrie said. She had chosen a multi-melta in place of her usual heavy bolter for this attack.

Helewise nodded. She had long awaited this moment. She remembered the tomb of Aoid's Sepulchre, and steeled herself with righteous fury.

The battle chapel slammed into the gantry-spines that jutted out from the central hub, meltas blasting a hole through the superstructure. The interior of the craft was dark and cold and airless as the Battle Sisters entered its corridors.

Across the vox they recited prayers of battle and vows of vengeance against traitors as the squads separated. Helewise's squad headed for the centre of the structure, seeking out the fiercest resistance.

Morgandrie blasted a way through a series of void locks. The citadel's corridors were deserted. They rang with distant howling.

'What manner of Astartes is this?' Morgandrie asked.

Helewise did not know. 'I am sure we will soon find out.'

The howling grew steadily louder.

'*Ave Imperialis!*' Helewise said, as the bestial sound came yet closer.

She took a position before her squad as its source burst around the far end of the corridor.

A corrupted Space Marine. He sprinted down the corridor, a chainaxe within each fist, both of them gunning furiously as he hurtled towards them.

Helewise had never got used to the size and speed of the Space Marines. Their bodies were genhanced to make them the ultimate weapon of war. This one combined that with an astonishing rage.

'Prepare for close combat!' Helewise shouted. 'Faith and courage!'

Blue voltaic light crackled over Reckoning's surface as she engaged the power stud.

The ancient broadsword balanced perfectly in her hand. It was as eager as she was to cross blades with this heretical beast.

The corridor was three hundred feet long, but her foe crossed the distance between them in a matter of seconds, wordless hatred spewing from its vox-grille. She had expected it to strike with one axe first, but it swung both weapons at her, sending her reeling as she narrowly managed to parry.

The Chaos Space Marine did not pause. It came on without care to defend itself, attacking with blow after blow until she could barely raise Reckoning in defence.

Even she, Helewise, started to doubt herself.

She could feel Morgandrie behind her. 'Stand aside!' she hissed.

Helewise was fighting too desperately to answer with words. Her only response was a grunt of pain as one of the blows landed, spinning steel teeth scouring across her armour. The strikes rained down on her. She was only human, but she was standing before this eight-foot-tall monster, and she was still alive.

The seconds dragged on with terrible slowness. Each moment brought a flurry of attacks, but Reckoning caught them, doing just enough to push them aside.

She was noble-born, trained from birth with blade and bolter, and yet she felt that all she could do was parry and retreat to stay alive. She ducked under another wild swipe, but as she did so a power-armoured boot connected with her helmet. There was an instant of confusion as she flew to the ground, but she quickly regained her senses. She tasted blood.

She rolled away a split second later as a chainaxe slammed into the floor, the weapon swung with such force that it stuck deep within the metal plating.

'Back!' she told her Sisters as she swayed to her feet. 'I have this.'

She felt their faith flow through her as they chanted a battle hymn. She gripped Reckoning with both hands and joined them. 'From the lightning and the tempest!' she whispered to herself. 'Our Emperor, deliver us!'

The heretic came at her, his remaining chainaxe swinging. Helewise readied herself. She knew what she was up against now. She had thought that the Astartes were sublime blade masters, but there was no grace to this battle. It was berserk strength against skill. Genhanced against human. Rage against faith.

The heretic Space Marine let out animal snarls, punctuating each kick and swing. Helewise could feel her body slowing, even as her enemy came on. He was not tiring, she realised, and yet she was. She passed up a chance to run him through. It would not kill him quickly enough, and then she would be within his arms' reach, an embrace she knew she would not survive.

No, she thought, *I have to kill him.* She lost focus for a moment, and he tried to grab her sword with his free hand.

She only just held on as the powerblade bit. She felt a cold sweat break out over her skin.

'Let us end him,' Morgandrie voxed.

'No,' Helewise said.

The words of the Fede Imperialis kept chiming in her head. Her Sisters spoke louder and louder, and she knew her moment when it came.

From the scourge of the Kraken, from the begetting of daemons… from the blasphemy of the fallen.

For Aoid's Sepulchre, Helewise thought, and let out a shout of pent-up anger.

And swung.

* * *

Justin D Hill

The citadel had been largely abandoned in the face of the Sororitas' attack. Why, the Sisters did not know – but they scoured the craft, slaughtered thralls and the corrupted servitors, and set holy wards upon the void-craft.

A handful of thralls were brought back so that they could be turned over to the Sisters Dogmata.

All the Sisters wanted to see the token that Helewise had brought from her battle.

They all marvelled at the size of the severed head. It was monstrous in its gruesome detail, its acidic blood burning into the metal plating.

Palatine Albreda came down to greet them. Helewise had removed her helmet. The force of the traitor's kick had slammed her head against the inside and cut open the skin of her cheek.

'The citadel was abandoned, but they left this one behind,' she said, throwing the head onto the floor.

'Crimson Slaughter,' Albreda said, recognising the icons carved into the heretic's flesh.

Helewise nodded. She had barely survived. But faith had given her strength. 'There have to be more of them.'

After her wound had been stapled closed, Helewise meditated upon her fight with the Heretic Astartes. She had expected skill, but had met with brute power instead.

She prayed that night with Morgandrie.

Afterwards, Morgandrie said, 'How is it that so many of the Adeptus Astartes have fallen to the whispers of heresy... and yet, we, unaltered women, do not? Do they not mortify themselves, or steel their hearts with prayer?'

Helewise considered the question. It was one that she had thought about many times. 'They are proud,' she said, 'and their pride leads them astray.'

Morgandrie paused. 'Are we not proud?'

Helewise thought about that. She was proud. She was proud of her lineage, her skill with blade and bolter; she was proud of her faith, her conviction, her leadership on and off the battle-field. 'We are,' she said. 'We are not so strong of body, but our strength comes from elsewhere.'

Helewise's pride, however, was wounded. That night she woke with a start and remembered the moment her foe had almost wrenched Reckoning from her grip. It was a back-alley move. A brawler's battle style, and she should have trained for that.

She recriminated herself for her pride, her foolishness, but the truth was there was no servitor, or number of servitors, that could bring even a fraction of the speed and danger of a Space Marine.

She meditated upon her pride as they processed along the Pilgrimage of Fire. Each of the venerated worlds had been stripped of humanity, and the sanctified places defiled.

It became clear why the citadel had been abandoned as they reached the next sector and found a heretic fleet waiting for them. The first was a picket of a few escorts that were swiftly destroyed. But with each warp transit, they faced bigger and bigger foes. On the fifth re-entry, at Diablo Prime, there was a Crimson Slaughter cruiser buried within the fleet.

But, for some reason, the enemy held off and disengaged into the vast emptiness of the warp.

'I think our faith is drawing them to us,' Albreda said.

'They're hunting us...' Lanete said, as the senior Sisters met for prayers.

'Perhaps,' Helewise said. 'Or driving us on.'

Albreda nodded. She had prayed on both these eventualities. 'We do not know, but we are committed to the pilgrimage. We must continue on that journey. To turn away and pursue our foes would be a neglection of our holy vows.'

Navigator Hemponia, who had been sitting in the corner listening, said, 'Your words chill me. But continuation is not without its own dangers. When we move through the warp, I feel the presence of an evil entity stalking us.'

They all looked to Albreda for a decision. The Palatine had the *Confessions of Dogmatism* lying in her lap. She put her finger on the page and looked down.

She read the verse before her and felt assured. 'We hold onto the course of the pilgrimage. The road lies before us, and we must follow, regardless of the danger.'

The next time they re-entered realspace it was to an ambush. The *Daughter of the Emperor* was rammed by a cruiser, which tore a great hole in the ancient vessel and damaged the shield generators.

Clawed boarding craft followed up, with the dread shapes of Chaos emblazoned upon them. Helewise was chosen to lead the teams that repelled the foe. The boarding craft slammed into the sacred hull and bored a hole through the void armour, like a tick seeking the soft flesh within.

Helewise ran her squad at a sprint to locate the point of assault. Boarders could do untold damage if they located the ship's vital systems. The location of attack was relayed to her via vox: ventilation shaft nine, beside the dorsal laud hailers.

Their boots pounded on the metal decking. They could hear the heartbeat of the ship thudding at battle pace and intensity, the scream of melta cutters, the thunder of battle.

They reached the ventilation chamber, and readied themselves.

'Our Emperor, deliver us!' Helewise hissed, as she slammed the void hatch open.

The chamber was unlit. Splashes of incandescent metal were visible in the darkness, showing the blunt snout of the boarding craft thrust through the melted hole. The boarding ramps were open...

Bolt-rounds slammed into Ruslana, detonating against her power armour.

Helewise shouted a warning as the boarders appeared.

They were vast, horned shapes, perversions of the Emperor's blessed design, the epitome of all that was unholy.

Morgandrie roared hatred as her heavy bolter barked, filling the chamber with shrapnel. Helewise's first shot hit a Space Marine in the visor. It punched straight through into the head of her foe, exploding within the helmet and decapitating the heretic.

A tentacle-armed warrior came behind, underslung flamer filling the corridor with swirling flames and roiling black smoke.

Helewise strode into it, the temperature dampeners of her suit screaming into action.

The Traitor Space Marine loomed up, filling the corridor like a wall of ceramite. A blade was swinging down towards her head. She had only a moment to parry, and she was once again astonished by the strength of these transhuman warriors.

She ducked and swung, and he parried her blow, his pistol whipping down to smash into her helmet. It knocked her sideways and she slammed into the ducting. Her body was protected by the power armour, but her right lens was shattered. She was fighting with one eye blind.

'Noxious witch!' the Astartes snarled. 'The False Emperor does not protect you. He does not care. He is a rotting corpse!'

Helewise let the words rouse her fury, parrying his killing blow then a second strike, thwarting him each time he tried to spear her through. He drove her back, but she was getting the measure of him. Her foe had every advantage. Height, size, strength and fury.

But she had the God-Emperor.

And she believed.

'You betrayed your vows!' she roared at him, and he laughed at her.

'Ignorant woman! Vows are not chains!'

She parried a fourth blow and stepped in, the sword lancing in through his guard and slicing through the cabling at his gut. Viscous coolants splattered over his thighs. He was so bent on killing her that he barely slowed. He chopped down at her, again and again, like an axeman hacking at a lump of timber.

Her powerblade crackled and sizzled as the stains about his waist grew darker, and his movements started to slow. He lumbered forwards, struggling to keep control of his suit as its systems started to shut down. With satisfaction, she saw him realise that he was a dead man walking.

With a roar of righteousness she swung.

The blade sliced through his pauldron, and into his neck.

His head fell backwards while his torso tumbled towards her, splashing her armour in arterial blood.

She looked at the remains of her foe, and felt a surge of pride rise through her. She had met and matched a real blade master, and more than that...

'I felt Him!' Helewise hissed. She gripped Morgandrie's arm. 'He is with us. Can you feel Him?'

Morgandrie sounded shell-shocked. 'Not yet.'

'He is with us!' Helewise hissed. 'Come, let us hunt!'

Fights were raging across the Sisters' cathedrum. It was hours before the threat of boarding had passed, and they could assess the damage.

Six Heretic Astartes had been killed, and a host of heretical cultists.

In return they had lost over twenty Sisters. Their corpses piled up before the gates to their devotional chambers.

The bodies of the martyrs were laid out in honour, as their names were inscribed upon the prayer wheel. The attackers were dumped into the plasma generators, which purged their physical remains in holy fire.

But Helewise had not been the only one to feel His will. Those like her glowed with renewed belief, and that night, when they met to sing hymns of victory, the diminished assembly sang out with renewed vigour.

Helewise returned to her armoury, where her attendants waited. Her armour was removed, piece by piece, the damaged sections set aside for repair and purification. Her wound was sutured closed then blessed and smeared with counterseptics.

'Done?' she said as the attendants stepped away.

They bowed as she marched out, and already a fresh suit of armour was being hauled up from the ancient armouries.

iii

As they prepared for the next jump, Sister Dovere distracted herself by scouring the cathedrum's microfiche librarium for details of the Pilgrimage of Fire. There were diaries of ancient Sisters and pilgrims, and a series of reports from Navy officers who delighted in detailing the dangerous approaches, and how close they had come to a rocky oblivion exiting from the warp too close to the system's inner Oort cloud.

The details provided a respite from the constant threat of warp-borne death. The cogitators were full of histories written by those who had taken part in the pilgrimage and those who had followed the route in years past. But she also uncovered pilgrim diaries, eyewitness accounts and Ecclesiarchy guides that listed the clothes a devout participant should wear and the prayers they should intone.

She sifted through the data. Each night she reran the route, boarding pilgrim barges at Aoid's Sepulchre and taking the short hop to Sohiri. Diaries spoke with horror of near-death entries from the warp. The Sohiri Mandeville point was notoriously close to the Oort cloud – a tumbling mass of asteroids that had been liberally mined. But all of them spoke in awe of Saint Katherine's feat of bringing her fleet safely in to attack the hollowed-out asteroids, which had been fitted with generators and lance relays.

She dreamt of the pilgrimage, waking up at night unsure if she was on the *Daughter of the Emperor* or landing on the Pilgrim Plains on Cion. She saw herself upon void-barges and private packet ships plying the short void hops, carrying millions of the pure and regretful from planet to planet, following the saint's pursuit of the Mnestteus Witch-cult. All the diaries showed that the pilgrimage was the culmination of a lifetime's prayer. Many of the diaries came to abrupt ends – the faith had cost the authors their lives. But death on pilgrimage was considered a great blessing, for past misdeeds were wiped clean.

They walked in the very tunnels that Saint Katherine had trodden, saw the ancient melta-scars, walls pockmarked by bolter fire, the burnt-out defences. All of them wrote at length of the deep impression these visits had made.

After five thousand years, each of these planets had become bloated with faith. The pilgrims all noted how they were covered in abbeys, medicae facilities, oratories, spires and hostel houses for every type of Imperial pilgrim – from pious nobility to the barefoot mendicants who spent a lifetime completing the journey, begging passage from planet to planet. There were chapels, halls of remembrance and regimental chantries. There were marble sanctuaries, the Navy bethel-chambers and plains filled with forests of ornate tombs, which, as space had run out, had gone underground with miles upon miles of quiet catacombs. Their wall-niches were filled with the carefully wrapped bones of the dead and burnt ashes, or for many millions, their names only, carved into plaques on the wall.

Each of these worlds had once been heavy with tokens, keepsakes and mementos left by grateful supplicants: the lasrifle of a Guardsman who lay in a crater and prayed to survive the hell that they were in; the doll of a cherished child afflicted with scales or unwanted appendages, who was cured of their ailment; the wedding ring from a grateful widower, who knew he had been blessed with a long and content marriage; the veil of a young woman, married into a noble family; a locket with the painted images of a pair of devoted lovers separated by life, class, fashion, war, warp travel or time.

Dovere made sure she was at the viewports at the moment they re-entered realspace.

She wondered at how little had changed. Hope flared within her as she saw how all was as the pilgrims had described it. The wall of asteroids, the burnt-out husks of orbital gun platforms and, here and there, the ancient mines, their spheres strung together with vast iron-linked chains. Then they slid through the narrow gap, and suddenly the system opened up before them, the dull red light of the local star staring balefully out.

The *Daughter of the Emperor* processed along the ancient pilgrimage route and Dovere took it all in.

She held her breath as she watched. The Sohiri System was renowned for being beautiful, dominated by a pair of great gas giants. The pilgrims had all mentioned these two huge planets, both slowly shedding their orbiting atmospheres, which corkscrewed between them, forming a whorl of coloured gases swirling about each other.

As they passed through the Oort cloud, Dovere saw them, the gigantic worlds' baleful gravities making the *Daughter of the Emperor*'s structure creak and moan. And then they were through another scattered asteroid belt, and they held their breaths as Sohiri swept into view.

The planet emerged from behind the red nimbus of the sun. It was hard to see it at first, its colour hidden in the glare. But the clearer it became, the more Dovere's heart fell. Sohiri had been described as being the most breathtaking sight of the whole pilgrimage. It had been a sapphire of a planet, hanging trans-cendent blue in the darkness. But she saw now that the planet was no longer so. It was black, like a lump of seared rock, turning slowly on its axis.

At Kald, Saint Katherine had broken the wychspell about the local sun and thrown back the darkness. Now, the local sun had been destroyed, and the world had been plunged into an eternal night. In Ituna, where she had slain the warlord twins Xaglun and Kaenictrum, the planet had been broken in two, the sundered pieces tumbling about each other in a death spiral. The heretics knew their histories. Each world was defiled in a way that related to the original acts that Saint Katherine had performed. Time and again, the Sisters cleansed the worlds of heresy and set up altars and statues to the Imperial creed.

The Sisters saw the desecration and mourned, yet their faith was not dimmed. It shone out through the immaterium, luring the Neverborn towards it.

'We are being pursued,' Navigator Hemponia told Canoness Albreda. 'And our pursuers are gathering in both number and power.'

Albreda nodded and called her Celestians to attend her. Some argued for them to make a stand, and sacrifice themselves in a battle against the traitors. They ran over familiar arguments. It went against the Sisters' fighting spirit to avoid battle like this.

But Helewise said, 'Palatine Albreda, we will all die in battle, and we accept that. Our deaths will come. The Emperor has set us upon the Pilgrimage of Fire, and we cannot choose to turn aside without scorning the trial He has set before us.

'Let us complete the pilgrimage, and once we have reached Holy Cion, then let us stand and face our pursuers.'

In the end Albreda brought the instruction to Navigator Hemponia, who was now as bent and wizened as an old crone. Her breaths were coming in short, rapid bursts. She closed her eyes and made the sign of the aquila. 'If that is your will...'

'It is,' Albreda said. 'Can we make it?'

Hemponia closed her eyes and pressed her fingers to her temples. 'I will do my best.'

Albreda knelt by her side. She had prayer beads wrapped tightly about her fingers and closed her eyes in prayer. She thought of the destruction they had found so far, and when she thought of what they might find on Holy Cion, her heart was full of foreboding.

The *Daughter of the Emperor* was preparing for the last jump to Holy Cion when klaxons abruptly wailed out. On the bridge, augurs lit up with sudden contacts – they had lingered too long. Weapon systems were charged and shield generators whined into action as defence batteries flared to life, searching for targets.

The void-cathedrum was caught in a ring of enemy craft. She fought like a cornered she-wolf, weapons spitting ordnance out at the most dangerous of their foes as her crew laboured to reload and fire, while Sisters repelled every attempt at boarding with flamer and melta.

First to charge was a slope-browed grand cruiser, an old slugger of a craft racing in to unleash terrifying broadsides at short range. The *Daughter of the Emperor*'s main armament swung slowly round, the magma warheads being blessed and loaded into the monstrous bombardment cannon.

The first shot hit the slugger amidships, the warhead ripping a vast hole in its side. It slewed sideways, venting atmosphere that froze into clouds of ice, bodies and debris. As the craft drifted it exposed its flanks, and even as it started to pound ordnance towards the Sisters' craft, a second shot delivered the coup de grace.

A squadron of heretic escorts were turned into fireballs under the incessant salvos of lance shots. From the other direction a fireship accelerated towards them, trailing fumes into the void. The course was a suicide mission, meant to blast a hole in the sacred craft.

Blessed armaments tore the bridge away, but the craft ploughed towards them, shedding fragments as it ran into a hail of ordnance.

There were shouts of alarm throughout the *Daughter of the Emperor* as defence turrets swung round, the accelerating fireship coming apart in a rain of debris that slammed into the Sisters' craft.

The way towards the Mandeville point was open, and they fled towards it, the heretic fleet falling behind.

There was no time for augurs, or blessings. They would have to make the jump, even though Navigator Hemponia was almost burnt out. Albreda knelt next to her.

'We cannot run,' Hemponia whispered. 'They will follow us. Your souls shine out. Your faith is like a beacon drawing the denizens of the warp. They swarm about us. Each time we jump into the warp, more are drawn to us. We can see the heretic fleet, but a gathering host of Neverborn is the greater threat.'

'Then we will face it at Holy Cion.'

Hemponia nodded.

The sound of prayer rose up through the craft as Hemponia made ready for the final jump. The doors of her chamber were sealed and locked. She was alone, except for the Palatine, who knelt at the top of the dais. Hemponia walked slowly up the carpeted steps, then turned and settled herself into the throne, adjusting the skirts of her robes.

The canoness' head was lowered. 'Are you ready?' Hemponia said.

'I am.'

Hemponia readied herself, untying the band about her head with both hands.

The cloth came away, and her third eye blinked against the sudden light, before catching its focus.

Her fingers tightened upon the Palatine's own, as her other hand reached for the inlaid lever that would ignite the Geller field. It was cold in her palm. Her fingers gripped it; she could feel her heartbeat starting to quicken as she paused for a moment, said a silent prayer and then pulled it back.

But nothing happened.

The Geller-field generator had been damaged in the battle.

'How long will repairs take?' Albreda demanded. But there was no way to answer such a question.

Albreda joined the other Sisters in the prayer hall. This was a moment that would need a great act of faith.

Prayers were ordered across the whole craft, and the corridors of the *Daughter of the Emperor* rang to desperate chanting.

The Marshal marched into the Dogs' hangar and lined them up. They were not prayerful men, and many could not read, but Mercy Cody stood before them, prayer book in hand, reading each line aloud so that the Dogs could repeat it in turn.

The whole process started with an air of angry defiance. They were Dogs. No one had expected them to worship before and none of them were used to organised prayer. The words were unfamiliar, and even though they were the lowest of the low, they resented the abject note in many of the prayers exalting the God-Emperor.

The Marshal paced slowly along the lines, and wherever he went the volume lifted. None of them dared to be singled out, or attract his ire. Even Colonel Salem looked troubled by the prayer. 'The God-Emperor can't hear you!' he told them. 'You have to shout!'

They did as they were told. They closed their eyes and yelled, and the troubled souls found solace in the roaring out of Imperial prayers.

'Though we march into the heart of darkness,
With faith as our shield, and conviction in our cause,
We shall smash through the wall of enemies,
We shall grind their bones under our boots,
The light of the Golden Throne,
Shall shine upon our hearts…'

They went through a year's worth of prayers in a few hours, and then started again. Mercy Cody led them until his voice was a bare croak, at which point Mercy Chapell stepped forward and took up the recitation.

The Marshal paced along the line, his mouth moving almost soundlessly. Bit by bit, he felt the mood of the Dogs softening. They were into the third year when Major Chalice fell to his knees.

Colonel Salem turned in irritation. 'Pick him up!' he called out, but he saw that Chalice was still praying.

And then, one by one, the other troopers followed his lead. The Marshal realised the Dogs were moved. He had never known such a thing, and judging by Salem's expression neither had he. The sound of prayer rose, lifting them all in faith until the whole regiment was kneeling.

The Marshal was suddenly aware he had followed suit, and as ordnance shots pounded into the superstructure, the Geller-field generator spluttered back to life.

They could feel it, and their prayers rose to a pitch of intensity that was like a scream of faith.

The Geller field ignited with a blinding flash. It was like the blast of an exploding star, and Albreda could feel Hemponia's terror.

The Navigator's breathing was desperate and ragged, as if there were someone with their hands about her throat. Albreda concentrated upon her own breath, slowing it down, and reminded herself of her faith.

It was all down to faith, and without faith they were nothing.

Part Seven

Now

Imperium Sanctus

'Execute great vengeance on the heretic. Smite them with fury. Bury your revenge into their hearts. Bring wrath on the wrongdoer.'

– Credo of Sebastian Thor

I

On the other side of the Great Rift, Battle Group Phaedra, of the Cursed Fifth, made its way in grand procession towards the edge of the system.

The *Vigorous* nosed into the darkness, augur discs slowly spinning, alert for any danger. Behind it the rest of the fleet followed – a magnificent column of battleships and cruisers, with a picket of Dauntless light cruisers and smaller escorts. The whole fleet in full pomp. A magnificent display of Imperial might that would terrify the Imperium's foes. But there was no joy on the bridge of Qartermayne's flagship.

As they approached the Mandeville point, the mood grew increasingly sombre. Admiral Jayn caught the eye of his officers and nodded as Commissar-General Oskarr Qartermayne stood at the wide windows that curved across the front of the bridge. His arms were folded across his carapace breastplate, his peaked cap pulled low over his face, his eyes glittering with the light of reflected stars.

* * *

The fleet had assembled a safe distance from the Cicatrix Maledictum, but it ran across the horizon, a poisonous purple bruise.

The admiral swallowed. He joined the commissar-general, and waited for a moment before speaking. 'Do you think we will be able to cross?' he said, at last.

Qartermayne was silent for a while. He was clearly thinking on the matter, and the sight of the *Pax Imperialis*, tossed back into realspace, gutted and broken. He pursed his lips. Finally, he said, 'That is a matter that you know more about than I, lord admiral.'

'You know my opinion.'

'I do,' Qartermayne said. 'And it has been noted in the records.'

Jayn nodded. The Navy were sticklers for protocol, and he would not have his fine career record blighted with an error that led to the loss of a fleet.

'But what are our chances?'

'House Ferraci say they are slim,' Qartermayne said. 'But that does not mean that we should not try. *The Voidsman's Primer* does not give instructions on working out the odds of a successful stand or assault. It lays down the rules, and we must abide by them, regardless of the hopes that we have of success, or failure. This mission is the same. It has been ordained that we must cross the Great Rift. It is like an assault upon a pillbox, no more, no less. We have prayed. We have done all we can to prepare, and now it is the time to take up the flamer and grenade, and to step forward with our fellows, knowing that many of us may die. But that does not mean we should not try.'

Admiral Jayn nodded. He understood the analogy. He himself had made his name, and indeed, his career, in a daring attack he had carried out while commanding the *Bellerophon*, a vicious assault on a heretic cruiser. Suicidal, some had thought. But the *Bellerophon* had had a stain on her history that he had felt it vital to expunge.

'I understand,' he said at last. 'I pray that you are right.'

Qartermayne turned to Jayn. There was the hint of a smile. 'I think that is one thing we can do. Pray.'

The Navigators of House Ferraci were praying too as they prepared themselves for transition. The lead Navigator was named Lord Sicil. He was the most senior of their number, a veteran who had come in from the house's grange on Yuzkiv Prime. He knew better than almost anyone else what they were going up against, and could feel a cold sweat starting to gather in the small of his back.

Sicil was almost disappointed. If there were any legitimate reason to call this crossing off, he would have been grateful. But the pre-departure rituals went through without any mishaps, the Geller-field generators were running at full power and one by one the other Navigators of his house answered his call. They were all ready and waiting, and watching him for the signal to start.

He started to count down from ten. It was as if he were counting down the last moments of life. His hands were sweating. His mouth was dry. He prayed that the end would be swift. He got to three, and knew he was consigning the whole crew to oblivion. His hand was shaking as he reached out for the power stud. He armed the Geller-field generator, gripped the handle, and counted the last few numbers until he reached zero.

His hand refused to engage the Geller field. It was trembling so hard, he had to put his other hand upon it, and then he pulled the handle towards him.

The Geller field crackled to life, and the ship dropped into the whirlpool mouth of the warp, protected by a thin sheath of reality.

The light of the Astronomican was only a bare glow behind

them, like the last light of the setting sun. And it grew darker and darker as they plunged into the raging storms within the warp.

íí

The warp jump to Holy Cion was tenuous and difficult. Hemponia feared that she had been lured astray. The warp could do that, leading the unsuspecting Navigator far out with bewitching lights, will-o'-the-wisps. And behind her she could feel a malevolent presence, and she knew, in her heart, that it was a swarm of Neverborn trailing behind them.

Cion was wan as a distant moon sighted through the veils of purple mist. It was just a faint glow, obscured by the swirling passing clouds of the empyrean.

Hemponia held the course, and slowly the light grew stronger, the clouds between them thinning out. At last, the system appeared, like a brief view of the sun on a storm-wracked day.

Sometimes she lost sight of the target, but then it would appear again, like the moon glowing briefly through night clouds. Cion grew larger and brighter, and its golden light flooded upon her face, and filled her with joy.

She had found it, the Navigator told herself.

The Mandeville point was a ragged scar in the light of the warp – a wound that had been opened up so many times before and crudely stitched back together. It was ugly, stiff with age. But she knew that she had to break through, before they were all overwhelmed.

At last she felt the lips of reality resist, as though it had a mind of its own. The shadow pressed in behind, racing forwards with insane speed. She could feel the warp spawn clutching at the cathedrum, and brought the *Daughter of the Emperor* right up to the edges of the tear, before pushing through, back into reality.

The suddenness of the transition was shocking.

At one moment, Cion shone out, radiant and golden in the warp. At the next, the *Daughter of the Emperor* fell with a thunderous jolt back into reality.

Albreda heard Hemponia's cry of agony. The Navigator slumped in her throne and toppled forwards, her life force spent.

The *Daughter of the Emperor* had arrived at the final stage of the pilgrimage, and its stained-armaglass windows shone with an inner light.

But even as the hailers blasted hymns into the void, an after-birth of noxious warp energies forced its way through the rift.

It was a monstrous cloud of black and purple, a bruise upon reality, flexing and tensing within the strange confines of real-space. It filled the augurs until it seemed to be all around them, and the *Daughter of the Emperor* was the glowing heart of an insane storm.

The clouds tightened into a shape of dread, a beaked mouth twitching at the centre of a web of claw-tipped tentacles that flickered with malice, hunger and anticipation, ready to drag the holy craft towards its fanged maw.

Warp fire flickered about the Sisters' void-craft. They had faced heretics, Traitor Astartes, and now they were assailed by creatures of the empyrean.

Tentacles of fury lashed out, driven by hunger for the feast of souls laid out before them, yet repelled by the sense of danger emanating from the fiery faith within.

Streaks of warp energy crashed against the silver shields and recoiled as if stung, and at that moment the *Daughter of the Emperor* readied herself for a counter-attack.

The whole craft rang with the rumble from the gunnery decks. Torpedoes were already being lifted from their gantry carriages, the massive claws swinging them into the loading bays.

Each torpedo was eight hundred feet long, their carved casings engraved with devotional texts and imagery, and stained with holy oils and the tallow-fat of martyrs.

Within each torpedo were the remains of the holiest members of the Order. Knuckle bones, fine parings, hair, the dust carefully gathered from the tombs of saints. As they exploded, these fragments were blasted into the mutating bodies of the Neverborn, banishing them back to the empyrean.

Each salvo punctured the warp cloud, but it quickly re-formed and regrew – and now it attacked with all its strength, swirling into the shape of a python and coiling about the *Daughter of the Emperor*, withstanding the agony it felt in its determination to destroy the vessel.

It was a battle of raw strength and power, and here, within the Imperium Nihilus, the forces of the warp were filled with an energy and fury that the void-cathedrum had never faced before.

The coils tightened, twisted into ropes of twined madness and, despite the shields, witchfires started along the length of the craft. The cathedrum glowed brighter even as it shook with the daemonic fury.

Klaxons rang out across the ship as systems failed. The shields struggled to fight off an overwhelming blizzard of warp energy that lashed at them with suicidal ferocity. On all sides warp creatures pressed in hungrily, wrapping, coiling, biting, burning.

Among the Chem Dogs, the weak of mind were driven to insanity.

The hangar was in uproar when the Marshal led the Mercies inside.

The Marshal did not need to call for silence in normal circumstances, but this time, not even his presence was enough to calm the fear the Dogs felt.

In the bowels of the cruiser, Wythers hung in agony, neural implants lacing through the grey fat of his brain, taunting his anger, storing up the explosion of violence, and blotting out the tendrils of raw emotion that swirled through the ship.

There was sanctuary before him. He could see it, just beyond his pain: echoing cloisters, filled with the uplifting songs of holy choirs. It was a sublime place. But he could never reach it. If only he went faster. He lengthened his stride, and felt his feet fall heavily upon the flagstones as the siren voice called him forwards.

The song of the choir was always just before him, but here and there were discordant notes that did not seem to fit his dreamscape. The shouts of harsh voices, the bang and clang of metal joists and void-locks, metal claws scraping hangar floors, the binharic cant of the tech-priests, and the hushed, busy voices of arming crews reciting their prayers.

These sounds were growing louder and more insistent, but Wythers was in a state of torment, the singing drawing him forwards into the shouts of loading thralls, the grind and hiss of hydraulic systems. The scrape of metal feet upon the grille plating.

* * *

As the Battle Sisters surged out to meet any foe, the non-militant Orders remained in the prayer hall. Their voices rose up, the sublime singing shrill and piercing as it was channelled up through the prayer amplifier until it was a searing funnel of sonic purity.

Their faith was a force that repelled the daemon, until at last the shields collapsed, and throughout the length of the craft those of weak will or shallow sanity succumbed to madness.

The heavy doors of the Repentia cells were unlocked, and the women inside grabbed their eviscerators with shouts of faith. Penitent Engines stalked the lower decks, hungry for enemies. And in the prayer hall, ancient reliquaries were unlocked and sacred weapons handed out to the worthiest of the Sisters.

Helewise took Reckoning and turned to face her squad as they fell to their knees. They each put their hands upon the blade, and all of them felt the righteous fury of the ancient sword surge through them.

'This is our last trial,' she told them all. 'The last step before we reach Holy Cion!'

Battle broke out throughout the Sisters' craft.

The Sisters Repentia were desperate for combat. They threw themselves into the fight, screaming their fury as they each tried to outdo the foremost, welcoming their death as a release from their immortal shame.

Helewise felt the incursion even before it flared up on her augur. It was a sickness in the pit of her stomach, rising like nausea. She was already running towards it as alarm runes flared inside her helmet.

The manifestations were all about them.

Her Sisters were surrounded, and each was fighting for her life.

Morgandrie's bolter barked out. Ruslana was singing her battle hymn. From Josmane's flamer came gouts of purifying fire.

'In Aoid's memory!' she shouted at a boiling cloud that formed a human skull with eyes of flame and a snaking tongue that ended in a fanged maw.

It lashed out towards her and her sword struck, severing the head. Another replaced the first, scouring a vicious scar along her pauldron.

As she cut that off, two more appeared.

'Helewise,' the daemon said in her mother's voice, *'they will not let me in…'*

Helewise was momentarily stunned, and the daemon struck. She parried desperately, but a tentacle hit her in the chest and bored through her power armour. Its touch was like a blast of flame. It seared her skin, but then an icy sensation spread out, leaving her struggling for breath. She staggered back, lifting the powerblade before her as a second blow set off a series of alarm runes on her helmet's display.

She wanted to beg for help, but she had her pride. She sucked in a deep breath as the skull stretched into a serpent that coiled about her.

As the daemon prepared a killing blow, Helewise closed her eyes and sought the inner strength that she had spent years cultivating.

'Thank you for your martyrdom,' she whispered. She prayed to Saint Katherine, but the image of her mother came into her mind. 'Thank you for the chance to kill your foes.'

As the daemon's tail scored her armour with unholy markings, Helewise called on Saint Katherine as witness, and her blade glowed with a golden light.

Holy fire burst from her sword and the daemon was consumed in cleansing flame.

* * *

Throughout the craft, each Sister battled their own daemons and vanquished them. Morgandrie found Helewise, bleeding yet defiant.

'You are wounded,' she said.

Helewise nodded. 'I am,' she said. 'But it seems that the Emperor has not abandoned us. Even here, in the midst of this dark night.'

There were lingering patches of warp energy in the void obstructing their route, clotting together like diseased blood cells, devoid of will or purpose. Precision strikes pinpointed each one, destroying them in turn, until at last the road to Holy Cion lay open.

The Sisters Repentia who had survived were taken back to their cells and locked away, where they meditated upon their deaths in a room just large enough to fit a cot and washbowl and lit only by the single grilled window that stared out into the Great Prayer Hall.

The Sisters heard the lamentations of the Repentia as they knelt in the hall and prayed in gratitude for deliverance. As they looked back, the enormity of their journey overwhelmed them all. They had lost half their number in the series of tests and trials.

All that was left was to touch down on the final world of their pilgrimage.

The *Daughter of the Emperor* was sorely wounded by its battle in-system.

An unholy cloud followed the Sisters as they sailed towards Holy Cion. It filled the system behind them, crackling with traceries of dark energy, and they were in no shape to face it in battle.

Sister Dialogus Dovere's greatest fear was that they would be caught and broken before they reached the planet. As repair crews worked tirelessly, she kept watch on their destination, urging their craft forward.

At first the planet was just a small dot. Pilgrim accounts all talked of their first sight of Holy Cion. The long trains of void-shrines illuminating the way, the orbiting statuary, chantry chapels and docks. All of it was gone.

'What do you see?' a voice said.

Dovere had become lost in thought. She turned. 'Sister Helewise.'

The Battle Sister strode up to the viewport. Her breath steamed on the cold glass. In the reflection, Dovere could see the cut across her cheek. The metal sutures had been removed, but the edges of the wound were still raw and red.

'So that is it?' Helewise said.

'That is the world we have come so far to reach...' Dovere looked through the window, gazing at it. 'I suppose this was how Saint Katherine saw it,' she said, after a few minutes' silence.

Helewise nodded, and turned away. 'How long until we are there?'

'A day,' Dovere said.

'I suppose it is too much to expect an unopposed landing,' Helewise said, half joking.

'It will be like that of the saint.'

Helewise nodded again. 'Time to clean my armour.'

Dovere was still there a few hours later when Lanete came down with Palatine Albreda.

The Sister Dialogus stood, but Albreda waved her back down. Nevertheless, Dovere remained standing.

Holy Cion had grown to the size of a small marble, gleaming white in the light of the local sun.

'There it is!' Albreda croaked. 'Holy Cion!'

Dovere could see tears sparkle in the old woman's eyes. She took a deep breath. 'Our last test.'

The whole company of Sisters gathered together for this final part of their pilgrimage.

Hymns filled the Great Prayer Hall as the brass wheel ground steadily round, sending prayers back across the length of the galaxy to the God-Emperor of Mankind.

Helewise stood at her carved throne. The empty places had grown steadily. She saw Ruslana, singing fiercely; Morgandrie's eyes closed as she sang; the lean face of Aiguell, her eyes lifted to the darkness of the vault.

At last the dusty ball of Holy Cion filled the viewports.

Hope was a sin, but despite their years of training, many of the Sisters had allowed themselves to believe that Holy Cion would not have been despoiled. That the Sisters of their Order, in the Abbey of Eternal Watch, would have held out against the darkness.

The disappointment was crushing. Holy Cion looked as dead as all the other planets along the pilgrimage – the dusty world wrapped in coiling clouds. But as they watched, there were shouts of alarm and anger. The planet was not dead. There was movement – its surface pulsed and shifted. It was as if the whole world were possessed.

Morgandrie saw the world as a rotten corpse, devoured from within by maggots. Albreda saw a skull – her own skull – staring back at her. Dovere saw a fanged maw, dripping ichor, hungering. Helewise saw her mother's face, looking up at her. *We cannot let you in.*

She closed her eyes, taking her rage within herself.

No one said anything.

'Contacts,' an augur officer reported. There was a moment's silence as the comms officer tried to make sense of the signs behind them.

The silence stretched on as more and more spikes appeared on the augur scans.

'How many?' Albreda demanded.

'More than a hundred ships at the latest count, though more are still arriving.' There was a long pause as the cogitators struggled to identify the craft; most were Imperial-built ships, defaced with chains and spikes and unholy symbols.

'The usual rabble,' he said, 'but we have identified grand cruisers and a battleship among their number.'

The words fell into silence.

Albreda nodded. 'Prepare for boarding. We shall fight!'

Throughout the great craft guns were loaded, their magazines stocked with thrice-hallowed ordnance. All this time the warp cloud moved steadily behind them, its un-light lit with a noxious storm of rotting yellow and bruise purple.

The Sisters of Our Martyred Lady had all witnessed martyrdom throughout their time of service. They had lived and slept with it about them. It had taken commanders, squad members, younger Sisters that they had seen come and die while they yet served.

And now the time of their own martyrdom had come.

Each had their own feelings about the moment.

None welcomed it more than the ones that Sister Lanete was to lead. As the others went to their battle chapels and armouries, she made her way up into the vaulting domes of the void-craft, to the Hall of Contemplation.

The circular chamber ran about the top of the Great Prayer Hall. It was a dark, windowless space, shaped like a doughnut, with a ring of cell doors within the inner wall.

There were leather harnesses; ancient blades, each as tall as a woman in armour; red candles burning atop nameless skulls; brown bones littering the floor.

Lanete went along the cells, ringing a bell as she unlocked each one. 'Rejoice!' she called. 'Rejoice! The hour of your deaths is drawing close.'

One by one, hooded women stepped out from the cells. Their naked limbs were dirt-stained. Each was dressed in a simple bodice, onto which they had stitched holy scripts and a belt of iron. Some had mortified themselves with holy spikes, which chastised them each waking hour, but each of them had listed their failings in self-confessionals that were stitched to their fronts.

Now they could feel that their chance of redemption was almost upon them, and their deserved sufferings were possibly at an end.

Lanete did not deign any of them with a glance. The Sisters Repentia fell into step behind her. They muttered prayers and exhortations. Lanete could feel their excitement. Each release meant the chance to kill, and the hope of death.

Sister Dialogus Dovere stood within the red lacquer walls of her arming cell.

Her thralls came forwards, their cowls pulled low over their faces. As they prepared her for battle, she remembered her words at the Unification Palace what felt like a lifetime ago, when she had explained how, as a Sister of the Order of the Illuminated Page, she had served through knowledge, faith and exploration, not violence.

'Blessings, Sister,' the attendant muttered as she anointed Dovere's power armour sockets with holy oils. And now she focused on the coming fight. 'Smite the foe. Chastise His enemies. Be the fire of purity on those who are tainted.'

The incantations went on as Dovere prepared herself with meticulous care, saying the appropriate prayers in the proper order as she opened the casket that held the symbol of her office: a staff mounted with the cross and skull of martyrdom. Her suit of armour had been handed down for centuries through her Order, ornately crafted with seams of golden script, an open helm, and a vox-horn fashioned into her headpiece.

She lifted the staff, closed her eyes, and prayed as the cowled attendant fitted each piece to her body. At last the power pack was lifted onto her shoulders, and she felt the weight of it all.

She bore that weight only for a moment, as the attendant invoked a ritual prayer.

'Awake,' she called, 'to His holy war!'

The last part of the arming was the most important.

The attendant led her to a pair of golden doors set into the wall between statues of the saint. She bowed three times, then untied the blessed cloth and opened the doors to a vaulting gothic chamber of ornate tracery and latticework. There was another door within, bound with heavy chains, each one slung with skulls and charms and symbols of the saint, weighed down with heavy brass locks.

The key turned with a click and the doors were swung open. The musty scent of ages billowed out, and she could see the glimmer of gold leaf, could smell the rich scent of scrolls of ancient providence, and vellum books of all shapes and sizes and binding, each as individual as a human face.

The thrall bowed before the holy objects. 'Which one, Sister Dialogus?' she demanded. 'Which will you carry into battle upon this great day?'

Dovere picked out the *Grimoire Opheliatus*.

The attendant brought it out and set it upon a table. The book was bound in velvet cloth, which had deteriorated with age. With gloved hands the attendant slowly unfolded the wrapping, and revealed the grimoire within.

It was one of the most ancient texts, clad in the leather from one of Ophelia VII's own commanders, the human skin dyed vermilion and embossed with curling silver leaf work. Dovere opened the book, moved past the marbled end papers of the finest vellum and turned through the ancient illuminated leaves, scarred and singed from a hundred battlefields, to find the page she had decided upon. The dark-robed figure made the sign of the fleur-de-lys before lifting it and setting it upon the integral shrine of Dovere's armour.

Already she could feel her anger building. A warlike spirit was rising within her like a force of nature, a flood or a typhoon.

Helewise took her place within the armoury as a cherub circled above her dragging a censer of blessed incense. Instead of her own armour, she saw that the suit that awaited her was one of the most venerable that the void-craft housed.

The Armour of the Vengeful Cloister, which had been first worn by Saint Ionna. The black lacquer surface was inlaid with silver tracery, and ancient prayer strips hung from its surfaces. Helewise felt her mouth go dry. It was a venerable suit, she told herself, and silenced her pride. 'No! I cannot accept this.'

The attendant bowed. 'It is the Palatine's express wish. All the great relics are being brought out to battle.'

'No,' Helewise said. 'Please.'

'It is the Palatine's *order*,' the attendant said.

Helewise closed her eyes and said a prayer of thanks as the sacred suit was fitted piece by piece, the sheaths of neural connectors plugged in at calf, thigh, shoulder and forearm.

It bore down upon Helewise, but she carried the consecrated armour with a sense of reverence. Each piece was a dead weight until the backpack was lifted onto her shoulders and the final sheaths of neural conduits were plugged in. There was a sudden lightening as power flowed through the suit.

There were a host of checks she went through as she mag-locked her bolter to her hip, then she attached a set of spare magazines and powercells to the small of her back. She flexed her fingers as the armourer made a last few adjustments and Reckoning was brought to her. She lifted it, clamped it to her thigh, and called out, 'We shall bring reckoning to all His foes!'

Last of all, she was handed the helmet. She could already feel the turbulence as they entered the high atmosphere.

Carrying it in the crook of her elbow, she marched out to her battle station.

Sister Morgandrie knew her death was not far off, and all tension and doubt fell from her. There was no room for anything but her bellicose nature, which swelled up until it filled her body.

She checked the magazine of her heavy bolter and the looped gun-feed, checked her spare magazines, then finally lifted her helmet and lowered it into place, slotting it into its fixings. She clicked the neck seal closed with a ten-degree turn and the helmet's circuitry whirred to life.

The rebreather unit showed available oxygen, and the ocular retinal display scrolled through her powercell reserves, ammo levels and prayers of moment. A background reel of chanting benedictions played in her earpiece as she said a prayer to test that the vox-bead was working.

The words she prayed were as familiar as the backs of her hands. She ran through the Fede Imperialis, but each word and phrase had new and forceful meaning.

And at the end, she repeated the lines:

From the lightning and the tempest,
our Emperor deliver us.

Helewise was waiting for her in the open doorway, Ruslana and Aliciel standing behind her. All her Battle Sisters. Superiors read to them from sacred texts as some hitched heavy weaponry to their harnesses, plugging in ribbed rubber hosing and cabling.

They embraced, short and fierce, in the manner of warriors, and waited as Aiguell, Josmane and Naoka all came, leading their own squads.

Senior Sisters were encased in Paragon Warsuits, stalking slowly towards their battle stations; armed with blessed relics, primed to purge the unclean.

Each took their place among the squads of Celestians and Battle Sisters.

Helewise led her squads to their station. 'Time is short.'

In the guts of the assault lander *Chapel of the Martyr's Tear*, Wythers hung within the steel embrace of the Penitent Engine. The account of his sins rang through his mind, scourging it with constant pain. The air about him crackled with ozone. The tension was building. Through the singing he could hear the moans of the other penitents.

There was the slide of metal bars releasing. One by one the locking gears uncoupled, and he heard the siren song lead him forwards. The cloisters gave way to a loading bay, a series of arched alcoves, flickering candles, and somewhere he could hear the manic roar of buzz saws.

The heretic fleet powered towards the *Daughter of the Emperor* as she stood alone and defiant, her shields flickering about her as her massive armaments charged and loaded.

Within the bridge, the comms officer reported with dismay as more and more Chaos ships converged upon the *Daughter of the Emperor*. They were all broadcasting their names in a cacophony of triumph.

The *Gibbering Gestalt*, the *Putrid Pact*, the *Afflicted*, the *Architect of Adulation*, the *Celebrant of Blood*, the *Befouler*, the *Pestilential Syndicate*, the *Foebane*.

The chorus of names meant nothing to the Sisters – they knew only that they were foul and profane.

Palatine Albreda remained resolute. 'We shall fight them. And we shall vanquish them all!' she hissed.

As the first Chaos ships powered into range, the *Daughter of the Emperor* unleashed fury upon the enemy, her bombardment cannon wreaking destruction upon the cruisers that surrounded her. As the minutes dragged on, lance batteries and ordnance turrets began to fire, until the skies above Holy Cion were a lightning storm of terrible proportions.

The *Gibbering Gestalt* was hit amidships, smashing through its lower bulkheads and setting off a sector-wide collapse that crippled the shield generators. The *Befouler's* bridge was torn from the superstructure and the spiked craft carried straight on, slamming into the *Pestilential Syndicate* as it tried to bring its dorsal armament to bear.

A flight of knife-nosed torpedo escorts came up beneath the *Daughter of the Emperor*, firing off a salvo before her gun turrets shredded them with a hail of hallowed ordnance.

Again and again she repulsed the attacks, but the Chaos fleet slowly enveloped her until she faced enemies on every side.

_The Sisters fought on, even as their shields failed and torpedoes and lance strikes struck home in a gathering storm of destruction. Wave upon wave of boarding parties slammed into the cathedrum.

Most were loaded with cultists, who raged out, firing wildly and praising the Chaos gods as they died. But hidden among the assault craft were Heretic Space Marines. They cut their way through the hull, severing vital systems, and Helewise led her Sisters to hunt them down, weapons flaring in the smoke-clogged corridors.

It was ruthless work. The Sisters carried fearsome weaponry – flamer, melta and blade all taking a terrible toll upon the enemy.

They had survived the first wave of assaults, but soon after fresh Chaos ships pushed forward, blaring their names out in a cacophony of insanity.

As the crew struggled to repair faltering systems, a series of fireships streaked towards them – rusting old hulks, packed with fyceline and powering ahead at full speed.

The danger was spotted almost too late, and the targeting matrixes were rapidly reconfigured. One by one the fireships were blasted into oblivion, but the gunners could not keep them all at bay. More and more streaked in: coal barges, void-skiffs and all manner of lesser craft.

It was only a matter of time before one of the fireships hit.

The first crashed into the upper decks and tore a gaping hole in the massed spires, secondary explosions tearing out huge chunks of superstructure. Fireballs roiled through the decks, causing dreadful damage throughout the craft, and the statue of Saint Katherine that stood at the top of the vessel broke free and tumbled towards the planet in a gathering fireball.

A second fireship hit them in the enginarium, and the *Daughter of the Emperor* groaned as her motive power failed.

'We cannot last!' the captain hissed as the craft slipped into the gravity well of Holy Cion.

The planet was pulling them down into a murderous embrace, and they were paralysed.

Albreda said nothing.

She had hoped to cleanse Holy Cion. Hoped for better than this, and they had come so close, she thought, and yet they were now powerless.

She looked about at the faces of her Battle Sisters.

Albreda made the sign of the fleur-de-lys. Alarms were already wailing throughout the enormous craft as it started to break apart, whole sections slewing off, the fragments wreathed in flames as they plummeted down through the atmosphere of Holy Cion.

Even wounded as it was, the cathedrum was one of the most devastating weapons that the Adepta Sororitas could deploy.

'Give the order,' Albreda said. 'We shall land upon the planet.'

Voltaic storms crackled and boomed through the upper atmosphere. Trails of black smoke billowed behind, and a mile from impact, battle chapels detached themselves, each one an ornate fortress in its own right, with statues and reliquaries, void shields, and lance arrays that could flatten whole districts.

The daemon world trembled.

It felt the presence of the hallowed craft plunging towards it like a bolt.

Flying warp beasts flung themselves at the craft, screaming in rage and frustration as they were incinerated by its blessed shields.

Cackling maws lunged for it and were thrown back. None could withstand the sacral bastions as they plunged downwards, generators raging with holy energy, laud hailers thundering songs into the thickening atmosphere.

'Ready for battle!' Major Chalice called out to his Savlar Chem Dogs.

They had huddled within the guts of the *Daughter of the Emperor* as the void battle raged about them, but now klaxons wailed. The time for their self-sacrifice was upon them.

There was no ceremony. No prayers. The armoury was unlocked, and each Dog found their own kit, buckled on scavenged armour, cleaned out inhaler filters, checked their store of powercells.

Major Chalice limped along the line, steadying himself as the whole craft shook, handing out combat stimms to each of his Dogs.

Shin took his and paused before slipping it into his rebreather.

He'd taken stimms before. He couldn't remember what had happened. He couldn't remember anything once the stimms took hold.

Chalice got to the end of the line and paused. One eye was still closed, his split lip had scabbed over. But he had the sacred wax seal next to his skin, and he was still alive. He looked over his troopers. *No more Wythers,* he thought to himself. They would have to do this without him.

His Dogs looked back at their commander. They felt his shame and his pride, and his fierce determination.

'How long?' Shin called out.

Chalice didn't know. 'Not long,' he told them.

They steeled themselves as the craft groaned with the trials of re-entry. They could feel the planet approaching. It was like a wave of hatred rising up towards them.

Chalice had to swallow back nausea. He reached inside his jacket and his fingers touched the vellum prayer strip within. 'You and I, we have all failed the God-Emperor,' he told them. 'Now is our chance to wipe the slate clean. Fight like dogs, and then, when your time comes, thank the God-Emperor for the second chance He has given you all.

'Now! Pray with me!'

Even those of little faith closed their eyes and shouted out the prayers, finding conviction and comfort in the recitation of religious texts, even as they felt the heat of entry through the soles of their feet.

* * *

Lesser daemons screamed as the assault of the Sisters approached, and even the possessed planet's surface recoiled against its fiery descent. The perimeter ring of battle chapels were only a few hundred feet from impact when flocks of Seraphim were released, swirling downwards on the furious blue flame of their jump packs, searching for targets.

Their pistols flared with incandescent fury, scorching any that stood against them. The creatures of the warp threw themselves forwards with fanged tongues and clawed limbs, and the circling Seraphim sang their hymns in praise as the *Daughter of the Emperor* made its last and most dramatic descent, burning towards the surface like a falling star.

The battle chapels thundered down first – seven of them, one for each of the mortal wounds that Saint Katherine had suffered, slamming down about the ruins of the Shrine of Landing.

Helewise exchanged looks with Morgandrie.

'We're going to meet Him,' Morgandrie said.

Helewise nodded. She smiled.

'Our struggle is almost over.'

At the last moment, the *Daughter of the Emperor*'s retro-thrusters raged against gravity. Blasts of sacred flame cleared the place where Katherine had landed five thousand years before, and the massive void-cathedrum slowed, before crashing down to earth in a roiling gout of dust and fumes.

Vox-horns trumpeted battle hymns as assault ramps slammed down, and there was a blinding flash of faith.

A shockwave of purifying light rolled out across the plain. Lesser daemons popped out of existence while larger ones lashed back and forth in pain and ecstasy. The planet itself pulsed and writhed, and for a moment the miasma of unholy clouds lifted, and the sun shone down on Cion once more.

But the release was momentary.

Darkness rolled back in with a *boom*, and from the earth an army clawed up on shaky legs and turned towards the Sisters with a hungry and malevolent hatred. A billion cadavers, imbued with unholy life, rose from the tormented planet and started in a dark tide towards the invaders. Each carried the rotting remains of their own pilgrimage: veteran guards carrying the bones of their beloved commander; an ornate servo-sarcophagus bearing the rotten remains of a once honoured cardinal; the countless men and women bearing tokens of faith – a lead badge on a steel chain, an icon of the God-Emperor, now defaced and rotting, the bones of their parents.

But they were pilgrims no more. Their pilgrimage had ended in heresy and corruption. They were a numberless army of the hate-filled dead. Their sole intent was to kill, their only emotion the detestation of the dead for the living, the corrupt for the sublime.

The numbers turned the Pilgrim Plains dark. They came on like ants, filling the plains, chilling in their silence, arms raised, fingers clawed, teeth an angry snarl.

Palatine Albreda stepped out onto the assault ramp, her standard bearer next to her, a bodyguard of Celestians about her, and took in the scene. She had seen these plains many times in the illuminated manuscripts that dated back to before the Great Catastrophe: the Road of Purification, the stone gateways, the vast mass of Lisanors Gate, and finally, across the plains where the armies of the dead waited, the great black cylinder of the Bolt. It loomed cold and menacing under the dark purple bruise of a sky that swirled insanely above them, balls of warp energy spiralling in the air above an army of the dead.

But at the top of the Bolt stood the Abbey of Eternal Watch, and from the highest spires, a golden light fell. The beauty of that place took the breath from her chest, and she lifted her voice in a song of victory.

The other Sisters saw it as well. It was like a holy vision.

The journey had sapped Albreda of so much. She knew that this battle would be her last, but the realisation filled her with divine conviction.

Albreda did not need to pray. The way was clear.

'Rejoice!' she called out in a clear voice. 'The Pilgrimage of Fire is complete! We have landed upon Holy Cion and our martyrdoms are at hand!'

Part Eight

Then

Holy Cion

'Lo! The dead awoke, and they came to me and cast down their idols, and bowed down to me in supplication.'

– The Grimoire of Skelos

í

Holy Cion was lost.

Across the Pilgrim Plains, the last pockets of Sisters were overwhelmed and drowned under the deluge. But even as all hope was extinguished, Ysolt pointed to the sky.

'The saint has come!' she hissed.

They looked up in wonder as a golden warrior swept down upon resplendent wings. Gloranthrax howled as the saint's sword bit into its inhuman flesh.

In the long years of imprisonment, Gloranthrax had known hatred and anger, but it had not felt such searing pain and recoiled like a serpent preparing for another strike.

The saint drove the fiend back, and all about the Sisters lesser daemons retreated with sibilant howls.

From the Abbey of Eternal Watch a golden light shone out against the firmament of night. Dominion Gahene pointed. 'Look!' she called. 'Saint Katherine has come, and the abbey yet stands!'

Ysolt's faith was rekindled. 'To the Bolt, Sisters! Let us go there, and make our last stand!'

Saint Katherine was a golden star that swept down to clear the encroaching horde from the plains before them. She rekindled fury and belief in their hearts, and with new strength the knot of survivors fought their way through the insanity, under her protection, until at last they reached the city perimeter.

The habs and streets were deserted and empty, the stench of corruption rising like a miasma from the ruins. Even the Bolt had been damaged.

It tilted at a dangerous angle, and many of the abbey buildings had sheared off and fallen to the city. Only their foundations remained, jagged as splintered teeth, with the Octagonal Tower rising up, lit by an inner light.

Slowly they carried Ysolt up the winding stairs, as the flood of madness lapped about its base.

'Set me down,' Ysolt whispered as they reached the tilting top of the Bolt. They did so, and knelt about her even as her strength ebbed away.

'I failed you all,' the elder Sister whispered, as the blight of corruption festered within her.

Her eyelids fluttered for a moment. 'Saint Katherine saved us!' she whispered.

At those words, they felt the saint approach.

The golden light came towards them through the air, and landed fifty feet away amidst the ruins of the abbey.

As she landed, the saint's light dimmed. Before them stood Sister Lizbet, her face streaked with sweat and pain, her suit of sacred armour charred and broken – even Chalybix's light was fading.

She saw her Sisters kneeling about the figure of Canoness Ysolt.

'She is dying,' Morcata said, and Lizbet hurried forwards.

The canoness' face was drawn, the skin grey, mutation writhing within her flesh.

'I have failed,' the old lady whispered.

'No!' Lizbet told her. She looked about at the ruin of this, the most sacred spot of this shrine world, and felt crushing despair. 'We have all failed.'

'Pray for me,' Ysolt said, as she closed her eyes and prepared for death.

The Sisters knelt about her and Lizbet said a simple prayer, such as one a child might learn in the schola.

'Place the sword upon me,' Ysolt whispered.

Lizbet took Chalybix and laid it on the canoness' lap.

A shudder went through the old woman. A low moan of agony that grew into a scream, and Lizbet pulled the sword away.

Ysolt spoke through gritted teeth. 'Fear not. True healing never comes without pain. Place the sword upon my wounds...'

Canoness Ysolt tried to hold back her cries of agony as the corruption began to lessen and then retreat, and colour returned to her skin.

'The saint is with us still,' Hospitaller Avalla said, and they knelt in prayer as Ysolt's breathing became stronger.

As they prayed, Ysolt put her hand up.

'Can you hear that?'

The Sisters exchanged looks. Hospitaller Avalla asked, 'What can you hear?'

'Singing,' Ysolt whispered.

It was like a distant songbird. Sublime poetry, in honour of the God-Emperor, sung to a tune that none had ever heard before, but which brought a warmth to their hearts. The purity of the song echoed down through the broken corridors. It grew in strength and potency.

Ysolt pointed upwards to the ruins of the abbey.

They listened. And, one by one, they heard it.

'Is it a miracle?' Brace asked.

'It is the saint!' Ysolt said.

Sister Lizbet lifted Chalybix. 'Tread with care, Sisters. I will lead. It may be a daemon sent to bewitch us...'

The stairwell of the Octagonal Tower was dark.

Lizbet could hear the howls of daemons echoing up from the plains below as she picked her way around chunks of broken masonry and shattered glass, sword in hand.

As she crested the stairs, she saw that the heavy wooden chapel doors were open, and a golden-white light flooded out through the doorway.

A dark figure stepped out into the stairwell, blade in hand. The voice was commanding. 'Who is it? Show yourself!'

Lizbet pushed the barrel of Morcata's bolter down. She raised Chalybix, and stepped forwards. 'It is I! Sister Lizbet!'

'Is it true?' the other said. 'Show yourself! I will not fall for any treachery.'

Lizbet stepped into the golden light, and the dark shape lowered the blade.

'You have come!' Sister Morgaulat said. 'She said that you would come.'

Within the beehive chapel, before the statue of the saint, knelt maid-of-all-work Branwen.

'Her song is holding them back,' Morgaulat whispered, as one by one they laid their weapons down and took their places about the kneeling figure.

The song washed over them, lifted their grief and weariness, and after a long time they realised that Branwen had stopped singing. Her eyes were closed, her mouth still, her hands lifted up in benediction, but her song still rang out through the tower.

At last Branwen roused herself. She turned to look at the Sisters about her, their faces stained with blood and battle, their expressions grave.

Branwen's face was weary beyond measure, but she forced herself to smile.

'She said you would come,' she said at last. 'I have held out until now...' Then she realised where she was and who was kneeling about her, and promptly fell unconscious, overwhelmed by the sight.

ii

Branwen slept.

But the song went on, echoing through the hallowed stones of the Abbey of Eternal Watch.

The surviving Sisters left the maid alone, and sat in silence. Each was stunned by the enormity of what had happened. There was a terrible circularity at play. The Festival of Landing was a point in a circle. It had marked the moment of cleansing, and then it had marked the moment of corruption.

Holy Cion was now a world lost to daemons. The population had been slaughtered. Their Sisters were dead, the God-Emperor had abandoned them. They could feel the lack of Him. It was an unbearable absence. A cavity within their souls, into which corruption might spread.

They all wished that they had been martyred rather than witness this.

Each felt uniquely abandoned.

They could not conceive that their emotions were multiplied

countless times across the Imperium of Man. That the fortress world of Cadia had finally fallen, and the Imperium had been torn apart.

As Branwen's song went on, Sister Lizbet stood at the chapel window, looking out onto the plains.

Elaifor stepped up next to her. They looked out in silence. 'If I had been purer,' Lizbet said after a long silence. 'If I had been more devout...'

Elaifor put her hand to Lizbet's arm. 'The saint chose you.'

Lizbet nodded, but she seemed unconvinced.

'I *saw* it,' Elaifor told her. 'We all did. Saint Katherine returned to Holy Cion. She came to all our aid.'

Canoness Ysolt spoke to Sister Morgaulat, who reported what had happened within the tower. How Branwen had started to pray, and how her song had kept the forces of heresy at bay.

Ysolt was silent for a long time. 'Should I have chosen her?' she said at last. 'To be the saint?'

Morgaulat had no answer for her.

Branwen slept for weeks.

She was so still that there were times the others feared that she was dead and put a hand to her cheek to check that she was still warm. And yet, her song went on, crafting ever more phrases to define her faith.

It was Brace who first saw the change within the maid. She called the others, and said, 'Look! Can you see what is happening? She has been touched by the God-Emperor's light!'

They saw it.

The roots of Branwen's auburn hair had turned white, just as Alicia Dominica's had, after she was taken to speak to the God-Emperor.

Canoness Ysolt prayed on the matter, and she announced her decision to the Sisters.

'This would be outside our customs. But at moments of great crisis sometimes we must alter our own strictures. We have been blessed. The saint chose one of the lowliest serving girls to pray here during this moment of utmost calamity. And now she has been marked. I believe the saint has chosen this child, and I believe we should welcome her into the Order of Our Martyred Lady, if or when she wakes.'

It was during Morgaulat's vigil that Branwen finally sat up and looked about.

'She is returned!' Morgaulat called out, and the Sisters looked upon her return as if it was a sign of hope yet to come.

'Sister Lizbet will train you,' Ysolt told her, and in the days that followed, Lizbet ran her through the novitiate drills.

'She is a natural,' she told Ysolt after the first few days. 'It is like duelling with Katherine herself.'

Branwen was prepared for induction into the Order. The rituals brought comfort to all the Sisters, for they saw within Branwen hope for the continuation of their Order upon this world.

After a week of rituals, the remainder of Branwen's auburn locks were cut away, her cheek inked with the skull and cross of the Martyred Lady. Hospitaller Avalla prepared her body for power armour, and on the day of induction the flesh-plugs were still raw, the wounds swelling red against the sutures.

They armed Branwen in a suit of black Sororitas power armour, and sang a hymn of thanks as they presented her with bolter and blade. Now she was a holy warrior, charged with the defence of humanity.

When all was done, she was finally brought forward to be accepted into the Order.

Ysolt's legs would not heal, but the other Sisters helped her up and stood on either side, holding her.

Branwen knelt before her, trembling.

'Let the saint speak through you,' Ysolt told her.

Branwen closed her eyes and took a deep breath. There was a pause before Branwen sang her vow to them, words of courage and defiance in the face of darkness.

Verses that were written down, and came to be known as the Song of Branwen.

That night, after the hymns had been sung, Lizbet found Ysolt dressing her corrupted legs with holy oils. The old lady winced at the touch of her own flesh, which writhed as if possessed from within.

'The corruption will not go,' she sighed.

'Shall I bring Chalybix?'

Ysolt shook her head. 'No. This is my penance.'

They sat together in silence. At last, Lizbet said, 'Canoness Ysolt, I wish to renounce my place among the Order.'

Ysolt's face showed concern. 'You did not fail. You saved us all.'

Sister Lizbet listened, stone-faced. 'I wish to take up the vow of the Repentia.'

Canoness Ysolt studied her. 'Sister Lizbet, we need your prowess and protection. You took upon yourself the role and armour of the saint. It is not mere costume. It is holy ceremony. The saint is our defender, and you have taken that aspect on. What would Saint Katherine do in this moment? She would not take the vows of Repentia. That would be a sin of pride. She would remain to protect her abbey.'

Lizbet listened, her expression unchanged. 'I insist,' she said. 'I failed us all.'

Ysolt tried to argue, but she saw that Lizbet's mind was already made up. 'I give you permission,' she said, 'but I ask one thing only.'

'What is that?'

'I cannot spare you now, and there is no Repentia Superior among us who might guide you to your end. Do not speak of this again, until, or unless relief shall come to us.'

iii

In the years that followed, Branwen's song continued, echoing through the stones, and the surviving Sisters defended the Abbey of Eternal Watch with unrelenting devotion. Despite all their efforts, Canoness Ysolt remained crippled by the affliction. She sat in her throne, and prayed for victory as Chaos warbands returned to assault the Bolt.

The Sisters marked the passing years with prayer and contrition. They defended the Bolt with ferocious determination, yet bit by bit their strength was whittled away to a bare handful of Sisters.

They fought, without hope of relief, but not without faith.

All the time they feared the return of Gloranthrax, but the daemon did not come.

'Maybe it has found easier prey elsewhere,' Elaifor said.

It was a fool's hope, many thought, though it was Lizbet who spoke their fears aloud. 'It is biding its time. It is waiting until we are at our weakest.'

* * *

Morgaulat died to wounds from a daemon of plague and corruption, and none of their prayers, not even the touch of Chalybix, could save her. Lucia was lost on the Pilgrim Plains as they sallied out to retrieve their holiest relics. Adelith had been old when the battle had started, and her body gave way to age.

Of the one thousand Sisters who had once filled the abbey with faith and prayer, only nine now remained.

The twins, Brace and Morcada, who fought side by side, their blades moving as if controlled by a single mind. Celestian Alird, whose pistols spat destruction at her enemies. Dominion Gahene, blessed by the saint so that her flamer would never run out of purifying flame. Elaifor the Pure, who was so weary that she thought every swing of her blade would be her last. Hospitaller Avalla of the Ebon Sword, who knelt at Ysolt's side, head bowed and lips moving in a devout prayer that had lasted decades, keeping the mortal corruption from consuming the canoness. And Branwen, whose faith burned with a fierce white flame.

Time and battle had worn them thin. The once young Sisters were now haggard with age.

Celestian Lizbet's faith had been severely tested, and she had aged more than any of the others. The relief she yearned for had never come, and she was just a shadow of the Sister who had once taken upon herself the role of the saint for the Feast of Landing. She was now bent and wizened, her strength ebbing with each enemy she faced.

As their strength faded, so did all thought of reclaiming Holy Cion. Now, all they could do was fight to hold the tide of corruption and heresy back. But it slowly drove them further up the Bolt, step by weary step, to the very gates of the abbey.

But here they stopped and refused to give in, faithful to their ancient vows, refusing to let any enter.

They formed a living wall. The twins, Elaifor the Pure, Alird, Gahene, Lizbet, and at her side Sister Branwen of the Blessed Song, her power mace crackling with the spite of judgement.

Even Branwen's face was no longer young. There were lines etched into her skin – some natural ageing, but most the raised welts of fresh scarring. Her rough-cropped white hair stuck to her cheeks with sweat. A veteran now of unnumbered years, standing guard upon the steps she had once scrubbed as a maid-of-all-work.

For days the skies had been darkening.

'The heresy grows,' Elaifor said.

'They are a relentless tide,' Lizbet hissed. 'They sense our weakening.'

They felt the daemon's return, even as they stood guard at the broken doors. Then they heard its name, blaring out: '*Gloranthrax. Gloranthrax. Gloranthrax.*'

Canoness Ysolt's skin was grey and wrinkled as old parchment, her eyes staring out from hollow pits, the slack skin hanging in bags over her cheekbones, and her teeth brown with age. The ornate power armour only served to highlight the shrivelled body within it, but she would not die, and faith sustained her.

She heard those words and closed her eyes. The end, it seemed, had come.

The Eternal Watch was about to end.

As if to reinforce that fact, fire rained down from the sky.

Part Nine

Now

Holy Cion

'Singing hymns shall they come, swords unsheathing,
Doom to their foes, death unleashing,
Faith before them, fealty unbroken.
Blade and bolter, both shall conquer.'

– The Song of Branwen

í

Palatine Albreda ordered the Sisters under Celestian Junestri to lead the defence of the cathedrum. 'Take a hundred Sisters. I give you the penal legion and all of our thralls. Hold the *Daughter of the Emperor* until our return! Do not let any despoil her!'

Junestri started to marshal the defences. She put the Dogs out in front as a picket around the perimeter of the battle chapels.

'We will guard it to the very end,' Aebram told her.

For the rest, they were to make a charge to the Bolt. Albreda's battle companies were ready. 'Be not afraid, though great danger awaits us!' she shouted. 'It will be a journey of fire and slaughter!' She drew her sword and it flashed like the ice on Titan, and then along its edge gleamed an eldritch fire.

'Follow me, all!' she called out. 'To the Bolt!'

First to charge were the Sisters Repentia.

Lanete goaded them with prayers as they sprinted headlong

towards the enemy, yearning for the absolution of death. In their wake stomped the Penitent Engines, the crude machines loping forwards, and at their fore went Wythers, who slavered and snarled, his mouth set in a scream of pain, of intimate secrets laid bare.

He fired and swung at every creature that might slow him. His buzz-saw arms tore through them, bursts of flamer incinerating any that remained in the way.

Lanete shouted prayers as the Sisters Repentia cut a swathe through the stumbling dead.

They fought with berserk fury, the teeth of their two-handed eviscerators ripping through dead flesh and bone. A rain of gore filled the air about their heads.

Gobbets of putrefying flesh showered down.

It was a battle between purity and corruption, and corruption was slowly enveloping them all. But just as they started to slow, Seraphim swooped down over the dead, sudden flares of hallowed promethium and flashes of bolt-fire cutting down their foes.

As Albreda led the forces of the Order across the Pilgrim Plains, the Dogs assembled a rough barricade from debris hauled from the ship and positioned themselves behind it. Their lines were thinly spread, the reserves being cannibalised to a small force led by Colonel Salem himself.

Colonel Salem had always bragged that his troops had faced down the worst the galaxy could throw at them. But as he looked out at their foes he understood how wrong he had been. His knuckles were white, his voice little more than a croak as he stepped out upon the assault ramp and looked at the horde of shambling, putrid bodies.

'Give your orders, Colonel Salem!' the Marshal told him.

Colonel Salem's orders were a bare rasp. 'No retreat! No surrender!' he called out and slammed on his rebreather. He needed the stimms for this.

Major Chalice had strapped his chainsword to the ruin of his hand. He gave the order for his Dogs to line up. Mercy Cody stood behind him. 'No retreat,' he reminded the penal legionnaires, his bolt pistol primed and loaded.

Trooper Shin was clear that his life was going to end here, upon this ruined planet.

He gripped his grenade launcher as he searched his pockets for a strip of meat. If nothing else, he was not going to meet the God-Emperor with an empty stomach. 'What did we do to end up on this Throne-forsaken expedition?'

Chalice said, 'Do you want a list?'

'Rhetorical question,' Shin said.

The two of them glanced to where Colonel Salem stood.

'I hope I get to see that bastard dead,' Chalice said.

He looked about and saw a column of tanks powering across the land. Among them he saw Sisters in black power armour, already charging forward with gouts of sacred flame flaring out.

He saw one, and imagined it was the woman he had met in the chapel on Ayaan. That sight and memory was enough for him. He did not need stimms; he had faith and it burned hot within him.

As the Dogs prepared themselves, the *Daughter of the Emperor* and the ring of battle chapels opened fire: void cannons and lance arrays now wreaking terrible damage upon the forces that filled the plains.

The Dogs had never seen such fury, a constant thunder booming behind them, turning the near distance into a hell storm of flame and shrapnel. Through it all the dead charged, and the Dogs put up a hail of fire, ready to slam their bayonets into the throats of any that stood before them.

The dead came on, relentless, and within minutes they were scrambling over the barricades.

Salem slashed one cadaver's belly open, and it tripped over its spilt guts. It tackled him as it fell and he had to slam the butt of his rifle into its head, but still it clawed up at him, snarling and biting.

He'd been an accomplished killer long before he had been turned over to the Dogs. And he'd done this many times, but now he carried out his executions with added stimm-induced ferocity.

He put his boot onto the creature's back as he took hold of its lank, foul hair. As he pulled the head back, he saw the glint of a pilgrim badge hanging about its neck.

He felt for the gap between the vertebrae and sliced the head free, kicking the remains from his boots.

The battle raged for what felt like only minutes as the Dogs held their line.

The Mercies were ready to make an example of deserters, but none fled. None abandoned their positions. Penal legionnaires though they were, they fought and died bravely, reinforcements rushing in to crush any breakthroughs or fill the gaps where others had died. It was ferocious, merciless battle. It was what the Dogs expected.

They fought as only penal troops could, their native ferocity honed to a serrated razor's edge by the toxic mix of stimms that pumped through their rebreathers. Illuminating their ring, the battle chapels glowed out like lanterns, and the tide of death began to fail. The heaps of dead lay seven or eight deep about their lines. But the furious assault had covered a far more dangerous action in the rear.

While the Dogs had been fighting, the heretical fleet had been landing its forces for a planetside coup de grace.

Assault landers plummeted earthwards and armoured columns approached, the industry of an invasion force preparing to strike.

Stretcher-bearers were carrying the wounded to Sawbones, and the whine of his buzz saw carried through the stillness.

'Hold firm!' Salem ordered as the first salvos of artillery fire began to rain down upon the ring of battle chapels. The void shields protected the Dogs as they dug in and waited.

Dust rose as the forces of heresy started to roll towards them. The Marshal marched along the line, calling on the Dogs to remember their sins, and to sacrifice themselves for the God-Emperor.

Major Chalice heard and puffed out his chest.

The sky was growing dark above them. The Chaos fleet was drawing itself up in orbit, ready to unleash a devastating bombardment.

He caught Shin's eye. Neither of them spoke. At this point, there wasn't much left to say.

Time to die like Dogs.

ii

Helewise's column was on the left flank of the attack, the Sisters riding in their blessed tanks, light flaring where flamers bathed the dead in sacral fire, storm bolters scattering the hulls with spent shells.

They roared along, crushing the dead beneath them.

'The Bolt!' she shouted, and fired off a salvo towards the dead. She could not believe that they were here, on Holy Cion, with the Bolt rising up before them. And this was where they would die.

Behind them, the *Daughter of the Emperor* was lost in the flame and thunder of battle as the defenders held off those that pursued them.

Albreda stood in the cupola of the lead transport, her white hair shining out against the corruption of the daemon world. The closer they drew, the fiercer the resistance. Enemy assault craft were landing ahead of them, disgorging armies straight into battle. As they approached the broken remains of the city, las-bolts flared from the ruins about them, and suddenly the air was thick with the trails of missiles and heavy las-bolts.

The lead tanks went up in roiling clouds of flames. Palatine Albreda's own Rhino was struck. She charged out, Celestians drawing close about her.

Their enemy was already running to meet them. There was no mistaking the horned helmets and hulking, armoured forms of their foe. The Heretic Astartes howled as they charged, raging their battle cries as their chainaxes roared.

The Sororitas answered with hymns of their own. The sound of their singing drowned out the discordant baying. It filled their hearts with faultless wrath. They were Sisters of Our Martyred Lady. They were steadfast and vengeful, and as the Astartes loped towards them, they drew their swords and charged.

There was a clap of thunder as the two forces drove into one another. Power armour against power armour. Chainblade against chainblade. Bolt against melta and flamer and faith.

Helewise was calm as a heretic Space Marine charged towards her. Heads hung from his belt, suspended by their knotted hair. She turned side-on and felt the glancing shots ring off her armour, and was still singing as Reckoning met his first blow, shearing through the weapon's shaft.

She ran him through, but the resilience of her foe was astonishing. He did not die. With the sword still embedded in his gut, he caught hold of her with one fist as the other slammed into her side. The force of the blow threw her sideways.

A knee caught her in the chest. Alarm runes flared suddenly.

She dragged her bolt pistol from its mag-lock and fired point-blank, throwing herself sideways and twisting out of his grip.

The first shot ricocheted off his nose plate, the second from his vox-grille, but the third struck true, slamming in under his chin and blowing up inside his helmet.

Even though they had come so close, the Sisters' momentum had been lost, and now they were pinned down within the shadow of the Bolt.

Through the melee a Helbrute raged, a twisted caricature of an Astartes Dreadnought. The maddened beast carved a way through the Sisters, shrugging off melta shots as its possessed form crushed and tore with berserk fury.

Space Marine kill squads closed in on Palatine Albreda as her Celestians stood about her. They met the furious assault with a flash of powerblades. The Helbrute took a melta shot to the head and it died with a scream of tortured metal.

But it had done its job. The Sisters had been distracted, and a wedge of Traitor Astartes barrelled through the Celestians, smashing through to the Palatine.

Albreda's sacred blade cut the first in half. The second slashed down at her with a chainsword. She sidestepped his blow, and a second swing took his legs out from under him.

Her powerblade glowed with a furious light as she drove it through the faceplate of a third. She called out to her Sisters, her words inspiring them all, her deeds rousing them to acts of vengeance.

The air began to fizz and crackle as daemons materialised among the traitorous horde. Ruslana was torn apart as she emptied her magazine into a pack of Neverborn that had the form of hounds, with coals for eyes and foot-long sabres for teeth. Aiguell was downed by a headshot from Throne knew where. Josmane shouted a warning to Helewise and the Sister Superior threw herself down as an inferno of raging promethium turned a Space Marine into a living torch.

He tried to batter through the flames, but Helewise was up behind him and carved a line through his generator, sparks flying and crackling about her blade.

His power armour slowed as he tried to turn and grab her, but Helewise eluded his grasp.

'From the blasphemy of the fallen,' she said, and then she carved him down from skull to groin.

The battle raged. There was no mercy, no quarter asked or expected – it was kill or be killed. As the Sisters began to tire, Sister Dialogus Dovere marched through them singing rousing verses from the *Grimoire Opheliatus.*

She drove them to a state of ecstatic violence. Helewise remembered Aoid's Sepulchre, all the Sisters they had left behind. She remembered her mother, who had sacrificed herself to let her daughter live.

To live for this moment. To die here, with the name of the Emperor upon her lips.

Heretics charged in amongst them. Reckoning swept round her head, chopping and cutting.

A chainaxe slammed into her side, the teeth gnawing through the cabling of her power armour and grazing her side.

She returned the blow, an uppercut that caught her enemy in the thigh joint. It was wearying work, and her muscles screamed for a rest as the relentless foes drove in, their huge forms smashing through the Sisters.

She felt her armour crack as a chainsword glanced off her helmet. It was a lucky escape, and she thanked the Emperor as she rained blows against the unfeeling opponent.

The enemy's fist caught her neck. She gasped for breath as its fingers pierced the cabling under her helmet. It was crushing the life from her, cutting short her prayers.

Helewise drove Reckoning at the foe, but the blade failed her. It did not bite, but skidded off the slabs of power armour.

She kicked and struggled as her strength lessened. Her vision went first as she tried to work her jaw, but no sound would come. As one fist crushed her throat, the other caught her right hand.

She snarled in fury but he was far stronger than her, and he was twisting her arm back and around her, to tear it from its socket even as he crushed her windpipe.

Helewise's vision blacked out. She wanted her last words to be a prayer, forced her lips to keep moving, even as her enemy squeezed the life from her.

She felt her death coming and she consigned her soul to the God-Emperor.

A voice boomed out about her. 'Smite my foes and bring them in chains for His holy judgement!'

At that moment the grip lessened.

She was thrown about as the Space Marine jerked back and forth. Blood poured down her eye-lenses. She was bathed in crimson as a giant buzz saw slammed through the Space Marine's chest.

It travelled up, the spinning teeth carving his body in two.

Before her stood a Penitent Engine, the operator's scrawny body lashed by chains onto a crucifix of rebar.

'Bless you!' Helewise called out as the engine stopped before her, its armaments twitching.

It doused the heretic's remains in a furious blast of righteous flame, then charged back into the fray.

From the Abbey of Eternal Watch, the Sisters watched the landing with a sudden hope. But while their voices were full of enthusiasm at first, as the hours wore on, and as they saw the armoured column reach the base of the Bolt before being hemmed in and surrounded, their tone grew increasingly despondent.

Lizbet turned away.

'They will not make it,' she said. 'We must abandon our watch, and aid them!'

'No,' Ysolt said. 'We must retain the Eternal Watch.'

'Let me go,' Lizbet said. 'I will take Chalybix, and together we will smite our foes.'

'No,' Ysolt told her. 'Look!'

As she spoke, they felt the unmistakable presence of Gloranthrax.

The daemon marched across the plains, bloated with slaughter, at the head of an army: tanks and bipedal engines possessed with daemonic powers, flaming Heldrakes swooping overhead, their metallic jaws spouting fire.

Their great enemy had returned to the Bolt.

The skies above them turned dark with fury as the daemon army approached. Palatine Albreda called on all her Sisters to gather around her.

'With me!' she called, and led the last, desperate charge.

The remaining Exorcists and Castigators came alongside, fire and shell raining into their foes. Helewise strode shoulder to shoulder with Lanete and a handful of Sisters Repentia – all that was left of the company that had come to battle.

Helewise felt uplifted by their sacrifice. They had made good their broken vows, at last – they had followed the saint, and taken martyrdom.

The Sisters followed after her, their blades slashing furiously as they cut a path through their foes. Penitent Engines marched alongside, throwing themselves into the enemy. One charged a Helbrute that was staggering along, blood and engine fluids leaking from a melta scar in its side. The two met in a screech of metal as each maddened creature tore lumps out of the other. The Helbrute's power fist crackled as it tore the cabling and hydraulics from the Penitent Engine, which fought back like a caged rat, kicking and snarling at the stronger foe.

Its buzz saws skidded over the Helbrute's armour, finding weak spots and tearing them open, seeking the imprisoned body within. Their armoured carapaces locked together. Each was death to the other, and the Sisters surged onwards, leaving the doomed melee behind as they grew close to the Bolt.

Their path was blocked by a daemon engine, a dreadful combination of six-legged tank and daemonic torso, one arm ending in a sword of warp fire, the other in a vast industrial claw.

'Out of our way, daemon!' Albreda commanded.

It answered her with a snort of fire, insectile legs powering the vast construct into a charge.

Helewise was at the Palatine's shoulder, her broadsword in hand, prayers on her lips. And with her came Morgandrie, Josmane and Aliciel – with the martyrdom of Ruslana and Aiguell fresh in their hearts.

iii

One of the battle chapels was burning as the Savlar Chem Dogs girded themselves for their last stand.

Shin and Chalice were bunkered down about its skirts. They had a problem. It wasn't the laud hailers over their heads, broadcasting thunderous hymns onto the battlefield, nor the cherubs that circled above, censers trailing behind them. No, it was the crackle and spit of the chapel's void shield.

'It's going to pop,' Shin warned.

Chalice nodded. And when it did, the Chaos fleet's batteries would pound it from space, and they'd be dead.

Chalice said nothing. The truth was, there was nowhere better to go. He felt better being in the shadow of the chapel. It wasn't just the aura of faith and confidence that flowed off it, it was also the sight of the Battle Sisters in their black armour, white hair framing their battle-scarred faces.

'How many do you think they have left?' Shin said, following Chalice's gaze.

351

He shrugged. 'I've only seen five.'

It didn't matter how many there were, it was their presence that counted. Every Dog felt them watching, and drove themselves to be better and greater.

'You know we're dead,' Shin said.

'Looks like it,' Chalice said, as he fumbled with his broken fingers for a fresh powercell. 'Here, help me.'

Shin sniffed as he slipped the fresh powercell into the laspistol. He handed it back. 'Want me to strap it back in?'

Chalice nodded. He didn't want to die without a weapon in his hand. 'Old gang superstitions,' he said.

Hearing movement to his left, Chalice turned and saw Mercy Cody coming along the line. As he made his way towards them at a half-crouch, something hit him. Cody stumbled for a few steps, then fell, plunging face first into the dirt.

Shin looked about. No Mercies. Nothing. He caught Chalice's eye.

'Is he dead?'

'Don't know.'

It didn't matter, dead or wounded. Both men were thinking the same thing. For this moment there was no one behind them with a loaded gun. It was a strange feeling for penal legionnaires. Despite the shit they were in, Chalice and Shin were, for the moment, free men once more.

Chalice clapped Shin on the shoulder as he took in a deep breath. 'Looks like we're at liberty.'

'What should we do?' Shin said.

Chalice looked at him. It was a stupid question and Shin knew it.

'We do what we always do. We fight,' he said.

Shin smiled. That was what he thought as well.

He reached inside his jacket for his last half-eaten piece of dried meat. 'Want some?' he said.

Chalice half smiled. 'It's all yours,' he said.

Shin smiled. 'Good. I was saving this one.'

The heretic land army rumbled towards them. The earth shook as the massed armour approached.

'They're coming,' Chalice warned him. He shouted along what was left of his line. 'Ready for battle!'

Shin scrabbled through his bandolier. He only had a handful of grenades left.

'Remember Dimok?'

Chalice didn't.

'Got himself shot on Ayaan. Before the Fang Takers attacked.'

Chalice nodded. He thought he remembered. 'What about him?'

'He was a lucky bastard.'

Chalice kept his head down as a shell landed just outside the void-shield perimeter. Another hit the shield itself and the whole thing flickered and crackled.

Aebram stood at Colonel Salem's shoulder as he assessed the strength of the army rolling towards them.

He lowered the monocular. It was hard to see through the smoke and dust, but it looked like the front row was at least five Gorgon armoured assault transports, with Hellhound variants mixed in.

Aebram put his hand out to Salem. 'Do your duty, colonel.'

Both men's grips were iron.

'You have led the Dogs well until this moment. Remember. Not one step backwards.'

Salem nodded. He wished someone would shoot this bastard so he could run.

'Thank you, sir,' he said. 'It's been a pleasure.'

Aebram paused. 'Has it?'

Salem laughed. 'No.'

'Good,' Aebram told him with a grin. 'It shouldn't be. You're a penal legionnaire, after all.'

The heretic armoured columns approached the ring of battle chapels in a broad front, turret-mounted weaponry laying down a furious fusillade.

The chapels returned fire, but a second one went up in flames – thick black smoke billowing from its vaulting domes. Shin kept his head down and said some brief words of contrition and repentance as autocannon rounds whined over his head.

Chalice fumbled for his whistle and gave it a single blast.

'Ready!' he shouted. Shin checked his hard-earned grenade launcher, his bandolier of rounds, found his footing, and waited for the next order to rise and charge.

The two men braced themselves for whatever came.

The heretic column was a hundred yards off when the battle chapels responded. Laud hailers broadcast hymns in a wall of sound that lifted the souls of the faithful, and struck fear into heretical hearts. Screaming salvos blasted out from defence organs and Exorcist launchers. The tube-launched salvos arced down onto the enemy tanks, smashing through the upper armour and wreaking havoc within.

The intensity of the salvo singed Shin's brows. He kept his head down and thanked the God-Emperor. Then the whistle blew two short blasts, and he threw himself up against the barricade and fired.

The Gorgons were burning just a hundred feet away. Shin could feel the heat on his face. He was glad of his goggles – they enabled him to stare into the inferno, helped him pick out the black silhouettes of the charging cultists.

The first grenade hit one in the chest. The dead man's legs kept powering ahead even as his body was ripped apart.

Shin pulled a fresh grenade from its webbing, found the loading slot and slammed it in, and picked out his target.

Chalice was firing his pistol over the parapet. A Chimera suddenly reared up on their left.

It slammed through the debris of burning wrecks, hull-mounted flamer spitting out a torrent of burning promethium. Shin saw a couple of Dogs go down before it. They rolled on the floor as the tank ran over them.

He put his eye to the sights, lined it up and fired as it mounted the barricade and crashed down on their side.

The grenade blasted into the track workings with a hail of shrapnel.

For a second nothing happened, then the tank slewed sideways as it shed a track.

The heretics responded almost immediately, the assault ramp slamming down and the carapace-armoured troops ducking out.

One of them had a plasma gun cradled in his arms. Shin saw that and his mouth went dry. He had to get that gun, he thought to himself, and slammed his last grenade into the slot.

iv

Gloranthrax roared across the Pilgrim Plains like a gale, swelling in size and fury, rising up with great bat wings, its jaws gnashing with teeth of iron.

Branwen's song still echoed through the halls, but it had lost potency with time, and Gloranthrax had grown in strength and power.

The daemon hauled its way up the Bolt like a dragon of legend. Claw by claw, right up to the abbey, tearing away chunks of holy masonry. Lizbet's mouth went dry as she saw the size of the thing. It was bloated with power and rage, and she was worn down and weary.

'Have faith, Sisters,' Lizbet rasped as the Sororitas on the plains began to fire up at the daemon. The surviving Sisters nodded, their lips moving in prayer as the daemon ripped a hole in the abbey wall. 'We will maintain our Eternal Watch.'

Gloranthrax's rise was relentless. They stood at the door of the abbey and waited for its approach. But rather than come across the ruins, it thrust its snout through the wall in a shower of masonry, roaring hatred into the chapel.

Branwen emptied her bolter magazine at it. The rounds were swallowed by a miasma of corruption. Lizbet leapt forwards, Chalybix in hand, her voice strong as she chanted lines from the Fede Imperialis.

'From the lightning and the tempest,

Oh Emperor, deliver us!

From the begetting of daemons,

Our Emperor, deliver us!'

Gloranthrax laughed at the prayer, and forced its massive form into the chapel. It filled the chamber, rising above them like a monstrous shadow, shedding flame and blood as it bellowed.

'Back to the warp, foul creature!' Lizbet shouted. She held her hand out and started to chant a prayer of banishment, but her words only fed it more power.

'*This* is *the warp*,' it told her, the words malformed through its inhuman snout. '*This is* my *world!*'

Lizbet saw eyes of black smoke that sucked in light. She saw a circle of leathery flesh, ringed with hooked fingers, a clawed mouth set within its centre.

And she was fearless as she stood in the middle of the chapel.

As the many arms clawed towards her, she cut and swiped, but each time she cut one arm away, two more took its place. The daemon crushed her with a claw, runes flaring within her helmet as the suit of armour struggled to deal with the catastrophic damage sustained. And even as she stabbed at it with Chalybix, the daemon caught the sword in its iron claw and broke it in two. It fell from Lizbet's hand and clattered to the chapel floor.

It tossed Lizbet aside, and would have stamped on her if Morcada and Brace had not leapt forward.

Their bolters barked but the daemon seemed untroubled by the rounds that hammered into its unholy flesh.

'When you perish, I shall devour your souls!'

Brace was the first to die as it caught her and lifted her to its mouth. Iron fangs tore her in half and tossed the remains aside. As it reached towards the canoness, Morcada stepped before it. 'I shall smite you down, foul creature!' she shouted.

Her fury halted the daemon for a moment, but its flicking tail lashed out and drove a brass spike through her chest.

'The sword!' Ysolt cried. She crawled over to it, even as the daemon turned towards her.

Branwen screamed a warning. Ysolt turned at the Sister's yell and, one-handed, fired her sacred melta.

It hit Gloranthrax in the torso and tore a hole right through. But before Ysolt's weapon could fully charge for a second shot, the wound had already sealed, and Gloranthrax made its way towards her. She turned and crawled desperately, stretching to reach the hilt of Chalybix, but as her foe drew nearer, the corruption within Canoness Ysolt's body boiled and she screamed with pain. With a flick of its tail, the daemon casually swatted the broken sword away.

'I thought to devour you last, old crone! But the creature inside you calls out to me with such a sweet song…'

It caught her foot and dragged her towards it, lifting her from the floor with effortless ease.

At that moment a chorus of voices chimed in.

Helewise stood at Palatine Albreda's shoulder, and behind them came the other Sisters of the Order of Our Martyred Lady who had crossed the Great Rift to sacrifice themselves here.

'Foul daemon!' Albreda roared. 'You were banished five thousand years before! Back to your hole, you worm!'

She swung at the beast, her sword scoring a gaping wound

across its chest. But again, the wound healed, and the daemon reached for her with a hand of fire.

Helewise swung with Reckoning, and cut that hand away. It blinked from existence as the stump slammed into the Palatine, and then another hand pushed through the wound, reaching out for her again.

Unseen by the daemon, Sister Branwen caught up the stump of the saint's sword and charged. She sang her own song, and the sword flared bright white as if with recognition, like the last sudden gleam from the setting sun.

The saint spoke through her as she slashed at the terrible thing with the stump of the sword. 'Out, vile daemon! This is hallowed ground, anathema to the unholy! Back to the hell from which you were spawned!'

Gloranthrax spun around, even as the Sisters unleashed torrents of holy fire, bolts and melta beams into its profane form.

It roared with pain as it clutched for Branwen.

In a moment of clarity, the young Sister understood that she could not fight this thing. There was no winning in a contest of power. Not here, not where this creature's strength was at its zenith. Victory lay through faith and sacrifice.

Instead of retreating before it, Branwen dropped her guard.

The creature snatched her greedily, and dragged her to its dripping maw.

There were sounds of horror as the daemon's fangs pierced her body front and back, but even as Branwen let out a cry of pain, she plunged the stump of Chalybix into the daemon's eye, and the blade hissed like a red-hot iron plunged into ice.

Gloranthrax let out a great moan of pain. Its blood gushed out like molten rock. Branwen's arm was burnt right up to the shoulder but she refused to let go, and drove the stump in again.

The daemon lashed back and forth as it was blinded. It threw

Branwen's body across the chamber. She slammed into the wall as Lizbet struggled to her feet.

'Drive it out!' Helewise called, and the Sisters goaded it with sacral flame out of the abbey gates; sent it tumbling down the steps, until it was standing on the precipice where the heretics had once been burnt.

The daemon scrabbled desperately for purchase. But it was blind and agonised by so many Sisters unleashing their blessed ammunition into it.

As the daemon cried out in pain and despair, Lizbet put her boot upon the belly of the beast and shoved it backwards. The daemon teetered for a moment before it toppled, crashing down from the high peak of the Bolt, down to the ground below in flames and ruin.

For a moment it looked as if it were trying to crawl back under the Bolt, but its life force was shattered. It flickered for a moment before it was banished with a clap of thunder, the air rushing into the void it had once occupied.

Lizbet ran over to where Branwen lay, unmoving. Her armour and body were in ruin. Blood ran in hot torrents from her nose and mouth.

'Branwen!' Lizbet shouted, calling out to her, but the young Sister was slipping away.

'Lift her!' Ysolt yelled.

They carried her to the altar and laid her down upon it.

Helewise came in, fresh from the banishment of the daemon.

'She is dying,' Lizbet said.

'Martyred,' Morgandrie said.

The Battle Sisters came in to pray beside Branwen as she lay on the brink of death. It seemed their words brought the young Sister a little strength, and Branwen opened her mouth to speak.

'Have faith, Sisters… Turn your grief into flames and purge. Do not grieve… Fire tests the quality of each of us.'

'She was touched by the light,' Ysolt said.

The words were true, for as Branwen died, her soul, magnified by her martyrdom, shone out through the empyrean with all the brilliance of a psychic flare. The Sisters all felt its light upon their anima. All their eyes shone with an inner light for the briefest moment, before it faded away, leaving the afterglow to comfort them ever after.

Battle Group Phaedra was stuck in the warp. Its time was rapidly running out, and Navigator Sicil knew that he had failed.

He sat rigid in his throne, knuckles white, teeth clenched in a grinding snarl. The battle group's Navigators were looking to him to lead them through, but he was lost and trapped, and another warp storm was boiling up about them.

The Geller-field generators screamed with the prolonged effort. They could not last much longer and he did not think he had the strength to lead them back.

The ship slammed into another warp reef, and blood started dripping from his nose. He let out a moan of pain and despair. There was nothing left for it. He turned to prayer as a death rattle sounded throughout the ship.

It was the prayer of a Navigator to the Golden Throne, the prayer that had steered generations of his house through the warp for so long:

'Guide me through the darkness,

Steer me through the bottomless channels,
Yea, though I steer through thunder and tempest,
Anoint the waves with your sacred oil.
Steer me with your golden light.
Let your soul shine out from Holy Terra.'

He did not expect to be heard. The prayer was one of pure faith, for they had sailed beyond the light of the Astronomican, and beyond His hearing.

But as he prayed, very suddenly, amidst the confused bruised purple of the warp, a gleam shone out.

It was not the resplendent light that came from the Golden Throne upon Holy Terra, but a blue-white flash, as searing as heated metal. It stood out from the maelstrom of insanity, as bright and sudden as a starburst, a serene glow amidst the benighted darkness of the Imperium Nihilus.

Sicil felt a surge of hope, and as the sudden flare began to fade, an image was seared upon the retina of his third eye – the shape of a young Battle Sister, etched in gold.

He steered his craft towards the light, and suddenly the roiling clouds and figures that had tormented them relented. He saw the scar of the Mandeville point and pitched towards it, and as the Geller-field generator gave its last, they plunged through into realspace.

The *Vigorous* groaned as the ship's iron skeleton returned to the laws of gravity and sanity. Qartermayne was on the bridge within moments as the ship's augurs scrambled to get their bearings. The servitors' brains were overwhelmed by reels of realspace information. They let out a strange mewling sound as the cogitator fans whirred into sudden action.

'Did we make it through?' Qartermayne demanded.

The bridge captain's staff were already bent over their screens.

'I believe so, sir, but I have asked the Lord Navigator for confirmation.'

Qartermayne strode forwards. 'Any idea where we are?'

'None,' he said. 'We are determining.'

'And the fleet?'

'They are arriving as we speak.'

One by one the whole of Battle Group Phaedra slammed back into realspace. A proud fleet of conquest, each ship's captain reporting their craft ready for orders.

'Sir!' an officer said after a moment. 'Lord Sicil confirms. We have crossed the Cicatrix Maledictum.'

Commissar-General Qartermayne's skin goose pimpled. He punched his open palm in a gesture of triumph and awe. 'Yes!' he hissed, though he could hardly believe it, and his voice trembled with the magnitude of that statement. 'Bridge captain, please hail the captains of the fleet, and let it be known that Battle Group Phaedra, of Fleet Quintus, has brought the light of the Emperor to the Imperium Nihilus.'

At that moment the augurs started to bring up contacts. 'Sir,' the gunnery officer said, low with concern. 'Look!'

The holo-display hummed into life, and a rough map of the system lit up in the air above the projector. Alarm klaxons rang out. There was a whole fleet out there, and whoever they were, they were drawing a target upon the *Vigorous*.

The nearest contact was immediately identified by the cogitators' data banks. A swirling holo-image depicted a brutal all-rounder, with lance, batteries and carrier capabilities.

'*Foebane*.'

'*Foebane*... I think some of you have met her before.'

'Yes, sir!' the gunnery officer said. 'Retaliator-class grand cruiser. Battle of the Brethren Hollow. Mutinied at Galan V, five thousand years ago.'

'That's right,' Qartermayne said, and allowed himself a tight smile.

At nearly five miles long and one mile abeam, the *Foebane* was a formidable opponent, containing a crew of nearly one hundred and fifty thousand souls.

'I have left a picket force around the supply and troop ships,' Admiral Jayn reported. 'Front-line craft are engaging at full speed. I assume we attack?'

Qartermayne clapped his hands together. 'Yes, admiral, attack at once!'

Admiral Jayn nodded and turned to the gunnery officer. 'How long to contact?'

The gunnery officer was tracking the targets with each sweep of the augur. 'Two minutes, sir.'

Admiral Jayn's voice was firm as he gave the order. 'Gunnery officer. Ready the nova cannon.'

Qartermayne's face was set, his arms behind his back, his heart beating steadily, his nostrils flaring with military intent. The seconds passed incredibly slowly as the gunnery officer called out the diminishing range. As they approached five thousand miles, the officer started the process of firing the nova cannon.

Step by step the orders were given over the gunnery-deck vox, repeated, confirmed, and then when the action was complete the information was relayed back to the bridge. The ship's lights flickered as the nova cannon began to charge. The commissar-general stood to watch as the gunnery officer continued counting down. Admiral Jayn stood next to him.

'Ready to fire, sir!'

At a nod from Qartermayne, Jayn gave the order, and the cruiser shook as the cannon fired. The darkness was lit with streaks of luminescent gases as the projectiles raced towards the foe.

'A direct hit,' the gunnery officer reported, as a second salvo was being prepared.

The heretic fleet had been caught at anchor above Holy Cion, their weapons trained on the planet below. Battle Group Phaedra steamed towards them at full speed, nova cannon salvos smashing the stationary vessels. The *Foebane* broke apart, and the Navy officers watched with intense satisfaction as the heavy cruiser's treachery came to an end. Ship by ship, they pummelled the traitor fleet as it struggled to respond.

The Chaos cruisers hauled in their grav-anchors, and attempted to raise shields, charge guns and channel energy to their motivational power all at the same time. As any Naval officer knew, it was an impossible task. The Imperial captains could barely believe the luck that had delivered the heretic fleet to them in this manner. The gunnery decks could not load and fire fast enough.

The Imperial carriers launched torpedo bombers in flight wave after flight wave. They powered through the void, the Chaos fleet laid out before them like a feast, big ships already burning under the weight of the Imperial onslaught.

As the attack craft sped towards them, the heretic captains tried desperately to bring interceptors up to the flight decks. But their hangars were crowded with troops and transport ships waiting for disembarkation. The torpedo bombers lined the Chaos cruisers up and unleashed their payloads, then swung back around, whooping and singing praises to the God-Emperor.

The *Pact Infernus* had brought up a store of bombardment ordnance to attack the planet. The gunnery officers were desperately attempting to switch the armaments when they were hit by a salvo of torpedoes that slammed through the ship's ablative plating. The gunnery decks were crammed with ordnance, setting off a chain of secondary explosions that gutted the port side and sent billowing clouds of burning gas venting out into space.

But worst of all, in their haste, the gunners had left the ammunition hoists open with stacks of propellant charges ready for loading. These ignited, and rapidly expanding fireballs rolled through the flash-gates, down into the armoured guts of the craft where the magazine decks were located.

Open cases of ordnance cooked off as more and more fyceline shells started to burn. Flames roared through the machinery decks and ventilation ducts that ran through the ship. Charge after charge ignited, as hundreds of tons of encased propellant were set alight in a bare fraction of a second. The reinforced deck armour contained the pressure for a brief moment, making the resultant explosion even more catastrophic. A hell storm of fire, ordnance and superheated air blasted through the craft, ripping the ship in half. Its plasma generators and rear section skidded forwards, as expansive explosions vented about the craft and the void sucked the crew out through a thousand rents in its armour.

Within seconds, the Chaos flagship was a burning wreck. Heretic captains desperately tried to flee, but the *Vigorous* led the line of Imperial craft into the middle of the enemy cruisers, and unleashed deadly broadsides port and starboard.

On the *Bitter Maw*, the captain saw the fleet of attack craft swinging towards him and vented the hangar decks without warning. Whole regiments were sucked into the vacuum before the airlocks were restored, and support crews scrambled to get their interceptors airborne.

They had barely launched when the first salvo of torpedoes slammed into the plasma generators, which exploded like an overheated star – tearing the craft in two, and sending the fragments spinning. The prow hit the *Annihilator*, which had managed to return fire at the approaching Imperial fleet, tearing a jagged rent along its starboard flank.

The scenes of destruction were multiplied throughout the heretic fleet. A few of the traitor ships managed to return fire, but the salvos were rushed and the few hits were deflected by the the *Vigorous'* reinforced prow armour. The Imperial flagship led its fleet into close quarters in a textbook action that would have made the commandants of the Imperial Navy scholams proud.

The void was lit with the burning hulks of heretic craft as the Imperial vessels unleashed broadside after broadside into the anchored fleet. The skies above Holy Cion flared with the incessant lightning of lance strikes.

vi

The pall of purple clouds had lifted. The plains were littered with bodies and wreckage. All that was left now was the smog and dust of battle. But the heretic assault had been halted, and the expected follow-ups did not come. There was a brief respite.

Aebram made his way along the line to assess the damage.

One of the battle chapels was burning, a column of thick black smoke billowing up into the sky. But the perimeter had held the initial assault. Aebram instructed Chalice to pull his Dogs back. 'Shorten the line,' he said.

Chalice gave a set of three short blasts upon his whistle. The Dog packs pulled back through the dead and the burning tanks.

Shin sloped back and led the Dogs to the ring of battle chapels. Chalice looked at him, and Shin grinned. He held the plasma gun in his arms with all the tenderness and care of a father with his child.

At that moment, there was a sonic boom. They looked up as a fireball appeared in the sky above them.

'What the frekk is that?'

The flame grew larger and larger, falling in a slow parabola. It took nearly a minute to crash into the plains.

'That's a voidship,' Aebram said, 'or part of one...'

They stood and stared in wonder as the sky started to rain debris. They felt the impacts as they prepared for another assault, but it did not come. One after another, hunks of battleship crashed to the ground.

The plains were littered with bodies and wreckage from the void battle, and from the sky they saw the shape of reinforcements grav-chuting to the planet.

The destruction of the heretic fleet transformed the situation upon the planet. The Chaos forces had been expecting an easy victory. Some of the troops had been only partially unloaded. Others were waiting for their armour or supplies, and suddenly all of them were stranded.

Despair had turned to victory, and the Dogs pushed ahead as wreckage was still falling to the ground and a mass-drop of Elysians reinforced their positions. The Chem Dogs and the Elysians drove the confused heretics back from the environs of the Bolt before retreating to the ring of battle chapels. And then the bombardment began, Battle Group Phaedra scouring the heretics from Holy Cion with a relentless barrage of flame.

The heretical fleet was almost entirely destroyed. Rather than face capture, the troop transport *Charnel Horns* was scuttled by its crew, the massive craft tumbling to the ground. The *Absolver of Blood* attempted to flee, and was devastated by lance strikes from the *Vigorous'* array of dorsal turrets. Last to die was the *Scarlet Scythe*, which was aflame as its captain tried to ram the light carrier *Mortis Redeemer*.

The captain of the *Mortis* swung his craft round as a swarm of bombers and interceptors descended upon their enemy. Attack runs shredded the *Scarlet Scythe*'s bridge, and its captain lost control of his craft as the steering mechanism locked. It spun towards the planet, straying too deep into the gravity well, and was pulled to the ground over Cion's southern continental mass.

The only troops to escape were the remains of the Crimson Slaughter warband that had attacked the *Daughter of the Emperor*. They left their drop pods, tanks and dead where they had fallen, littering the land about the Bolt.

Sawbones shuffled through the piles of dead, sucking on his opiates, tutting as he turned bodies over and looked at the faces. One trooper waited for him, his hood pulled low over his head. Sawbones made his way towards him, his rebreather hissing between his clenched teeth.

'You look well, major.'

Chalice smiled. 'I'm a fast healer.'

Sawbones laughed. 'I didn't think you'd make it...' he said, sucking on his rebreather.

Sawbones shuffled right up to Major Chalice, who was rolling a fresh lho-stick for himself. When he saw who Chalice was staring at, he laughed.

'You've not killed him yet?'

'Salem?' Chalice tapped the lho-stick onto his knee, and then stuck the end in his mouth and lit it in a cloud of blue smoke. 'Not yet,' he said. *Not yet.*

Helewise picked her way back towards the battle chapel that she had landed in.

It had survived the battle, she saw. Tech-priests were already at work, one of them moving along the line of surviving Penitent

Engines, hosing them down, the bloody water swilled away through the drains before they were returned to their chamber.

It hadn't been decided yet what to do with the *Daughter of the Emperor*. They had to establish if she was still void-worthy.

Until then, she remained their home.

Helewise caught a scent that reminded her of her father. She turned, and saw a man smoking a lho-stick.

She paused as she caught his eye. Just a Guardsman, she thought, and turned away, but something made her look back.

'I know you,' she said, her voice a rich, gravelly sound.

The man stood to attention, and slipped the lho-stick behind his back. 'Holy City, Ayaan. The Chapel of Saint Thor. Your name, begging your pardon, is Sister Helewise of the Order of Our Martyred Lady.'

She smiled. It wasn't an expression she was used to, but now it all came back. 'Your name is Chalice.'

He blushed. She went on, 'Your mother was religious.'

'That's it,' he said.

She paused, and coughed. 'You have also come all this way?'

He nodded towards the *Daughter of the Emperor*. 'We came with you. In the bilge deck.' He fumbled for a moment, and said, 'I have something of yours. I hope you do not mind. I did not want to leave it in the dirt.'

He held it out to her. A wax seal with a prayer strip.

She took it from him and looked at it. 'A purity seal. Keep it!'

He didn't want to take it, but he hated to let it go. 'There is writing on it…' he said. 'What does it say?'

'You cannot read?'

He shook his head.

Helewise knew the words. They were in High Gothic, and she translated them for him. 'By bolter shell, flamer burst and melta blast, the mutant, the heretic and the traitor are cleansed of their sin of existence. So it has been for five millennia. So it shall be until the end of time.'

He smiled. 'By bolter shell, flamer burst and melta blast... I like that!'

She turned away, but she saw something lying on the ground by his feet and picked it up.

It was a simple lead token, stamped with the fleur-de-lys. 'A pilgrim badge,' she said, and looked at him. 'You have completed the Pilgrimage of Fire. That is a great honour. It cleanses you of many sins.'

'I have many to cleanse.'

'So do we all.' She placed the lead token in Chalice's palm. 'Keep it,' she said, 'and remember.'

As Helewise returned to her cell, she met Sister Dialogus Dovere leaving her own.

While most of the Order were to accompany the rest of the fleet to battle, some were staying behind to rebuild the Abbey of Eternal Watch.

'You are staying behind,' Helewise said.

Dovere's expression was hard to read. In the blank data-goggles Helewise could see her own reflection: the scar on her cheek, the bruising on her throat, the cuts and grazes she had suffered.

'There is much to do. Miracles to record!'

'So I heard. A foundling...'

Dovere nodded. She would dedicate herself to the preservation of the tale of Sister Branwen, she who was touched by the God-Emperor's light.

'Farewell,' Helewise said.

Dovere blushed and bobbed, and was about to pass by when Helewise spoke again.

'I should thank you.'

'Me?'

'Yes,' Helewise said. 'You gave me strength out there. It was a line you said, from the *Grimoire Opheliatus*. "Smite my foes and bring them in chains for His holy judgement!"'

'Ah!' Dovere said. 'Actually that was not from the *Grimoire*. It was a line I had heard from the sadhvus. It was one of their battle-cants. A rousing line, I thought.'

Helewise nodded. 'I will inscribe it onto a purity seal. I shall have to find the sadhvus' verses. Have they been collected yet?'

'Not yet.'

'Next time,' Helewise said.

When Helewise returned to her chamber, it was as it had been, before they landed on Holy Cion.

Reckoning hung on its stand, the blade cleaned, oiled and freshly blessed.

Helewise knelt before it, and offered thanks to the saint for her precious blade, her sword-arm, and her fierce spirit. And thanked her that her martyrdom had not yet come.

Not yet.

Epilogue

Holy Cion

'I am far from absolution. Lost to any exculpation. I offer myself to repentance. Before the Emperor I have sinned. Beyond forgiveness. Beyond forbearance. Beyond mercy.'

– Oath of the Penitent

A week later, Commissar-General Qartermayne landed on the Pilgrim Plains, as Saint Katherine had done millennia before.

They had the stink of death, and the whole plains were white with bones of the ancient pilgrims. The whiteness stretched away as far as they could see. But despite the scent, the breeze had an uplifting air to it.

Some had reached this place before them. Between them and the Bolt stood the ring of battle chapels. There were streaks of black soot, burnt-out windows, battle damage where the shields had failed. But from others the light shone out. And from the laud hailers came the sound of sublime singing, which lifted the hearts of all who heard it.

They were all veteran warriors, but none could listen to the singing and not stop and stand and stare, and feel, for a moment, just a little of the faith that moved the Adepta Sororitas.

A crowd stood and stared at the ring of chapels. More came

than left, so the gathering slowly grew. It was silent, contem-plative, thoughtful.

Qartermayne was already planning the expansion out from Cion. Battle Group Phaedra had many objectives that it had to capture, linking up with the rest of Fleet Quintus and driving deep into the Imperium Nihilus.

Munitorum emissaries staked out camps across the Pilgrim Plains. Tents and perimeter fences spread as far as the eye could see. The remaining battle chapels formed a circumference about the *Daughter of the Emperor*, and the ground within was empty except where the Dogs had raised their camp.

Their simple bivouacs of stretched tarps huddled among the ruins of the shrine. Within each the Dogs hoarded their pitiful worldly possessions. So few of them had survived that they each inherited five other Dogs' possessions. Each of them felt like a rich man.

The whole regiment only needed a handful of tents. At the far end was the one belonging to Sawbones.

Trooper Shin waited his turn. The file of Dogs sat hunched against the wall, each one nursing their wounds. One by one they limped inside, their pockets full of things they thought they might barter for healing.

There was a long silence as they waited, and time and again they heard the whine of the buzz saw, the note changing as it cut through flesh and bone.

Some did not come out. Others held cauterised stumps of arms and legs, or wounds stained purple with iodine. Shin waited, chewing on a hunk of slab that he had found in a dead man's pockets.

The meat was covered with a red powder. It was some kind of flavouring. He sucked on it thoughtfully. It tagged some distant memory, but he could not think what it was. He wanted to ask someone, but he didn't want to share it. It was his and he sucked on it, and remembered a time before this. Before he was sent to Savlar...

When it was Shin's turn he pushed himself up and pulled the cloth aside.

Sawbones' clinic was a ruined hab, with a few beams and a scrap of roofing remaining.

There was a pile of amputated limbs lying to the side.

'That will keep you going!' he said, sucking on his rebreather as he chuckled at Shin's arrival.

Shin said nothing. He pulled out a whole chunk of slab, still in its foil wrapper. He tossed it down. Sawbones picked it up and slipped it into the folds of his robes.

The medic did not move.

Shin looked at him. 'You want more?'

Sawbones sucked on his rebreather, and let out some thin blue smoke.

'You frekking bastard,' Shin said.

Sawbones sucked on the pipe again. Shin wanted the slab back now. After all the gifts he'd given this bastard, he thought, and reached into his pocket. 'Here!' he said.

He held out a pict. It was a woman in a black lace dress with net gloves that reached up to her elbow. *Mamzel Hilma*, the name said, in worn gold lettering. 'Salem's girl,' he said.

Sawbones sniffed and reached out.

Shin pulled it back. 'Counterseptic,' he said. Sawbones pulled out a small bottle of red pills. He tossed it to Shin, who caught it in one hand, checked the label and slipped it into his pocket.

Shin touched Mamzel Hilma to his cheek, and then handed her over. Sawbones looked at her for a long time.

'Salem's?' he said. 'I didn't know he was dead.'

'He's not,' Shin said. 'He wanted my plasma gun, gave me her in return.'

Sawbones chuckled as the trooper sat down before him and pulled his clothes aside to reveal the injury. It was low on his left side. The bruised flesh was purple. In the middle was a wound, the jagged lips discoloured, weeping pus and clear fluids.

'Shrapnel,' Shin said.

Sawbones nodded. He leaned towards the wound and sniffed. 'You're lucky,' he said.

Shin laughed. He had never thought that.

'This will hurt,' Sawbones said, and handed him a biting rag.

It was wet. Shin put it in his mouth and bit down as he slid his hand into his pocket and wrapped his fingers about his battle knife.

Sawbones found a scalpel, flicked on his brow-lumen and made tutting sounds as he cut the flesh open. Shin gritted his teeth, but the real pain came when Sawbones picked his long-handled tweezers from the tray and probed inside.

An hour later, Shin put one hand to the wall and swayed in the doorway. He'd kept the piece of shrapnel. It was still dark with his blood, the curved metal shell casing jagged where it had been ripped apart.

The next in line pushed himself up, and Shin shook his hand and spoke in a bare croak. 'Good luck.'

That afternoon, the surviving Dogs stood on parade. Aebram was at the front of the surviving Mercies as they made their way along the line. Colonel Salem carried his plasma gun slung over one shoulder. The Marshal nodded. 'Very good, colonel.'

'Thank you, sir,' Colonel Salem said, and saluted. He turned and looked at the survivors, and Major Chalice met his gaze. Salem nodded for the order to be given for the regiment to fall out. The Dogs would be brought back to strength, which meant he'd have to deal with a frekk-load of new penal troops.

There was always trouble as the pecking order asserted itself.

As he turned back, the Marshal appeared to be waiting, and Salem moved towards him and waited for a signal to approach.

'All good, sir?'

The Marshal nodded, but said nothing.

Colonel Salem paused. 'Did Wythers survive?'

'I don't know,' the Marshal said. There was a pause. 'I hope not. I hope he is laid before the Emperor's judgement.'

Salem looked away. He didn't much like the word 'judgement' and he fell silent, thinking about the crimes he'd be judged for, when his time came.

Helewise and her Sisters were busy in the weeks that followed, roaming across Holy Cion, cleansing the place of any lasting heresy and purifying the tainted world. They cast down heretic shrines and emblems, burnt icons, and flushed out any remaining forces.

At the end of their final campaign, when Helewise and Morgandrie returned to the Pilgrim Plains, the reconstruction was underway, and the vox-chatter was of where they might go next. The Shrine of Landing was already being restored and rebuilt.

The two of them strode up the marble steps and down the long corridor to the amphitheatre within.

They looked down at the sacred spot where Saint Katherine had landed. The heretics had burnt the wood and filled it up with filth. That had all been cleared away, and now the plaster had been restored, the stone cleaned, and even though it was empty, there was something beautiful in the stark white simplicity.

A familiar voice broke their reverie. It was Sister Dovere. She looked down at the blessed space. 'The Palatine has put me in charge,' she said.

'You have done much already.'

Dovere was pensive. 'Yes,' she said. 'I am already working on the murals.' She looked up at the freshly plastered vaults. 'There are archives… but I was considering approaching the Palatine. I thought our arrival should also be memorialised.'

Her augmetic goggles looked from one of the Sisters to the other. 'Of course,' Helewise said. 'Despite all the barriers before us, we have reclaimed this world from heresy. There will come a time when these events will be distant history. The faithful will look back upon this moment and read our story, and they will find comfort there.'

The two Sisters walked about the shrine, feeling the weight of loss and destruction.

They would not see it restored. Not in their lifetimes.

As they returned to their cells, Morgandrie was the first to speak. 'This journey has tested me in ways that I did not imagine.'

Helewise nodded. They had plunged into the darkness of the Imperium Nihilus.

'I still miss His presence,' she said. 'But we shall have to be more perceptive. The God-Emperor has proved His grace extends across the whole galaxy.'

'He is with us yet.'

Helewise put her hand on Morgandrie's shoulder. 'Our pilgrimage is done. A new one must begin.'

'This must have been how the saint felt, five thousand years ago. You know your histories, where did she go next?'

'Agnet Tor. Pursuing the Witch-cult of Mnestteus.'

'And martyrdom.'

'And martyrdom,' Helewise said.

Sister Dovere's team consisted of the finest illustrators from her Order. They sketched out the most important moments from their pilgrimage, starting with Battle Group Phaedra, the *Daughter of the Emperor* plunging into the darkness of the Cicatrix Maledictum, Albreda kneeling at Hemponia's side, and proceeding on and on through their journey.

But there was one part of the story for which Dovere had to go to the Sisters of the Abbey of Eternal Watch. One by one she recorded their testimony. It was all vital information. She had faith that the Ecclesiarchy would want to know, once the Imperium Nihilus was reclaimed.

The last Sister she interviewed was Sister Lizbet, who came reluctantly and sat down before the Sister Dialogus.

'You were selected to take the part of the saint, in the Ritual of Landing.'

'Yes.'

'How did you feel about this?'

'I did not want it.'

'No?'

'No.'

'Was it not a great honour?'

'I was not worthy.'

Dovere paused. Sister Lizbet was rigid, her face set almost in pain.

'I'm sorry,' Dovere said. 'I know this is difficult. But these are important details.'

Lizbet nodded.

'I wanted to ask you about the child.'

'The maid?'

Dovere's goggled eyes reflected Lizbet back to herself. 'Other witnesses say that she claimed her powers of healing came from you.'

'Yes, she said that.'

'Is it true?'

'No.'

'Did you heal her?'

Lizbet paused, remembering that moment, so long before, when she had been walking to the refectory, deep in thought. 'I laid hands upon her,' she said. 'And I prayed.'

'And were her hands healed?'

'So she said.'

'Would she lie?'

Lizbet paused. 'No. The saint moved through me.'

'And she banished the daemon?'

'She helped.'

'How?'

There was a long pause. Dovere wanted to know what happened next.

'I had fought it,' Lizbet said finally. 'It was a terrible foe.'

'And you hurt it?'

'I did. But I could not kill it.'

'So how did she?'

'I cannot say.' Lizbet pursed her lips. 'It needed a great sacrifice. And... my own life was not precious enough.'

Commissar-General Qartermayne turned over his flagship, the *Vigorous*, to the Sisters to replace their own craft. They renamed it the *Eternal Watch*, and filled its corridors with prayer and devotion. Within its bowels, the man who had once been Wythers hung from the front of the Penitent Engine. He had earned a little grace upon Holy Cion, and the God-Emperor was beneficent.

While the other penitents hung in states of tortured agony, the neural implants within his brain soothed his mind. He was, for the moment, in a state of tranquility.

It could not last, of course. At the next battlefield, as the agony returned, the shock would drive him to yet greater deeds. But for the moment his mind believed himself in a cloister, calm and at peace, his heartbeat slowing to a bare twitch as the sound of pure singing drifted down to him from a distant chapel.

The Bolt rose amidst the tent city. A leaning black cone of rock, with the spires and domes of the abbey rising from its summit. Once again the bell tower sounded, as songs of gratitude filled the chapel.

Branwen was laid out upon the altar, with the shards of Chalybix next to her. The Sisters of Our Martyred Lady stood as an honour guard about her as Canoness Ysolt led the prayer.

When the prayers were done, Palatine Albreda entered to pay her respects. They stood over Branwen's body and each of them felt envy.

'She was just a maid-of-all-work,' Ysolt said. 'But one of pure faith.'

'And the saint chose her?'

'Yes. Who would have thought that the humblest among us should have been the vessel of the Emperor's grace?'

Palatine Albreda nodded.

The two women looked on in thought. Albreda was the first to speak. 'But you had faith.'

Ysolt paused as she looked back. Her faith had been tested many times, but it was true. She had never lost faith, even when they had seemed doomed.

'And the wounds?'

'Healing,' Ysolt said, and forced a smile. 'It is a blessing to be able to walk again, however slowly.'

The canoness smiled as she paused at the bottom of the ramp. 'We must carry the flame of faith to each world within the sector. And we must purge the darkness!'

After she spoke, Sister Lizbet came to her. She had dressed again in her own armour, and now stood, looking grave as she waited to speak.

She knelt before Ysolt. 'Canoness,' she said. 'You promised me that I could take the vows of the penitent when the planet was saved.'

'I did. But you did not fail. Without you we would have been lost, long before.'

'Please,' Lizbet said. 'Give me the grace of martyrdom.'

Ysolt nodded sadly. 'If I cannot dissuade you, my child, then you may take the vows of Repentia. Go with my blessing. And may the God-Emperor bless you with a suitable death.'

Sister Lanete was summoned by Ysolt to the Abbey of Eternal Watch, to observe the vows of Repentia. Lizbet had spent the night in prayer. She knelt before the altar.

'I leave this company of my own free will, and by my will shall I return. I shall seek the Emperor's forgiveness in the darkest places of the night,' Lizbet pronounced.

Lanete wet her lips. 'Sister Lizbet, I condemn you to a life of contrition, purgatory and penitence. Only in death do you have any hope of absolution. Seek the Emperor's forgiveness in the darkest places of the night. Only He can offer you hope of absolution. Only He can purge your soul of its misdeeds.'

Sister Lanete removed each piece of armour from Lizbet's body. When she was done, Lizbet knelt bare-kneed upon the tiles. Her limbs were naked, the flesh stretched tight over her lean musculature. Her body was covered with a simple surplice, upon which she had diligently inked her sins and failings, so that all might read them.

When she had stripped Lizbet, Lanete took a pair of shears and cut her hair away, right down to the skin, clumps falling to the floor.

Lanete's hands were rough. Here and there the blood ran as she nicked the skin, and blood trickled down Lizbet's face.

'When forgiveness is yours, we shall welcome you back. Until such time you are nameless to us,' Lanete told her.

Lizbet closed her eyes. 'See me and do not see me. Know me and know fear, for I have no face today but this one. I stand before you a Sister Repentia, until absolution finds me once more.'

'So shall it be,' Lanete intoned. After a pause, she added, 'You have chosen an extra chastisement.'

Lizbet nodded.

'Speak it!'

Lizbet coughed to clear her throat. 'A vow of silence until death.'

An attendant handed Lanete a needle and ball of steel thread.

'In silence shall you serve!' she declared, and pulled Lizbet's lips between her fingers, put the needle to the flesh and pushed.

The needle came through with a bead of blood, and she pulled the steel thread so that the knot caught on the entry wound, then looped it through the knot and made another stitch.

'Muzzled shall you strive for death, for forgiveness and a cleansing of your sins.'

Lizbet made no sound as the thread was pulled through her living flesh.

She closed her eyes as Lanete went on, and felt relief wash

through her. She would no longer be Lizbet the paragon. Those pressures had gone.

She would be nameless, faceless, silent.

And so she would serve.

Lanete was rough as she pulled the thread through its final loop and used Lizbet's nostril to finish the stitch. When she was done, she took the leather hood of the penitent from her belt, and placed it upon the Sister-once-named-Lizbet's head.

Then she locked the belt of penitence about the Sister's waist and manacled her wrists.

The cells that ringed the chapel were all empty. None of the penitentiary Sisters had survived the battle for Cion. The room was just as the last occupant had left it – strewn with straw, with no more furniture than a bare metal bed and a washbowl.

'The Emperor protects,' she said, as she swung the door closed and turned the key. And left the Sister who was once named Lizbet alone in the darkness.

As the new Repentia was consigned to her cell, Major Chalice lay on his back, the pilgrim badge hanging from a chain about his neck.

He filled his lungs with sweet smoke, closed his eyes and exhaled slowly.

She was imprinted upon his memory, white hair hanging about her face, stark against her suit of battle-stained black power armour. All he could think of was how fierce, how pure, how beautiful, how steadfast she was.

When he died, it would be for her, he told himself.

One day.

ABOUT THE AUTHOR

Justin D Hill is the author of the Warhammer 40,000 novels *Cadia Stands*, *Cadian Honour*, *Traitor Rock*, *Shadow of the Eighth* and *Pilgrims of Fire*. He has also written the Necromunda novel *Terminal Overkill*, the Warhammer Horror novel *The Bookkeeper's Skull* and the Space Marine Battles novel *Storm of Damocles*, as well as several short stories. His novels have won a number of prizes, as well as being *Washington Post* and *Sunday Times* Books of the Year. He lives ten miles uphill from York, where he is indoctrinating his four children in the 40K lore.

YOUR
NEXT READ

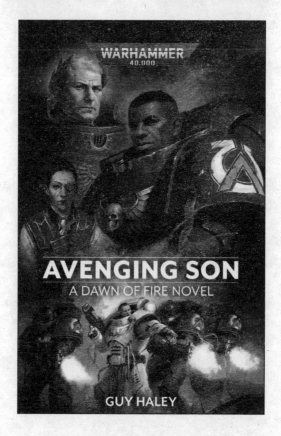

AVENGING SON
by Guy Haley

As the Indomitus Crusade spreads out across the galaxy, one battlefleet must face a dread Slaughter Host of Chaos. Their success or failure may define the very future of the crusade – and the Imperium.

An extract from
Avenging Son
by Guy Haley

'I was there at the Siege of Terra,' Vitrian Messinius would say
in his later years.

'I was there…' he would add to himself, his words never meant
for ears but his own. 'I was there the day the Imperium died.'

But that was yet to come.

'To the walls! To the walls! The enemy is coming!' Captain
Messinius, as he was then, led his Space Marines across the Penitent's Square high up on the Lion's Gate. 'Another attack! Repel
them! Send them back to the warp!'

Thousands of red-skinned monsters born of fear and sin scaled
the outer ramparts, fury and murder incarnate. The mortals
they faced quailed. It took the heart of a Space Marine to stand
against them without fear, and the Angels of Death were in
short supply.

'Another attack, move, move! To the walls!'

They came in the days after the Avenging Son returned, emerging from nothing, eight legions strong, bringing the bulk of their numbers to bear against the chief entrance to the Imperial Palace. A decapitation strike like no other, and it came perilously close to success.

Messinius' Space Marines ran to the parapet edging the Penitent's Square. On many worlds, the square would have been a plaza fit to adorn the centre of any great city. Not on Terra. On the immensity of the Lion's Gate, it was nothing, one of hundreds of similarly huge spaces. The word 'gate' did not suit the scale of the cityscape. The Lion's Gate's bulk marched up into the sky, step by titanic step, until it rose far higher than the mountains it had supplanted. The gate had been built by the Emperor Himself, they said. Myths detailed the improbable supernatural feats required to raise it. They were lies, all of them, and belittled the true effort needed to build such an edifice. Though the Lion's Gate was made to His design and by His command, the soaring monument had been constructed by mortals, with mortal hands and mortal tools. Messinius wished that had been remembered. For men to build this was far more impressive than any godly act of creation. If men could remember that, he believed, then perhaps they would remember their own strength.

The uncanny may not have built the gate, but it threatened to bring it down. Messinius looked over the rampart lip, down to the lower levels thousands of feet below and the spread of the Anterior Barbican.

Upon the stepped fortifications of the Lion's Gate was armour of every colour and the blood of every loyal primarch. Dozens of regiments stood alongside them. Aircraft filled the sky. Guns boomed from every quarter. In the churning redness on the great roads, processional ways so huge they were akin to prairies cast in rockcrete, were flashes of gold where the Emperor's Custodian Guard battled. The might of the Imperium was gathered there, in the palace where He dwelt.

There seemed moments on that day when it might not be enough.

The outer ramparts were carpeted in red bodies that writhed and heaved, obscuring the great statues adorning the defences and covering over the guns, an invasive cancer consuming reality. The enemy were legion. There were too many foes to defeat by plan and ruse. Only guns, and will, would see the day won, but the defenders were so pitifully few.

Messinius called a wordless halt, clenched fist raised, seeking the best place to deploy his mixed company, veterans all of the Terran Crusade. Gunships and fighters sped overhead, unleashing deadly light and streams of bombs into the packed daemonic masses. There were innumerable cannons crammed onto the gate, and they all fired, rippling the structure with false earthquakes. Soon the many ships and orbital defences of Terra would add their guns, targeting the very world they were meant to guard, but the attack had come so suddenly; as yet they had had no time to react.

The noise was horrendous. Messinius' audio dampers were at maximum and still the roar of ordnance stung his ears. Those humans that survived today would be rendered deaf. But he would have welcomed more guns, and louder still, for all the defensive fury of the assailed palace could not drown out the hideous noise of the daemons – their sighing hisses, a billion serpents strong, and chittering, screaming wails. It was not only heard but sensed within the soul, the realms of spirit and of matter were so intertwined. Messinius' being would be forever stained by it.

Tactical information scrolled down his helmplate, near environs only. He had little strategic overview of the situation. The vox-channels were choked with a hellish screaming that made communication impossible. The noosphere was disrupted by etheric backwash spilling from the immaterial rifts the daemons poured through. Messinius was used to operating on his own. Small-scale, surgical actions were the way of the Adeptus Astartes, but in a battle of this scale, a lack of central coordination would lead inevitably to defeat. This was not like the first Siege, where his kind had fought in Legions.

He called up a company-wide vox-cast and spoke to his warriors. They were not his Chapter-kin, but they would listen. The primarch himself had commanded that they do so.

'Reinforce the mortals,' he said. 'Their morale is wavering. Position yourselves every fifty yards. Cover the whole of the south-facing front. Let them see you.' He directed his warriors by chopping at the air with his left hand. His right, bearing an inactive power fist, hung heavily at his side. 'Assault Squad Antiocles, back forty yards, single firing line. Prepare to engage enemy breakthroughs only on my mark. Devastators, split to demi-squads and take up high ground, sergeant and sub-squad prime's discretion as to positioning and target. Remember our objective, heavy infliction of casualties. We kill as many as we can, we retreat, then hold at the Penitent's Arch until further notice. Command squad, with me.'

Command squad was too grand a title for the mismatched crew Messinius had gathered around himself. His own officers were light years away, if they still lived.

'Doveskamor, Tidominus,' he said to the two Aurora Marines with him. 'Take the left.'

'Yes, captain,' they voxed, and jogged away, their green armour glinting orange in the hell-light of the invasion.

The rest of his scratch squad was comprised of a communications specialist from the Death Spectres, an Omega Marine with a penchant for plasma weaponry, and a Raptor holding an ancient standard he'd taken from a dusty display.

'Why did you take that, Brother Kryvesh?' Messinius asked, as they moved forward.

'The palace is full of such relics,' said the Raptor. 'It seems only right to put them to use. No one else wanted it.'

Messinius stared at him.

'What? If the gate falls, we'll have more to worry about than my minor indiscretion. It'll be good for morale.'

The squads were splitting to join the standard humans. Such was the noise many of the men on the wall had not noticed their arrival, and a ripple of surprise went along the line as they appeared at their sides. Messinius was glad to see they seemed more firm when they turned their eyes back outwards.

'Anzigus,' he said to the Death Spectre. 'Hold back, facilitate communication within the company. Maximum signal gain. This interference will only get worse. See if you can get us patched in to wider theatre command. I'll take a hardline if you can find one.'

'Yes, captain,' said Anzigus. He bowed a helm that was bulbous with additional equipment. He already had the access flap of the bulky vox-unit on his arm open. He withdrew, the aerials on his power plant extending. He headed towards a systems nexus on the far wall of the plaza, where soaring buttresses pushed back against the immense weight bearing down upon them.

Messinius watched him go. He knew next to nothing about Anzigus. He spoke little, and when he did, his voice was funereal. His Chapter was mysterious, but the same lack of familiarity held true for many of these warriors, thrown together by miraculous events. Over their years lost wandering in the warp, Messinius had come to see some as friends as well as comrades, others he hardly knew, and none he knew so well as his own Chapter brothers. But they would stand together. They were Space Marines. They had fought by the returned primarch's side, and in that they shared a bond. They would not stint in their duty now.

Messinius chose a spot on the wall, directing his other veterans to left and right. Kryvesh he sent to the mortal officer's side. He looked down again, out past the enemy and over the outer palace. Spires stretched away in every direction. Smoke rose from all over the landscape. Some of it was new, the work of the daemon horde, but Terra had been burning for weeks. The Astronomican had failed. The galaxy was split in two. Behind them in the sky turned the great palace gyre, its deep eye marking out the throne room of the Emperor Himself.

'Sir!' A member of the Palatine Guard shouted over the din. He pointed downwards, to the left. Messinius followed his wavering finger. Three hundred feet below, daemons were climbing. They came upwards in a triangle tipped by a brute with a double rack of horns. It clambered hand over hand, far faster than should be possible, flying upwards, as if it touched the side of the towering gate only as a concession to reality. A Space Marine with claw locks could not have climbed that fast.

'Soldiers of the Imperium! The enemy is upon us!'

He looked to the mortals. Their faces were blanched with fear. Their weapons shook. Their bravery was commendable nonetheless. Not one of them attempted to run, though a wave of terror preceded the unnatural things clambering up towards them.

'We shall not turn away from our duty, no matter how fearful the foe, or how dire our fates may be,' he said. 'Behind us is the Sanctum of the Emperor Himself. As He has watched over you, now it is your turn to stand in guardianship over Him.'

The creatures were drawing closer. Through a sliding, magnified window on his display, Messinius looked into the yellow and cunning eyes of their leader. A long tongue lolled permanently from the thing's mouth, licking at the wall, tasting the terror of the beings it protected.

Boltgun actions clicked. His men leaned over the parapet, towering over the mortals as the Lion's Gate towered over the Ultimate Wall. A wealth of targeting data was exchanged, warrior to warrior, as each chose a unique mark. No bolt would be wasted in the opening fusillade. They could hear the creatures' individual shrieks and growls, all wordless, but their meaning was clear: blood, blood, blood. Blood and skulls.

Messinius sneered at them. He ignited his power fist with a swift jerk. He always preferred the visceral thrill of manual activation. Motors came to full life. Lightning crackled around it. He aimed downwards with his bolt pistol. A reticule danced over diabolical faces, each a copy of all the others. These things were not real. They were not alive. They were projections of a false god. The Librarian Atramo had named them maladies. A spiritual sickness wearing ersatz flesh.

He reminded himself to be wary. Contempt was as thick as any armour, but these things were deadly, for all their unreality.

He knew. He had fought the Neverborn many times before.

'While He lives,' Messinius shouted, boosting his voxmitter gain to maximal, 'we stand!'

'For He of Terra!' the humans shouted, their battle cry loud enough to be heard over the booming of guns.

'For He of Terra,' said Messinius. 'Fire!' he shouted.

The Space Marines fired first. Boltguns spoke, spitting spikes of rocket flare into the foe. Bolts slammed into daemon bodies, bursting them apart. Black viscera exploded away. Black ichor showered those coming after. The daemons' false souls screamed back whence they came, though their bones and offal tumbled down like those of any truly living foe.

Las-beams speared next, and the space between the wall top and the scaling party filled with violence. The daemons were unnaturally resilient, protected from death by the energies of the warp, and though many were felled, others weathered the fire, and clambered up still, unharmed and uncaring of their dead. Messinius no longer needed his helm's magnification to see into the daemon champion's eyes. It stared at him, its smile a promise of death. The terror that preceded them was replaced by the urge to violence, and that gripped them all, foe and friend. The baseline humans began to lose their discipline. A man turned and shot his comrade, and was shot down in turn. Kryvesh banged the foot of his borrowed banner and called them back into line. Elsewhere, his warriors sang; not their Chapter warsongs, but battle hymns known to all. Wavering human voices joined them. The feelings of violence abated, just enough.

Then the things were over the parapet and on them.